"Pull out your cock for me."

"Not out here, Day."

She smiled, wickedly. Wickedly, is the only way to describe how she smiled at me, as she pressed with delightful insistence through the soft cotton fabric of my chinos, making my breath catch. My buttocks, of their own accord, tightened, pushing me to be with her.

"Don't say you don't want this, like this, Benn. That woman you were engaged to before, who wouldn't openly show her pleasure at being with you; she never risked everything of herself for you, did she? You really wanted her open to you, to entirely expose herself to you, shame herself even to the world.

"Yeah, especially that, because you needed for her to want *you, more* than anyone or anything else." She winked playfully. "And, we both know *I* have no shame or pride or any of that. Right? *Especially when it comes to you.*"

I thought I heard a sound in the house but I must've been wrong. She was so deep inside my head, rattling around inside me where no one else but me had ever been, skillfully wrapping her will around the most protected, most delicate part of my ego.

Day was being a touch playful but *she knew,* and she knew I knew, that she had me by more than my balls and enthusiastic cock.

And, I never answered her questions because I could barely think at all or manage to form an audible word.

That Steve would be heading back faintly occurred to me, but my knees widened, giving her more access to me. She buried her face in my crotch and gently gnawed at me through the fabric; the enticing novelty of it, making me precum, as I pushed her head into me.

She licked at the wet spot and huskily restated her previous request, and I complied and finished unbuttoning . . . .

"Hobble is a story of lust and obsessive sex . . . I was so moved . . . I went back to my (Franklin) dictionary . . . hobble means to limp along . . . to impede . . . to tie-up, shackle or leash . . . all of [which] were used in this steamy story, of sex, incest and betrayal!"

—Delores Thornton, BlackRefer.com Reviews

"Hobble is a book that you *must* read."

—RAWSistaz Reviews

" . . . the narrative style is rather appealing . . . an interesting story . . . I would read again . . . it rather intrigued me. The heroine is unique."

—Sensual Romance Reviews

"The numerous sex scenes . . . show . . . natural spark."

—Absinthe Literary Review

"When's your next one coming out?"

—Several Cleveland, Ohio Readers to the author

—for trade paperback edition

HOBBLE

A Novel by

Neale Sourna

PIE: Perception Is Everything

A **Book**

"Doing for the mind, what the body shouldn't."™

Copyright © 2007 by Neale Sourna

ISBN 978-0-974195-03-2 / 0-9741950-3-0 Trade Paperback

also available in ebook formats

HOBBLE Cover Concept © Neale Sourna

HOBBLE Photos by the effervescent Sonya Cheren
Makeup by the charming Barbara D'Avilla, both of
Studio f.64, Cleveland OH. 440-888-9317, **www.studiof64.com**
Model *(Author)*: Neale Sourna as "Day"

Crossed Battleaxes graphic & Aegis graphic © Neale Sourna

Updated publisher's book file December 2012

First Print Edition (Trade Paperback) published October 2002, Infinity Publishing

Published by

"Doing for the mind, what the body shouldn't."™

PIE: *Perception Is Everything*™   www.PIE-PerceptionIsEverything.com
12600 Rockside RD Box 192   www.PIE.Percept.com
Cleveland OH 44125 USA   www.Neale-Sourna.com

TABLE OF CONTENTS:

HOBBLE: The Full Novel

* * * *

From the Author:

Stories are important, fiction and nonfiction: news stories, fantasy stories, work stories, wishful stories, school stories, "nothing but the truth" stories, band bus stories, even stories about stories, plus our dreams *(awake and asleep)*, and especially our nightmares.

They are a gift to be shared, a lesson learned, a journey taken, a wish fulfilled, a proposition considered—as translated through the intellect and heart.

Stories fine-tune our inner vision, because . . .

PIE: *Perception* Is *Everything*™,

Neale

Neale Sourna

"Doing for the mind, what the body shouldn't."™

PS

To my fun and articulate family with three special irreplaceable "thanks" to The Reynolds Brothers *(Ira, Levi, Armin)*, to my bodacious life friends, and most especially to my perpetual enemies—*THANK YOU*.

Now you know what I was doing when I was too goofy to write you.

—S

PPS

Hank Centa, Ken Horner, and Joe DiLallo thanks big time for the time and support.

—S

Hobble
by

Neale Sourna

I literally fell for her; tripped over and fell on her, on the sunny, gritty beach of Virginia Beach. I wasn't spiritually or emotionally lost, I believe, but what we "believe" is so very often wrong. I suppose I was inactively, instinctively hunting something, something I *almost* felt, but couldn't as yet begin to verbalize.

Anyway, because of muggers, mad dogs, and badly driven cars, I'm always very aware of everything and everyone around me, when I take my morning run, but it was late in the day. So, maybe because my flight'd been delayed or because I'd become strangely out-of-synch or . . . ?

My mind was fixated on a problem, now entirely forgotten, as I turned my head toward the frightened, anguished cry of a lone sea bird, which sounded terribly and despairingly lonely to me; and, somehow, devastatingly lost. And, in gazing aside at the bird, for all of two blind seconds, I knocked her down, onto the sand—a brown woman, in a long, potato sack, calico dress.

What a face!

An American face of excellently blended African and Native American genes, with a healthy little dollop of European blood, a terribly agitated face, as she fetally balled up in great pain and wouldn't let me look at her injured ankle.

I explained that she could "trust me," that I knew what I was doing, when I wasn't "knocking defenseless young women to the ground." She didn't laugh, slightly chuckle, or even crack the tiniest of a smile, and from furtive, dark eyes, she gave me a shaky, cursory once over—at the brown skin over hard-angled facial bones, at my black hair and dimly Asian eyes.

I have a lot more than "a healthy dollop of European blood" myself, from Dad's side, which explains the beard *[a recent addition]* and the general curliness of my hair, which I've let grow to its own rule for months now. But, despite the Old World genes, I look most like my mother's Peruvian-Incan/Mexican-Mayan, New World genes.

I told my hapless victim my name was Benn, Bennet Gillespie.

She took a more thorough, ill-at-ease view of me into her head, which was covered with tousles of dark brown ringlets, which in the sunlight had auburn streaks, speckled with *very* premature silver. The sterling was incongruous with her physical youthfulness, but the heartrending glance from those eyes hinted that it was well earned.

Finally, she stared into my eyes, then nominally stopped cringing and gazed downward —as her *("demure" came oddly to mind)* . . . as her demure signal permitting me to have my way with her, so to speak.

I checked her injury.

She had the shapely legs of an athlete or dancer, and wore battered out, low-heeled ankle boots, that were slightly Victorian or Edwardian or one of those old "-ian" styles, laced over soft, thick socks. The ankle moved stiffly, painfully.

The footgear was in the way, so, I began unlacing to better ascertain how bad off it was, because sometimes there are hidden breaks and misleading damage.

She abruptly realized I was actually opening her boot and flinched away, shrieking at me, but the small boot and sock slipped off into my hand.

She fell silent, completely mortified, before starting to cry; wailing, in fact, lying flat back in the sand.

Besides the swelling I'd caused, her ankle had a deep cut. Not an immediately recent slice, that I might have caused her, but a deep, nicely healing, surgical one—and I know this because my mother was a surgeon and she'd made me take "real" medicine classes and be her assistant, to go with the rest of my training.

This cut was nicely, cosmetically stitched, but I bet you, and I'd win, that the seam was there to repair something grossly traumatic.

She was lying there sobbing actual tears. I know because I pulled her hands away from her face and checked.

However, whether the tears were also actually genuine . . . ?

I glanced up and down the beach and saw absolutely no one else around for continents. The nearest anything was a lonely looking, one-story beachhouse behind us, that was showing no life or interest in us.

I had an insight.

She attempted stopping me, though, as she sat up and wordlessly defended her secret, until finally allowing me, in mute, humiliated resignation, to unlace the other boot—that stiff and pained ankle was also restitched. Both of them were sewn quite a way around, like a can opener makes a cut around a lid, until it's nearly severed.

However the original lacerations had been made, it hadn't been by small penknife or thick train wheel—I've seen the resulting cuts of both of those on the human body; these'd been done by something in between.

I asked if she lived nearby, I suggested I call for an ambulance, or I could carry her to my car at the hotel a mile or so back up the beach, and she obviously hated all my ideas.

Noisily so.

Who'd think so much mournfully, piercing sound could come out of such a perfect mouth.

I began considering that she might be completely inarticulate, before I had another insight. With her ankles this raw, she had to've come from nearby. I asked her, quite specifically, where she lived.

She clammed up like a petulant child and really didn't want to answer that, so I told her if I couldn't take her home, I'd have to take her to a hospital. I couldn't just leave her there, like a beached wha—.

"What are you doing to her, young man?!"

It was a Scottish accent, hurried and harried, from a probably usually pleasant but now distressed, slimly roundish and handsome, middle-aged woman in her fifties, who glared at me, as if she already hated my very existence.

"I fel— . We bumped into each other and she's bruised, maybe even sprained her ankle. It's a little hard to tell with all the other damage."

"My young lady hasn't torn open her wounds, has she?"

"No, ma'am; but she refuses to go to the hospital, or tell me where she lives. Where—?"

"For shame, Ms. Day. You know, quite well, you're not allowed out here alone. Why did you come so far out, without me? And so close to the water?"

The Scot wanted to chastise more but apparently felt my rocking and sobbing victim/patient was already in enough piteous grief.

"Is she all right? Can she walk?"

I shook my head "no." The younger woman's leg was . . . . Well, both legs were enough of a problem, but her tremulous demeanor wouldn't get her anywhere.

I told the Scot I'd play beast of burden and carry—"Ms. Day," if I could be pointed in the right direction.

I picked the young woman up and she smelled of fruit, of peaches and vanilla; some sort of shampoo, I thought. The weepy thing stiffened, then calmed and relaxed in my arms, as I followed the older woman, carrying her socks and boots, to the same beachhouse I'd spotted behind us.

If it had a style name other than beachhouse, I wouldn't know. I have cousins in the Yucatan with a shack on the beach, at the edge of the jungle where, on our vacations as children, we caught snakes and milked them of their venom for cash from a New York City researcher, who "wasn't good" with poisonous serpents.

This house wasn't huge but it was no shack, either. The Scotswoman was its live out housekeeper, as she led us in and found a proper place on the sofa for me to place my shapely charge.

I know that sounds a bit . . . but, a man gets a fairly involved idea of a woman's body, when he's carrying it against his own.

"What's this all about, Mrs. Gorbachev?!"

The Scot, Mrs. Gorbachev, explained our situation to the late sixties, early seventy something, Anglo-English master of the house, a Mr. Hopkins, who seemed even more suspicious and disdainful of my presence than the Russian Scot. He didn't want me touching his . . . whatever "Ms. Day" was to him. Then, he called her his "daughter."

Plenty of people don't look anything like their parents; plus he could be a foster or step—. It didn't matter what they were to each other, the logic loving part of my brain reminded me.

I suggested my hosts have someone look at her injury and in the meanwhile I could make a poultice—.

"A what?"

Yeah, like he wasn't old enough to have heard or probably worn one himself sometime. Probably back during The Blitz, The Great War, or that little altercation between Generals York and Washington even. Something about the man pissed me off. I think it was just him—not because he was English, or much older, but because he was him—whoever he was.

I took a step to leave and Ms. Day grabbed my hand, tightly. She dug her sharp, natural, and hard, little nails into me, not to hurt me, but plainly because she was afraid for some reason.

"Let the man go, Day. He must leave."

She shook her head "no," then began saying "no," over and over, and when I moved, she stood up abruptly, which had to have hurt her legs a great deal.

She continued clinging to the flesh of my arm.

Her begging me to stay could have been nice, if her short, hard nails hadn't been gouging me, nearly to drawing blood, and if the other two people in that uncozy, expensively appointed house hadn't glared at me, as if I'd put her up to it.

I tried peeling her off me and getting her to lie back on the sofa, but she wouldn't heed me, and she certainly wasn't listening to either of them. Actually he was no help at all, and managed to make everything worse, as he barked sharp orders at her. Condescendingly, I felt.

I did wonder if Day's middle name were Night.

He snapped at her to "behave like an adult" and to let me, "the stranger," go about my business, etc. That sounded condescending, too. It was getting out of hand, and I was losing needed skin cells to her clawing.

Mrs. G, however, had a simple idea.

"You know, sir, how she detests all those surgeons you brought her here to see. Ms. Day, do you want the gentleman to stay?"

Day instantly looked at the woman in relief, without letting go of me. Hopkins, old bean, was very pissed at the question. I thought I could, perhaps, help all concerned, and suggested, if I could leave for an hour or less, I could grab some things from my hotel, some herbs—.

"'Herbs'?" He pronounced it like a man's name.

I explained to him that I was a curandero, a trained and licensed healer. That got a big harrumph. I also added I was the son of a surgeon. He asked why *I* wasn't a real doctor. Maybe it was his stentorian tone of voice that annoyed me. Then again, it was none of his business what the hell I—.

Okay, it's a sore point of mine.

I merely reminded him, instead, that since she was refusing to go to the hospital, her leg might become infected or at least hurt a hell of a lot, for a hell of a long time, making her more lame. Even in America, gangrene still occurs, which can lead to amputation.

Also, as temperamentally high-strung as she'd been since I'd met her, neither of them would get any rest sleeping or fetching and carrying for her every second, which they'd . . . which Mrs. G'd most likely had just stopped doing recently, because of the ankle surgery.

I explained that as a well-trained, experienced, and highly sought curandero, I always carry or can find herbs, oils, and teas to soothe, calm, and take down the swelling of most any infection or injury. The treatments might even urge her to sleep for a while. I kept it to myself that I thought she was being juvenilely bitchy; however, I suspected the beauty was something of a head case, or at least terribly spoiled rotten somehow.

What a waste.

Neither of them had a better idea of what to do with her, in order for them to handle her, as she refused to listen to or be touched by them; so, Hopkins, in extreme reluctance, agreed to let me return.

The really hard part came when I tried to extricate myself again from their Ms. Day.

Finally, I convinced her I was coming back, soon, by setting her attention on the ancient gold locket I wore around my neck.

It has a childhood photo of my sister and me, and one of my mother; my dead mother. I was reaching for simpatico involvement from Day, to affect her and get her out of herself and more focused. I slipped the locket, hanging on its black cord, from my neck onto hers. Her possessing it, in payment against my return, seemed to satisfy her enough, and she let me go.

I—*unfortunately or fortunately, depending on your perspective*—never actually gave it serious, full consideration, but it crossed my mind, more than once, while I was gone from Day, to not go back. Which wasn't disputable. The heart-shaped locket was not emotionally or psychologically replaceable; and Day's ankles, especially the one I'd bruised on top of the old injury and surgical repair, needed my attention.

I'd said I'd take care of it, and I was most likely the only person she'd allow near her who could help what was wrong with her—*in the leg department, at least.*

I also had to admit, when I took a few moments to rinse off, change, and grab a bag, that Day intrigued me. Maybe, I should've sat and thought about that a while longer, perhaps in a chilly shower.

Her intriguing me was probably not a good thing, as my newest, gratis client; especially, since Hopkins was so clearly defensive and overprotective of her, and I had no possible clue about whatever it was that kept her so stressed way up there on that thinly taut high wire of hers.

It didn't help that I didn't believe the father-daughter equation. Not fully. He did act somewhat brusque and fatherly toward her, but that could've just been the vast age difference.

Plus, my gut said there was something else about them.

My brain logically said their personal relationship absolutely wouldn't matter, once I took my scheduled flight back out, so, I left it at that.

I parked my rental car in the drive, and heard her before I got to the porch extending all along the oceanside of the house and around the one side nearest the drive and garage. She was shrieking again, "keening" Mrs. G called it. It was an effectively poignant sound, if keeping the household at bay and stepping gingerly around her was the goal.

"Ms. Day, here he comes now!"

The young woman had her palms and elbows up, defensively barricading herself from being touched, especially by Hopkins, who threw his hands up in total, practiced impatience with her.

Day looked around at me.

My first impression this time, at the sight of that extraordinary face, was that she was indisputably bright; it was in her eyes, but there was also a coldness there, and again that look of fear—an old fear.

The sunny eagerness she stunningly expressed at my presence warmed me more than I should have let it, and it never occurred to me that I'd fallen down the proverbial rabbit hole.

But, I was plainly needed and it was a smart thing that I'd returned, because she was feverishly exhausting herself, in fending them off, and now both naked ankles were in incredibly bad, unusable shape.

She shouldn't have been on the shore in the first place.

I had Mrs. Gorbachev make her tea from the leaves I'd brought and she had to hold the cup for Day, who was trembling too much to maintain it herself, while I gently massaged then wrapped the damaged ankles in poultices of warm castor oil and herbs.

Hopkins had no tolerance for any of it and went outside to chain-smoke.

Day fell asleep and Mrs. G had me carry her to her room, where Day obviously spent *a lot of time,* by the look of the presence of a great number of books and old VHS videos.

Her bedroom had a full bath attached; shared with another room alongside. From what I could see of it, it had a large folded futon, some boxes, and little else, as if someone had half moved in, then forgotten it all. I was fairly certain Mr. Hopkins' room was behind the closed, smoky door across the hall from hers.

Mrs. G opened Day's windows, which were tall, large, deep silled, and placed comfortably for sitting, then she pulled the curtains partially together, leaving only a narrow view of the waning afternoon.

"Have you eaten?"

Mrs. Gorbachev's gentle question was an insightful one, and kind. I hadn't eaten, not since very early in the morning on the flight in to the convention, then I'd had seminars *[one I conducted]* and meetings at the Association's facilities with some others, who do or are interested in what I do.

That's the Association for Research and Enlightenment™ (A.R.E.™), the Sleeping Prophet, Edgar Cayce's people.

She set a place for me at the dining table. The cramped dining area openly adjoined the living room and a tiny bar area.

The house was basically made for only one or two people to be in comfort, and probably *never* any guests, if Hopkins' attitude were evidence.

"You're a good cook, Mrs. Gorbachev."

"Thank you. And, you're good with Ms. Day. Most people aren't." My value had definitely gone up in Mrs. G's desirable esteem, since her first words to me.

"'Most people aren't?' Really? She's so . . . soft. So sweet. He calls her daughter. Is he—?"

"She *is* sweet, normally, although, Ms. Day has a . . . vagueness and ofttimes becomes confused. Plus, the injuries to her legs trouble her a great deal. That's all." She seemed to remember something unpleasant she didn't want to, before adding, "He's quite responsible for her."

A little cryptic, and said in a manner, that heavily implied nothing else would be said about it.

"Gorbachev? Scottish accent? Is there an interesting story there?"

She laughed. A warm, pleasant laugh. There *was* an interesting story. Nice, sweet story. I avidly listened, although, I was becoming really tired. A good bedtime story. Her narrative had all the elements: immigrants in a new land, romance, love, children, widowhood, a job opportunity taking care of—.

Day was awake, and not happily so. The girl had way too much electricity going through her brain and should've stayed asleep. Mrs. G went to her young lady, who wanted to know where I was. I went to her and asked Mrs. G to bring her another cup of my herbal tea.

Day had shed her dress to the floor and had slipped on a soft, *thin* robe. Except for my wrappings at her ankles, it was clearly the only thing she wore. *I notice those kinds of things.*

She was trying to walk, and making a turtle's progress, which meant my attention to her legs was working, but obviously, she shouldn't have been on her feet yet, as she looked like she was seriously considering getting down on all fours to crawl to wherever.

"Where're you trying to go?" She hesitantly, petulantly pointed to the bath.

We all hate it when we need assistance with going to the toilet, because it's all part of being a mature and independent person. I scooped her up and carried her in and told her to call me back when she was ready. Finally she did, she was too incapacitated to do otherwise. Tea. Massage. Rewrap.

Mrs. G had to go for the night, and hoped I'd have a wonderful life, since she wouldn't see me again. Too bad, I wanted to hear more specific details of how a Scottish widow of a Russian immigrant had ended up playing nanny to this particular woman. And man.

I'd forgotten about Hopkins. He was somewhere, out of the way. Day's swelling, the one I'd caused, had gone down noticeably.

Thank you, Mr. Cayce.

She took my hand and I thought she was just going to hold it. People do that, sometimes. They're grateful to be out of pain, to not be alone, to be gently touched. No one touches anymore, not without first considering if they could be sued for it. She slid my hand up the inside of her firmly inviting thigh.

"*No.*"

It was bad enough I didn't want to say "no," and of course, Hopkins picked that moment to check in. I didn't think, or at least hoped he hadn't seen. Which all probably didn't matter because he'd made it clear the first moment he'd seen me that my presence was absolutely not something he wanted. He took me aside, out of sight and sound of her.

"Mr. Gillespie, Mrs. Gorbachev has pointed out that your skills might be required, in the night; should Day become distressed again. She has . . . a condition, besides her ankles. In the past, we've given her various drugs, but the 'way she's wired,' as the experts here say, the chemicals only aggravate her to horrid distraction or inordinately depress her. You . . . you seem to have a . . . somewhat calming affect on her."

He didn't like saying that, and wanted even less to say the rest. Finally, he did.

"Mrs. Gorbachev prepared the sofa for you. There's a rest-room off the side." His face screamed that it pained him to have me there, killed him to need me, and if he could've dropped a house on me right then, I know he would've.

* * * *

I slept for only about an hour, an hour and a half, maybe. Theirs was not a house of rest. I got a glass of water, then wandered out, onto the beachside porch, and followed it around to where it becomes a balcony over deadly rocks above the road below.

I'd never before seen a home porch railing with what appeared to be . . . jumper bars.

There were weak, sharply distressed sounds, hers, and a man's calmly wheedling voice, his. I could see and hear them between the wide crack in the drapes of her open window.

Hopkins was murmuring unintelligibly to Day, as he lay beside her, in her bed. She plainly didn't want him there, she was stressed and cringing at his touch, dodging her face away from his, as he endeavored to gaze at hers, but she wasn't shrieking or physically keeping him at a distance, as she'd done earlier, when she'd wanted me to stay.

Whatever their true relationship was, I couldn't, didn't really believe, not in the pit of my stomach, that they were blood or stepwhatever. I normally can trust my gut's input. Anyway, despite what my eyes saw and whatever the roiling distaste was churning my dinner, I didn't feel I should . . . interfere.

Day turned her mouth from his, and I believe she saw me, as he whispered something in her ear, unheard by me, which made her flinch, before he more loudly coaxed and instructed her to "close her eyes," "as always," because it "would be all right," it "would be better that way."

It did seem to help calm her, as she lay still as death in her unenthused, desireless body, as he stared at her, touched her in his coveting of all of her.

And, I was no better—watching.

I didn't mean to stay, but I did. He flung open her robe,

through which I'd already judged that I liked her body immensely. In his revealing her . . . . I *loved* her body.

Oh, great. Now, I'm officially a friggin' peeping tom!

I became hot with shame, anger, and confusion—probably pretty much what she was feeling; unless this was some convoluted game of theirs.

Then it became worse when I felt desire for her rise in me, and when I discovered I was unable to move away, because the floorboards creaked in alarm, which caught his ear for a fleeting moment.

I remained where I was, anchored to that spot, unable for some reason to close my eyes or turn away; with the sensitive stomach I'd puked my way through stressful oral reports and other sick moments in elementary school now making a nauseating return.

He took his self-indulgent, inconsiderate time with her, but it was probably not as long as it seemed.

Or, perhaps, it was much longer. For her.

I managed to look away, but not for very long, as I watched him take possession of her—.

My Mother'd slap me on the back of the head for that thought. We men always say and truly believe we "take," "possess," "have" the women in our lives, just because we can hold them tightly and force our entry into their bodies, whether they want us to or not.

We mentally and emotionally fashion ourselves as great conquerors or fantastic invaders, or merely because women are often stupidly overkind.

What else could possibly explain why we can also get them to do *pleasing* things for us, which are *abhorrent* to them?

I find many women often don't think so, but they're powerful. And, they never have to prove it, with egotistical feats of derring-do and parading of a chest or shelf of crystal and gold trophies or blue ribbon honors or showcase houses with showcase spouses and showcase bank accounts—offshore somewhere.

We men overstrive to prove we're so different and separate from "females" and that we're not "you ladies" or "you girls," which are the usual male insults at boot camp, training camp, and whatever other "pussy" male camps we pull together.

I guess, it's not an insult to call the guys "you women." What'd I say? Women = Power.

We men clothe ourselves in our business, sports and other uniforms of organized, hierarchal conformity, in search of and to protect our precious balls.

Don't believe me?

Try to get a frightened-for-his-entire-future-career male intern to correct or merely question the judgment of a surgeon, his superior, about that surgeon's mistake, especially when the intern's actually in the absolute right but final grades are pending.

You don't want to know the percentage of spineless men with empty scrota or of the ova-less women, as well, who entirely buy into the I-couldn't-possibly-question-the-doctor-surgeon-mentor-as-god syndrome, while your loved one, or you, are getting *miscalculated* care, that can cripple or kill you.

I know. I'm making your head split in screaming, writhing pain. I'm a "feminist," and you spit out that word like bile when you say it.

Like it's an insult.

Like calling a male a "girl" or "lady" or that all so familiar pet *cat* name is an insult; and as a male feminist I'm perceived as a complete traitor to my own, as if what I am has to be validated by—.

All I know is, my mother was always a feminist. If believing in being a woman, who is independent and decisive, is *a good* thing. All I know is, is that when our Dad couldn't cope and she couldn't cope either, he left and she stayed. She learned to deal with it and us.

When she couldn't, if necessary, she shared her burdens, the family burdens, with us, her children, which was perfectly fine. We were only kids, but we were . . . are family.

She helped us; we helped her.

She taught me, as a kid, that when I got my underwear dirty, I could wash them and my nasty butt just as well as she did; that when hunger struck, a stove and the dishes would let me handle them without my dick falling off from doing chick's work.

Think about it, what better way to become a slave yourself than to require someone to wash your filthy briefs and cook your meals, and therefore force yourself to marry said launderette/chef to keep yourself in fresh eats and clean undies.

Just to pretend you were "in charge" of your own life?

You're *in charge*, but you can't even make a bowl of one-minute oatmeal?

Incredibly stupid.

Once Hopkins finished with Day, he stiffly got up and left, without taking care of her needs, if any, or without even a basic thank you.

She stared after his retreating back, as if surprised at his leaving her side, but she never glanced my way again before she turned out the light. Afterward, from the darkness within, I had the eerie feeling for a long while that she was staring back at me, but it was probably my guilt.

I saw her silhouette rise from the bed and head toward the bath.

When she was out of sight, I ran to puke over the rail, as best I could through the bars. A lone car drove by below, windows open, letting out the tune, "My Heart Belongs to Daddy"—Marilyn Monroe's version. Ick. *The thought not the song.*

I distantly heard water inside, a shower running, as I rinsed my mouth with the last of the water in my glass, then spit it out.

Hopkins was abruptly near, scaring the hell out of me, smoking. He nearly always seems to be smoking, which, from the looks of him, he shouldn't've been. He was flushed and still breathing a bit heavily from his . . . exertions.

Day's probably his only exercise regimen.

"Enjoy the performance, did you?"

He spoke his next piece before I could sputter out any explanation sounding like reason.

"Be gone when I get up. I rise early." Fine. He turned on his heel—.

"Wait! She's not *really* you're daughter, or stepdaughter, is she?" He left, without answering.

* * * *

I never got back to sleep. I left way before sunrise and returned to my hotel, then to a scheduled seminar, which I conducted badly, with many apologies, then I did a few hours of distracted research at A.R.E.™

An urgently tense Mrs. Gorbachev was waiting for me in the lobby when I got back to the hotel.

It didn't seem appropriate to lead her to my room, so we found a quiet corner in the cozy restaurant. I loosened my tie as she spoke, as the blood vessels in my head throbbed, with what she was saying, because I was and should not have been so deeply involved so soon.

She said Day had become distraught to find I was gone, and, after the next thing she told me, I advised . . . .

I often step out of myself, "watch" myself in situations; in this one, I kept smoothing my expensive, imported silk tie, over and over, as if keeping it ordered; it already was, as Mrs. G stated frankly that I was "good medicine" for her frantic charge.

A flattering statement, from a woman, who probably never flatters.

I advised that she or Mr. Hopkins "should call professional mental assistance for Day."

I could give them several names of worthy people I'd definitely highly recommend, and whenever they got her calm, Mrs. G could please send my mother's locket back to me. I abruptly excused myself, turning my back on her obvious disappointment.

"Mr. Gillespie, he's not her father. 'Not by blood or by law.' That's an unfortunate affectation of his. Ms. Day wanted me to be certain you knew that."

She fell impatiently silent; her reflection in the wall mirror showed plainly that she wasn't certain what else to say to me, to my backside, to convince me. I looked back at her, while still tie smoothing, assessing her motives—*like I would know what a stranger's feelings and thoughts might truly be in all this.*

It was a critical time for her, and she clearly didn't like me making her wait, so, I'm sure she had many interesting words, in English and Scottish Gaelic flashing across her mind, but she merely watched me, and waited. Waited for pearls, rubies, and diamonds to drop from my lips.

"I'll follow in a few minutes."

I left a voicemail for my sister, on her private number, of where I'd be and that I'd contact her soon.

Day was sitting on the sofa, quiet as that proverbial, little church mouse, as long as no one else approached her. Hopkins sat across the room, smoking, glaring at her, as if he despised her—in his inability to control her, in his inability to take his fatigued eyes off her.

I sat beside Day, who had a serrated breadknife in her hands and was holding the deadly sharp point at her throat. Her hands were steady.

"Day, if you don't mind, I don't want blood on my mother's locket."

She held the blade, handle end out, and allowed Mrs. Gorbachev to retrieve it. The poor woman had left it alone a few seconds, while cutting bread, to answer the phone, then turned to find Day had it.

It turns out that "Ms. Day's not allowed to handle sharp knives."

I didn't ask about pointy forks. Or hard, plastic sporks.

Hopkins sighed deeply, before retreating to his bedroom. I tended Day's inflamed ankles, and she wasn't happy that I was being wholly professional, emotionally distant, and a bit sullen.

I don't like being manipulated, without my permission.

That night, I was still not able to sleep, on their sofa, in all the strained tension, which also seemed to live there. I heard him again, late night, somewhere in the middle of my restlessly checking the email off my Mac Titanium Power-Book®.

I heard him with Day, who I remembered was still wearing my locket, as I absently scratched the area on my bare chest that missed it.

It was very notable that I had forgotten to get it back from her. I closed the computer, and for some perverse reason, rose and went toward his grunting and snuffling to stand near her door. His rutting noises peaked, violently, and were followed by a bout of strained coughing.

Then the light went out.

Eventually, I heard water running and Hopkins snoring. He was all tuckered out, I guessed, as I stood there a long while, not really thinking or feeling, *just there;* then finally roused myself from my stupor, realizing what I was doing, or not doing—not leaving this *mess* and—.

Day was only a few yards from me, having gone from her bedroom through the connecting bath and out through the empty adjoining room. She was wet and shivering in a large towel. Taking a few steps to me, she faltered, her towel fell, and I caught her.

She smelled of peaches and apple soap or shampoo and was enticingly naked; closer scrutiny of her body telling me that it was athletic but slightly gone to softness for lack of activity.

Did I mention she was naked, shamelessly, casually naked, which, of course, caught *my* attention, but she seemed to take no particular notice of it, while in my arms.

Part of me was thinking of what Hopkins did with her, which was soon flushed from my mind, when she brushed her electrifying hand down my bare chest. She placed one of my very warm hands on her gooseflesh cold, round breast, warming the plump flesh of it, as I ran my thumb tip around its dark brown, hard nipple.

She took my other hand and swept it across her soft, damp bush of gentle curls.

Then, I slipped my probing fingers deep into the inviting, warm cleft between her thighs; she was dry, having just bathed and evidently assiduously douched; until my touch was rewarded by generating liquid heat.

People with heightened, excited minds, like hers, are often unerringly prescient; she preempted my better judgment of stepping back from her, by grabbing me "below the belt," through my boxer briefs, causing me to swell and harden faster in her hand than I already was.

And, like most men, grabbed by a desirable, naked woman, who's every look and touch most clearly states she greatly wants him, I kissed her.

A moment of stray logic halted it though, until she smokily spoke.

"Benn, I only want you." That's an ego booster.

I glanced back at the closed door between Hopkins and us, and unlike how so many of us swear—"one thing" did not "just *uncontrollably* lead to another," as we quite plainly chose to be seduced by each other.

I carried her back through the short hallway, past the intimate, small dining room to my bed for the night, his sofa in the front room. Her ankles were cold and uncovered and I asked if the wrappings had come off in the shower. She nodded and said they felt fine.

I got a pinprick twinge in my gut, which made me suspect she was probably fibbing a little, to be with me, which I let go, because I wanted her *badly* and because she still had that look for me, you know—*that* look.

I kept my fingers swimming in the carpeted, hot pool between her legs, as I kissed her deeply for a long while, because she has an incredible mouth and because her whole body partakes in her kisses. Then, I asked what she wanted me to do to please her; she graciously said whatever I wanted.

"Yippee!" was my first mental response, followed by, "Yeah, but does she really mean it, and what exactly does *she* mean when *she* says it?"

It's amazing how much miscellaneous crap and white noise goes through a person's brain, at such crucial times and situations.

Or how enjoyably and/or annoyingly aware one's senses become: hearing her quietly tense responses and my own hungry responses; and whether or not he's making a response from the back of the house to our not completely discreet responses, which he thankfully wasn't, as he snorted then snored on.

I was kneeling on the floor beside his sofa, making my pleasant dining journey downward; from her responsive lips and tongue, her tantalizing, plump breasts, the little softness of her belly, and below, where I was dawdling, before devouring.

One hand kneaded a breast—*all natural, the best kind*—while the other was still happy to be knuckle deep in the oven between her softly peachfuzzed thighs, as I watched her react to me, writhing seductively as a serpent, until she looked at me oddly in her impatient breathlessness.

She actually pouted in indignation.

When you're with a woman, especially a new-to-you woman, in such a vulnerable position for you both, it's always best to ask and not imagine exactly what she might be thinking.

Then, take what she says with a big grain of salt; depending on the lady and whether you think she says precisely what she means or whether she couches her phrases. I asked her if I were doing something wrong, and her answer . . . .

"You don't like me?"

It was a strange, pleading question and because of the way she said it and the way her face appeared made me reconsider *the entire situation,* as I removed my hands from her and sat back on my heels.

"How old are you, Day?"

It was her turn for another perplexed look. Then she smiled, as she sat up, and I half realized that even the simple thing of her hand sliding gently up my arm made me want to be hers.

"Old enough for what you want of me." She saw by my expression of suspicion that that wasn't the best answer to give me. "I'm legal, in every state of the Union. I wouldn't lie about that, not to you."

I chose to believe her.

We choose everything we do, somewhere along the line—the stuff we swear we don't want to do, even the stuff we're terrified of, probably even the stuff that kills us, too.

Day'd been a strange girl since I'd met her, but she hadn't lied to me, not seriously anyway, I was certain of that. Conversely, I didn't ask about the other *thing* hanging about in my mind. I harnessed it, bound and gagged it, and temporarily buried it somewhere—the relationship between her and . . . him.

"I'm old enough, Benn. My people just look young. Really." She peevishly frowned. "I'm not lying, or is there something else you don't like about me?"

"What makes you thi—?"

"You're not inside me, yet. You're avoiding and stopping, so you don't have to. You even still have your underwear on."

I decided then that even after living, working, and dating in some very large metropolitan cities and traveling the world, rural and otherwise, quite a lot, I hadn't yet heard everything, after all.

"You want me to rush?" She didn't seem to understand slight sarcasm; yet, she wanted to answer my somewhat teasing question.

"I . . . . You . . . . Isn't that what . . . ? It's the way *he* does it, and the way the—." She stopped, abruptly, censoring herself.

Odd girl. Woman. I also took note that I didn't seem to want to face the fact that her mind was . . . .

"Day, do you like me touching and kissing you? Licking you? If you don't, I'll stop."

"*No.* I mean y*es.* Yes, I do like it. A lot. It's . . . it's just not—."

"What you're used to?" She eventually nodded, uncertainly, as if fearing I might not like her answer. "I very, *very* much like and want you, but if you'll let me take care of you, Day, let me please you, before I take care of me, I'd really love that."

She didn't acknowledge what I'd said at first. It was my impression that no one had ever said such a thing to her before.

No. I didn't ask. About him.

Sometimes asking questions gets you in too much trouble, or at least adds to the searing hot H_2O you're already parboiling your head in. And, yes, I was feeling a little . . . a *lot* selfish. I really, *really* wanted *this woman*—her body, *her.*

I "predewed" my pants then, as a certain smart-ass cardiologist I know calls it, and Day put her palm on the warm, wet spot.

I liked her hand there, but I sighed deeply and moved it.

"Stop overstimulating me."

I made certain that both my tone and facial expression were playful and light. The innocent tone she gave back almost spilled me over the edge.

"But, I wasn't doing anything."

I hugged her, because I needed to and because I wanted to slow my desire for her. Although, holding her naked flesh to mine wasn't the best idea, but I didn't want to get up and go far across the room—not away from her.

I know, I could've just *taken* her, I achingly wanted to; or one of us could take me manually, to take the edge off; I achingly wanted that too, but the self-inflicted, excruciating wait for her seemed right, particularly after what she'd just said about him.

I'd seen his selfish impatience first hand and I didn't want to be like that, *like him,* with her.

I wanted to wait for her, so to speak.

I felt her relax against me; then started over, a little quicker this time, to get back to where I'd stopped. I put my lips and tongue to her natural fruit scented and flavored body and strove to delight her however I could, which plainly was a great deal.

She'd been a bit tense before; evidently waiting for me to strip and hurriedly dive in like good ole Hopkins would've; without any joy in it for her.

But, this was *my game,* and when I play it, the way I play it, nobody's better at it.

All modesty aside, of course.

Besides, a man's . . . or a woman's rewards are greater, with a little patience and tender care. Especially, with the special ones, and Day was proving to be quite special, as she writhed in softly whining pleasure and harshly whispered something, which seemed to be more for her sake than mine.

"'You know you have to be quiet!'"

That one sentence had the ring of a quote, as if someone might have told her that. Warned her with that, because the tone she'd spoken in felt slightly ominous.

Then again, maybe the sinister feeling I had was coming from me—*assiduously making love to a woman, who so unmistakably belonged to another,* beyond and despite whatever odd thing bound them together.

Day's incredible, *incredible* body joyfully peaked and the breathless depth of her final reaction to my lip, tongue, and finger service alone quite clearly shocked her. I loved the pleased, amazed expression on her face, after cumming in my mouth, crushing my head between her strong thighs.

Pleasure on a woman's face, bliss even is a great thing, but awe?

Perhaps, my hormones were just dissolving my egotistical brain too much, as I removed my underwear and knelt on the sofa, as she opened herself wider to receive me.

Another stupid, not so stupid, just unfortunately timed, thought streaked across my mind; that he hadn't worn any protection while with her, but theirs clearly was a long-standing deal.

She didn't have a diaphragm, IUD, or sponge, etc—trust me, by this time I definitely knew that.

There are also less obstruction-based ways for the Tantrically initiated, at least against pregnancy, but they required a certain kind of control and concentration, which I was losing more and more of, by the second, by being with this particular woman, whose body was worldly, yet she herself didn't appear to understand certain basic things; man/woman things.

This "innocent" woman, who was suddenly inside my head, knowing my unspoken thoughts.

"Don't worry. I'm taken care of. In the 'baby department.'" Her voice sounded more than vaguely bitter to me. "And, the last hospital—*for my ankles*—gave me all kinds of infection tests and shots, to cure God practically. If you're afraid of something like that."

While I weighed what she said, she kept my eyes locked with hers, as she scooted closer, stroking her cool palms over my hard nipples and down my taut belly to take me into her delightful hands and guide me, into heaven.

All done. Day was soundlessly crying, by the time I was too quickly and blissfully finished, and I asked what was wrong. If I'd hurt her.

Which was probably not the most realistic question to ask a woman, who'd taken her second man for the night.

She didn't answer at first, although she clung to my arm, as if its skin, muscles, and bone were fascinating to her, as was my face and hair, which she completely, tactilely examined, in teary silence.

Deep emotions can silence the tongue, besides I was, in so many ways, a stranger to her.

"You're real. Still."

I barely nodded "yes."

She was surprised at the reality of *me*? *Wow.*

That silenced us both, for quite a while, but thirty minutes or so later, we realized we were entirely unable to sleep, because we both wanted the other again.

She boldly, yet sweetly asked. She wanted to make love to me and I wanted to look at her while she did, so, she was on top and doing a fantastic job of it, until she curled up in great pain.

Stupid, selfish me!

Her position, in straddling me was too stressful for her sorely damaged ankles. I removed her from me and made her lie down in my stead, while I rechecked and massaged her tortured limbs, releasing her pain.

A lot of the formal medicinal education my mother had me train in was . . . .

Doctors. Surgeons, especially, were, *are* taught and grossly rewarded to be distant, unreachable, smart-ass know-it-alls. They don't touch their patients, literally or figuratively, because, frankly, all that "playing God" aloofness goes to their heads, brains, and dicks.

Or clits.

I always preferred the way of the curandero; touching people, literally and figuratively, helping people heal and feel whole, instead of merely like a stitched up garment.

Mama though felt the old ways were "out of date," but healing is from the inside out, is timeless and has a certain, indescribable sensuousness and intimacy. The feeling of connecting, of intimately making contact with another individual person has always remained with me longer as a healer than any time, during or after, in which I had to handle a formal med rotation.

Caring for Day's legs was an arousing affair to me, not in a tacky way, mind you, but in an it's-good-to-touch-her-and-do-for-her way.

She'd become very comfortable and relaxed in my presence and was innocently, pleasurably fingering herself, as I tried not to be overly distracted by the moist activity of those lucky masturbating digits, and by her combined reaction to them and my massaging touch.

Then, she clearly realized she was messing with my mind and boldly slipped one of those Day/slightly peachy-tasting fingers into her mouth and sucked, before slipping the rest into mine.

A delectable signal that reasonably seemed to imply that she wanted me back inside her, so I kissed her ankles then held her legs safely up out of the way against my chest, as if I were her chair, and we resumed where we left off.

It was "damned near, electrifyingly perfect," as my buddy Chuck used to say. No. It was closer than that.

Day, in her oddly peculiar manner, had barely spoken directly or coherently to me, since I'd met her.

Though, she now spoke faintly *for my ears only*; her eyes were soft and *only for me*; and her incredible body and more incredibly seductive intensity were *only for me*. All the former petulant childishness was, at least temporarily, gone from her.

There is . . . there is something most extremely intoxicating about a woman, who actively, completely desires you, and who actively, openly responds and entirely yields to you.

Or, entirely controls you, for that matter.

She slipped my mother's locket, which still hung between her breasts, from her neck back onto mine, as sleep began to claim us.

I still hadn't asked for it back.

Day whispered before we slept, as I spooned against her, that the next time I could have her from behind, on her knees or side, because that wouldn't hurt her ankles.

* * * *

Hopkins startled me awake, early. I'd been deeply enveloped and lost in sweet REM dreams. He must've been there, watching me, for quite a while and was smolderingly pissed, standing on my underwear, exactly where I'd dropped them. I was naked under the thin cover and grateful Day was not in sight.

He pointed to my locket, which she'd been wearing when he'd last been with her. He shouldn't have awakened me so abruptly—*the main two reasons being; that I'd been dreaming of Day and that Hopkins, therefore, wasn't at all happy at my all too apparent, morning hard-on.*

"Mr. Gillespie. I knew her mother, before Day was born and have known her all her life. You will not *touch* her, ever again. This is *my* house; she's *my* responsibility. And, I will not have it. I want you out. *Now.*"

I thought he'd storm out or at least stop standing on my boxer briefs. He didn't move, so eventually, I threw the cover back and stood, fully naked.

He didn't like the sight, which was fine, she did, as he judiciously decided to be elsewhere, and I sat back down, knowing I should leave and that I completely didn't want to. I also thought I'd better get dressed before poor Mrs. Gorbachev clocked in for the day.

As it was, she'd get an eyeful, since she was the "family" housekeeper and launders the sheets.

I dressed for a meeting I was scheduled for, before checking, massaging, and rewrapping Day's ankles, which took a while, as she wouldn't stop distracting me, until I told her that *I really had to leave.*

She asked, poignantly begged really, when I was coming back to her, and was watching me too closely.

I didn't want to lie or say the wrong thing and trip her hair-trigger emotions, but I told her; then waited for the storm. It didn't come.

"You should have something to eat, before you go, Benn. Where's Hopkins?"

I wasn't certain I should tell her where he was, but since she was calm; extremely, eerily calm, and without sharp objects in reach.

Mrs. G and I both watched as Day, in her little boots, walking gingerly on her own, found him outside, looking at the ocean from the beach, called to him; then gently, respectfully requested something of him that we couldn't hear.

It angered him. *A lot. Loudly a lot.*

She'd apparently expected his anger and didn't mind, as she quietly said something else, which abruptly shut him up, with a surprised look on his face; then she sat down and put her high-topped booted feet up.

Mrs. G took Day her breakfast and remained with her, while Hopkins came in and spoke to me in the kitchen.

"Mr. Gillespie, you have a choice. Two choices really. The room adjoining Day's, you may . . . sleep there. For now. We store her old things from . . . . There is a mattress, one of those horridly flat, portable Asian things and linens."

"And, the other 'choice'?"

"You, sir, have no idea what we're about. What she is."

"Why don't you tell me. You certainly want to." He smiled in agreement, but wouldn't be baited.

"I suggest you listen to reason, young man, not your . . . . Just go. *That's* your '*other* choice.'"

He drove off, unwilling to stay and await my decision, smugly certain I wouldn't or couldn't take her away. He shouldn't have been.

"Day, what did you say to him?" She shrugged, unwilling to answer. We were alone outside. "What *exactly* is it between you two? What am I getting . . . ? What *am* I into here?"

"Benn, do you want me?"

"That has—."

"Yes, it does. Is there *anyone* anywhere, in your imagination even, after last night that you want more than me? Is there?"

What brazen ego.

You find a lot of that, too much or too little ego, among the patients, when you do a psych rotation. You find a lot of that among the doctors and surgeons for that matter, especially the surgeons.

But, it was an excellently insightful question on her part—*there wasn't anyone else.*

She'd whispered into my mind the night before, while I was still deep inside her, that I was hers, as she'd completely held me fast and claimed me, as she'd lain open her defenses and given herself to me.

What accumulation of choices . . . ?

How had I gotten here, this deep, with these people, this childlike, strange woman, in less than two days?

It was like being in one of the diversional movies or novels Mama loved. I get the names confused, but they were always some "Games"; "Hush, Hush Sweet Charlotte"; "Gaslight" kind of thing. Mama'd liked treacherous, intrigue-ridden mystery and horror stories.

By the way, "Charlotte", with its intimate treacheries and betrayals; punishment-ridden, triangular sexuality; and severed body parts, completely creeped me out, until I was an adult.

I kept that gem private from Stephanie, my sister, as long as possible.

Oh, yes, and Mama had also warned me to stay away from crazy girls. Peculiarly, she'd done that more than once.

"They'll make you crazy, too, or just mess you over, until you'll beg to be crazy." I had never really taken Mama's advice seriously, not until that very moment, while mulling over Day's question; and it was probably already too late for me.

I'd walked away from her, down off the porch to the beach, which was too far from her, as I slowly moved back.

I'm never like this with any woman, not with this kind of overwhelming intensity, not this soon.

And, without a condom?!

Hell, I've been known, on occasion, to wear two simultaneously.

I didn't know her, *them*. The situation was emotionally and sexually scary enough with just two, let alone three of us. My chest was hurting, and my emotions were sliding out of my control—Charlotteing me.

It's not a word, but it's how I felt. I had questions, to say the least.

"Why is Hopkins 'responsible' for you? You're an adult. Why don't you just leave here?"

She'd tucked her legs, boots and all, under her long dress, in that catlike fashion women do. She was just as cryptically sphinxlike, as well, as she hugged her arms tightly to her.

"He is. And, I can't."

"If that's the best answer you can give me, I can't stay here." That got to her. I was afraid it wouldn't. I was only bluffing.

"He's . . . my . . . guardian. My 'legal guardian,'" she spat the words out in disgust. "I can't . . . I, literally, can't leave, or he'll send me back. To hospital." Living with him, she'd picked up an occasional Briticism. Like "to hospital" not to *the* hospital.

"And, I don't mean the hospital that fixed my ankles. Another one. A mind one." The light in her eyes changed in a flash.

"Hopkins isn't like you. He won't bluff me, like you just did, Benn."

Damn.

"He can have me . . . *willingly* recommitted, whenever he wishes. He's proved that to me before. And, lately, too many things have gone wrong for me.

"If I go back again, even Hopkins, with his big money and powerful connections, won't be able to get me out again. *I don't like it here, with him,* but I detest *there* more."

She pushed away her chamomile tea and uncurled her feet from under her. They'd stiffened terribly and were cold even with socks on, when I checked, so I removed her boots and held the icy things against me and massaged the ache from them.

She relaxed to my touch; stretching her sock covered, cat feet, flexing them against my hard runner's thigh—*silently generating a different sort of reciprocal ache in my crotch,* while Mrs. Gorbachev came out to check on her.

Their closeness was obvious, seeing them interact together.

Day even playfully did a very good copy of Mrs. G's accent. Mrs. G did a less fair North Coast American one, while mindfully fingercombing Day's perpetually disheveled hair, then removed the breakfast tray, and said that since I was with Day, she'd go out to "take care of a few chores," like buying "some soap."

I suspect she just wanted to leave us alone together.

"Why were you 'there,' in that particular kind of hospital?"

Day's eyes dropped in remembering something that made her draw up and hold herself more tightly this time, as if freezing. It was a sweaty, warm morning.

"Day?"

"I didn't need to be there." That statement twisted my bowels like wet spaghetti, so I gently countered her declaration.

"Don't lie to me, Day." She stared at me momentarily, as if unexpectedly caught with the proverbial cookie jar.

"M-Mommy. I was there because of her."

The look on her face cut me through.

"How is it that men always have rights, especially white men, like Hopkins? Women have rights, *most* times, children have almost, well, none, really. There's always someone to push a child around 'for her own good.' Always someone to tell her what she *has to do*, to please the free-to-go-and-come-as-they-wish grownups.

"They totally make you a child again, when the court says you have no rights to control yourself, to say where you want to live or sleep. Or with whom."

Her face suddenly lit up.

"I always loved Sarah Connor. Linda Hamilton as Sarah Connor?" I leaned back against the porch rail and shook my head to say the woman sounded dimly familiar but not really.

"She's the *real star* of 'The Terminator' and 'Terminator 2' movies. She always out-survives the heartless thing chasing her, even though, she's this small . . . .

"And the others, they hurt and vandalize her body, mess with her mind, lie to her, put her in . . . in a place, like I was—."

She bit her lip, glanced at me, then away, as if playing *something* off, as if she'd said more than she'd meant to.

"Can you take me down the stairs and closer to the water, or would that ruin your clothes?"

"Not as long as I don't go in."

I chose to treat her to a little piggyback ride.

What a joyous little laugh, and that soulwarming smile.

She said she didn't know anyone else as strong. I *am* strong and it's one of the reasons I do so much orthopedic work, like what's wrong with her ankles. Ortho work can often take considerable physical prowess; manipulating bones, sinews, and muscles.

I commented that a former girlfriend loved my body's overt physical strength, too, more than me even.

Day's blunt answer to that was that the other woman "was stupid."

Mrs. G was right; Day *is* a sweet person.

I spread a blanket out for us. A few people strolled or jogged by, as I had her bury her bare feet above the ankles in the warm sands of Virginia Beach. Another one of Mr. Cayce's brilliantly simple and effectively soothing remedies.

"What happened at the hospital, Day, that makes you so afraid?"

Other than her smile evaporating, she didn't actually move, yet she emotionally drew up into a defensive ball. I wrapped my arm around her, and kissed and stroked her soft, springy curls.

"They take away *everything,* even your basic sense of time, and your will to—." She segued abruptly, "Sarah, no, Linda's a twin. I always wanted to be a twin."

Her bright flash of a smile was broad and heartrendingly innocent. After an extended lapse, in which her happy mood swiftly tumbled, she continued.

"*There*, they don't heal, they don't use natural stuff that helps like you do, and when they touch. That disgusting orderly licked Sarah's face, when she was strapped to that bed and couldn't do anything. He was pressed for time.

"When they're not pressed for time, they make you do . . . whatever they . . . . Sarah stuck him pretty good later, though."

She took a big sighing breath.

"I never really liked Hoppy, but I'd . . . I'd rather just do him than—. Benn, what's wrong?"

My throat muscles had constricted. I couldn't swallow. I could barely breathe. What she'd been saying upset me. A lot. I was failing at trying not to let it show; losing my objectivity fast. It makes your clients nervous and diminishes your effectiveness, when you get too . . . .

"I-I'm sorry I brought it up, Day. Are *you* all right?"

"Of course not," she giggled, "that's why everyone treats me like a child or wants to use me. 'Pretty face, prettier cunt's' what Mo—. It's okay. Everything's . . . everyone's a weapon. My wise, guy friend, Roger, taught me that, and he's *really* crazy. The Marines? Green Berets?"

She shook her head.

"Anyway, they taught him to kill when he was only fifteen or sixteen, then—."

She frowned in her confusion.

"Or did I see that on cable, at the hos—? Roger and Vincent and . . . ." She shrugged. "Hoppy's always liked looking at me, touching me. I learned from Roger that I should use whatever I have, even if it seems like nothing, to do what I need to do, to get what I need. I need you."

"Not if it makes you do things, things you don't want to. What did you promise him?" She shrugged, casually.

"He'd make me do him, anyway. If I didn't do at least the bare minimum, he'd send me back. It's all he's ever wanted me for. But, now it doesn't matter. I'd do *anything* for one special thing, one person I really wanted. Wouldn't you?

"I mean, personal ego's not that damned important, is it? It's all conceit being who we are; trying to be big shots, and smarty-pants, trying to have absolutely everything we want. Controlling 'all we survey' but unable to even control ourselves. That is such bullshit!

"*One* really *special* thing, *one person* outside of our self-indulgent selves, and how we take care of it or them, is *all* that matters. It says tons more about who we really are than anything else. Doesn't it?"

She waited, but I wouldn't answer her.

I'd heard and *felt* her every word, as I watched two seabirds in flight, far out over the waves, they swooped drastically, erratically it seemed, then plunged out of sight toward the rolling vast expanse of water.

It looked very much as if they'd drowned below the tidewaves together.

Day slipped her palm into my lap and touched me, intimately.

"No."

My "no" was a great deal less than a definite command or chastisement, as she ignored it and leaned into me, straight into my head.

Her words, her tone, the very warm, chamomile flowered breath from her lips aided her will into slowly, deftly, securely enwrapping mine, like a muscular, famished jungle boa around a juicy, death wish vulnerable rabbit. Her authoritative hand remained, claiming and owning my crotch, as her other palm sensuously wooed my nape.

"I want to feel your mouth and tongue again, tasting me. I want . . . . I need to feel you again. Your hard power deep inside me, filling me, till I burst." I closed my eyes against her. It's interesting that it's so difficult to close our ears, our hearts—.

"Take me inside, Bennet, take care of me."

I couldn't seem to stop allowing her to seduce me. I shouldn't even have been listening to her. I should've been the adult of the two of us, the leader, but the woman is usually the true leader in such matters.

Willingly, I did as she asked. Too willingly.

I was beginning to fear that if she asked me to kill, I would. I'm not certain why that particular thought kept popping into my mind, but it did, probably because every time I touched her, or she touched me, her reaction to me was so overwhelmingly "intoxicating" is still the best word for it.

* * * *

I awoke in my new room among her "old" things, which were actually all new or mostly unused. She was gone. I'd missed my meeting and cell phoned my profuse apologies—something came up?

I redressed and stepped out into the hall. Cooking smells and sounds said Mrs. G was back and busy in one direction from me, to the other I heard *him*, murmuring to himself, before realizing he was speaking in approving tones to coax Day.

His door was open, revealing several mounted photos—*all of her at different ages, including a life-sized, expensively framed photo of her joyously dancing.* That one caught my attention a long second, until noticing his head resting back, while she sat on a low stool, back to me, her dress down off her, revealing her to the waist.

His liver spotted fingers were roughly shoved deep into her thick tousles of dark hair.

She was . . . she was between his soft thighs, before his unzipped pants, and she . . . she . . . .

Well, y'know. He didn't perceive me, but she did, and she

didn't look around, but I saw her back and neck stiffen, as she ceased her . . . activity. That's when he remotely took notice of me.

"Ah, you already had your go at her, Mr. Gillespie. This one's mine. Do you mind?"

I closed the door, surmising that his leaving his door open had only been for my benefit, as I went for a run, an extremely long, hard run.

Being with these people had put me off my routine, off my own life.

When I got back—*and, I'd truly considered not going back, not for anything*—I ran into her in the bathroom and watched her brushing her tongue so furiously I thought it'd bleed. She also took such a large portion of mouthwash that she swallowed most of it, then violently coughed and half-wretched, to spit it and the feel and taste of him out.

She was becoming more and more frenetic about cleaning herself, when she reached for the shampoo. I physically stopped her.

"He touched my hair."

"I touched it first."

I know, but it made sense to her, and she let me put the vanilla-laced shampoo back. Mrs. G'd mentioned buying "much" mild, natural soap and shampoo; this must've been why. "Much" must've been the only way Mrs. G had been able to warn me. Without ruining the surprise.

Perhaps I should consider buying stock in The Body Shop™.

Day wouldn't look at me.

"You promised him *that*, didn't you, to keep me here? I'm not worth it."

"Yes, you are."

"No. I'm not."

She shied away abruptly, tearing up, as if I'd reproved her personally. She kept rubbing her soft, full lips harshly, as if scouring away something horrid and vile, while her voice came in harsh, frantic whispers.

"You shouldn't have seen. He wanted you to see. Wouldn't let me close the door. We always close—. *His* house, *his* rules."

She nodded confirming some thought in her troubled brain.

"Knowing it and *seeing* it are different. I meant it. I really did. I'll *do anything*."

She was getting beside herself and still swiping too hard at her lips. I was becoming afraid that she'd bruise herself—.

"Don't hate me. Don't leave!"

She abruptly pulled back, emotionally, trying to control the situation, to control her rampant fear.

"I'll . . . I'll promise him something else. To keep the door and curtains closed, when we . . . when he . . . he—."

I shushed her, and held her to me to calm her.

I wasn't going to mention the following; however, I will because . . . because I should. Part of me was unreasonably glad she'd "do anything" for me to have me, and another part of me hated, no, feared that same thing.

Being truly human, I know every day one or two paradoxes and ambivalences make an appearance; in my actions, in my feelings or thoughts.

Most of the time, I ignore them or I'm even entirely oblivious of them, but at that moment, I was wallowing up to my neck in them. I'm not like that. I make saner choices than that. Not necessarily safer, but certainly . . . .

I'd have to talk to Stephie to get a second, outside perspective on my impulsive choices of late.

However, my sister wasn't around, right at that moment, as I felt Day's expressive body melt against mine.

I removed her hand from her overflushed lips and claimed them and her tongue, with mine, as if I really wanted them, which I most certainly did.

Then, I let her do whatever she pleased with me; I gave her complete control over me, which generated a puzzled look.

No man had ever offered himself to her in that manner before.

Her brief puzzlement was followed by a crooked little smile that lit up her eyes, with a smoldering flicker.

She sniffed me, deeply, after run sweat and all, then led me by the waistband and sat on the toilet lid, pulled down my pants, and unabashedly buried her face in the pungent scent of my pubes. Her subsequent "activity," with my happy cock and balls . . . .

Her gloriously well-educated mouth erased most of any memory of what she'd just likewise done for Hopkins, except that I noticed she hadn't done it for him with this kind of dedication and passion.

With a vengeance.

Because of the sounds of approval I was making, she teasingly asked if I liked what she was doing.

"YES" screamed through my brain, but somewhere, after reflecting that she had incredible jaw, tongue strength, and flexibility; in full innocence and stupidity, I said—.

"Where'd you learn that?"

She immediately stopped.

Looking down at her, I suddenly realized she'd taken it as a literal question and was speechless, angry, shamed. There was too much going wrong with her expression to tally, as she slipped down off the toilet to the floor and inched back, away from me, until the wall stopped her.

I apologized profusely.

I seemed to be doing a lot of that, lately.

My pleading regrets took awhile to take effect, because my juvenilely simple comment, my stupid, simple, and teasing comment, sent her somewhere inside herself that was hard for me to reach or woo her back from.

I'd never seen that kind of fear or shame before. My generation usually fears next to nothing. I only barely managed to get her part of the way back to me, before we were called to dinner.

* * * *

I stopped wondering that exact night, barring Hopkins' bedroom visits, why Mrs. G, as much as she obviously loved Day, would leave for the night, instead of staying in what was now my room. I also realized that Mrs. G had impeccable radar; she left a little early.

Hopkins was in a terrible snit, despite the post blowjob endorphins and a full belly of dinner.

Neither Day nor I finished our meals.

He still wasn't satisfied with our "arrangement," even though his opportunities in it had improved tremendously. He was presently mentioning, that before Day's hospital stay for her ankles, she'd—.

"SHUT UP!!!"

Day bit her lip, looking sheepishly embarrassed, realizing how loudly she'd shouted, as her words reverberated in my ears. I was sitting beside her on the sofa. She then seemed to be quoting someone.

"'Anger, even justifiable anger, especially *loud* anger, appears crazy, insane,' when institutions are mentioned."

"Tell him. Your young man should know. Or, shall I tell him?"

She softly insisted, "No."

"Tell me what?"

"We wouldn't want you here, Mr. Gillespie, under false hope and pretenses, with misguided desires. Tell him." She was instantly angry.

"What? That you had a nasty little itch? A thing for Mommy? Our darling Hoppy lost his chance to a friend, my Daddy. Now, he's using me as a substitute for her."

Which is, of course, enough information to cause a look of

disgust out of almost anyone. He also most certainly didn't like the way she was telling the story; if the piercing lasers darting from his eyes were any sort of sign.

"There's more to it than that. A lot more. True, she does, sometimes, remind me of her mother. But, I've known them both, quite well, and Day is really nothing like Twyla. Absolutely nothing like her. I *did* miss my chance, long ago. Then, even after Twyla . . . .

"I remained her good friend. I even interceded time and again for her headstrong, young daughter. Took care of her, as if she were my own."

Day was about to comment, but I beat her to it, which pleased her.

"I hope it was completely different then, because, at the moment, I think you have another definition of 'care' than I do."

"Caring for Day has been an honor. I've asked nothing special of her, nothing she wouldn't do ordinarily in showing her appreciation."

She made a sound, a Bronx Cheer raspberry, as she slouched back.

He gave her a nasty squint, then added, "Day's last 'accident,' the one affecting her ankles, changed many things between us. I was long overdue."

"What could possibly change to get *that* result, Mr. Hopkins?" Hopkins spitefully glanced her way. She straightened tensely and sat forward.

"Shut up, Hoppy." He gloated at her discomfort.

"Your Mr. Gillespie needs to know the truth, young lady, especially if you're going to continue confusing him with your pliant body."

"I'm not confused." I lied. Well, not completely.

"Surely then, if not the *first* 'accident,' involving your mother, then tell him about the second one, about your ankles. How they were injured, months before he, so fortunately, tripped over you."

She became retiring, reticent; as she fiddled with a thick sock, with one leg bent and her foot on the sofa.

"I don't . . . I don't remember, you know that."

I looked at her, slightly thrown. That statement, her statement . . . my gut—it felt like a lie to me.

"I only know, my delicate flower, that that is so very convenient. Everyone around us assumed I somehow caused her pain. It's maybe because I'm such a nice, loving person. That's one of the reasons I moved her here, to stop overhearing how the 'sweet, innocent child' didn't even blame me."

His malignant facial expression actually became *more* so. Talented fellow.

"You've tasted her, boy. There's nothing 'innocent' about her, which is why you're still here, isn't it?" A *very* talented fellow, this *Mr.* Hopkins. "If not *that* story, my sweet flower, then, please, do tell him about your mother."

"No." She sounded weak, pouty even.

"All right. Did you tell him what *kind* of hospital I removed you from, when I received custody?" I fielded that one.

"A mental hospital." He stared at me a long while, then decided he'd chance something.

"Tell him what kind, Day."

"I just said she told me, plus I saw a partial wrist I.D. among your things, when—. Day?"

Her face had changed, considerably. Alarmingly.

"*Day*?"

"I take it, Mr. Gillespie, the full name of the institution was missing? It wasn't merely a mental hospital. It was a state prison, as well."

They both were watching me, as I got up, not certain if sitting still or walking around would make me pass out sooner. Sudden unconsciousness would be good.

I heard the blood rushing as noisily as rapids in my ears;

felt my heart pounding heavily against my ribcage; and saw, as if nothing else at all existed in the entire world for me to see—*his cigarette's end, as it burned.*

I heard and felt nothing from her, she'd suddenly become aloofly frozen, waiting, holding her breath.

"Why . . . ?" My brain was shutting down.

"The first 'accident' landed Day in that institution for the criminally insane—."

I was choking to death, asphyxiating on the thought.

"To be in a place like *that* . . . ."

"It was for homicide." He was very ready to answer more—.

"That's enough, Hoppy."

"Is it, Day?"

He'd just gotten a very strong taste of having more of her, of having her attention, of her more enthusiastically doing exactly what he wanted of her—because of *my presence.*

But, despite that, to spite her and me, even if he couldn't get rid of me, ripping me apart, by slashing her open to my viewing, was keeping a smile on his mean face longer than I'd seen one there.

I needed a place to hide in plain view, so I slipped around, into the darkened bar area against the wall, then grabbed and drank a beer; some nasty British import, all in one long, warm draught.

She followed me.

"Benn, Mommy and . . . . We argued. Very badly. A hideous row." Pronounced like cow, like a Brit. He wasn't only just getting in her body, but in her head, as well.

"Hopkins'd told Mommy *things.* Lies. Partial truths. I told her the *whole* truth. It didn't matter. She . . . she never liked me, not the way I looked, once I . . . ."

She didn't say what she was thinking, only brushed her hand down over the womanly curves of her body.

"Mommy restricted me. Punished me. Took me to a *doc-tor* she had . . . she had hurt me."

I couldn't see Hopkins, but I heard him, as he breathed noisily, overexcited at our little talk, I suppose. So much so, he decided to participate.

"She wanted you to be a proper young lady, that's all; to stop being the promiscuous, wild little—!" She limped back to face off with him.

I half followed her.

"I wasn't like that!" She gave it serious thought. "I *never* ran the streets, and I only had *ONE* boyfriend, then . . . you—. *Liar!*"

She collapsed onto the floor, which must have hurt her damaged limbs, but some other deeper pain curled her up in a ball, as she pulled her hair, her eyes pleading him not to say whatever he appeared about to utter.

He merely said, "The court psychiatrists deemed there was an 'unfortunate, ungovernable pathology' in Day's manner, a condition they didn't feel was temporary. That is why they locked her away."

"Just 'cause they saw it that way, Benn, doesn't mean it was. They saw 'intent' in history. Of course, we had *history*, she's . . . she was my mother!"

She paused a long moment, her breath frozen, locked within her.

"Mommy's anger was so . . . . I never meant . . . . I *had* to push her off me, she was *hurting me,* again."

Day became completely forlorn, remembering her fear and loss, her anguish. He was sitting back, getting comfy, lighting up another.

"But, Twyla's the one who is deceased and buried in the ground. And, she so hated cold and dirt. I eventually went to see Day in hospital many times, to try to understand her. Perhaps forgive her, if it were possible. I finally had a change of heart."

Day's bitter anger erupted again.

"'Change of' lust! Why jerk over it when you see a better opportunity to jerk off in it, whenever you want!"

I didn't like the sound of that. I didn't like the sound of any of it, as I moved back behind and slumped against the bar, keeping its shielding thickness between them and me.

He coolly stood to look down on her.

"With my dedicated advocacy and, in time, with a reassessment of the evidence and her *many* varied states of mind, I did 'grease the wheel' a bit, a lot actually. Pulled a few 'highly placed' strings. Day was given into my custody for her own good."

She petulantly corrected him, "*Your* good. He *never* had her."

His burning cigarette end flared, as he hard dragged on it, and reseated himself, with as much dignity as an old Asian emperor.

"That's not true. I did."

She surged forward in her intense agitation.

"*Did you?* Must've been *one* supremely unremarkable experience. It didn't stop her from turning to Daddy. And, she obviously never regretted it, as if she'd missed something *great*, which I *know* she didn't."

Many a man, too many to count, detests being hit below the belt by a woman, especially one he's extremely attracted to, even an Englishman.

"I should have left you rotting there, you evil little bitc—!"

All their tensions were draining the energy straight out of me. I didn't know how to get out of it, or just out of the damned room. Running, screaming from the house and them both never quite fully formed in me.

I didn't have the juice for it at the moment, anyway, which made me consider later how some people complain about being drained sexually.

It'd been my experience that that only occurs when you choose to lie down with the wrong partner; the right, loving partner invigorates you, balances you, makes you feel certain of your place and reason for being dropped naked and screaming alive from a loving, warm womb into *this* cold world.

I'd been feeling that way . . . certain, with Day.

It was a good thing we weren't having sex at that moment, because something was grossly wrong; with her, with me, with the universal fabric, and she'd probably kill me; drain me to the last drop of my death.

They were still tearing viciously at each other's throats, without me; severing jugulars, splattering bloody emotions and acrimonious viscera on all of us.

"—always keeps me in isolation." She plopped back onto the sofa.

"You don't do well in crowds."

He appeared done with his incessant smoking, focusing all his attention instead on her. Her voice was becoming distant, resigned.

"So. He . . . he took me to live at his forest house. Out far from anyone else, but better than this horrid place. I like the forest better than this fish smelly, humid ocean.

"Or a lake's better. A freshwater lake is so—. You should see the pictures Mrs. G has of Scotland, Benn. I could very much love it there."

The pendulum that carried her moods back and forth changed directions again, as she snorted in distaste.

"If it hadn't been for the need to be close to the specialists here, we wouldn't be *this close* to other people. He'd hired Elise. *[She means Mrs. G. Day's the only one, who calls her by her given name.]*

"She was to take care of me, at the forest house, but she'd just started and was away at her sister's wedding, when he said he *wanted* me. In *that* way. Whether I—.

"He had *no right!* Said I *owed* him. Said, if I *chose* to continue to be 'selfish' and 'immature,' I'd soon 'be back in lockdown,' with the restraints and the overstrong drugs. Benn, my body doesn't like those chemicals. I can't tolerate them."

She was becoming acutely distressed, and I could feel her anxiety pulling on me, as I listlessly stalked around the room, in my own distress.

"The guards, orderlies, nurses, doctors, administra—. There're *too many* people with access to me, *there*. You'd think you'd be safe in a place with so many locks and doors and bars, except everyone . . . *everyone wants* . . . ."

I missed some of what was being said. I was getting a general mind overload, so I sat, plopped really, onto a chair at the dining table in the cramped dining area.

My sister, Stephie, argues with me constantly, as if her life depended on it, that all my most serious, emotional reasonings are mistakenly done in my heart, which is too close to my dick.

If I could leave my heart out of it altogether, like Stephanie says she does; or if my heart were closer to my wallet, she'd understand.

She and Dad love money like horny lovers; I'm more our Mama's child, because cash isn't everything, although one can probably never really have too much, but that might be Dad's part of me talking.

The only thing in my favor, Stephie once said, was that even though a lot of women like me, I don't like a lot of women. In "*that* way," as Day'd said. I'm not that casual with my heart.

But, my twin clarified, as she so loves to do, that once my heart was seized and secured by my lower anatomy, I was lost.

Stephie also says—*and maybe, she's right*—that I have a little hero-damsel complex.

I knew I should've left, crept away on hands and knees, slithered away on my flat belly, if need be, while they argued, but I couldn't, wouldn't leave. Not even in spite of the horrendous things I was hearing and feeling.

I was no longer certain whether I could ever leave.

Great, the one time I can't run.

When I was ten or something, Mama'd caught me talking "like an idiot," about how obviously stronger men were over women.

I'd been gesturing emphatically, making my point to some little buddies of mine, until she grabbed my forefinger, and held it. She'd asked me which is stronger, the finger or the vice that holds it; then instructed me to pull.

I pulled, for all I was worth.

Her grip was like a pair of Chinese handcuffs. I couldn't pull out.

Mama said I should remember the one finger versus the many fingered unity of the hand, or more precisely, the single, *hard* penis—*Ah, jeez, Mama! Not in front of Jeffrey and the guys!*—versus the many muscles of the *soft* vagina—*Ah!!*

Mama, however graphically, had made a valid point, then. But now . . . .

If it'd just been the sex, I could leave, but Day had me gripped with ALL of her, because slipping inside her, she'd gripped me and held me there, like Mama's finger vice. Tighter even.

Day held me fast with her intelligent eyes, with her *diverse* emotions, with her luscious, petulant mouth, with her . . . with her everything.

I literally was so screwed. I knew I'd never, NEVER want to leave her, even while hearing the horrid things I was hearing.

But, we don't always get exactly what we believe we want, do we?

It also occurred to me that I was obsessing.

Needless to say, her horror stories were upsetting me, but they still weren't scaring me out of that house.

After all, when Bette Davis and Bruce Dern in "Hush, Hush, Sweet Charlotte" had frightened me out of my wits as a kid, I'd sat through it all the way to the vicious, bloody end; a love story puzzle for horror freaks that scared the hell out of me.

I saw it again a few years back. It's no longer scary and

pretty over the top.

It's real life that's scary.

I got up again, too restless to be still and Day was saying that at his forest house . . . .

"He . . . He shouldn't have *ordered* me. He used to ask, at first. He'd been nearly shy about it even, but he tired of me not bending to him.

"*Why is it everyone thinks they own me?* Always ordering me around, telling me to do *things*, for *my* 'own good' that's more good to them than—. In hospital, they said I'd . . . . I . . . . I forget." I sat near her.

"What do you remember?"

Asking questions is a good way to get information, and to draw attention from the fact that your brain's invisibly bleeding out your ears. So much for being sane.

"Being tired. Exceptionally tired. The two woodsmen Hopkins had to cut wood and do repairs left a circular saw unattended and went *somewhere.* Lunch?"

She shrugged.

"I didn't want him touching me, again, not like . . . ." She held her breath a long time, then finally let it go. "I used to help my Daddy with carpentry at home, and—."

She made an abruptly quick knifeblade gesture across her throat. That chilled me, especially realizing how warm and alive her throat was to my lips. I also acutely wanted another beer, cold or warm, or boiling hot, for that matter, but I couldn't move.

I thought it, but no movement.

"You can snap out the safety guard, Benn. The blade spins, like a wheel. Wait. It is a wheel. A sharp wheel. A Frisbee®? It'd be like that Japanese Bond guy had thrown his razor hat at me."

Her head flipped to the side after she made the knife cutting movement at her warm throat again. I held her hand to stop her from repeating the gesture anymore.

"Hoppy shrieked, startling me. You shouldn't startle someone holding something dangerously sharp and unwieldingly heavy. He was screaming, and grabbing, and I . . . . We . . . ? I fell. He pushed me?"

She paused, unable to get it straight in her memory.

"Or, he grabbed . . . ?" She abruptly remembered, and it made her snarl.

"*He touched me.* I hit him. At him. Lost my footing." She giggled sleepily at the word "footing." "I fell; it fell. On both legs. How shocking. No pain. No sound.

"It was funny; Hoppy and his two tall woodsmen running headless all about, the car seat and floor filling with . . . so much bright red blood from . . . somewhere."

I feel now, despite my own emotions running "headless" and rampant, I can tell most times when she's boldface lying to me; it's harder, if she's confused or truly believes it herself.

There was truth in what she was saying, in her now lax, nearly hypnotized manner, but someth—.

"When the blade fell, Hoppy, did you find something more immediate to do than trying to pry apart my legs and hump me? Always taking such intimate 'care' of me."

She stared at Hopkins, who was leaning in, as if to pounce, to clarify any of her statements, perhaps.

"Benn, you should've seen his face. So ashen white, and horrified. Oh. Yeah. The saw. I dropped it on me. On purpose."

I bounded out of my seat and got another nasty, warm English beer and drank half or more, before she took it from me.

She polished it off, gazing at me, making certain my eyes were on her and her pink tongue, as she licked, then sucked the last foamy drops from the dark, hard bottleneck.

I heard Hopkins laugh at me as, with a flash, he lit another cigarette.

"I'll make the decision easy for you, boy, get out while you still can. She tricked me into believing she'd be safer with me than in the asylum, and now she's expertly playing us against each other. I have the money, you have the . . . hard youth, and she has each of us, by our manhood.

"There was truth in what she said. Somewhat. However, since I'm her guardian, what better way for a 'delicate,' insane, young woman to control her older, male keeper than to suggest. I repeat. *She* suggested I lie with her."

She stared round at him, in astonishment.

"Hoppy, that's not true."

She had lied some, but I wasn't sure when. And, now, she didn't exactly seem to remember herself where in their history they were, and I certainly didn't know.

"Mommy's really mad, mad that . . . that I let you—."

"Mr. Gillespie, when I said 'no' to her, Day came to me, naked. You've seen her considerable attributes and I may be old, but I am a fully functioning man. She said she'd 'close her eyes' and I could 'do whatever I wished,' 'pretend whatever I wanted,' and 'use her however'—."

"*NO!* No. No. No. No. *NO!* That's . . . that's . . . !"

I was getting very much confused and was about to edge away.

She uncannily, instinctively sensed it, shook her head "no" at me. I shook mine and shrugged. Abruptly, she was with me, kissing me, her whole body seductively against mine, as her tongue in my mouth was usurping any independent volition right out of me.

I was so screwed.

Hopkins growled, deep in his throat.

"No!"

He pulled us apart. Well, attempted anyway. She glanced at him for just a brief moment.

Nothing was said, just a stiff, intense nod from her, which he—*it seemed to me and to my great surprise—accepted,* in triumph.

He left.

Something'd passed between them, something important, that I missed, standing mere inches away.

"Wh-what just happened?"

In that brief moment, underwater, out of my depth, I'd suddenly been sucked deeper into darkness by an undertow, without knowing exactly . . . .

There'd been a quick, deadly skirmish, in a battle for . . . for me; and in that concise insurgence, she'd won. He'd won. I felt I'd won, but simple reason didn't confirm that; especially, since I still didn't know what war I was in.

It didn't matter.

I was like a diabetic confronted by his favorite forbidden and deadly sweet delicacy. I ate, hungrily, fearing it would kill me, yet not giving a damn, as she kissed and touched me, until I'd forgotten my question, as we made love where we were, her desire for me entirely burning out my reason.

She left me there on the floor, and after realizing I couldn't use my mind for anything except thoughts of her, I sought her.

He was in her room, door closed, grunting and huffing, while speaking her name and begging her to be vocal.

I heard her, faintly.

Then louder, which meant she was most definitely participating, as he wished. She was no longer merely lying there, as before. She was, evidently, paying him for my continued residency.

First, she'd seduced me to keep me from running. Correction. I'd let her seduce me; then, she'd gone straight from me to him, from my body to his.

Day didn't come back to me that night, which she couldn't've, if she'd tried; I'd locked my hall door and my side of the bath and turned my Mac to an Internet radio station, to drown out their sounds and too many thoughts of them. In there. Together.

I changed the station, though, after getting a painful third of the way into the all too prophetic Dave Matthews Band's "Crash

Into Me©".

Everything was just great. Having a fantastic, extended sabbatical on The Beach, far away from all formerly intense life and death decisions and unseemly demands on me, my mind, and soul.

This was much worse, much more personal, and bore deeper under my skin than my "conflicted career choices" ever had. I wasn't sleeping properly or resting, not in *his* house, where "Hoppy" was right—she *was* "confusing" me.

Terribly. Probably detrimentally.

Day, this child-woman, whom I'd seen come to tears over the decision of which fruit preserve to put on her peanut butter and potato bread sandwich, knew exactly what she wanted, when it came to me, despite having been treated harshly, in ways I can't and don't want to imagine.

Her violent affections for me frightened me. Mine . . . mine for her frightened me even more. Most times I was swept up in her like driftwood in a Gulf/Caribbean hurricane battering the Yucatan shore; caught in a force of nature, that was wild, emotional, and beyond deadly.

There was something truly addicting about that for me, and I don't have an addictive personality. At least I'd never thought so. Not until her.

* * * *

I ran *much* earlier than usual the next morning; then breezed past Day expectantly waiting for me on the sofa. I relocked myself in and called the hotel, which still held my room. No, no arrival yet, sir. Thank you. Click.

I went to the kitchen, when I knew both Day and Mrs. G were elsewhere, and was heading back to shelter, when I spotted the pretty blonde woman outside speaking cheerily to Day.

I couldn't hear either of them, but I could tell by their respective demeanors that the blonde liked Day, and that Day hated the blonde's presence.

I went out in time to have my hostess glare at me, before

she guardedly crept down the stairs, while holding tight of the rail, to sit on the last step, strip her feet bare, and bury them up past the scars in the warm sand.

"Gee, Stephie, still have your winning way with people, do yah?"

If you think Day's a bitch, when she doesn't get her way, you've never spent time with my twin sister, who couldn't keep her eyes to herself.

"Your Day has a good eye. Identified me right away and I look nothing like that ancient locket photo. And we certainly don't look alike, shaggy. Tell me you didn't toss that expensive travel razor I gave you, while you've been purging your very enviable life."

I hugged her from behind, as she put an arm back around me; which is a standard stance for us.

"You like her."

"Snake Boy, she's gorgeous, and a more petulant bitch than I am."

"Yes, and maybe. Stop staring at her. You're always trying to steal away the other women in my life." We'd let each other go, as Steph peeked in the house before gazing again at the back of Day's windtossed curls, then dipped her eyes to thoroughly view again the rest of Day, who intently ignored us both.

"You always have great taste, Benn. This one's even managing to look delicious with no makeup and absolutely nothing on under that frumpy potato sack of a dress.

"Even so, she must be incredible in the sack to have both my Bennet's swelled heads on backward, so swiftly. She does look like a definite *gotta-have-her-latex-free-lay*, though. Am I right or am I right?"

My Stephie is not subtle or able to speak below a stage whisper.

"Not here. Checked in yet?"

"No. Came straight here in the cab."

"Nose."

"Like I instruct my cardiology students everyday, how else am I to give you viable advice, little brother, without examining, up close and personal, the voluptuous subject in question?"

Stephanie's three minutes older than I am which makes her at least three minutes more know-it-all.

I visibly clammed up, so she knew, if the conversation were to go any further, she'd have to play on my terms. Passive aggressiveness works on bossy older siblings. I let her in, so she could see I wasn't being strung up and tortured; not physically anyway.

She ducked into Day's room, behind my back. When I caught up to her, she was going through the woman's things.

"Well, she most certainly knows the way to get down on her knees and suck the bucks out of a sugar daddy." The mental visual of that sentence was just too infuriatingly close.

"Steph, not everyone loves a dollar, as much as you and Dad. Hey! Get out of there!"

"No, really, guano brain, your woman has no panties! I don't see one pair. Or a bra." I'd never seen a pair, on or off Day, never thought about it—. "And, oh, please, Benn, you do pretty damned well yourself getting a dollar. Or would that now be an English pound?"

If I had thought about Day's panties, I'd have assumed she didn't wear them at home or—.

Stephie was laughing at me, which cured my panty preoccupation. I tossed my rental keys to her to go out and put her bags and herself in the car. On my way out, I stopped beside Day, who was still feigning indifference, as I stooped down, to speak eye to eye.

"I'm putting Stephanie in my room at the hotel; I'll be there a while. I need to talk to her."

"About me? About all of us?"

"*Yeah.*" Of course. What else?

"She doesn't like me."

"Stephie likes you just fine."

"*Not like that.* Not sexually." Uncannily quick instincts, this girl. "She doesn't like that I have you. Period." The truth of that statement made me wince, on so many levels.

"I won't be gone forever, just a few hours." She grabbed my wrist.

"*Don't leave me here.* Alone. With Hopkins." She did a very good job, Oscar® caliber, but I could feel, I *knew*, she wasn't afraid of him. She wanted to manipulate me. I pried her fingers from me.

"No histrionics, Day. Just continue doing whatever it is you need to do with 'Hoppy.' That's your business. I need to be with my sister for a while—."

The bitch hit me. A full-knuckled backhand across the face, hard as she could.

It didn't get the response she wanted, so she leaned back from me. She didn't exactly shrink in fear from me, but she definitely got back, proof that the little bitch was very tough.

I've seen men, larger and stronger than myself, run from me, when I'm abruptly like this. I spat out bloodied saliva onto the sand at her feet, realizing she'd planned to make me red or white hot angry; unfortunately for her, my rage was a cold, colorless one.

"Try and stop me today, try and get me back here before I want to come back, and I won't come back. To you. Ever. Am I bluffing, now?"

Day was plainly anxious, as I waited, blank in my anger until she sadly, almost imperceptibly, shook her head "no."

I left.

Stephie and I hadn't seen each other face-to-face in months, so we had a lot to catch up on; the bulk of which was analyzing the quagmire I was presently in.

The sun'd gone down, someone knocked. A pizza guy. We

hadn't ordered any.

You're sure? Yes. Wrong address? Yeah.

It was probably a scam, or the guy was just lazy. We bought the large off him for five bucks. Not bad. My favorite toppings. He got a good look at Stephie in her nightshirt, pleasant guy, totally wasted on her.

I thought I'd go out for ice before resettling in and glanced out the hall window; Pizza Guy was about to settle behind a smallish driver onto a motorcycle; a little, beat up Harley.

The driver was completely covered, leatherclad, head-to-toe; with a polarized, full-faced, visored helmet, yet seemed familiar.

Pizza Guy's cocky attitude outside reminded me of a few stuffed-full-of-shit medical residents I'd dealt with over the years. He seemed absolutely pleased with himself about something and grabbed hold of the driver's middle to hold on, as they pulled off, erratically, as if the driver weren't used to the machine.

Maybe it's just me, but I find men, who aren't gay, seem to feel that holding onto the guy driving the bike is a "girl's gesture" and therefore a "homosexual gesture." So, they don't do it, even upon pain of falling off and breaking their one and only neck.

Pizza Guy seemed terribly interested in girls to me, if his eyeballing Steph were proof.

Two hours later, niggling thoughts were still active; annoying and preoccupying me with every recalled gesture and movement I'd seen between the two of them. I finally grabbed my car keys and told Stephie I'd be back in a bit.

She asked if I were going "to the house for a quickie with the cripple."

She's a sweet girl my big sister.

I did go "back to the house," the garage actually. There's a tarp in there with wheels under it that I'd never bothered looking under, until then, as I uncovered a banged up and deeply scratched small Harley-Davidson™ with fresh sand and dirt on it—Day's machine, I bet.

I was tossing away a stray fast-food bag that had blown into the garage, when I spotted two freshly used condoms lying discarded on top of the rest of the garbage.

My mind blanked numbly, before I went back to the hotel and stayed over.

Stephanie, the next evening, didn't want me going back to my "self-inflicted, sexual prison" and wanted me to leave with her on her flight out, but I had to go back, her joke about "a quickie" was no longer humorous.

Mrs. G was glad to find I was back for the night, Hopkins had gone out to a dinner meeting with his "solicitor"—his lawyer, Sid; Mrs. G was exhausted and relieved for my presence, having dealt with Day being "bit of a problem, a bit difficult" all day.

"Ms. Day" was in her room, lying down, her head on a pillow covered with the shirt I'd done my last sweaty run in, her feet and lower legs were covered by a thick afghan. She solemnly watched me with serpentine interest, as I rummaged back deep into her closet of soft, flowered dresses, to find her riding leathers and helm.

She volunteered, in near monotone, that Hopkins had gotten her the bike and the other things in my room long ago, as an appeasement for her having nothing of her own. She was "allowed" to tool around the grounds of where they were staying, and no farther.

Then, he'd pointed out that she had nowhere to go, especially nowhere he couldn't, literally, have her dragged back to him from.

The futon mattress was collapsible and had given her the sense that she could pack and go; while it also fixed the fact in his mind that he didn't like bedding her on the uncomfortable floor. He'd eventually gotten her back into a bed that was a decent distance from the floor and had mothballed the bike.

"I ran away on it once. He sent bounty hunters—didn't want the law to know I was 'on the loose.' They did what he'd promised, literally dragged me back to him.

"He always brings the bike and the mattress with us, wherever we go, so at the critical times I'm 'bitching about my free-dom' he can ask, 'Why don't you pack up your things and take a ride?' Why doesn't he fucking screw himself, and you too for that matter."

I let that one go because I didn't want to get more enmeshed in their "history," but she was still in a nasty mood, feeling screwed over and busted by him and screwed and abandoned by me, I guess.

She graphically pointed out how she'd "let" Hopkins seduce himself last evening into taking her, which wasn't hard, not with the way he always obsessively watched her, salivated for her. More than I did, in literal fact.

She said she'd "poured it on," about "missing" me, "need-ing" me, could he "make it better." In short, she gave me more insightfully specific details than I wanted to hear about how she'd thoroughly tuckered him out, before coming after me.

I dimly wondered who Pizza Delivery Boy was, but didn't re-ally want to care. I've seen far less interesting women, than Day, attract and manipulate men to do their whimsical bidding; like moths to a flaming pyre, without hardly trying. Moths like me.

So, I put the freshly used, discarded condoms out of mind.

"I'm surprised 'Stephie' let you come back."

"I'm surprised you can't go anywhere, but you can leave here to check up on me—when I'm with my twin, at that."

The "milk-filled" condoms and Pizza Boy were out of mind, but not out of some other, deeper, more sensitive part of me and I blurted out some outraged, indignant, and regrettably needy comment on my part.

I'm sure Hopkins would have guffawed very loudly at it.

Gist: Pizza Yutz was some Surgical Attending Physician from the hospital where Hopkins had had her ankles cosmetically repaired.

She'd called him before, well, paged him; Day doesn't like conversations on the phone. She'd paged Pizza Junior Surgeon once before, just to give herself a sense of power and independence; to feel another man's . . . hands on her, a man *she'd chosen*, "anyone" besides old Hoppy "groping and poking" at her.

I could tell through her words, that she was indifferent to our young medico; nevertheless, his very existence still irritated me.

Her reasoning was that, at a time when she wanted to bust my nuts keeping tabs on me, she preferred "paying him for his eager assistance with a few lame fucks on the bike tarp, rather than get [Mrs. G] fired for helping."

How considerate. Warped. Evil.

She then called me a long string of obscene epithets, the least of which was "fucking bastard" before turning her back on me. That shouldn't have bothered me, but it did.

I walked around to address her face, she turned away again; we repeated the process, which pissed me off further. *I know.* She was yanking me. She was sincere about her feelings, but she was still yanking me hard, because she could, because I allowed it, and we both knew that.

I got on the bed with her. I shouldn't have. I shouldn't have touched her.

Or seen the hot, salty tears on her cheeks.

Or kissed her trembling, soft, yielding lips.

Or . . . .

Somewhere in the night, I heard an overfed, slightly drunk Hopkins open her door, then curse when he saw me with her. She was happily cuddled and spooned hard against my back.

He slammed the door.

* * * *

I'd just rounded the corner into the hall, midmorning, next day, having heard nothing, before Hopkins seethingly bellowed—.

"You whore!"

He backhanded Day across her high, rounded cheekbone. She moved with his action but still received a great deal of that percussive act, causing her to hit the wall.

I roughly grabbed his hand to stop him from striking her again. It was the first time he and I'd ever touched.

The thought of striking him, like he'd struck her, occurred to me, but there were no blows between us, because with about forty odd years difference, his smoking and no exercise versus my physical strength and outrage, I'd shatter him.

And, be promptly arrested.

Day for her part, remarkably, didn't shatter and break, despite his rough hand, as she'd apparently been prepared for it.

She didn't stumble as much as I would have thought. Her eyes didn't water up. She didn't whimper. She didn't touch and soothe her brilliantly bruised face because this had obviously happened before, and explained how and from whom she'd learned to deliver a blow like that herself.

She straightened her dress and ignored both of us, as she limped away, using the wall's surface as a support guide while avoiding his contempt and my concern. She headed through the front rooms, then out onto the porch to sit, nervously tugging at her worn footgear, as she gazed far out at the water, as if starved to be out, far out beyond it.

"Hopkins! How could y—? What is wrong with you?"

I can't express the heat that radiated from the hatred and anger in him.

If I had gone any further with my obvious rant, he unmistakably would've barred me from the house, from her. He might even have run away with her, in an attempt to do so, before I'd take her, because that sort of unspoken desperation, which so often hung about her, now hung like ice floes around him.

His anger and fear were justified, because despite Day's behavior in the previous forty-eight hours, I'd've taken her from him at that very moment, but legally that wouldn't have gotten us very far.

I let it go for the present.

"I don't understand, Hopkins. Wanting a woman, who so obviously doesn't want you. Forcing her. For how long?" I left out, "not since early childhood, I hope" and trailed him to the living room and its beachside, French doors, from where he assiduously observed every breath she took, while sitting on the topmost step.

"We came to a point, when she was yet a girl, but not a girl. She would tempt me, in her calculated nonchalance, to make me want her, beyond all reason." That sounded familiar. "Then she'd callously refuse me, feigning indifference. But—."

He discontinued abruptly, as if flash frozen, like a thought, a feeling, a memory freezes in the mind and chills the soul. There was a lie or something in what he'd said, I was nearly certain of that, but I never could feel him, read him like I could her.

"She has the right to refuse you."

He smiled, if glacial blue ice can smile.

"Like I have the 'right' to toss an unwanted resident squatter from my house, who eats my food and fucks what is mine."

He had a certain valid point of perspective, though, technically, he had personally invited me to stay, but I wasn't in the mood or mind to sympathize with a man, who'd been keeping the unwilling woman under discussion, for his own quite prurient self-interests.

"Hopkins, I'm not blind and she's not stupid. It's more than anticipating the fulfillment of having her want you; you entirely get off on controlling her, knowing she's dependent on you for every scrap of food, every piece of clothing, practically the molecules of air she breathes."

He stared at me a long while, weighing what I'd said.

"I do. I really do 'get off,' is it, on that; and no little slut deserves such treatment more than she. I rightfully, legally control the cunt and still she defies me, keeping *herself* from me, hating the touch of the hand that feeds her, yet trying to play me for a fool, the ungrateful little bitch.

"Steve *[from next door]* saw her steal away the other night—

after you. But you know that, don't you? You forgave her, didn't you?

"That's what I overheard her whisper to Mrs. Gorbachev. That she'd whored herself with two men she detests to pursue you, even though she was in no position to actually do anything to stop you, or force you to come back. *And, you gave into her.*"

A shake of his head indicated a shift in his mood.

"I was ever so basically satisfied, before you arrived."

"She wasn't. Isn't."

"That doesn't concern me. What does, is that *sometimes* her body would forget its indifference and respond to me, not fully or willingly, but respond.

"You wouldn't understand the significance in that, because her response to you is so 'all-encompassing,' I believe is the term she uses. She was like a barren, lifeless tree with a spot or two of greenery left to signify a lack of total death, but still worth keeping to gaze at and possess.

"Then you tripped over our horizon and she's suddenly full and ripe everyday, every night and I can see and feel and taste the edge of that difference, while she continues holding herself, her emotional attentions from me; and I resent her restraint greatly."

He made a sound, a wounded deep growl.

"If I appear . . . . If I am greedy and harsh it is your fault, Mr. Gillespie. Her body now confuses parts of my touch for yours, warming that incredible body to mine. She detests that, even while she more obligates herself to me on your behalf.

"So, young man, this continuous stream of vicious discontent and acrimony you see, you have generated it. Which gives me heart."

I'm glad it gave him something because his little speech had eviscerated a gaping emptiness in me, as he swallowed like he was ingesting bile before staring through me.

"There is no secret in that I have always wanted Day and

that I was, despite the tragic circumstances, glad to find an opportunity to make her indebted to me.

"And, I will be quite blunt and apparent. She will fulfill her proper sexual and emotional obligations to me and give me what I want of her or she'll never completely have what she wants.

"You, sir, came running down that beach to my Day and gave me a screw to tighten right through the very heart and soul of her. I didn't have that before. In fact, I had nothing. Other than her nominal freedom, I had nothing with which I could get the better of her.

"Now, I know *exactly* what she wants. Exactly, *who* she wants. No. She'll never have it. Have you. Not completely. Not 'without strings.' Not ever. Not her. Nor you, either, Mr. Gillespie."

"You can't seriously. . . . I don't understand how—?"

"Please. *Please.* You understand it all just fine, my bright lad. And, you are an extraordinarily bright lad, aren't you? Winning her to you, winning yourself free room and board, and especially bed?

"Look at us. Two grown men of the world, as our lovely, hothouse flower sits out there on her delectable buttocks and here we stand, her two industrious bees, flying busily around her, nearly always just about to fatally crash into each other over her.

"She's ignored me, said 'no' to me, and even grievously injured herself to keep herself from me, but *now,* suddenly, she freely offers herself. To *me.* On the gold platter that is you.

"So, come now, we both know we need each other. Without me, she goes away. Without you, I can no longer control her. So it always is that the most valuable objects always come at a higher price, then that price, *if you're so very fortunate,* increases in value while you own them."

He smiled in his malignancy at my obvious disgust for his calling her an "object" he *owned.*

"Bee to bee, Mr. Gillespie, I may be grizzled; however, I will have mine, even if you do register more trips between her soft, fragrant petals than I."

He stared harder at me, if that can be possible, trying to read me.

"Mr. Gillespie, just who the hell are you, besides a highly unwelcome guest?"

"If you want rent and board, fine. I'll pay it."

"Now, wouldn't that document me as a pimp." I didn't like his implying prostitution.

"Keep your currency. When I have you tossed out on your ear, I want to be able to do it freely and clearly and spur of the moment.

"But, do tell me something. How thoroughly should I have you investigated? Give me a small hint of what they would find? What are you always running from out there, Mr. Gillespie?

"What is your personal world and business life like, that a vital, strapping young fellow, such as yourself, never has any-where else to be, except here?

"What are your true intentions?"

"Investigate me all you like. Knowing more about me won't make you any happier, and they certainly won't find I was, for all intents and purposes, a former pedophile, keeping a woman prisoner, for my own sexual benefit."

He smiled sourly in thought.

"I suppose that is a fair description, Mr. Gillespie, in your mind. But, let's not forget that you're benefiting, too. And, as long as I am benefiting, I have no desire to know more about you.

"Except perhaps, slightly wondering, excluding young Ms. Day, and since there's no ring on your finger, no talk of wife, husband, or significant other, that it would seem that maybe you too have been wanting the unattainable and waiting for some-thing, for someone. Who have you been waiting for, *Benn*?"

He said my name with distaste. It was the only time he didn't say "Mr. Gillespie," "young man," "lad," or "boy."

It's psychologically notable that I glanced out at Day, who, in characteristic-synchronistic-out-of-earshot-eeriness, was staring at me with the bruise he'd put on her cheek plainly noticeable. Then, she glanced away and so did I.

I'd, again, forgotten the question, when confronted with a query that could be construed as asking about my deepest feelings for her, before realizing Hopkins was laughing, loudly, at me; the laugh almost sounded empathetic, almost.

* * * *

It'd been awhile and my unofficial pact with Hopkins, which "benefited" us both, had been declared long enough ago that I'd nearly forgotten it, much in the same manner fresh beans simmer ever so slowly in an iron pot on the back burner.

On the way to being completely consumed.

Or burned to blackest destruction.

I'd unintentionally startled her, and she'd had that look one has when waking abruptly from a potent and far away dream, as if discovered naked in court or, as Steph insists, "caught masturbating at Mass."

Day'd been half hiding behind the corner of the porch and intently watching the woman next door, or more accurately, I think, the toddler next door—a rather plain kid with a certain charming sweetness.

Day became incensed, upon being discovered.

Y'know, instead of trying to control Day's sexual life, her mother should have worked on finding ways for the girl to learn how to constructively channel her virulent temper, but it was far too late for "Mommy" on that one.

I grabbed Day up in a fireman's carry hold—*to diffuse her anger*—but she didn't perceive it as the fun I'd intended, as my walking with her down the stairs and toward the neighbor's caused her to pound my backside with her fists and scream at me to stop.

Her voice was in that same mortified range from our initial collision on the shore, so, I called out a quick and casual "hi" to mother and child, then headed back with my enraged cargo, up the front steps to deposit her delightfully charming ass on the table.

Let's just say, she was seething.

"I'd kick you in the crotch for that; but it'd hurt me more than you."

"You can knee me, that'd hurt me more than you."

And, it would've, since our legs were interspersed, as I took her leg and rubbed her knee against my crotch. She plainly liked the feel of my cock against her, but fussed her skirt down to glance back guiltily toward the neighbor, Penelope, I believe the name is. Steve's wife.

Day didn't seem to want her seeing us so intimate, which was odd because she had never cared before if anyone saw us, except sometimes Hopkins, when he's particularly under her skin and she's exhausted with his perpetual, hyper attention.

Besides, we were only displaying public affection; it wasn't like she was "going down" on me, or vice versa.

The whole neighbor affair became quickly nonexistent and dismissible when the mother walked away with the boy, whose name I hadn't bothered to learn. He stared over her shoulder, waving at us. Cute, for the most part.

I should restate that. *I'd* thought that it was a dismissible event, but Day didn't seem to, as she appeared to let it affect her mood periodically the rest of the day and wouldn't clarify why. Then, the next day was worse and long for other reasons, as we fought.

I've never been involved in so many nasty and intimately vicious fights with any woman before, not without a complete parting of the ways. Stephie doesn't count, she's blood family, and I have absolutely no sexual inclinations for my sister.

I tried exceedingly hard to stay even and mellow, but Day thoroughly pissed me off, knowing intuitively how to burrow under my defenses.

We fought because I was leaving—*despite my warning her two days ahead that I would be gone only briefly.*

I slept alone, her choice. I'd gotten over most of it by the next morning, but she was still sharply pissed when I left.

I was a few states away the majority of the day, for a long-standing, personal commitment—an extremely depressing memorial service. At least it was to me.

Our fight before leaving and my depression for the duration of my short trip was crowned by an exhausting three-way fight amongst Hopkins, Day, and myself, as soon as I arrived back.

The usual bull: "ownership," abandonment, sexual hierarchy, etc. Mrs. G hovered quietly in the background, getting a gutful, despite apparently deciding on her own hopeful misjudgment that I'd successfully keep the body count down.

Mrs. G hadn't liked Day's situation before I'd ever come over the horizon, and with me added to the mix, the extra tension was wearing on her. She unreasonably insisted on retaining great irrational hopes for me; that I'd bundle up her little confused and dangerous darling and make an illegal run for the "happily ever after."

There was some wistful merit to her thought.

The right person taking Day and becoming completely invisible with her . . . .

"Invisible" is something most of us entirely can't manage though, not between paper trails AND ego, and state of the art skip-tracing techniques.

However, disappearing, slipping into the ether with her might be possible. If there were a sufficient absence of paper, of: checks; contracts; credit cards; and, more crucially important, a sufficient absence of one's ego.

Ego's always the hardest to get away from and cast aside.

You'd think, for some reason, that a practical Scot would be more down to earth about such things.

I'd stayed to myself the evening after returning from the service, but was certain Mrs. G had something that was crucial to her to ask me, but wasn't finding the right moment to ask, before leaving for the night.

The next morning she managed to inquire if I were well.

I told her that I was feeling better; actually I wasn't, but'd decided I should get out and do something for someone else. I'd become morbid and distant from everyone important to me, because I kept obsessing on all the things I'd done or hadn't done for my friend, way before it'd become necessary to attend memorial services for him.

It seems to me, and I have proof in my mother's life and death, and especially with Chuck's, that what we can do for people, especially those we love, is never, NEVER enough, to soothe our ravaged hearts, once they're dead and buried.

"Mr. Bennet?"

I playfully scowled at Mrs. G, since she insisted on calling me "Mr." when I'd repetitively begged her otherwise.

We were at a local media store; I'd asked her to accompany me to pick out some new books, CDs, DVDs, and player for the woman of our mutual interest. Day "wasn't permitted" to watch or hear live broadcasts but most prerecordings were fine.

There is just too much Der Führer in that last sentence to calmly comment about.

I'd asked Mrs. G out, because I'd gotten tired of her looking like she was about to burst.

"Ms. Day says . . . . She believes you don't love her. I told her she was mistaken, that she was merely feeling insecure, trying to undercut herself so she wouldn't fly to high with her hopes and emotions, in case you should—."

"Leave her in the lurch?"

She nodded tersely and tried not to sigh, but she did, annoyed with my lack of urgency. Or tack. Mrs. G likes me; but she'd definitely prefer that I'd take some of my energies and steer them to more actively finding a warm, cozy place for Day, besides psycho lockdown.

She knows, though, whether she wants to face it or not, as well or better than I do, just how hard and thoroughly constricting the situation with Hopkins is. She's asked him herself, more than once, to name her as inheriting custodian of her Ms. Day, but he refuses.

He always refuses. He will always refuse. Period. No reasoning. No sympathy. Just "no."

Not one iota of whatever "yes" would bend anyone else, who had a heart, or a conscience.

So, Mrs. Gorbachev was playing another card. She's like an aunt, so I tried to be less infuriating and more focused on letting her get whatever point of hers out, but the point was always the same for her—wanting me to keep and take care of Day.

"The situation's difficult, Mrs. G, and you know that. You both know that."

"I know, Mr. Bennet, that you look at her with love and respect, and that you've worked heroically to not let your fears about her get the better of you."

"You 'know' all that? Are you so sure?" She nodded in full conviction.

Her use of "heroically" wasn't lost on me. I also don't care to be praised too highly, even by someone like her. The higher and harder the pat on the back, the more likely it is to break your neck.

I almost told her not to underestimate a man's innate, complex fears when it comes to amour; especially, when sharp objects, blood, and the legally criminally insane were involved.

"I understand what you want of me, and it would be . . . nice. Day is a challenge, a surprise, a story I don't think I'd ever truly get tired of. Or at least, could come back to over and over again.

"But, I wasn't in a great place when I crashed into her, and two somewhat lost people finding each other doesn't negate them still remaining lost. Perhaps, even becoming more so, because they're also lost in each other."

"What's wrong with that?"

I made a face she took as a challenge.

"What's wrong with being lost, if lost is better and more invigorating than where you were, when you knew *exactly* where you were?" I hated that. She was just like Mama sometimes. I blindly picked something off the shelves, to distract her.

"What about this one?"

She shook her head "no"; smugly so, was my impression. And, she's not my mother.

"Maybe, just maybe, Day's just merely an incredible and easy lay, that's keeping me amused for the moment in my extreme boredom."

Her face reddened, brilliantly, but she didn't fall for being goaded.

"Maybe she is. Maybe you don't cherish the feeling of being lost. Maybe you don't—."

"'Maybe,' just 'maybe,' people beat down, kill, and destroy what they love the most." She was aghast.

"Ms. Day said that. *Precisely.* How sad. How very sad for you both." We fell silent a long while, as we pretended to focus on shopping.

"Mr. Bennet, I only want her to have some happiness, some peace; someone, who truly loves her enough to sacrifice some of his pride and will for her. I don't believe that's too much to ask, because she is quite special and deserves . . . .

"I'm not asking him to 'give her the world' or 'the stars' or the entirety of 'all' his love, as if no one else mattered or existed.

"Simply a man she can hold onto when she's frightened, who comforts her when she's lonely; a man, who understands and isn't afraid of what he can't fix about 'what's wrong' with her, nor of her bold and great, unbounded capacity to love with every atom and breath of her."

I thought she was going to cry, but she didn't.

She did, however, tell me that I knew, as well or better than she did, what Day liked, and that I should pick whatever I thought would please her. Nevertheless, she picked out a special edition

DVD and said Day really liked it for some reason, then went out to the car to wait for me.

It wasn't a "Terminator" movie, but in a way, it was.

"The Searchers" is a 1956 American Western about two desperate men hunting for a lost little girl, who grows to teenaged womanhood with her assumedly "cruel" kidnapper; forced to be his mate, his pawn, and his trophy.

One searcher, her adopted brother, wants to rescue her; the other, her blood uncle, wants to kill her, since she's perceived as sexually tainted and entirely ruined, with premature *[nee premarital, not prepubescent]* sex, with an Indian.

Oh, dear. How heinous.

I joke, but it is oddly, topical. And, bonus points, it had Natalie Wood.

Geez, what would Jung AND Freud say?

* * * *

You've come to the conclusion, by now, that I'm a leech, a heel, or—optimistic gasp— a hero. Such a wide choice.

You know, you really shouldn't jump to a conclusive assumption, before the full spectrum of facts is in, but it's hard, isn't it?

* * * *

I know it was late in the game to be "cautious"; however, the test results were back and posted in detail to my email, from a few samples I'd finally sent out of Day's and mine.

Imagine me asking Hopkins for blood, or any other body fluid sample?

I didn't. I had wanted to send in a "sample" from him, that he'd left in Day, before she furiously douched, as usual, but she absolutely would not permit me to touch her, until she'd scoured him from her—as *usual.*

More important were the lab test results. Day and I were healthy.

I had been, before meeting them, but I hadn't worn any protection, had barely considered it, since I'd met her, which was very odd, since her past was sketchy at best, and again there's the old man. I'd mentioned it to her a day or two after we started, that I'd wear something and had gotten a box.

"*No.* I don't want to be protected from *you*, Bennet. *Not ever. Never.*"

* * * *

That got to my ego, and it shouldn't've; well, at the very least, I shouldn't have let it. At least, she'd used them with Pizza Guy. Yet still, without a doubt, I shouldn't've deferred to her wishes, but I nearly always did.

How sane is that, heeding a documented headcase?

Letting her play my ego so effortlessly. I evidently needed more protection from her than a simple latex rubber shield could ever provide.

* * * *

Day was in a playful mood for the evening; first sitting, then lying on top of me, on his front room sofa, tickling the hell out of me; and, we'd gotten to that place in adult play, when you fall silent for significant moments, knowing you'll presently be doing more intimate things.

Then, we'd resume tickling and laughing, before falling silent again.

I'd been in our "situation" long enough to pretty much block out his existence when she was giving me her full attention, which was quite often now.

She was softly but mercilessly teasing me about my growing hardness, which was sandwiched between my thigh and hers. Her cool palms were inside my shirt, against my hot skin, and I'd just snuck one of my hands, the one hidden by our bodies against the back of the seat, under her skirttail, where it found a nice, hot, wet welcome.

I know I seem to mostly only inform you about the sex between us, but think about it. It can be so telling. I know couples, too many couples, who said sex wasn't important and then the official or hidden reason behind their breakups and divorces was always sex, and/or $.

Can you ever have too much of either? Good or bad?

Probably, but that's less important than sex being a test—a proof.

It's a test of how open, how naked, how vulnerable, how giving, how receiving, how willing to truthfully communicate, and how bold you are. "Bold" enough to *just ask,* because some people never get exactly what they want, especially in bed, and the ones who do, often selfishly squander it.

In general, however, sex has usually been, in my experience, a pleasant test to take; especially the make-ups. Which, for no particular reason, reminds me that I once asked Day a normal, simple query; sometimes, I'm just ignorant because it simply wasn't such an ordinary question in her mind.

"What do you want, Day?"

We'd been on the beach most of the morning and had re-treated to the relatively inexpensive, wooden lounger I'd gotten for her, on the side porch with the high bars. Why he hadn't had the bars styled more subtly to allay what they truly were is typical Hopkins.

She was curled up at the head of the chair and I sat facing her, straddling the chair's foot, "at her feet," so to speak. She'd asked if I had always wanted to work in medicine and I said it had always been an indisputable point, with Mama in the field and with having a natural knack, as I was told, when quite young, by a powerful shamaness-curandera.

I had "a skill," she'd said, that I couldn't "avoid using."

Personally, I industriously ignored it for many years, but it's amazing how often the Powers That Be can plop people, who desperately need you, right smack into your lap, over and over again, whether you can *actually* help or . . . .

I, at least, was lucky that my services generated good word of mouth and good money; if lots of money is the exact same as good money.

But, again it was sort of a moot point, at present, because, except for Day and other extremely rare reasons, I wasn't doing any of that anymore.

If it were all okay with the PowersTB. Which it probably wasn't.

Day asked why. I simply said I needed a *very* and, perhaps, *permanent* vacation. She made a pouty, dissatisfied face, when realizing I wasn't going to say anything more than that.

"But, you help people feel . . . . You've helped me. Bennet, are you hurt that much? That profoundly?" What a word—"profoundly." I didn't answer.

She was absently toying with her supplies, the ones I'd gotten her; a large color pencil set with paper. She wasn't half bad and preferred making scenes of eagles and other birds flying high on the wing.

Day uncurled to tuck her cold, sock covered toes under my warm thigh, a thing she does often; her feet are almost always cold, no matter how warm it is. She, herself, hadn't answered my next question of what she'd wanted to be, when she grew up, except to gently snipe that she hadn't grown up. Eventually, I asked . . . .

"What do you want, Day? I mean, *really* want. Now? In the future?"

"You."

She spoils my ego rotten, with statements like that, spoken without a second of hesitation; then, her face darkened. It was a brooding look I'd caught her wearing several times before, and she'd always seemed embarrassed whenever I'd seen it, but this time she ventured an explanation for it with—.

"'Now' and 'in the future,' you can keep me 'on the side.' That's what people do with me."

I choked out a loudly explosive, "WHAT?"

Then, realized, by her self-conscious, yet determined expression, that she'd given the matter much forethought and that, since I had asked, she was giving me permission to use her, as I liked, while still keeping a "normal" life and a "normal" wife.

"*No.* No, Day. Not what do you think *I* want. What do *you* want, if you can have *exactly* what and who you want?"

It sounds like I was fishing for compliments, but it was very possible she just wanted to be ultimately left alone, by everyone, including me, or that there was some other guy, she'd met or hoped to meet.

Maybe a handsome someone with darker skin than mine, who'd deck "Hoppy," kill him even, then sweep her off her feet and completely out of the house she hated.

Her tears silently cascaded down. I don't think I've ever known anyone, female or male, adult or child, who cried more disturbingly silent tears. What she said was almost as inaudible, as she stared down, afraid to meet my eyes.

"Do I have to answer, now? Would you be . . . angry at me, if I—?"

"*No.* Why would I be angry? It's just a question, a friendly question."

She nodded, but the easy conversation we had going was dead. I let its corpse lie there between us, as I sat with her, as my simple question mutely stalked around inside her mind.

She never answered me directly, although I overheard her from the hall, later, whispering to Mrs. G.

"Elise?"

Mrs. G was fixing something in the front room by the bar, which had gotten broken in the last "row," and was listening to Day, in that distracted way experienced moms do when they have many things to do.

"Benn asked me something, something personal, I couldn't answer." She received an "uh-huh" from her companion. "He asked me *what I wanted, who I wanted.* No one's ever asked me that; except, maybe you. What do you think he meant?"

"What do *you* think, Ms. Day?"

"*I don't know.* I-I told him I wanted *him.* That he could . . . he could keep me hidden, if he wanted someone else, too. Someone he can take places and be seen with. Was that wrong?"

Mrs. G composed herself before looking at Day. The woman has a good heart, which I'm sure I saw break in those brief moments.

"No, it wasn't wrong. Not if that's how you honestly feel. I think, however, and I don't know Mr. Bennet as well as you do, but I think he wanted to know what *you* want, not what you think would please him."

"That's what he said." Mrs. G waited silently on her charge's next words. "I want Benn. I don't want to share him. Not with anyone. I don't have anything of my own, not one thing that can't be taken away, nothing without . . . ."

Day stared downward, and Mrs. G noticed me then, as Day sighed deeply.

"He already knows I only want him, but do I have to tell him again, since he asked?"

"No, Ms. Day. I'm quite certain he knows."

Which takes us . . . me back to the matter at hand, somewhat, of what she wants or doesn't want and her personal power in it.

Of Day in a playful mood, on top of me, on the front room sofa, with my hand deep under her skirttail, where it'd found delightful purchase—before he called her, bellowed for her, in truth. Not unlike a dad checking on his errant daughter, who's hanging out with that skuz of a boy he can't stand.

"Day!" His disruption of our playtime irritated her, and it showed in her voice.

"*What?*"

"Come." She didn't move. "I would have you. Now." I felt her body stiffen and her head shook, in a slight, uncommitted statement of "no." "Remember, Day, you must keep up your installments on Mr. Gillespie's room and board, so come."

He wasn't normally so open, so blatant about his private dealings with her, except when pointedly getting my goad. He glanced at me, alpha dog to beta, to see if I'd challenge him.

His house, his rules. His ward.

Isn't that what they always called a girl or boy under some nonrelated man's care in old books?

Maybe I had a dirty mind, but it usually, if not always, had sexual connotations to me. Maybe because Chuck's dad worked vice and so we learned early that a *lot* of men can't keep their hands off their own blood, let alone a "ward," who was just as vulnerable and dependent on them.

And earlier, as a kid, I used to read anything and everything, and that gothic ward type of story was Stephie's book of choice. She thought the same way I did about it, except she pretended the brooding guardian men were brooding, older women, which helped her identify with the "sexually blossoming," young women wards.

Imaginative girl, my sister.

Day made a choked sound only I could hear or perhaps cared to hear, as she felt me remove my hand from its cherished home under her dress, relinquishing my temporary physical claim of her back to the master of the house.

I whispered in her ear that I'd wait up for her, no matter how long he took. When she moved, I pulled her back briefly to also whisper, "Thank you."

It logically was an odd thing to say, and probably "unmanly" and "nonheroic," but it felt sensibly right. She was putting herself out for me; the least I could do was say a simple, verbal thank you.

Her resulting expression was even more odd than my sentiment.

I'm certain she instantly realized why I'd said it, and I'm pretty damned certain no one had been courteous enough to thank her for anything, in quite awhile.

If ever.

I watched Hopkins coldly observing her, in his imperious impatience, as she limped past him and he bird-dogged her to her room. It was strange that he almost never took her to his room, and never to his bed. Not that she wanted to go there or that I wanted her to. It was just strange.

He tried to keep her as long as possible, I felt, or, and I wasn't sure how long he'd watched us at play, but maybe seeing us together had gotten his juices up.

The things I'd overheard her saying to Mrs. G, about what she wanted, kept running through my brain that night as I waited, for no other apparent reason I could fathom than to torture myself.

It was a long time before she could slip away, scour him from her, and come to me. I would've met her in the bath and bathed her, but she abhors me touching her, when his "filth" [her word] is still on and in her.

I also would've been happily content with no sex and to just hold her and, literally, merely sleep beside her, except Day always preferred to have my body remove the residual feel of him from hers. Inside and out. And, to have my taste in her mouth, my scent on her skin, because soap, hot water, and a vinegar douche never quite fully erased him from her psyche.

So, though it was very late and delayed, we finished our love play on Hopkins' sofa.

* * * *

The house was all ours, again. He'd been called away to a funeral of a "dear old friend." *Didn't know he had any.* Mrs. G had the day off, since we'd both agreed not to tell Hopkins.

Day was sitting on my windowsill. I'd started by tickling then kissing her toes and the soles of her feet, followed by kissing her ankle wounds, which were healing admirably under my ministrations. Then, I'd worked my way up and up, and was pleasing her and myself; first, by dining on her cunt—*there's a good reason we associate women with fruit, and other tasty things.*

I love Day's juice and how the more she wants me, the more

her slightly changing, salty liquor hotly flows, as her flesh heats and plumps in answer to my licks and kisses.

Then, I was fucking her.

But, at the moment, she was holding me away from her. She does that sometimes, to tease me. She still has very strong upper legs, and alternates opening wide to me and letting me deep within her, holding me there; then releasing me and closing her thighs a few inches to block my full reentry into paradise.

She let me back in deep, before hugging me by the shoulders, and whispering what she wanted in my ear.

It didn't entirely register on me at first, so she repeated it, and I saw in her eyes that I had heard her correctly.

"No. I won't do it." She nodded that I would.

"*No.*"

She was still fucking me, although I'd paused. I began again. She asked again. My third negative to her request caused her, in unexpected peevishness, to shove me completely from her, back on my ass.

She was halfway to the door, when she said *it.*

"If you won't, Hoppy will."

I grabbed her arm. She pushed me off again, and I didn't like it. She hit me with all she had, which didn't physically hurt a great deal, but I disliked that even more. I knew she was trying to anger me, I also knew she wasn't bluffing. She would go to him, and she was right, he would.

The plain fact that she would petulantly, actually wait for him to return, then go to Hopkins, in her misplaced stubbornness, all because I'd . . . .

I couldn't remain calm.

I didn't get "colorless" in my anger this time, which became hot and red, bordering on white.

I snatched her by the hair, dragging her back to me, pulling her incredible face to mine.

"You won't go to him."

Her eyes were indifferent, completely empty and cold, and she didn't answer back. Day couldn't take care of herself for very long out in the world, especially if her sexuality were taken from her. Nor could she run very far in it, but in her own way, she ruled us all.

She was definitely ruling me at that moment.

"I don't want to do this, Day."

Her eyes softened a little. I was still physically exposed, so she touched me "below the belt," at the "root of my problem," Steph would say, not harshly, but to make me want her, to get me ready for what she required me to do.

What I knew I had to do, or completely leave her, because she would go to "Hoppy" and he would hurt her, which would damage her beyond, way beyond that delicate edge her mind was presently already balanced on.

I grabbed hold of her and Day struggled uselessly, as I pushed her to the futon, roughly held her down, and forced her.

I'd never done such a thing in my life.

That's not quite true; yet, here I was ripping at the soft fabric of her dress, restraining my lover face down—.

Which is exactly what she'd repeatedly asked of me. I stopped and turned her to face me; I needed to see her, to have an idea of what—.

I can't say what I saw in her distant eyes, because I'd never seen that particular expression before. I'd never realized how many expressions a face *could* have, especially one as expressive as Day's, even while she was remote, tottering on catatonia.

I wasn't going to . . . .

She managed to half focus on me, to tell me to finish my task or she'd ask Hopkins to. I reached for the tube of lubricant she'd provided and hidden from me under a sweater.

I would've liked to've seen Mrs. G's face when she read *that* on her shopping list.

This *activity* wasn't like, yet was *too much* like, being back with Arabella. I was engaged to her, until a year and a half ago—*I don't know why but I was.* Ara liked sex rough as violent rape and she liked to be assfucked, neither of which is so very strange in comparison to so many things in this world.

She also liked that I "was so very strong and commanding, yet sweet."

She also "wanted to wait" before "losing" her "virginity," so I couldn't touch her vagina with anything longer or thicker than two of my fingers.

Where she came up with *that* rationale, *that* particular number of fingers and length, et cetera, I never could find out.

Nor find how she truly got any enjoyment out of being only violently assfucked; other than it was to her a *forbidden, shameful* thing, but fun. A *forbidden, shameful* thing; yet less so, in *her* mind, than the whole world-destroying, mandatory and perpetual VIRGIN burden?

I read a comment once, which had a fantastically bright point. That in The Bible it was never stated just *exactly* what the Sodomites and the Gomorrahans did that was *the* last straw and was *soooo* bad that they had to be entirely obliterated off the face of the earth.

Nothing was ever mentioned about buttfucking in any version I, or anyone else, ever saw.

There was also a recent statistic somewhere that said most sodomites, in various countries, including this one, weren't homosexuals but heterosexuals, who put a very high premium on a woman's lack of vaginal sex.

Historically, the male of the human species, once he finally figured out, in various culturally-sanctioned forms, how babies were made by two people—*female AND male*—seized control of his favorite vagina(s) to insure only *his* babies issued forth; which is also one of the most basic reasons of many for switching anal for vaginal sex.

Chastity of vagina is the only chastity of necessity for them, and therefore *true* sexual intercourse doesn't include any other body part that's not a dick in a pussy.

How anal.

Sex in that fashion is okay for me but not my preferred method. What really made sex and life with High Mistress Arabella truly joyless was her lack of openness.

I didn't care if she didn't want to tell the world the most graphic details of our sex life together, or tell her mama, who was *adamant* about the virgin thing; but keeping *all* PDA *[public displays of affection]* out of the game, in truth, pissed me off. Especially, with all the unsatisfying things unsweet Arabella had me doing.

Myself, I've never really gotten off, all that much, on . . . on being with someone, who didn't overtly, completely want to be mine.

I don't know what I was thinking when I engaged myself to her. No, I do. I was caught up in all the "shoulds"—*what I should have, who I should have*, and not what or who I actually needed, or truly wanted.

But, that was more than a year and a close death and a career ago, and Day is not Arabella.

I can't say Day enjoyed what she'd demanded I do, I certainly didn't. I was harming her. Physically and . . . .

Besides, the more oddly startling fantasies one sometimes or often gets in one's mind, and whacks off to, are not things that are fun outside of the head, once dressed in tender and real flesh.

Day didn't climax, which she normally does with me, and I just barely reached orgasm myself, with reluctance.

The fact that I did says a great deal about me, doesn't it?

It appeared somehow that this *activity,* performed in this manner, was a part of her, an unfortunately familiar and dark part of her that she needed acknowledged by herself and by me; a part of her, I think, even she feared because she shivered, as if freezing or going into shock.

I had wanted to end it, and didn't, because she would only make me start over; and because I finally understood, too well, how it must have been for her, in *that* place, to have others control and have her when she didn't want them to.

I gave myself over to her dictate, by taking control over her body, because she needed to do this fearsome, destructive thing and experience it with someone she trusted and perhaps loved, to get another view of it.

At least, that's what I told myself in my deeply unsettled heart of hearts, as I roughly, fumbled and finished with her, then freed her of my iron grip.

I would have preferred to've been naked and lost, far out to sea, in a frigid Atlantic tempest. I've been in that situation, it's not as bad as this.

I lay on my back, my arm thrown over to shield my eyes, fleetingly recalling I'd learned the gesture from Mama, who'd slept that way when we were small, to keep out the bold daylight. The thought didn't seem to have anything to do with the present, yet it came, without conscious invitation.

From under my arm shield, I was acutely listening to Day, acutely feeling her there beside me, and more than acutely afraid to look at her, hoping I hadn't hurt her, too much. And terribly afraid that I had. In a few minutes she got up and went to her room. I watched her go.

I'd torn, shredded her dress.

It's amazing my insides didn't pitch inside out, but my spirit did, before I got up and took the most scalding shower I've ever taken.

The sun was still high and disturbingly beautiful, as I sat outside on my sill, which was a waste, since my head was down and in my hands. I was finishing my third or fourth cigarette, well, the third or fourth cigarette belonging to Hopkins that I'd pilfered.

What's a little theft and the resurrection of a smelly, asphyxiating habit of slow suicide after . . . ?

Out the corner of my eye, I saw her stick her curlyhaired head out her window, see me, then step across the sill and come to me. I never looked directly at her, just at that space a foot or so before my toes, a space her feet and healing, mutilated ankles now occupied.

She'd at least changed out of that torn dress, and some icy, smug part of my brain registered that I hadn't heard her bathe *my* residue from her, as she always did Hopkins'.

Day ran her fingers across my scalp, through my long, damp hair, then leaned into me and stroked my neck and across the width and down the length of my back. She often strokes my neck and back, my chest and belly, my limbs, like an inventory, she never says why, but I feel she likes the solid strength of me.

I could feel the firm softness of her body, as she leaned against the hard crown of my head, which contained my besieged physical brain, who's mind was—.

"Day?"

I said her name as a check, because I wasn't certain if I were actually audible; like waking within a dream and screaming with great force, yet finding it silent to the actual ear—an alarm without sound.

I had a roommate in college, an idiot film school freak, who'd go on and on about "the silent scream" in movies of horror, especially the Alfred Hitchcock thrillers. My naïvely, unrealistic roomy had no idea just how soulsearing a reality that concept truly was.

I most obviously did now.

"Never ask me to do that again. Never. Not with you."

I turned my face into her abdomen and clung to her hips. As I was desperately trying to find and pull my soul back into me, my brain blithely catalogued my sensory input: from the wind and sun and ocean, the smoke of my cast off cigarette, the hard seat under my ass, the intoxicating scent of her past arousal through the soft dress fabric, and the warm woman's flesh of her.

"Never blackmail me like that again. That brought no joy to either of us."

"Thank you, Bennet." The souring smoke taste in my mouth turned to tin.

"For *that?*"

"For obeying me. For not enjoying it. For not wanting to do it. For not wanting to do it ever again. For not enjoying it. Hopkins would have. *He always does.* So did . . . . I . . . apologize . . . to you, I would have stupidly kept my threat and gone to him and it would—. You saved me. From me."

"By r-raping you?"

"You didn't hurt me much, at all. I just needed to feel . . . if there was . . . a difference, and there is, with you."

I wasn't sure of that nor was I entirely certain what that meant. The sun was brilliantly highlighting the deep bruises I'd left in her skin, which, as far as I know, no one else in the house ever asked about. I didn't have one mark on the outside of me.

I avoided her the rest of the day; and though tired, I stubbornly postponed turning in for the night.

Day finally grabbed my hand and led me to bed, whether I wanted to go or not; and even though I was excruciatingly exhausted, I still didn't, couldn't sleep.

Beside me, she sat up to look at me, and I pretended to be asleep, which was a fat chance because she did a thing one of my little cousins used to do when she was a toddler—plaster her face to mine. No kiss, just plaster her face; forehead, nose, mouth against the side center of mine, as if she were peering through a glass window.

It's very charmingly distracting, and impossible for me not to acknowledge.

When I confirmed I was awake, Day took her time arousing me, wooing me to her. I knew holding out against her was futile; I've never been more a man than with her, especially when she . . . when she was being gentle with me.

Not something you hear of as advice to young women in the proper care and maintenance of their men—to be gentle.

Slowly, gently, and sensuously thorough.

I mildly pushed her away a few times, which she ignored in her slow, gentle, sensuously thorough, all-body pursuit of my lust, which I could no longer withhold, as she managed to get me hotter than I would've expected possible after . . . .

Then, she leaned into me and said it.

The first night we'd been together she'd told me I was hers, and she'd said it again the next morning, in the light of day. I couldn't deny it then, I certainly couldn't now, after obeying her hard wishes earlier, when she'd taken me to a Christian's Hell, where souls, alive and dead, are tortured for *both* their indulgences AND their virtues.

Equal opportunity perpetual torment.

I don't know if you've actually felt your spirit or your heart grow, expand, or change planes of consciousness, it's called a quickening. It happens in less than a lightning's flash.

Women can experience it when their babies move independently inside them, especially the first time.

It happens when you have a true "aha!" or "eureka!" moment; some realize it when they fall in love with "the one"; or when men realize their entire *everything* is different.

In an excellent way.

As they fully accept that they really aren't the center of the whole damned universe but are fathers with children, who want and need them, like no one else on the planet wants and needs them.

Someone, who is completely dependent on them and open to them, who deeply, "profoundly" needs their father to love them like no one else can love them, and to take care of them like no one else is truly capable of. *Aha!*

Day was leading me from my agony to elsewhere, and had me on the brink, when she said it.

"All of me, even the pain in me, is yours."

Her words peculiarly reverberated, like an echo through my mind for half a millisecond, before my famished heart opened and eagerly sucked them in. She knew precisely what effect the entire day, now night, *and* her words of power had within me.

I wasn't tired anymore and there was nothing else in the universe, except her and me. I was more than incandescent for her, as she let me take the upper hand, but I found myself hesitating.

She bewitchingly egged me on and I found myself doing what I'd feared, pinning her, nearly as hard as before; but in a different, intense way, allowing me to hold her and take her as I think a woman should be taken, without harming her, without bruising or tearing—.

We were . . . .

At first I thought it was only me, but she was plainly exactly where I was, as that aha! moment shifted and the heat I had for her cooled but deepened, and the light I imagined emanating from us seemed brighter, yet softer.

I wasn't hallucinating, my people believed . . . do believe in such things, as Day and I passed a barrier.

Not all the barriers but a major one.

* * * *

Stephie'd flown back and was on the porch speaking with Day, who had her head half burdened down with the browbeating, when I got back from a tiresome and unavoidable breakfast meeting, with a couple of unavoidable someones, about money and other inescapable things.

I know my sister, I know she was verbally cutting the girl apart; it's a sure way for me to tell if the other women in my life are special.

Day retaliated—*she abruptly kissed my twin, on the mouth,* long enough to get the upper hand, as Stephie openly responded to her desire for Day; then my woman brazenly gazed in Stephanie's eyes, smiled her triumph, and went inside. Stephie sucked her lips, savoring the kiss.

"Steph, I told you not to mess with her."

"And I told you—and *that* was proof—that you can't keep staying here, she's . . . she's too . . . ."

"'Too' what?"

"Too under your skin."

"And, not under yours?"

"May-be, but, it was *you* Mama always warned. She's crazy. A normal woman wouldn't have done what she just did. Knowing you were watching? How else is she messing with your mind, or this."

She poked me hard in the chest, over my heart. I only half listened. Stephanie wanted Day badly, and if she couldn't have her, I certainly couldn't. And, if she could get me to run, she could step in, especially with someone as trapped as Day, because the rescuer, "the hero always gets the girl."

And, please, stop thinking I'm being too hard on her, I know Stephanie well, she used to break my best and most favorite toys.

"Maybe, it's her way of teasing you or me, Steph, or both of us. I've got enough odd behavior from her, so don't add to it. In fact, I'm more fine than I've been in years, so you really shouldn't come back here again."

The glare she gave me would've cut diamonds.

"She's totally got my little Bennet straining his inseam, lapping at her skirttail, doesn't she? I'd say panties, but the bitch doesn't have any." She didn't get her desired reaction out of me. "Okay, little brother, my advice is useless to you, falling on choosing-to-be-deaf ears. I'll get the complete hell out of here, tonight."

I didn't argue. When she's being imperious, it's usually because I'm being stubborn about letting her tell me what to do, and bending to her only makes her worse, because then she believes she's right.

Don't even think what you're thinking; it's a moot point now, isn't it?

She's a total pain in the ass, but I missed Stephie horribly the next few days, I always do when we intensely disagree and I have no idea when I'll see her again. I finally closed out my tab at the hotel, too.

I'd kept it as a lifeline, but it was plain that I might as well sever it and wait to see if I'd also cut my own throat.

Hopkins was his same hospitable self, Mrs. G was glad everything was "normal," and Day was Day. Except, even with me by her side, in her bed, she couldn't sleep the night my twin left. Something, some agonizing fluxom from deep within her kept her restless.

I carried her to my room, where she always seemed more comfortable and massaged her scalp to soles, with an occasional kiss on various sweet parts of her keeping it from being a legal massage. She relaxed yet fussed and refused to sleep, until I held her once more, nestling against me, which appeared to cancel whatever Stephie's presence or absence had disturbingly triggered within her.

If it'd been about my big sis and the kiss at all.

A cold night, about a week or so later, I made a nearly fatal mistake.

I have a titanium alloy ballpoint, which, because of its strength, I often use for prying things open or to poke holes in overly secure, plastic chip bags and such. Day was using my Mac when the battery died, and having had the thing a long while, and having dropped it many times myself, the battery packs won't come out, unless I pry them out, and the AC jack long since was killed, which is another story about Stephie.

I used the pen to pry out one pack, rammed in another, and jabbed myself in the finger somewhere in the middle of all that. It kept gushing, so I went to the bathroom to rinse and bandage it.

When I came back, Day was gone, with the pen.

I found her in Hopkins' room, standing over the sleeping

man. I hissed her name, just as her arm reached the top of her arc, the downside of which would find my titanium alloy pen, which I've punched holes in beer cans with, in Mr. Hopkins' neck or eye. Probably eye, which would cause brain trauma, if not death, I somewhat coldly thought.

I also thought why hadn't I yelled, only whispered; but she paused at the sound of my voice, freezing in mid-arcing swing.

I moved behind her, the only sound in the room was Hopkins' snoring, as I gently slid my hand up her arm and retrieved my pen from her hand. She took a few steps toward the door, but the adrenaline rush inside her crashed. I caught her up . . . caught her and carried her out and across the hall to her room.

When I returned to close his door, Hopkins was still snoring in resounding ignorance, never knowing how close to early oblivion he'd come.

After missing her shot at him, I was next. *Okay, that probably sounds too dramatically morbid, but she said . . . .*

"Benn, don't tell anyone, yet."

I listened. Stunned. It was possible, very possible; but . . . .

So many buts. I held back saying "don't lie to me" because I wasn't sure, if she were lying to me, but my stomach lining was sweating excess acid.

She'd been atypically happy the last few days, except for those recent few aberrant moments of trying to murder dear ole Hoppy in his sleep. Then, she became extremely, *(as Arabella would say)* "pathologically delighted" again, once telling me her news, as she glided from killer mood to happy mood, like an overhead lamp switches on then off.

I barely got her to reasonably calm down, while I stole a breath for a moment of serious thought.

It was as if she didn't recall trying to kill him, as if being happy had been all she'd been doing the past half hour, and, for me, the day got pretty long, once she said her piece to me.

Now, she wasn't happy at all.

"Bennet, you don't trust me? I wouldn't lie about a *baby*. Especially yours. I'd never want *his*, but *yours* . . . ."

I was silent; intensely doing the mental math and gymnastics, again and again, counting the time I'd been with her. I stupidly realized, in belated, full consciousness, outside of my overweening desire for her, and male blind spot, that when she'd said she was "taken care of in the baby department," she wasn't on the pill nor had she had a period since I'd been . . . .

All of which could mean many things, so I tried not to get too wound up and stubbornly refused to give in fully to her. I put her in the car, taking her with me for the short trip, which she enjoyed immensely. I hadn't wanted to leave Hopkins alone with her, while he was unconscious, and undefended.

There's a thought, *me* protecting *him*.

She was presently no longer immensely happy. We were in our bathroom, and she'd snatched the container from me, after I'd asked her to . . . .

I had a drugstore pregnancy test kit.

She gave back the urine sample, then locked her door between us. I heard her muffling a crying jag, as I tested. Negative. I reached into the bag and pulled out a second kit. Negative.

I didn't know how or if I should approach her, but I chanced it. Both of her doors were locked from within; however, Day was sitting in her open window, coiled into a tense ball. She half whispered to me, as she heard me behind her crossing the porch from my window to hers.

"Are you terribly angry with me?"

"No." *Absolutely no lie, I really wasn't.* "Why'd you lie to me, Day?"

She shook her head and was starting to cry again and not wanting to, which of course made the tears larger, faster, hotter. I let her be and sat beside her on the hard porch floor, resting against her soft hip.

"It's so stupid of me. I . . . I'd wondered what it'd be like to be . . . pregnant by you. A child with your . . . . You're smart and handsome, and well-adjusted. I wanted it too much. I just forgot. I forgot it wasn't . . . real. I'm . . . I'm too irregular with my cycle, since . . . . So, don't worry about babies."

I felt there was something else acutely wrong, but she was too clearly reluctant to reveal or give up her pain.

So, I took the easy way and I let it go, knowing full well I couldn't merely take Day at face value, like most people, not without digging deeper into whatever it all was that had made her like she was.

* * * *

I hadn't felt well so I'd cut my run short. Mrs. G was out, leaving Day alone with Hopkins; which didn't seem a completely good idea. I came upon them in the kitchen and he had her pinned against the counter and fridge/freezer.

I hung back, watching, because he'd expected having more time alone with her, although accosting her, in the open, outside of her room or his, hadn't been his style, since I'd been around.

I thought to interfere, then to not interfere, and either way my feet and mouth just never got in gear, as he groped her, with one hand under her skirt, and his other fondling and squeezing and then his mouth nursing on her breast. He fully opened her dress, which, like most of her frocks, unbuttoned collarbone to ankle like a coat, he stared at her and at how his hand wetted and warmed itself in the furrow between her thighs.

He obviously caused only an autonomic physical reaction and no ache of desire in her. He never did, as far as I could tell, when I was around.

If he had, it would've been plain on her face, or at least her desire had always been blatant with me.

Day looked terribly distressed and I was about to step in when she pushed him off her. He came back and she shoved him away again and drew the dress closed around her before shrinking to the floor, slumping against the refrigerator and counter.

He wasn't pleased with her withdrawal and rebuke, and for a moment I was afraid he would force her, well, force her more than he normally did, but he had his head down storming from the room, until stopping to turn back, when he caught sight of me.

He flushed beet red; not from anger but from embarrassment and in that second I realized he had approached her, as he knew I must when he wasn't around. He looked disgusted with life in general, glanced back at her still slumped and curled up on the floor, then walked out.

I heard him drive off.

He most likely hadn't planned to leave, or give up, despite her rebuff, not until he saw me, anyway.

I stepped around the corner and she was trembling, nearly uncontrollably, but perceived that I was there, even though she didn't look up from staring blankly at the floor about a foot or so ahead of her.

"I can't, I can't do what he wants."

"What does he want?" Besides your body, I thought.

"He wants me to be, with him, like I'm with you. To *respond*. I can't. I won't. I can't."

She looked up at me. Her eyes pleaded but she didn't say anything else and I had no clue what I could say, so I stooped down, held her face in my hands a moment before kissing her forehead. I only meant to kiss her forehead, but I looked in her eyes again and then kissed both of her cheeks, then that incredible mouth of hers, which slightly responded though something stayed distant within her.

I sat down beside her and let her relax in the comfort and security of my embrace.

Day leaned against me and eventually I felt her shaking cease, not long after which Mrs. G came in. She and I made eye contact, but said nothing, as she went about her activities.

After a while, I picked Day up and was carrying her to her room, until she begged me to take her to mine.

I know she was afraid he'd come for her, as she glanced at

his unoccupied bedroom. He never comes for her, if she's with me in my room. I put her down on the futon and was just going to watch her rest and not lie with her, but she made me lie beside her, then, a while later, she asked me to "make love" to her, "softly."

I did.

* * * *

I had an obligation. An unbreakable obligation, which meant I had to leave again. I didn't want to just leave Day thinking, assuming, I wouldn't come back to her, that she'd frightened me away, especially knowing Hopkins would tell her that I wouldn't return, so I put my mother's locket back around her neck for safekeeping.

A close friend of mine was lucky, that despite my "tune out and drop out" attitude, I was still checking my email. She's a Hip-Hop artist and dancer, a famous musician even you nonmusic types might know, and she needed me.

There'd been an accident, her husband was pretty messed up, and she didn't like the counsel she was getting from the top-drawer doctors working on him.

She wanted and only trusted my expertise, because she was afraid the damage, so like that which had crippled her highly cherished father, could be permanent and because, frankly, I owed her immensely for personally getting me through the horrible aftermath of Mama's abrupt death, during which my beloved sibling wasn't any help at all.

Stephanie never is under such circumstances. It's just the way she is.

I left for ten days, until both my good friend's confidence in and her spouse's health were secured, before heading back to Day.

* * * *

I've been reasonably polite about my word choices so far, but some things need to be what they are. Common terms—"bad words" are what the average person instantly understands and has definite feelings and mental concepts about.

"Bad" words, "common" words remove the distance and vagueness that "proper," "nice" language bestow.

We have these bad words for things we don't want to be caught talking about, despite that we continue thinking *and* talking about them, so we euphemistically change their names . . . and, continue to do what the words mean, as often as we can.

Which means, I somewhat apologize in advance for my language, from this point on, but if I described the "good stuff" in properly clean English or clinically sterile Latin, I'd bore myself and most likely unduly confuse you.

* * * *

When I got back Mrs. G had a package for me. It was a personally recorded DVD from Stephie. Mrs. G also said that my sister was "a delight" and had even managed to "completely charm the sir" [Hopkins], who let her stay a few days and nights, so that Day wouldn't miss me so much.

Hopkins cared that she not miss me?!

And, my dear Stephie is only "completely charming" and "a delight" when she's very much up to something.

Her note said I should watch the recording with Day, so I didn't bother to change clothes and popped the disc into Day's new player. I was highly involved in getting "reacquainted" with her, until I realized what was on the screen.

Day finally did, as well, when she'd lost my attention to the monitor, on which she was in the very same bed we were, letting my sister become *extremely* "acquainted" with her.

Day tried to stop the playback but I snarled "no" and she knew better than to argue. She tried squirming away from me, but I held tightly onto her, as I watched her and Stephanie . . . together.

Mouths, fingers, strap on dildos, double dildos and vibrators, you name it—*all my sister's favorite playthings*, including what . . . who's mine.

Something snapped in me, maybe it was seeing my sister, flushed with arousal and fucking in general, let alone seeing with my eyes *exactly* what she did with another woman, especially *my woman*; even though I already knew from our many conversations; but—"seeing is different."

I mostly snapped, of course, because it was Day.

"Part One" *[Yes, it was actually titled this.]* ended with some very familiar groans and moans . . . to climax, from the woman trapped in my grip, who still wore my mother's gold heart locket on its long black cord, which was also on screen between more breasts than I cared to see. From all the fumbling about, it must have been the first night, but lucky, fortunate me . . . .

Every time she'd taken Day—*and let's just say it was more than twice in the three or four days she'd stayed over behind my back, out of reach of my anger*—Stephanie had recorded every occasion.

Excellent camera and microphone.

My sister's fascinated by the latest electronics that snoop, especially the smallest kinds, hideable in watches or pens or whatever.

Day had no idea there'd been a camera and certainly didn't want to talk, think about, or acknowledge anything at the moment.

When the second session *["Part Two"]* came onscreen, I let her go; she limped to the window, crawled out and sat on the porch floor where I could see her, by the balcony railing, as I watched every damned "exciting and new" thing they did together.

"Why'd you fuck her, Day? You don't even like her." She was holding onto the rail slats like a jailed prisoner, and had jumped at the sound of my voice, even though she knew I was beside her. *"Day?"*

"They both said you weren't coming back."

I stooped beside her, to reach between her breasts, which had been last tasted and fondled by my sister, for the locket. I didn't want to mentally review what else of hers my sister had tasted and probed, even though it was already scorched into my optic nerve and brain.

Day looked at me, silently pleading for forgiveness with her perpetually forlorn sadness hanging on her heavier than usual.

"They . . . they wouldn't leave me alone. She said you'd ask to have it sent to you, that I should ask Elise, that you'd asked her to send it to you before. Elise said 'yes.'"

I have to remember not to tell my twin things that are too utterly important to me, especially when it comes to a cunt she might want as much as I do.

That wasn't quite true, I wanted Day a hell of a lot more than Stephie.

"What else did my *beloved*, big sister say?"

I was angry and I don't think Day was certain at whom I was focusing that anger: on her, on Stephie, or both. I didn't have the energy or the feeling of generosity at the time to say what my choice was, nor did I really care.

If I could've cracked open her warped, little skull and gotten my brain physically inside hers, to see exactly what was going on in there, I would've, but I had to settle with extreme, exterior closeness; uncomfortable for her closeness.

"What else did she say to you, to get you so quickly on your back, on your knees, on your belly with her?"

I was extremely pissed and she clearly wanted to cower from me but was afraid to.

Smart girl.

I'll never be sure if she wouldn't've gotten severe and violent blowback, if she'd triggered my wrath then, by trying to remove herself from the scorching heat of my rage. She didn't budge. Incredibly smart girl, when it comes to survival.

"She and Hoppy said he wouldn't live forever, or that he might just get real sick and have to send me . . . back. He's been sick before. He said we, she and I, 'should be friends,' like I was with you. He didn't say 'am' with you, but 'was.'"

"He left us alone together and she said if I liked you, I would like her. You 'came from the same womb,' had 'the same heart.' *That's a lie, she's nothing like you; I don't care if she is your twin.*"

Perceptive girl; perceptive, overly vulnerable girl.

"She asked if I could 'take the chance,' did I have '*that* much confidence' you'd never leave me, because, even if you came back, this time, for a while, my 'moods,' my 'desperation' would drive you away.

"And, that even if you stayed, after he'd die, you'd never visit me, not *there*. Not once. Stephanie's right, you wouldn't."

I stood up. They say if you really love someone, you really know them. Funny, both my sister and my lover were right; I would 'never visit [Day] *there.*'

"She said *she* would. Stephanie *would* visit me, even there, particularly if I . . . . She's always wanted me, but—. *Shit.* She wants you to be mad at me, she and Hopkins both, don't they? I should've known that. She was too . . . hungry for me."

I didn't look down at her, her voice sounded like she was exhausted, resigned, completely whipped even. I know the feeling. She was still in my peripheral vision though.

"I was, am incredibly hungry for you, too, Day; I always am." She nearly looked up at me but didn't.

Fear is a prison in itself, but that's not news, is it?

"You'll always be hungry for me, Benn, until you get fed up."

That had the ring of truth, too, and somewhere inside me, something Mama once said was trying to get me to see that we all have "different hungers"; that "some are forever," others can "be satiated," and that some do just get fed up. And move along.

My skin was crawling with too much energy running wild inside me and there was no one I could reasonably beat the shit out of, to make myself feel better. It was bad enough dealing with Hopkins alone, but him with Stephie as well was too much.

There's nothing like an enemy, who knows you inside out and isn't afraid to use that knowledge to cut you off at the knees.

My only personal redemption was that we'd spent a lot of time apart these past few years and there was no way she knew my *every* thought, plus there was no way Stephie could know my *every* reaction when it came to Day.

I didn't know that myself.

Day touched my trousered leg, I pulled away then reached for her to rip the locket off over her head. I went back inside to get my keys and drove until I was afraid I'd run someone over in my preoccupation and rage. I found a patch of green and, inappropriately dressed, just ran until I'd run the circumference more times than I could remember, and it was getting too dark to see.

Eventually, I drove back to the house where Day was sitting outside, her eyes hidden in the darkness by black shades, with her knees pulled up tight to her chest. All she had to do was tuck her head and she'd be the embodiment of the human football she seemed to be. Mrs. G was stroking Day's hair, and it was way past her usual knockoff time, which meant Hopkins wasn't around.

I asked if Stephie had called recently for him, she had.

I'd spoken with Steph and she'd known when I'd get back. The bitch had warned him not to be around when she tilted my temper over the edge, with her visual gift. At least she didn't want me going to jail for assault and battery, or homicide.

Also, Stephie, in her usual quest to control anyone and everyone, obviously hadn't imparted excessive info about me to fellow control freak Hopkins, or he would've been around breaking my balls about it, giving me grief in front of Day.

I told Mrs. G she could go, I wasn't going anywhere for the night and I'd "keep an eye on our little knifewielder." Mrs. G didn't like my joke or the fact that "Ms. Day" was "so extremely upset." I walked past them and inside, then heard Day softly beg her to "just go," that she'd "be fine alone" with me.

Day's voice didn't sound rock steady on the matter.

Thankfully, Mrs. Gorbachev left for home.

I like Mrs. G a lot and have a great deal of respect for her, but she misses a lot of the crap that goes on, no matter how much Day tells her; plus, she's deferentially partial to Day's side of nearly everything, whether the girl is "extremely upset" or not.

I was sopping with sweat and still "extremely upset" myself, because the past few hours hadn't actually abated my emotions much. I was pissed at Day for being Day, at my sister for being herself, at Hopkins . . . always, and was throwing a little self-loathing in for letting my libido and ego suck me so deep into all of this.

I also still greatly wanted to hold Day tightly to me, soothe and coo to her, and make it all better, take care of everything for her, which seemed a bit null and void after only less than two weeks gone. Despite that and more importantly, I'd been without her for all that time and, despite the video, I still wanted her badly.

Being pissed is such a burdensome bitch.

I'd reemerged from soaking my head in the tub. I would have stayed under longer, but I haven't yet acquired Aquaman's® useful knack of breathing underwater.

Or, of not wanting to be with Day.

I was massaging myself, my masculine self, shall we say. Geez, I had my dick in my hand, hazily thinking of her, when I turned to see she was at the door on her side of the bathroom.

"Come here, Day."

She looked at me oddly then disappeared; perhaps my emotions were too raw and naked on my face. I jumped out to pursue her.

"Day!"

When I entered her room she was half way across it, her back to me, frozen in place, evidently, since I'd last barked her name, knowing there was no way she could outrun me in this life or the next.

I was leaving a bathwater trail, as I went to her and took a good look at the back of her; at her thick hair, the slope of her back, the round promise of her ass, which I covetously touched before spooning her against me. I know she felt my desire for her pressing hard along her spine, as I harshly whispered in her ear.

"Get on the bed."

She didn't move and I scooped her up and threw her on it. I made her face me and she modestly tugged her dress down, as I took my first really good look at her, since I'd returned and ended up watching homemade porn from my loving, big sister.

Day's not to everyone's taste but I've seen men trip, while staring at her, as they jog past, even when she's frowning, let alone smiling.

She closely watched me reach over her for a pillow for her head, her gaze was suspicious and resigned; I hadn't known such a thing could be managed. I resumed masturbating, partially conscious of buying time in a losing attempt to decide what to do or say, or not do or not say, half wanting to release myself from the shapely, humid destination my body was already leading me to.

I pushed her skirt out of my way and immediately thought Mommy and Hoppy weren't totally wrong in saying "pretty face/ prettier . . . ."

My lonesome, drying palm wasn't good enough, not with the house to ourselves, days since we'd last . . . indulged, and the raging anger I still felt.

Sometimes I carry a bit of a grudge, even when I know I shouldn't.

There's seeing what you shouldn't see and feeling inside you what you know you're too smart to be feeling.

I unhurriedly slid inside her, which was the greatest feeling, as she made a pretty sigh, which I liked *exceedingly* much and which almost made me forget I was still angry, especially once the pleasant humid heat of her snugly enveloped me. She yielded to me, letting me have of her whatever I wanted, as she moved with me.

When I felt her really wanting me, I pulled out, leaving her empty.

Leaving myself feeling starved, chilled, and alone.

Her expressive face silently questioned what have I done, are you still pissed with me, how can I make it all the way you want it to be?

I couldn't stay out of her, parted from her for long, as I re-entered and fucked her a little longer before pushing all the way into her and resting my full weight on her, pinning her down, as her panting, heated passion held tightly onto mine.

"Day, if you want to be an adult, be treated like an adult, you have to take the responsibility of the blind choice, just like the rest of us, Little Girl. And, you have to stick with it, without knowing whether your choice will turn ugly, disappointing, or devastating."

She stirred, uncomfortable, but couldn't move with my body as her prison.

"You can't just scramble to do anything, to merely survive, Day. You can't be just . . . anyone's, whenever it's expedient. You can't allow any one of us to make this one decision of yours."

"What 'one'?" Her voice was a frightened whisper.

"Whether you think, believe, or hope I'll stay or not, you've got to choose a path . . . a person and stick, even if it sucks. Hopkins' path, his being in charge of you, you know what that's been . . . is, and most likely will be. Do you want to stay his course?"

There was no hesitation from her, not about *him*.

"*No.*"

I pulled nearly all the way out of her, to pump a few shallow, circular inches into her over and over, causing her body to arch against mine, before I slid my fully swollen length back inside her. I again thought of Steph's vid, which wasn't all bad.

I don't mean the visuals. Those were bad to me in disturbing ways.

No, it was Steph's . . . intent behind it, *besides screwing me over.*

It had been quite apparent to see, above and beyond when I wasn't blindingly pissed at them both, that Stephie in her own Stephanie way hadn't been just having sex with Day but was intensely making love to her.

I still didn't appreciate it, but I understood.

"Stephie will visit you when he dies and you're sent back. The trick with your ankles, and I checked with a lawyer friend of mine, that trick will pretty much ensure that you 'won't see the light of day without some sort of *extreme* intercession.' Do you understand that?"

Day nodded mutely, with that lost, sad expression she often, too often had.

"Stephie's often heartless and she has a cruel streak, but once she makes a commitment to a woman she sticks, especially one she wants as much as you. If that's the direction you want to travel, if you want to give control of yourself to her, I'll call her and she'll be here before I pull my cock out."

I didn't want to say anything else about Stephie, I don't get angry at her often, but when I do, I nurse it a long while, and I wasn't being completely fair to Day, she knew it and I knew it. If I had wanted to be fair in the matter, I would've been dressed and not buried to the hilt in her, slowly rubbing my naked pelvis around against hers, distracting her.

Stephie cheats. I can too.

Day rubbed her face against mine, lost in a small, soft orgasm. I know the feel of her when one hits her and knew I could coax more out of her, deeper ones, as I let her clutch to me, while I stopped moving to keep myself from flowing over the edge of my own control and waited.

I silently mused that I didn't think this was exactly what Mrs. G had had in mind when she'd asked, "what's wrong with being lost, if lost is better than where you were?"

Oh, *yes*. Such fun we were having now.

"Lost," though romantic, is not that great a concept in physical actuality.

Day was frustrated that I wanted her answer immediately.

That I was forcing her to decide and say out loud whether she wanted Stephie as her backup lifeline.

That she'd cut that cord, merely because I plainly, perhaps unfairly, wanted her to. That she could only have Stephie or me and not both; she couldn't have two knights in armor poised to give her aid and comfort.

I was conscious of the fact that she was well-versed enough in the vagaries of lies and lust to know that I might still drop her, no matter what she said.

"I don't want her, Benn."

Her statement, her decision was clean and simple. Logically, I shouldn't have been so territorial about Day, for Christ's sake, but I was sharing her with too many, and I was fed up with it.

I ripped open the top of her dress and clearly reminded her of what it felt like to have *my* strong hands and *my* hot, hungry mouth on her breasts, then I fucked her and she fucked back.

When we both were . . . close, and I was fucking her with a tinge of anger still in me, I heard her starting to make a delightfully seductive and familiar sound that she never makes for "Hoppy" and certainly hadn't made for sister Stephie.

That's when I pulled completely out of her and forced her to let me go. Her fearsome temper blazed hotly, as she rightly accused me of torturing her, even if I had to torture myself, as well, to do it.

Ain't love grand?

"I don't want her, Bennet! I only want you!"

I snatched the pillow out from under her head and laid it under mine at the foot of the bed, as I stretched out on my back and watched her beyond my Day-drenched erection.

"Come and get me, Ms. Day, if you *really* want me."

She didn't hesitate and seductively crawled over my feet and legs, only pausing to stroke and kiss them, my thighs, my balls, all of me was aching for her, as she then rubbed my penis along her throat and against her breasts, with her eyes always on mine.

She deeply kissed my mouth, and made certain my eyes were still fixed on her, before slowly removing the dress, so I could see all of her, then she sunk me deep into her, completely swallowing me, taking me.

She fucked me so furiously, I knew I should make her pause long enough to check her ankles, but my lust was great and self-centered, as the heat in her eyes for me said they were fine. Or, that if they weren't she didn't give a shit, as she continued with me, until she completely finished me, completely finished us both.

Our lovemaking, considering our circumstances and sur- roundings, had always been reasonably, discreetly quiet, but this time, the otherwise empty house reverberated quite nicely.

I held her tightly to me and whispered in her ear, as if someone were sitting close by her bed observing us, and trying to hear.

"Are you mine, do you trust my control?"

She didn't question why I asked this, only looked me full in the eye before answering "yes." It was plain on every part of her that she truly meant that "yes." Such trust, such faith is an honor to receive and its own reward.

I wasn't a bit angry anymore; but she was starving for a waffle with maple syrup, spread with crunchy peanut butter, topped with Pierre's® Coconut-Pineapple Ice Cream. All great elements, but a little too much altogether for me, although it's a joy to watch her heartily consume it.

Curiously, the Pierre's® is the one thing Hopkins has im- ported from Cleveland for her.

Maybe there's a truly fatherly part of him somewhere deep inside him. I'll assume that's the reason and try not to project anything else more probable and negative about his intentions.

* * * *

I'd like to mention that Day has her weak moments, but she also has this independent, resilient, titanium-strength core she can access when she's not too far out there and truly wants something, or someone.

That core was stronger now, after our little DVD/fucking match.

Even the old man mentioned it. He mentioned it because he'd expected me to throw him the key to her center and to run far, and for her to unravel and entirely collapse and leave him to conveniently do whatever he wanted, with whatever little of her was left, after my exit.

I didn't depart and her overt commitment to me was stronger. And, the promise she had sworn with her words, her heart, and her body—to never let anything or anyone come between us, well, we both had enough damaged "baggage" to trip ourselves up, without further outside help.

* * * *

Mrs. G, soon afterwards, had an emergency, a long distance family thing with her kids here in the U.S., so she was expected to be gone for at least two days or more.

Hopkins was actually almost sweet and drove her there; she has a fear of driving long distance and also detests flying.

Guess she must've boated to America from Scotland?

I also think he just didn't want to deal for a while with any of the "kids" in the house, which was fine; we had a *very* good time without him, which caused me to sleep well, awaken late, and . . . .

. . . . she was gone. Period.

Day's bike was still under the tarp, my car was still parked. It occurred to me to hit the redial—she'd phoned for a cab. It took awhile, but I found out where she was. With Hopkins' "solicitor," Sid.

His outer office was empty of an assistant. His inner office was making sounds; sexually grunting, moaning male sounds, and a few feminine ones I recognized.

The one thing I know too damned well is how Day sounds through a closed door, when another man's fucking her.

I left. I stopped, in front of a smoke shop because it happened to be where my feet stopped. I purchased cigarettes and without actually thinking, returned. Sat. Lit up. And waited.

I smoked as a teen, quit when I wanted to join the high school track team.

When Day, in a rather svelte, classy dress over stylish ankle boots, exited the office, her hair stylishly pinned up with combs, repinned up in that slightly disheveled, just-got-out-of-bed or just-got-off-some-fucking-dickwad . . . any-and-every-fucking-dickwad's way.

She saw me, she was . . . . The word is crestfallen.

The "little snip," as Mama would have called her, did at least blush with acute shame.

Sid was fixing his tie, then self-consciously checked his fly and wanted to know who I was and could he help me. I did not shake his hand—*washed or not I wouldn't've*—and made her introduce us. He obviously knew my name, as his face flushed a bold red, before mentally noting my physical build and deep annoyance with his very existence.

He quickly backed his unhealthily stooped shoulders and spindly legs away and excused himself to attend to alleged "important affairs" at his desk, which had a discarded empty condom wrapper lying on the floor.

No way was I looking in the trash, again.

Sid ducked back behind his impressive office door, which he locked with an audible click, before I heard his muffled sigh all the way through the bolted door.

I snatched at her purse, which was shoulder strapped over her head and resting on her opposite hip. Yep. She'd brought the rubbers, the very ones I'd bought and never used, per her insistence.

I followed her limping, treacherous. . . .

I followed her out into the office mall corridor, which was fairly quiet. She was leaving altogether, unto finding me blocking her exit, then she decided to take refuge in a nook between the brass railing and a marble pillar, as I required her to explain.

Day saved time, by not lying about working on Sid to undermine being sent back to lockdown.

I quietly, heatedly reminded her that I'd recently asked her to trust me, and that she'd specifically chosen me to be the one, who took care of her. She stood there, looking guilty as hell, as if trying to figure out how to say she'd "forgotten" to a man, who knows exactly when she's lying.

Part of me did feel sorry for her, she looked so boxed in. She *was* boxed in, in too many ways, like a demoralized bird of prey I once saw. It'd been caged so long that even with the door open—it was too afraid to leave, to fly away.

I mentally gave her points for trying to do something for herself, instead of waiting for enough crumbs to fall her way, but everyone had used her and now she was ruthlessly using herself to bribe this pathetic paper pusher, because even though she'd said the words . . . .

Even though she'd said the words to me and had meant them, and had sealed our binding deal with her heart and body, she still wouldn't, couldn't have complete faith in me.

In my helping her. In my taking care of her. In my being in control of . . . .

Not with all those who'd gone before me having used her. Not without her digging herself deeper into the water filled hole she was already drowning in.

Pizza Guy, the video, this . . . legal yutz.

I'm way too tenacious for my own good, I'd avoided controlling anyone or any situation in the horrid, past few months because it'd gotten to the point that, that seemed *all* I ever did, at every moment.

And, yet, I was standing before this delicate-minded beauty, whom I'd so fervently, devotedly offered my abilities to, in that vein; a public school dropout beauty, who was ripping the control from my privately well-educated hands.

I was abruptly, intensely aware that I very deeply wanted, no, *needed* Day to put herself in my hands, to let me care for her and handle everything, to let me not merely try, but to actually fix this somehow for her.

I wasn't sure how and it was stupid to think I could, but I *knew* I could—if she would only fully and unquestioningly yield to me, like she did her body, that proverbial mustard seed's worth of faith and trust.

And control.

I was also aware, as she blurted on, that she had absolutely no reason to have faith in or to trust or heed anyone and that experience had taught her to fend for herself as best she could.

She'd prostituted herself—*giving her body,* her pretended interest to Sid, as a bribe, another "down payment" in Hoppy-speak for Sid "to add" my name, for Sid "to find some way to sneak" me into the paperwork for Hopkins' Will, as inheritor designate, as her guardian.

I didn't hold back my rage after that; I barely held back the decibels, which truly wasn't fair on my part. I was just as angry, more so even, at myself as I was at her.

What I needed she couldn't give me, certainly not at the moment, as she cringed at every one of my emotional inflections, while the returning, boisterous, lunch crowd moved way around us.

In mid tirade, she agoraphobically cowered to the floor, begging in a muffled whisper.

"Please, take me home. *Please,* Benn?"

My heart didn't really soften at that, not with my resentment bathed in sharp disappointment and revved up high. I was tired of her bending to everyone else's whim, like wheat in the wind and I was very tired of her ruling me.

Of me allowing certain women to control me, by my heart and/or nads.

Mind you, Day controls me better in both ways, than any-one else ever, but at that particular moment, she was barely in control of herself.

I reached down and touched her face, she looked up at me, her skin ice cold and so starving for my touch, you'd have thought my palm a defense shield between her and the hundreds of people in the vicinity.

I had to carry her, while she clutched to me in terror the whole time, back to the car and into the house. We were still alone, but she was content to wash and go to bed extremely early and stay in her room the night, as I left the doors open between us and lay down alone.

My body, my everything managed to still want to be with her, despite or because of my anger, knowing she wouldn't have turned me down, but also knowing that would be a bad idea . . . for me.

I was at my limit or more correctly, way beyond it.

Stephanie'd left a fortuitous message on my private voice-mail, which I happened to rise and check in my now habitual disquiet.

I decided my sister, the treacherously vicious bitch, may have a valid point, this time, about my lover, the other treacherously vicious bitch in my life. But, since I'd been playing the rutting beast of a dog myself, I really couldn't bitch about bitches.

Hopkins arrived late, and I made the old cur's entire retire-ment by leaving before he'd unpacked his overnighter. He took silent notice that I had *all* of my stuff and that I'd said nothing to Day, still in her room.

I backed out of his drive, leaving the lord of the manor coolly standing sentinel on his porch, with his cigarette's smoldering end the only light burning at his house.

* * * *

I took a red-eye flight to where Stephie was, getting there on numb autopilot.

"You're smoking, again?! You haven't smoked since, we were

fifteen, and you wanted—. That little bitch!"

Her overly outraged, slightly smug tone was pissed, yet laced with jealousy, envy, and a definite note of covetousness. And, no, we didn't discuss or fight over the recording of her little backstabbing visit with Day.

She knew it hadn't worked, but now something had, so she was basically satisfied for the moment.

I also knew better than to tell her exactly why I was walking dead.

We were at Hopkins' forest house. We, well, actually Stephanie, spoke to the two pleasant, concerned, and gentle workmen there and to Day's competent, caring doctor and nurses at the nearby little hospital, who all still thought the circular saw incident was "an accident."

Stephie found nothing "juicy," as she kept calling it, while we "investigated." I also didn't bother telling her Day had nearly sliced off her own feet on purpose. My twin, as it was, wasn't letting anything go, and to tell you the truth, I believe she just wanted to know more about the woman, because the more you know, the more control.

Maybe. The more you control something . . . someone . . . the more of yourself is lost to it . . . to her, attaching and binding yourself to it . . . to her. Stephie's not big on being attached or bound by anyone, not if that someone needs constant attention.

Steph got us to Day's original hometown, a working class Cleveland suburb. The perverse irony of flying the commuter into Cleveland *Hopkins* International Airport wasn't lost on me.

We, she queried the neighbors, culled the newspaper morgues, and court transcripts. I was useless and smoked or slept like a narcoleptic through most of it, including the extensive drive to *there, the lockdown*—which finally woke me.

The more we learned along the way, especially *there*, the more my stomach tempests returned, pitching and roiling like November on Lake Superior. Day's "Mommy," wittingly or unwittingly, had used her, not unlike the lazy, desperate mother in the novel "This Property is Condemned."

The movie had Natalie Wood. Day became Mommy's bait.

Hopkins had spoiled Day's mom until she found a better deal or made a mistake, or whatever goes through a woman's mind or loins, when deciding between two men.

Day's father turned out to be something of a bust for Mommy, though, and she had to go back to working, about when Day hit her early teens, and certainly only the edge of the well-proportioned face and body she grew into. Just enough to get ole Hoppy's mind permanently off mom and onto the girl, who appeared to've been held like a carrot in front of him.

He paid quite a few of the family bills it seems, and just how the woman thought she could dangle the child like a tantalizing mouse before a starving lion, without him trying to devour her, is beyond . . . ?

She really seemed to have wanted Day to be a grand young lady of the old stories; to marry "well," which means to take care of mom; and for her to "keep her legs together"—*to use an old euphemism for abstinence.* Day was innocently being used as sexually charged bait, while her "Mommy" expected the old friend to just look and not touch, while yet coughing up the cash.

This is why "Reasoning Skills" should be added as a fourth to the all-important ancient three R's taught in school.

It was also highly possible good ole Mommy's intentions were far more suspect and self-centered.

Most people Stephie spoke to didn't know as much of the official record as they had thought. A lot was sealed because Day'd been underaged. It did turn up that she'd been pregnant, and her mother had had it removed, then had had her "fixed," with a tubal ligation; no doubt by a doctor who "hurt" Day, just as she'd said.

A middle school mate . . . friend said Day'd always wanted kids, but wisely realized she was too young.

She'd also told her that her mother's friend, some foreign guy, stalked Day—that the old guy would try to catch her in the bath and had, at least once, hidden and watched her from her closet, while she was "making out" with her middle school boyfriend.

The boyfriend had sworn that he'd never really touched her, which didn't matter in the long run, apparently, since the foreign friend took sexual advantage of the child, Day, when she was grossly confused during her abruptly traumatic breakup with said boyfriend.

The older man was rumored to've impregnated her. The mother barred him from her home, then caged Day inside and continued to resentfully control and push the sterilized girl viciously around, more so than before.

I met Dr. Carlyle of Day's hospital/prison lockdown alone at a nearby watering hole, as he requested. He was one of Day's doctors, and he'd been very interested, too interested, when he'd found out a Dr. Stephanie Gillespie and brother were hunting out details about her.

Stephie had clarified that Day hadn't killed anyone *("Lately.")*, not even Hopkins, but that we were just trying to find out more about her, to help her; the whole soft soap. Stephie would've made an excellent salesperson of some kind.

Guillotine sales probably.

Carlyle was smart, personable, a movie handsome, intense African American with clear, dark skin and a soft, processed wave in his hair, or maybe it was natural. It's not the kind of thing one man asks another—"Do you perm your hair?" Carlyle took an instant liking to me and seemed reluctant to talk around sister Steph, so it was presently just him and lucky me.

The mutual likeability factor might've been real and lasting, under other circumstances, but it was quickly tainted by the subject and emotions present.

Liking him wasn't something I would continue doing, because the man turned my guts.

"Can I call you Benn?" I shrugged my indifference, as he proceeded, warmed by whatever warms a person like him.

"A few of the orderlies would corner her and 'party' with her. When she got the backbone to complain, the chief doc on her case said she was lying to get sympathy. The idiot actually believed it was all a ploy to seduce him.

"I knew those little shithead orderlies, that she was most likely telling the truth. But, I didn't have the professional juice at the time to get those clowns investigated. So, I did it myself and kept at it until the unequivocal truth finally came out, and the hospital and all those high, important muckety-mucks on the board needed to save face.

"Those same little shitheads finally got fired, her case was transferred into my hands, and I got her to myself."

He smiled, gloated at me, conspiratorially would be the word.

"She was extremely grateful, and things were fine with just her and me. *Real fine.* Until dear, sweet Karen. The fund administrator? You met her. Administrators don't even usually see the inmates, but she got a gander at baby girl Day, then started asking about her, dropping in to see her, wooing her, plying her with guarantees of privileges.

"You know: nicer food variety for, a touch; fewer drugs for, a juicy taste; a trip off the grounds for, a leisurely crotch grind. Then, her 'wooing' and 'plying' got nasty."

No wonder Stephanie was able to turn Day around so fast. It was old territory for her. I wondered if Ms. Sappho, illustrious founder and patron of the Lesbian Nation, would approve of such expedient coercion.

Unfortunately, Carlyle was still yakking.

"Her blackmailing Day was an interesting approach, since I don't even think either girl was naturally inclined and disposed toward women, or bisexuality. For Karen, I really believe it was just because it was Day.

"Have you ever watched others stare at her? Male or female, it doesn't matter. She's just odd and, *you know*."

He stared at me, hard, with every look and every tone of his voice constantly implying we were in the same inner club.

"You have to admit, Benn, there's something so . . . m-m-m about her. Like some tangible promise of incredible sex, the most forbidden kind, that just exudes from her. Then, there's that whole *other* thing—like she needs to be protected.

"Or, at least, we men like to believe so. More likely, considering the final little talk she and her "Mommy" had, and being the complete ball buster that she is, I think we both know that *we* men need to be protected from *her*.

"Still, it's hard to shake, wanting to be her hero, to see yourself reflected, like a beacon light in her eyes. That light's incredible and seductive beyond belief, when she's wanting you and beaming that rare smile at you; too bad, she's so sad, so much of the time. But, it gives a man a goal, putting a smile on that remarkable face.

"Besides, the hero gets all the best tail. And, Day is *the* 'best tail,' isn't she, Benn? That's why she attracts the big, big boys, like the old man, and you."

I didn't say anything, I didn't want to talk or even listen to the putz, but I wanted to know, without wanting to know, and inertia or sheer masochism kept my ass in the booth seat.

"Oh, you want to pretend you haven't been banging that tasty shit. I'm surprised that old man, what *is* his name . . . Hopkins, lets you anywhere near that choice bit. Even when she doesn't want you, she's 'delicious to take advantage of,' as ole Karen'd say.

"Good 'ole Karen' said she'd tell my fiancée. I should've let her, would've saved me . . . . That's how she got Day to herself. It seems Day breeds fantastic amounts of territorial possessiveness to go along with the lust."

Great.

He'd taken it into his head that I was his competition, no wonder he preferred the private talk. Mano-a-mano, hand-to-hand, man-to-man, yada-yada-yada. Just what I needed, another man or manly woman *[re: Stephie]*, giving me crap about Day.

I wasn't even hers anymore, just merely curious about how she'd been made, and I was still getting crap, from envious strangers now, as he leaned in to make my brain constrict and contort into a few stroke-inducing tight knots.

"You already know, don't you, Bennet Gillespie. I've heard some tough old surgeons say you know shit hardly anyone else knows. A goddamn genius. Everyone talks about you, even before you showed up today, like you're a mothafuckin' god; hanging with the famous and getting your picture taken.

"They say you hit a brick wall when some close buddy of yours exed himself out after you, the Big Kahuna himself, couldn't handle what he had. Made you drop out of sight. Now, here you are, sitting across from little ole nobody me?

"Yeah, I bet you know all about making sweet Day want you, about 'taking care' of her. She needs that, craves it, because no one ever does. We all want her but none of us, not a one truly care for her, not the way she wants, not even you, sir, not without using her for *our* needs, not without cutting her off at the knees."

He chuckled.

"That's what that old foreign cracker what 'owns' her did. Just like the old slave days—*cut her, so she couldn't, can't run,* like a Mandarin and his prized, crippled, little Chinese bride. A real shame."

I was glad that he didn't know the truth about the saw accident and he smiled, closely observing my sullen silence. There wasn't any point in pretending he was particularly wrong or that I found him offensive, he clearly knew that, and I knew there was no way in a cold, hard fuck he'd get near Day again.

"Benn, Benn, Benn. I can't imagine Hopkins letting someone *like you* anywhere near her. He had trouble, as it was, controlling her from the moment he received court permission and signed her out. She ran off, rode away on a Harley and got dragged back. Literally dragged, I hear.

"Then, out the blue . . . massive bloodletting, which got all hushed up. Nice little place way out there. Like a gingerbread house in the forest. Used to call her out there and drop in, 'to check on her,' before and after the 'accident'; I wasn't the only one, but he's got the right friends, the powerful friends, and more money than . . . .

"That crazy little whore should've been sent right back to us, to me, for cutting herself like that."

So, he did know. What games of the mind these *people,* if that is what you could call them, play with the sane, let alone must play with the confused and disturbed.

Carlyle made me sick to my stomach and not because he was lying, which *I knew* he wasn't, as he waited.

I vaguely shrugged.

"Married, Benn?"

I shook my head "no."

"Divorced?"

Another "no."

"Lucky there, too, huhn? Believe me, you won't like it, especially with a house and baby in the mix. She accused me of being 'obsessed,' y'know. My levelheaded half Jew, professional wife jealous of a nutcase I couldn't even have anymore, thanks to Karen, The Mother Fuckin' Selfish.

"There was plenty for both of us, and she leaves me holding my own dick. I mean, my bride was really something but she couldn't top . . . ."

He got lost in some particularly volatile memory in his head, before he could proceed.

"I didn't give a shit after a while about what details Karen might say. I'm sure her husband and kids would be surprised to find out she's a cunt-eating, crotchbuffing, little bitch of an extortionist, when she's not at the PTA.

"Heard he took Day east. Is that where you been, hiding out? Buried all warm and deep and snug, as a hard, swelled prick in that hot, sweet cunt of hers?"

He laughed suddenly, loudly, then became conspiratorially hushed.

"That's exactly it. You're exactly like me, after all in all. You fucked her, then abandoned her, didn't you?

"It won't work, Benn. I tried very, very hard to play the faithful and dutiful to both the Hippocratic and the wife. But, I promised to 'take care' of Little Day. Meant it most of the time; hell, anything to get my aching dick into her deep sweet shit.

Sound familiar, Big Benn? Did you use the same line?"

He didn't seem to care that I never answered.

"Myself, I backslid, like a mothafucka. At full force. On my anniversary. Left in the middle of the night, after the celebration, after fulfilling my husbandly duty. I left for 'an emergency,' for a wild, randy itch my wife couldn't touch. Hard as a rock, way before I got to Sweet Day.

"Ripped off the pretty psycho's PJs and dove in. That bitch welcomed me back, with wide-open legs, and broke my balls six ways to Sunday. *Goddamn, I miss that.* Then she says . . . . Get this.

"'I'm not free, so neither are you. Your cock's got my cunt's name branded on it forever, now, but try and fuck me again and I'll break it off in a may your urologist will never fix right. Explain *that* to wife and boss and certifying board. Bye-bye.'

"Such delicate words from such pleasing, cocksucking lips. Seriously considered having her gangbanged to punish her, but even if she was shutting me out, I didn't want to share that incredible bit of ass with anyone.

"Besides, she loves my dick way too much to . . . kiss it off forever, especially in our lovely little place here. Then, ole granddad steals her away.

"Oh, yeah, don't forget to generously thank the orderlies and myself for her mighty skills in deep throat cum-eating. The orderlies and I taught her very thoroughly in that department, along with how to take it front, back, and on her knees."

He was silent a moment, an all too brief moment.

"Won't be baited, huh? How big of you. Left her behind, did you? But, Crazy Little Day's still got your brain all seared, because she's got her name cauterized into your cockhead, too, and, by the look of you, a ring and chain through it, and she's yanking it back and forth, however she pleases.

"No matter how far you get from her. And you don't like her having control of your meat, do you? Tough. She's a total man-eater, that one."

He was silent for a while. A blissful to my ears, too short a while moment.

"Tell me where she is and I'll take the murdering little bitch-slut off your hands."

"Carlyle, you'd never get past Hopkins. I barely did. A second man definitely won't." I thought but didn't say that she yanks me very well and I like it just fine.

"Accidents happen, Benn. Don't they?"

He actually said it with a sincere, straight face.

"Old geezers, like him, die 'accidentally' all the time. We medical professionals 'academically' toy with the dangerous ideas because 'we know' *things*, don't we? And, he *will* die, with help or just because he's not the healthiest stud around and she's, well, Day.

"Something sharp and pointed will get left out or she'll just fuck his broke-down old ass to death. Or you, you might . . . . However it happens, she'll get sent back home. To *here*. To *me*. *Oh, my*."

He creamed his shorts, "copiously" would be an appropriate adjective. *No, seriously,* the proof was there when he stood later. For the mere anticipation of her returning.

He shrugged it off and smiled in that eager way his competition, Karen, had when hotly questioning how soon Day would be back.

In *their* loving embrace(s)?

People work where they get the best salary, can do the most good, or can do the most damage, without being caught. Sometimes, and I've seen it before, especially in fields where you have control and power over people's lives and minds, sometimes, good people let their inner demon overtake them.

Certain people and certain situations bring out the best or the worst in these people.

Day herself, or Day plus the impossible situation she'd been in, would be in again, if, when she returned here, had triggered something ugly, in Karen and Carlyle. Or they triggered something in her, and got the blowback. Whichever or whatever it was, they were wholly addicted now and wanted more.

Remind me to thank Stephie for bringing me here.

I take that back. I thank myself for being stupid enough to come with her, knowing I did and didn't really want to get a better, full color, in-depth picture in my head of what, of who came before me. Just having a vague idea of who disgusts you is much better than a specific one with name, face, and graphic details.

Day had long ago had all of what we'd seen and heard—*and much, much more not mentioned*—stamped and burned into her tender brain and into her sensitive flesh; yet, she opened as much of her body and heart and her mind to me, as she could, nearly instantly.

I wasn't sure if that was merely extreme desperation, perversely fatalistic optimism, or just what on her part.

All of *this,* however, did say a great deal about her resilience.

Myself, I probably would've folded like a house of loose playing cards. I know I would've. That's why I was already seized up into an emotional fetal ball, before I'd fallen hard at her feet and . . . .

Day had rescued *me* on the beach.

I know, I know. Yes, she killed her mother, but . . . .

I know she was, *is* "confused", but it seems no one actually helps her, just helps themselves to her.

I've known a few people, who *always* get their cars stolen or are *always* socially meeting the same kind of wrong person, who's exactly like the one they've just excised from their life, over and over again. I think, maybe, that's Day.

Most of *these* people *(and I use the term "people" extremely loosely)* smiled wistfully and asked when Day was coming back. They reminded me of a pack of rapaciously hungry dogs, off the leash, gone wild in the city, and spotting an unarmed child alone.

I abhor unrestrained dogs.

I called from a pay phone and Mrs. G was ecstatic to hear from me and immediately put her on. Day sounded distant, vague . . . lost. And perpetually used to being lost.

"No one ever calls me. I don't like to be called. I don't need . . . other voices in my head. Benn, are you all right?"

"No, I'm not."

She was silent a long while, I didn't mind because I knew she was still there. I heard her sigh softly; I swear I felt it within my own chest, as if it had been my own.

"Bennet, wherever you are, whatever you're doing, do you have, do you really know what you want?"

She didn't wait for an answer and quietly hung up on me.

I'd been listening to her voice with my eyes closed.

I opened them and stared out the plate glass window before me. A bird, with a damaged wing, hop fluttered, hop fluttered, then rested, panting heavily against the glass, in a little corner of the building, out of the rushing way of passersby.

The fragile thing seemed terrified, and plainly, painfully familiar to me.

Maybe I do have a hero-damsel complex.

Stephie cursed a horrible blue streak when I told her and then, not too gently, reminded me, that I had a home of my own, a business, and important and valuable commitments. She also promised to my retreating backside, that she'd find the Kryptonite® against Day, as I left, to go back.

I'd forgotten to leave my key in my previous haste, and used it to get in.

It was late, Mrs. G gone for the night. The door was open to Day's room, the logistics of which, I can see inside when turning to my room. He was under her, grunting and straining, staring up at her as he always does. Oblivious to me, or maybe he'd expected me.

He wasn't at all surprised to see me the next morning.

Day glimpsed around at me. She wasn't happy, as she docilely continued her "obligation" to him.

I deeply hoped she'd kill the lecherous bastard—"obligate" him, fuck his very sorry ass to death. Unfortunately, my unkind thoughts and feelings were instantly curtailed, as he came and the view became appallingly worse when she moved off him and he slipped heavily out of her creamy slick.

I all but ran to my room, opened my window and considered leaving right back out of it, like a burglar, but instead, I burned and polluted my lungs again with another "fag," as Hopkins insists calling them.

Then, I lay on my, her mattress on the floor, without undressing, face down on it. Maybe, I'd smother to death, instead, as I heard him snoring atrociously and her washing her body spotless, of him.

Of his contamination.

I, eventually, felt her steamy body lie on top of mine, heard her speak tenderly to me, coaxing me. She didn't ask where I'd been, who I'd been with or seen, and I certainly didn't volunteer it.

She pulled out my shirt to kiss my back, before lightly nipping at my buttocks through my chinos, anything to coax me.

There was no reason for me to hold out on her. I'd come all this way back for her, or at least for myself, as I continued ignoring my own many "obligations," after I'd listened and seen vile things on top of the horrid things I already knew.

As I, presently, without question, gave myself into her care, capitulated to her, because I wanted her, needed her even more than she wanted and needed me, which quite, quite plainly was a great deal.

* * * *

The house was quiet, had been for weeks. In fact, it was always quiet, except doing the high tension and high drama of arguments and tests of wills.

What is it with Anglos and their lack of music in their homes, in their lives?

Perhaps it's just me, but I've rarely seen a home of a "colored" person, especially one of Mexican, South or Central American, or African descent that didn't have music, laughter, pleasant conversation, or all the above constantly buzzing in its occupants' lives.

So many Anglo homes I've been in have been dead quiet.

That's why I hate movies and television shows with bland Anglo families in them. They always seem so distant, cold, and, well, silent.

Hopkins' beachhouse was dead quiet, until I happened to open a computer file sent by my twin. She likes to send me musical messages. And, she obviously missed me in her way, so this particular note had a MP3 music file attached; which reminded me of younger years and of my meeting and befriending Chuck, off campus in our undergrad days.

In true actuality, he had befriended me.

I was seated on the floor, back propped against the sofa, when I opened the message. I'd had it for days.

Hopkins glanced up from his newspaper and glared at the sound—*80s British rock probably isn't his favorite;* he rubbed his eyes and looked like he was about to bitch that I was giving him a headache. "His house, his rules."

Probably needs to get his eyes checked, with all the squinting he's been doing lately, that or keep his pants zipped for a while, anyway . . . .

I was about to close the file, except Day unexpectedly begged me not to. She was entirely focused on it from the first beat, and it had a lot of beat, for an Anglo band.

Day has a tendency a lot of people of color have. She hears music in her head. She may not sing or hum but her head and body moves; "Hoppy" once said it was a "symptom of her illness." I explained the concepts of music, beat and rhythm to him.

He didn't get it and thought I was crazy or at least filled to the rim with bullshit. His opinion changed with Stephie's music gift of Depeche Mode, as Day closed her eyes to let their beat and words . . .

" . . . only when I lose myself in someone else, that I find myself, I find myself,©" enveloped her, penetrated her.

Hopkins was about to complain; but; the visual sensuousness of her listening with her *whole being,* her *whole body,* stopped him.

And, that particularly obsessed man, who rarely takes his eyes off her when she's within sight and still, fixed harder on her, as she began to move. I was no different in that regard; in those five minutes or whatever the dance tune runs.

" . . . did I need to sell my soul, for pleasure like this? Did I have to lose control, to treasure your kiss?©"

I've seen her feet flex and twitch, when viewing dancers on a video of some danceable musical or ballet; and she has many more of them than I've ever heard of. It's all so much a part of her, and he's plainly loved that part of her enough to have that expensive, enlarged, dancing portrait of her, yet he denies her new music, which would benefit her, in many ways, music therapy-wise and . . . .

He and I blatantly stared, fascinated.

Day was entirely oblivious to us, to everything except feeling and movement within herself, and the music. Sensuous, fluid, seductively innocent pleasure.

The supple woman was unwittingly driving us both over the edge of desire, lust, passion, whatever you want to call it, without any regard to anyone's existence but her own.

It may have been the only time we two men were ever truly in accord. We didn't want to interrupt her *(for our own sakes, if no other),* and watching her blissfully journeying inside herself drew us in, which meant neither of us moved or hardly took a breath.

Peripherally, I saw him shift in his armchair; to accommodate that previously mentioned growing desire, lust, passion. I was wearing looser pants, but I drew up my legs, to hide my rising hard-on, while he was repositioning his newspaper strategically for cover.

When the song ended, she paused, eyes still closed, and then the rapture on her young face swiftly became disappointment, as she opened her eyes and quickly limped out into the chilly, early night.

Hopkins and I made brief, vulnerable eye contact, before I glanced away long enough, so he could skitter off to his room without me getting a visual confirmation of his dance-induced want.

At the time, I assumed . . . .

He seemed dizzy and stumbled a little, probably from jumping up too fast, and all that blood in his dick. Myself, I remained still to let my own blood passion *too slowly* dissipate, and soon heard a strangled sound from his room.

I appreciated the fact that he "handled" his own dissipation without bothering her, then I felt her small, cold hand on my neck, as she leaned on me, to help her sit down beside me, wedging herself behind my arm and shoulder, between me and the sofa. It's a comfort place of hers. I could barely hear her question.

"Would you play it, again, please? I'll just sit still, this time."

She said it apologetically, having finally realized what we were going through. Women, it seems to me, always catch more hell, than we do, for simply being who they are and for openly expressing themselves.

All because *we* can't handle it.

I turned the sound low, so he couldn't hear it and she leaned forward and stared at the computer while it played.

When it was only halfway through, she shut the machine— quieting it. A ragged breath escaped her, but she refused to let the excess water behind her eyes fall, as she said a quiet "thank you," before she went to her room, shut the door, and snapped off the light.

* * * *

Five minutes after her bedroom light went out, I became conscious of something . . . of something I'd apparently suppressed or . . . .

I'd been so deep in the middle of my own traumas and dramas so many months ago, buried thoroughly under my work, my life, my . . . .

How can I say this? I really don't think I acted on it subliminally, but only Freud or one of that ilk [think Arabella] *would assume knowing for sure, right?*

On my laptop's desktop is a secured medical database, housed behind a solid firewall access on our . . . on my corporate website.

Doctors without a clue for treatment or with doubts in general often send me files, complete with detailed histories and past regimens, photos, or video even, for me to peruse and give opinions on. Sometimes I take over where they've become stonewalled.

I haven't accepted a file from anyone in quite awhile, not since, not since a lot of things. However . . . .

Day's file is in there.

Eventually, I went in to check and make certain she was all right. She said she was, as my stomach twinged inside, as if pricked with needles and I knew she wasn't.

I gently spooned against her and held her to me and softly sang Native and Spanish songs to her, until she'd been asleep for quite awhile, then I let her have her bed to herself.

* * * *

Mrs. G found Mr. "early riser" Hopkins in Day's bed late the next morning. Guess he hadn't "handled" his own needs well enough. Day'd woke me late into the night and I'd noted he couldn't leave her be for one friggin' damned night.

She and I touched, stroking the other's body tenderly all over, and we lightly fucked, a goalless fuck, since we didn't bother to drive it to climax for either of us, but just to feel each other's affections, to have each other's attentions, then she'd slept the remainder of the night with me, as usual.

"Usual" is an interesting term, isn't it?

Mrs. Gorbachev woke me, begging me to hurry and look after him, as she called an ambulance.

Hopkins had stroked.

I drove to hospital, after the ambulance took him away and stayed until I was certain about him.

When I got back to the house, Day had her knees drawn up tightly to her chest, sitting in one of the big chairs—*the sturdy one I prefer*—waiting.

She had on a cardigan sweater of mine, which swamped her in size, making her look more childlike. Her new drawing pad and a few color pencils lay on the porch floor, discarded in her distraction and Mrs. G was right by her, sitting on the arm of the chair stroking Day's hair, trying to soothe her.

I hadn't "profoundly" comprehended until that second that the one very good thing Hopkins had done for Day was to hire Mrs. G, because the woman was the only girlfriend or friend of any kind that she had and was the only one, who sincerely mothered Day, as best she could.

I'd inadvertently stopped in my tracks, lost in the thought of the two women together on top of the previous thoughts about his health and well-being, and eventually realized Day was silently grieving. She was pulling and worrying out of shape the sweater's sleeve ends, as she quietly sobbed in forlorn dread.

I glanced past her at my reflection in the large window behind the chair and saw my morose expression, which she'd read as full loss for her.

"Day, he's all right. He's weak but alive."

To say she was relieved, not to be going straight back to the strong, waiting arms of Dr. Carlyle and his competition, Karen, would be a bit of an understatement.

It was also interesting that none of us missed Hopkins. At least no one admitted it aloud, the entire time he was gone.

Day and I certainly didn't.

It was a joy, for me, to not have her constantly scrubbing and scouring herself copper shiny, from head to toe, inside and out; because there is absolutely no more pleasant scents on the planet than those of your lover; at least that's my opinion.

With him gone, I could wallow in how she truly smelled, and tasted.

With him gone, I even managed to take her a few places. Nothing too, too overwhelming, just a *little* loud—she LOVED the long car drive, during which she *screamed* and *bounced* up and down and *squirmed* in her seat belt restraint, as she watched things zoom by in her perpetual overexcited freedom, while toying with the satellite radio's many choices.

We arrived at an out of the way, yet homey, as I was told, bed and breakfast. I'd gotten a nice bonus check in my account for past "services rendered" and was planning on not servicing anyone else but Day.

With Mrs. G's help, I'd splurged on clothes and underclothes; the works for Day, which we'd packed for her and I gave to her when we got to the inn. Male or female, young or old, she caught the eye, which embarrassed her, even though it was obvious she quietly expected the attention. Not so much because of ego, but because it was her past experience.

She looked so great, in fact, I felt better-looking being with her and was completely grateful Stephanie was no where in line of sight of her.

Her Mommy would've been proud of her. Day truly was a "well-mannered, well-bred lady" on my arm, as her mother'd constantly berated her to be, when she hadn't been undermining those same words with more vile ones.

Day danced quite a bit and shyly refused everyone but me. Then, she picked from the jukebox "The Shelter of Your Arms" by Sammy Davis, Jr. During it, I had her place her feet on top of mine because she'd refused to stop dancing, though overtaxed, and breathlessly gushing about loving the song from as far back as she could remember, but not knowing why, except that she just did.

Then, she made me program it to play three more times, during which I adamantly made her sit.

When we got back to our room, I immediately stretched out on the bed, but instead of being completely exhausted, Day looked beatific and said she felt "every numbed nerve ending" she had was "finally alive." She said, "thank you."

And, "Bennet, tell me what you want me to do for you," which was plainly a loaded solicitation.

That surprised me. I just wanted to make her happy, give her a chance to feel freedom, not to make her obligated to me, and I told her so.

My answer unmistakably confused her.

Day sat down on the loveseat a long while, mulling it over—that a man or woman giving her a few things and a little freedom or fun didn't and shouldn't entail her being indebted and obligated to do anything for them in return.

Oddly enough, the two days and nights we were there, we merely cuddled and nuzzled and kissed but never fucked once. It was enough to make love to her with my eyes, by watching her enjoy everything; to see her allow herself to get involved in a gentle, yet animated, conversation with a wonderful great grandmother and her new and younger husband; or simply to watch her dress, and undress.

Oh, and we watched more than a few hours of broadcast TV and cable.

Take that Master Dictator Hoppy!

I'd spoken with Mrs. G and he wouldn't be home from the hospital for a little while longer.

So, I extended our trip, and on the spur of the moment, took her on a friend's private jet. During the short flight, she gazed out the window in delight and showed me things, that I'd probably seen a thousand times, from a thousand planes, like clouds you could nearly touch, but which she made interesting again with her enthusiasm.

Then, she took to staring at them, lost in a far off thought.

I leaned to her and half whispered, not wanting to disturb her, but curious.

"A penny for your thoughts?"

"Eagles. They mate for life and still manage to fly so very high together, completely and entirely unfettered by all the crap and shit down there." She nodded with distracted satisfaction. "Eagles."

That pretty much explained why she nearly always drew birds on the wing.

I drove us the rest of the way to the house of a friend, an abandoned house for which I still possessed keys and alarm system codes.

By the way, Day always chatters a lot more when away from Hopkins, and in that house she had a lot of questions, especially about me and mine.

"This is a *beautiful*, expensive place. A place Hopp—." She stopped herself from mentioning him. "Your friend, who owns this house, what's he, she do?"

"Orthopedic surgery, like the ones who fixed your ankles, that's why I knew they'd done a great job." She snooped around, as I opened a few windows, to let out the dust smell and general stuffiness.

"It's such a really beautiful house, Benn. Why's it empty? Why's no one been here in such a long while?"

"Because 'Hoppy' has nothing on the master of *this* domain, not when it comes to having *his* way or filing billable hours for heaps of cold cash. 'My friend' is a driven, overconfident shithead of a know-it-all surgeon, who's never home, always connected, and always on the fast go."

"Your friend's a 'shithead'? You call him that to his face?"

Having only one friend, one lover, and one "owner/dictator" in her life, she didn't really get my friendly hostility and contempt for someone I loved.

"I don't call him that anymore. He *was* a shithead. Now, he's just a dickhead."

I half smiled, leaving her uncertain how to take the intent behind my meaning, as I followed her, while she mulled it over a while and further investigated the place, which was still furnished, but'd been stripped of more personal items.

"Benn, is that better? Being a 'dickhead'?" I shrugged.

I like that about Day, that she let's me be a little cryptic, on occasion, when I'm cryptic. It's not that I particularly endeavor to be, but you know, there are some things, some people you just don't have the energy or the hard scab protection to talk personal things about.

She understands that.

"Is he a better surgeon than the ones I had? Because, I was thinking. I was woozy then." She giggled, oddly. "People talk around me all the time, even when I'm 'well.'"

She sounded increasingly bitter.

"Like I'm not there, like a child, a slave, a wall. Sorry. Anyway, the doctors working on me were afraid and considered consulting some high-priced surgeon from around here."

She shrugged a shoulder.

"*THE* 'BEST' man for 'both surgery and therapy.' Of course, Hoppy was immediately screaming and demanding they get Dr. pricey big shot very badly—'no matter the expense' and that kind of overbearing bullshit; but—.

"*Holy Mother, Benn, these floors are beautiful, positively, sensuously beautiful!*

"Y'know, I don't think they even gave him the guy's name. Hoppy was *hopping* mad when he was turned down. Via impersonal email at that, as relayed by the other doctors. How cold. And, to Hopkins, too. He hates 'technology,' except as stock investments.

"This floor is . . . it's *like velvet*. And, the pattern. How expensive is—? *Yeah*, blowing Hoppy off, that was cool. Very cool. My Docs said their pricey big shot'd 'glanced over' my case, said

I 'should be fine' in their hands."

She frowned, staring out at the first class view, then shrugged, before deciding to say whatever she thought, anyway.

"I remember feeling that I wasn't worth that important, expensive stranger's . . . . His answer though, that email message was still cool, as far as pissing off and snubbing Hopkins, but I think the guy just wanted to get them all off his back. And, maybe, his 'glance' *was* worth more and was 'more accurate than' someone else's full examination and consideration.

"But, at the time, I felt deeply slighted just the same, which is silly and childish, but I was probably just taking it too personally. Too many drugs. They make me weird and crazy . . .-er. Anyway, I wasn't exactly fully focused at the time."

Her face scrunched up in thought.

"I thought they'd said that the surgeon, no, his friend had been terminal but had committed suicide." She glanced off in deep consideration. "'Committed,' like a well-thought out determination. *Benn, you live here.*"

Her tone was more revelatory than accusatory. Eventually, she found a dust covered, framed photo of me with an Asian guy my age. The picture'd been lying face down on the abandoned grand piano.

"*Lived* here, Day. It's too big for one. We shared it, but now . . . ."

"He's got a great face and you two look so . . . comfy together. He doesn't look a bit like a 'shithead.'"

"That's . . . Chuck. Dr. Charles . . . . He . . . he's—."

"Dead," she said. I nodded, unable to audibly answer. She blew dust off the photo before putting it in my hands. "He's not your 'dickhead' former 'shithead,' is he?"

I barely shook my head "no" and we left it at that, as she slipped her arms around me, her body flush against mine was pure comfort and felt like home; lush, warm, intimate, inviting— nothing like this empty, lifeless, and equity-filled building had ever been.

All personal items in the house were long since relegated to storage, except the photo, which'd been most significantly and unfortunately forgotten.

Sometimes you examine, reexamine, evaluate, and reevaluate your checklist; you know the one, THE checklist with exactly and absolutely everything on it. You check more times than you can say—and you still miss something, or that something hides from you, whichever.

It's still soul-severing death.

Day wanted to make love, in my former bed, but I refused, not there. I thought she'd get mad at me, she has for a lot less, but she left it alone and let me have my way.

"Can we fuck on the jet, Benn? I've never, not in the air."

I didn't answer, but she smiled, as my abruptly preoccupied mind feverishly worked out the preliminary details. And, upon quitting the house, she wouldn't permit me to leave Chuck's photo behind; I was glad about that, sometime later.

After I'd granted and fulfilled her wish.

We stopped at the beautiful A.R.E.® Meditation Gardens, on our return to Virginia Beach; unfortunately, being in mere proximity to Hopkins made her tense, clingy, and childlike, but the Gardens captivated her and distracted her hypersensitive mind from our final destination, as we roamed about.

Their beauty and the overwhelming feeling of relaxation and peace overtook her, plus the shadow of a sadness that this beautiful place was so close and she'd never visited before.

She became silently retiring, after poignantly begging to stay as long as we could, which we did. It was always disconcerting to see childhood and womanhood alternate so swiftly across the planes of her face. And sometimes coexist simultaneously.

I let her enjoy the place on her own for about twenty minutes, as I chatted up . . . spoke with a visiting acquaintance, while keeping an eye on her and wishing deeply that I could take Day away more often.

Then, she could play . . . *be* an adult for a longer time.

We were sitting side by side; she was nearly under me, since she was behind my arm, holding on to it as my hand rested on her outer thigh.

"Benn?" She'd said my name so softly that I almost hadn't heard her.

"Hm?"

"I know . . . I know I've seemed *very* experienced . . . sexually, but I . . . I didn't participate with them, as much as people did . . . with me . . . . My body was . . . just there, a—. What does Hoppy call that? A 'commodity,' and I felt nothing or . . . or worse, with them."

Guilt then shame crossed her features and I had to lean to hear her nearly inaudible words, while her fingers strangled my biceps.

"Sometimes, sometimes my body . . . betrayed me and . . . and felt, it felt more than *I* did?"

She made a wincing, hesitant glance at me.

"It made them want me more. And, there was one . . . one, who seduced me with illusions of true affection."

Her words sometimes. I love them. All that reading and her desire to be open with me often came out in great, passionate eloquence. Like her lovemaking.

She sighed a huge sigh.

"But, he was a total fake. He wasn't anything like you—."

"My Beautiful Dayita, it's amazing you don't hate being touched." She nodded in her misunderstanding of my meaning, as she bitterly quipped.

"Because I'm a 'whore.' They all say—."

"*Day, that is not what I meant.*" She shrugged in offhanded indifference.

"Of course it's not."

She looked regretful, immediately, not about her doubting retort, but only, I think, because she'd said it to me. She leaned tighter into me, in confidentiality.

"There's this place, a secret place inside me, far from *all* of them. The best thing I've ever kept in there was how I wanted . . . how I truly wanted and needed to be loved, and . . . who, what kind of lover I wanted. You'll think it manipulative or just silly, childish even, but without knowing exactly who you were, Benn, you're *exactly* what I always hoped, and . . . ."

She giggled.

" . . . wet dreamed of. *I was right* in knowing how it *could* and *should* be. With the absolute right—. Benn, I . . . I've never been with anyone else in the same way I am with you, *not ever,* not in spirit and not emotionally, honest, in spite of—."

"Shsh."

I put my arm around her and I know what she said sounds somewhat . . . absurd, but there is a perpetual innocence to her. And, it's not faked; it's real and completely genuine, completely Day.

"Hopkins was right, this time, Benn. You *should* know everything."

I stroked her soft hair, then held her face between my hands. She seemed so fragile in my palms, as I gazed into her eyes to make certain this time that she didn't misunderstand my words or my intent behind them.

"Day, he isn't right, not about this, or—. You don't know everything about me, and you never will.

"Even if we confessed to each other every second of everyday that we could remember. That's the nature of life, and something I would never change about it because I rather like having that bit of privacy, that 'secret place' or whatever we want to call it.

"Sometimes a person needs it and *really* needs it to remain . . . secret, completely private or mostly so. In fact, it's my right. You have that right as well."

She stared at me for an extremely long time, a slightly uncomfortable time, before finally asking her question.

"*I* have a right?"

"*Yeah.* In fact, you have *rights.*"

She smiled, shyly; then, abruptly, was ready to leave, but on the short way back "home" to Hopkins,' I had to pull over and park, because she . . . I . . . we *needed* to pull over.

* * * *

He'd been back for weeks, and between Hopkins' regular His Royal Majestyness power trips and his added, extra, new illness-generated orneriness and her many divergent moods eating away at mine, she'd managed to royally piss me off, again, in that pierce through me way only Day is able to do.

Stephie busts my balls but Day, unintentionally or intentionally, can bust raw places in me no one else can touch.

And, despite my knowing why she was doing it, she still managed to get to me; only this time, I had no where to go, or run to, because I'd finally learned, slowly but clearly, that it was pointless to run.

From her. Or myself.

I'd no where else I no longer wanted to pretend to go, or pretend to run to, because I would come back to her. No matter that she was repeatedly convincing herself to anger me to make me go, because she still feared I would, especially now that she'd gotten a peek at how I used to live.

So, I sat my butt down on my favorite big armchair on the beachside porch, to stare out to sea, ocean, whatever. Considering her innate ability to get inside and read my most tenaciously secret mind and heart was as sharp as ever—*her perpetual fear of abandonment by me wasn't completely groundless.*

I was riled yet comfortably not going anywhere, as I half waved at Steve, our neighbor Penelope's husband.

He habitually stretches in front of Hopkins' house, instead of his own. The stair to the beach floor is convenient to lean on and he likes to get a close peek at the lady of the house, when possible. No one but me was in sight, so,' unfulfilled, he jogged up the shore toward my former hotel.

Hopkins was inside "doing his books."

Actually, what he was mostly doing was staring at them and not triple checking and rebalancing his accountant's balances, as usual, because his numbing illness now thoroughly affected his ability to correctly understand that kind of blandly intense detail.

And, he was gloating, since Day had me thoroughly pissed at her.

The man was always hopeful in the idea that I'd get tired of her and go. And, probably just as hopeful that I'd never leave, since without me, he could no longer control her, especially now that he was too ill to manhandle her.

So, though they disagreed on just about everything, my personal potential for abandoning her was the one concept Day and Hopkins mutually shared.

Poor Mrs. G had half mumbled that she was going to the store a half hour or more before, apparently off to buy pepper or such just to get a breather from us all.

Day wandered out, without saying anything to me, as she stood smack in front of me, blocking my line of sight of ocean, with her calico covered backside. I was trying to decide if I should let it go, move, lean to the side, or close my eyes—.

She turned around. Her skirt was up, her hand under its tail, her fingers wet from their warm activity between the "bearded lips of her womanhood," as my Peruvian, maternal grandmother might've said, once you translated.

I sighed.

The bitch was not going to fight fair or leave me be; she was going to drive me terribly insane by pushing me away then dragging me back by the delicate nads.

I stared at her gently moving fingers, then glanced away after I realized I was "smelling her," "tasting her," "feeling the soft contours of those hidden folds" in my sense memory.

She recaptured my eyes' fascinated attention when she slightly fucked her pelvis against her fingers, with a grunting sigh, then came to me, letting the dress' hem drop. I pulled my head back a bit from her, but it wasn't much of a defensive tactic, and only halfhearted at best, as she wiped the taste of her cunt across my lips.

I pulled her hand away, which wafted her scent past my famished nostrils, as I barely managed a short wait before I licked up her flavor, which I believe she took as her cue.

Day pulled a large pillow from the next chair to kneel on, between my thighs, which she ran her palms along the insides of, until finding the fleshy lump she sought, causing me to shift in my chair, but not to push her from me.

She kissed and licked and nipped at my bared stomach, unbuttoning my pants to hungrily explore me down to the pubic line, as, through my pants, she petted me, molded me, forced me far from my initial, aloof anger, and to a lusting hardness.

"Pull out your cock for me."

My gut and balls yearned after the possibility she'd now aroused in my mind let alone the true physical ache her successful mouth and hand techniques were generating in me, as I glanced over the beach in harsh daylight, stretching wide and empty to either side of us.

I glanced back through the window behind me and couldn't see anyone inside, only the reflection of myself and her and the world.

"Not out here, Day."

She smiled, wickedly.

Wickedly, is the only way to describe how she smiled at me, as she pressed with delightful insistence on my perineum; on a guy, that's that real sweet spot between his nads and anus. She pleasurably pressed on it through the soft cotton fabric of my chinos, making my breath catch, especially as I had nothing on under the pants.

In my remaining at the house with her, I'd taken to rarely wearing underpants when I wasn't going out. My buttocks, of their own accord, tightened, pushing me to be with her.

"Day."

I'm afraid it came out more as a faintly restrained plea than warning, especially after she unbuttoned her tightly bodiced dress, to the point of her breasts cascading out, which helped her petition to me a great deal.

"Don't say you don't want this, like this, Benn. That woman you were engaged to before, who wouldn't openly show her pleasure at being with you—*not even privately*—she never risked everything of herself for you, did she?

"And, you really wanted that, didn't you? You wanted her open to you, to entirely expose herself to you, shame herself even to the world."

She paused briefly.

"Yeah, especially that, because you wanted, needed for her to want *you more* than anyone or anything else, including her pride and her hardhearted self-importance."

She winked playfully.

"And, we both know *I* have no shame or pride or any of that. Right? *Especially when it comes to you.*"

I thought I heard a sound in the house; but, I must've been wrong.

She was so deep inside my head, rattling around inside me where no one else but me had ever been, skillfully wrapping her will around the most protected, most delicate part of my ego. Day was being a touch playful but *she knew,* and she knew I knew, that she had me by more than my balls and enthusiastic cock.

And, I never answered her questions because I could barely think at all or manage to form an audible word.

That Steve would be heading back our way faintly occurred to me, but my knees widened, giving her more access to me. She buried her face in my crotch and gently gnawed at me through the fabric; the enticing novelty of it, making me precum, as I pushed her head into me. She licked at the wet spot and huskily restated her previous request.

I complied and finished unbuttoning.

My pants were loose, with a wide opening, and it was little effort to pull my eager, thickly stiffening cock forth for her, the sensitive head of which she took immediately into her mouth, sucking off what was left of my "predew," which hadn't smeared inside my trousers.

Her mouth was hot and exactly what I wanted, her grip on my shaft, firm and commanding. I barely cared that Steve was in sight and getting nearer, and would doubtlessly stop again at our stair for a last cool down stretch and "lookey-loo" for Day.

A "lookey-loo" being what Chuck's wife, who was in real estate, always called those, who looked but never bought.

Steve waved.

I didn't acknowledge his existence, as he paused for his cool down, which never happened, once he saw Day's curl topped, dark head between my thighs, with a good substantial bit of my thick length rammed down her gluttonous throat.

He made some kind of noise, and she glanced around without letting go of me before pulling up and off me so he could see all, as she licked me, kissed me, reswallowed me, to the beneficial pleasure of both him and me—*teasing* him, *pleasing* me.

The notion *(another of those stray, stupid, inopportune thoughts of mine)* came unbiddened—of how she'd come to her high skill level, which still bothered me.

Not the skill itself, but . . . .

Thanks a bunch for fucking up my head, Carlyle, your job is done.

Mrs. G was right about her though, Day is a nice girl, a woman a man can't help but like, most of the time.

However, Doc-tor Car-lyle's descriptions *[I didn't tell you the half of his explicit details.]* of what he and the others had *taught* her, flared and burned in my mind.

It was the visualizing of Carlyle and those faceless others with her, hurting her for their own entirely selfish pleasures, but I let them fade with the warm manipulations of her tongue and lips and my own lust to be taken by her, in that public and masterfully obeisant manner.

I know guys, who have a preference, a taste, shall we say, for sexual virgins and not often fucked "nonvirgins." These guys thrive on a woman's inexperience—if she doesn't already know what he can do to make her crotch ache, then he doesn't have to sweat it that she never gets hers, while he gets his.

I was never like that and I always liked that Day was experienced, accomplished even, which heightened the sexual high stakes game between us.

I just never liked *how* she had gotten her higher education.

Which probably is a half-hidden mental and emotional quandary for me, a little landmine filled quagmire that'll probably one day go BOOM.

Another reason, in case you hadn't noticed, of why I was still with her, was that Day was very right, more than right that I completely got off on her open, violent affections for me. On her open lust for me in general.

On the fact that Steve couldn't take his eyes or ears off what she was doing with me, as he crept up to the top step, while massaging himself through his jogging shorts, before half pushing them down to pull out his stiffened rod and balls, none of which fazed me.

She was most likely a masturbatory sex fantasy of his already.

Even probably while he and Penelope went at it.

The fact that Day was messing with the minds of both of us simultaneously was something that should have horrified me, perhaps, but I was the one who'd moved in, knowing she could only come to me after Hopkins, literally, came first.

She paused a moment, as if she'd heard or seen something then released the throttle control her hand had held on the base of my exposed shaft, so that I could pump up and fuck her throat deeply.

Not something every woman volunteers for, or can manage, and with any other woman I'd try hard not to pump and fuck her throat, but Day's nearly spoiled me with it.

Swallowing a cock of any length or thickness is something I know I could never manage, without tossing the full contents of my gut. The fact that she says she doesn't permit Hopkins to throat fuck her makes it especially sweet.

On second thought, she has *completely* spoiled me, perhaps even to the exclusion of anyone else.

While I recall long discussions in the dressing and locker rooms for years at work, where other men said they wanted oral or more oral, and also anal sex, as well, from their beloveds, and were not getting it, Ms. Day now had me entirely hooked.

Another thing you may not have perceived by now, because you fell asleep or have been jacking off, is that there's so much that goes on in a man's head, about rewards and punishment, lust and love, public and private. Evil and Good.

Perhaps, I should've thanked Carlyle at that moment, as she attended to my need, as I benefited from his astute and useful tutoring, which probably sounds like some sort of betrayal of her, by male bonding.

Well, someone once said, "Women want to be appreciated."

Well, men want to be cherished and spoiled too, and worship of a man's cock, which is a major focal point of his own, by the woman he desires, goes a very long way.

Day rethrottled my penis, curtailing my deep thrusting, because, in full mastery of my body, she knew I was about to cum, and that she was in total control of this part of this fuck.

She taunted me, instead of letting me cream her esophagus, by making me wait further, as she pulled off then rubbed her astonishing face against my hard cock, while she fingerfucked her cunt, which smacked in its extreme wetness, audible even over the ocean's call.

I so very acutely wanted her more than anything in any universe—.

"You fucking, controlling, little queen bitch. Mount me . . . fuck me."

The chair was big enough for us both, as I picked her up, not wanting to wait for her tender ankles to propel her up. She eagerly slipped onto my lap and I wasted no time entering her, the feeling of which pulled an enormous groan from me, and a sweet, throaty, little whine from her, as she put her hand on the large window behind us for leverage.

I only remembered Steve when he shifted his position on the step, which seemed to hold him transfixed, as if to say one more step up to standing *onto* the porch with us, was too close, but where he was, was okay.

I didn't fucking care.

His new spot gave him a better view of her breast closest to him, as it jiggled voluptuously to our fucking rhythm.

She whispered in my ear—*making me party to her driving him over the edge,* as I hiked the fabric up high off her ass, per her instructions, to let him clearly see her getting enthusiastically spiked on my dick.

She never again glanced at him, not even at his reflection. I know because her eyes stayed locked on mine, until she came.

I was glad she came quickly because I'd misplaced my usual composure and restraint.

I couldn't hold back, not once her strong vaginal muscles squeezed me, convulsed around me, and *she sounded, like she sounded.*

I came hard, blowing strong within her, and felt my hot, sweaty crotch drenched by her lust and my own.

The humid air between us was filled with the thick scents of our individual arousals, which combined and thoroughly mixed into a deliciously heady perfume.

A dull, embarrassed, extended grunt came from Steve, as his strangling grip short-spurted and dribbled his wet, splattering tribute to Day onto the porch floor; a little too damned close to my bare toes.

I was still inside her as I covered up her backside and breathed in her ear.

"You amazing, incredible cunt. No one's ever 'taken care' of my needs like you. *No one.*" She liked that—her face is so easy to read about what she's feeling.

I kissed her a long while before finally rebuttoning her into her dress. Meanwhile, good ole Steve hadn't bothered to make eye contact or even say thank you, while putting "his business away," before running off, down the beach and not directly home, as usual.

He went past home up the other way, out of sight.

I don't recall ever seeing him face-to-face again or him stopping by to "stretch" or "cool down" at the staircase while looking for Day.

I smelled cigarette smoke.

The sun had shifted and when I looked back through the glass, Hopkins was just inside, panting heavily. Must've been a great show. Better than the one he'd put on the first night.

My cheeks flushed, not for what we'd just done, but for entertaining my smug, pain in the ass host. There was a wet spot on his crotch where his pants were wrinkled, as if he'd clutched them tightly for a long time.

He stepped out, dragging the foot that no longer did all he wanted it to, and flicked his fag carcass to the beach floor. Litterbug.

He looked at me oddly—almost like he *admired* me. Not merely envied me, but *admired* me.

Then he stared at Day, who, in his presence, now crashed down off her hard rush for me, blushing horribly, in that strangely disconcerting manner of hers, of shifting from in-charge adult to lost child in a second, as she turned completely away from him.

Her movement said she wanted to get off my lap, but not to expose me to him.

Odd, huhn?

I put my dick back where it belonged and buttoned up my fly under the cover of her dress tail, before she dismounted, shook the tingle feeling from her lower limbs, then slipped past him back into the house without the tiniest glance at him.

He hungrily watched her retreating backside the entire time she was within his view, then he stared at me again, as if he had a question in mind, but didn't know how to ask it, yet seemed very certain I had the answer.

He never said anything though or even grunted before he left; and almost right away, it occurred to me that she'd known he was there all along and had teased and entirely, thoroughly fucked . . . or mindfucked, as the case may be, the hell out of three grown men.

All at the same time.

I decided not to think about it too, too much and was still on the porch, facing the darkening eastern waters and sky, when Mrs. G got back.

I kept it to myself that I loved the dried, slightly "starched" feel of my pants.

* * * *

Hopkins, now my second "client," had cut down his "obligation" factor to me for my therapy services to him by paying me the rate I asked—room and board and sex privileges with Ms. Day notwithstanding.

However, his doctor, Mrs. G, and I were having a hard time getting him to properly stick to his full medical rehab regimen.

But, my ancient teas and deep tissue massages were noticeably helping. So, dear ole Hopkins, grudgingly, gave me more respect—someone easing your pain and discomfort can trigger that sort of thing.

My skills and knowledge and all our cautions, though, including Day avoiding arguing with him, were probably to naught anyway, because he was becoming more adamant, week by week, about not taking all of his stroke meds.

He wouldn't listen to anyone on the matter, just sit and

smoke, and, eerily, compulsively observe Day.

He detested the meds because they deadened and utterly destroyed the man's libido.

Like he needed a dickload of blood, when his brain needed, REALLY needed every drop.

What the hell; his choice, his life.

* * * *

I believe, in the way that it's nearly "always" a man's fault when dealing with the woman he desires most, that somehow it was "my mistake" to accompany Mrs. G on a difficult errand, which in and of itself was a good thing to do.

I left Day alone with Hopkins, which she'd always been, long before I'd fallen for her on the beach out front. Hopkins, despite being weak in his physical incapacitation, was yet still locked with her in their longstanding civil war, and in his blatant, stubborn way, had slurred his patent refusal to let us take her with us.

I hoped for the best, as long as he wasn't asleep and I had my titanium ballpoint with me. Mrs. G needed a strong arm for this errand, but similarly, in the way Day gets to me, *he* knows how to burrow laser slice by bloody laser slice, into the most remote and tender parts of her.

Mrs. G dropped me off before heading for her place, since it was so close to her knockoff time. I stacked what we'd gotten in the garage storage. When I arrived inside, Hopkins was agitated and Day barricaded in her room, sniffling and pathetically sobbing.

I dealt with him first, figuring his health was in more danger than hers. He refused to take his meds.

Meds or hospital, were the only choices I gave, short of me beating the shit out of him—*that was a joke, kind of.*

He finally, at least, took the one dosage that would calm him and eventually ease him to sleep.

Day wasn't heeding me in any fashion, neither unlocking either of her doors, nor ready to communicate like an adult at the moment, so I rechecked the old man, who was calmer but still nominally awake, and evil.

I never usually asked about their "private" conversations . . . incursions, but I asked this time, as I squatted by his bedside. He was drifting off, but was tough and defensive.

"What'd you say to her?"

"That's between my property and myself."

In private conversations between us, and sometimes even with Day within earshot, he calls her his "property," as you well know, because he gets a response from me, a silent one, but a response.

I didn't know what to say back to him that wouldn't include me physically hurting him, so I said nothing and he fired a blurry direct volley before sleep overtook him.

"I riled her good, lad. Yes. You'll see what she really is and it'll make that ever-hard piece between your legs withdraw up into your chest cavity, boy. See if you can control her when she's her *true* self."

He chuckled on happily, until full asleep.

I picked her lock, or was going to when I recalled Mrs. G told me where she kept her spare house keys.

They'd removed the locks completely at one time, but Day'd become so unmanageable they'd been afraid they'd have to keep her sedated or return her to lockdown—neither option palatable to Hopkins, let alone Day or Mrs. G, so Day'd gotten her locks back.

I was told that she never gave an explanation of what the locks truly meant to her.

I found her sitting high on the bed with her back against the headboard, legs curled under her and hands frantically buttoning and unbuttoning several buttons on the front of her dress.

"What did he say to you, Day?"

She didn't acknowledge my presence in any manner, not until I reached to comfort— .

She drew away, repulsed. And it wasn't like before, after the Pizza Guy thing. I tried again and the whole world felt cold, as she glared at me, and physically and emotionally withdrew more. It was like that old phrase, "iron curtain," but this was harder and colder—a steel curtain. Rain abruptly poured outside.

"Day I'm not leaving, until—."

She spoke then or more precisely she began to pick and pick with me like a scab you know you should leave be but, in personal, grievous discontent, don't. Nothing I said or didn't say pleased her. Eventually, as Mama would've said, "She took great umbrage," as she refused to be pleased by me in any manner, and, fell into a horrid, frightening rage.

She hurried from me, in her dogged, labored way, to the kitchen, which has new cabinets she violently tested. They held fast. She repaired to the dining room, to the less sturdy antique sideboard, where she commenced rattling a drawer; the one that held the pointy forks and sharpest knives.

Mrs. G keeps anything sharp or pointy under strong lock and key, of which I had a copy in my pocket.

It may sound stupid, but Day's behavior was pissing me off; not directly but because she should, could do better than this, than let her emotions blow on every tiny breeze of her imagination, and at Hopkins' infernal, fucking meddling.

Luckily, in the morning, I'd have the great pleasure of sticking him with a needle, to draw test blood on his doctor's orders.

But, to the immediate matter, considering my own lack of discretion of temper under his roof, perhaps Day was managing all she would ever be able to manage, and I was very wrong to think she could accomplish more.

It was thundering outside, as I took my personal key and slipped behind her, where she was furiously yanking with all her weight on the drawer's handle. She stopped when she felt me behind and around her, and studiously watched, as I unlocked and slid open the drawer.

"I suppose you want one of those?"

Not until you think how much damage a knife can really do to a human body, do you consider, when opening a drawer for someone a bit knife crazy, just how many we keep lying around in our lives—for bread, butter, and steak; the Swiss Army; and the larger ones for cleaving and *butchering*.

She chose well, a broad, sharp, step-down from a butcher knife, that was big enough with its nine inch blade, to do serious damage to a man of good size and musculature, yet manageable for her smallish palm.

Day, when she's not in one of her many choppy, petulant moods, moves fluidly, with smooth, nearly languid motions, which, I suspect, is natural to her, being a dancer.

I also suspect she knows she has a lot of time on her hands, so why hurry; besides hurrying pains her, but she would have been a formidable professional dancer, if her feet had been anything like her hands are.

Her hands are fast. Frighteningly fast.

Which is something you didn't need to know until now, because the scary thing was just how lightning fast she took the blade, once she'd chosen it and then just as quickly moved away from me, to get a good maneuverable distance.

She'd grabbed it by the handle, flipping it under, hiding its length behind her forearm, which fell, tranquilly, to her side and slightly behind her.

Having it in her palm seemed to give her some comfort, a sense of power even.

I backed away; you don't turn your back on a pissed off, legally documented, insane woman with a knife in her hand.

I wasn't certain if she were still enraged at me or not.

Her temperamental fits with me never usually lasted long, but this one was so abruptly brought on and more intense and laserlike that I was reconsidering beating the steak tartar out of Hopkins for whatever he'd taunted her with, while we'd been gone.

The wind shifted abruptly and torrents of spray rain hit

the porch and glass doors, as the Atlantic kicked up violently, disturbing the beach.

Day's always expressive face kept changing, undecided, as I waited for any of her many "normal" expressions—but *none* of the sad, calm, or fleet-footed, happy ones settled on her.

The appearance of a simply benign expression would've made me ecstatic, as she half-faced me, looking almost bashful, except for the blade clutched tightly in her fist. An indecisive little jungle viper.

I made it easy for her, by sitting down and exposing my bare chest to her, while I softly, calmly spoke to her.

"Here's your target, Day, you can see exactly where it'll go, whether you've hit your mark clean or not."

I'd mistakenly thought, yet another mistake of the day, that putting her thoughts into tangibly audible words would forestall her anger; instead, she glacially progressed toward me, staring at my chest, plainly more as a target than as an object of desire.

Her eyes shifted up, to my throat.

The possibility of losing this one occurred to me, especially when, to accommodate my nervous change in position, she flipped the blade edge around in her palm. Her strike would probably be a lateral throat slash.

I've been in similarly rough situations before, just never with a lover, as I tried to look and stay placid, while surmising it was highly likely I wouldn't be fast enough to stop her from doing considerable damage to me.

Plus, a defensive approach isn't always the best or smartest approach, with someone as volatile as Day.

And, offensively punching her out beforehand just wasn't a thought. Not yet, anyway.

She moved at me suddenly, and it took everything in me not to reflexively move to my defense.

The bitch was stalking me, testing me, and her calculated threat was to see if I would start. When I didn't, she smiled, but she didn't let up, because she'd smiled, snarled actually, with her shapely lips only, not with her eyes, which remained cold and distant.

That's when I shouted at her.

"Fuck it, bitch, strike me! It's what you do, isn't it?!"

I'd abruptly stood to my full height over her. She slightly flinched, more from the shear volume of noise assaulting her eardrums, I think; but, she didn't really jump or cower. She was used to overbearing men.

I couldn't stay that way with her though, and cut back in volume and attitude almost immediately.

"You're better than this, Day. You're better than your mother and Hopkins have forced you to be, better than how Carlyle, Karen, and the others've made you to be. I *know* you are."

She'd been staring, apparently, at a point of soft flesh just above my clavicle, then glanced up, while the tip of the knife, below in her hand, pulsed to some vague beat inside her, as she looked me in the eye.

"You don't *know* that. You just want to fuck me for your own selfish amusement, just like everyone else does."

That got a reaction out of me and whatever my mute expression was softened hers, as she glanced momentarily away, as if shamed and regretful, but not too shamed and regretful to not verbally machete her way through my unspoken, private reasonings.

"It is why you came to me that first time, after Elise went to the hotel for you, and why you came back after you packed and completely left me, isn't it?"

"Partly."

She searched my eyes to know what the rest was, I thought perhaps she'd might already, better than I did, because she was always inside my head, one way or another, but she didn't know this.

I wasn't certain I did.

"Day, I'm not your mother or 'Hoppy' or any of those others, am I? I make you feel *differently, good* differently, in your head and in your body and . . . in here?"

I pointed to her heart. She eventually nodded yes.

"It's like that for me, with you. The feeling I have for you, Day, with you is different, *very* different—*huge, uncontrollable, scary*; wonderful, exciting, 'profound'; home even—. I don't know how else to say it without it sounding trite, or more absurdly trite, as the case may be."

She suddenly flicked the blade, with great force, from between us, flinging it to the side, where it broke through glass and imbedded in the eye of a framed photo of Hopkins with a past Republican president.

She'd barely glimpsed in that direction, yet she'd hit bull's-eye. I numbly, stupidly wondered if given another knife, could she pull a "Robin Hood"? In archery, that's that little skillful trick of splitting an arrow with another arrow.

It was quite plain that she'd forgiven me and forgotten her anger, in those few ticking seconds that I'd glanced at his picture, as she carefully stretched up on her toes to put her warm, desirous lips to the hard throbbing carotid artery in my throat.

"Benn, you're cold." I was.

Primal fear does that.

She carefully shifted her weight back on her heels, making a little sound of pain; I hadn't had a chance to massage out her ankles since early the day before and the present general stress alone wasn't good for either of us.

I put my arms around her, and she reached hers around my neck, as my small cousins do. I told her about it once and we had, for whatever reason you want to imagine, we'd automatically taken to emulating the movement.

I picked her up, one knee on either side of me, and held her there, sitting on my hands, before depositing her on the dining table.

"Do . . . do you really think I'm 'better than' . . . ?" She shook her head, dismissing the concept entirely.

"I wouldn't say it, if I didn't believe it."

"People 'believe' a lot of things that are wrong. They were in the same ward with me. And, Hopp—. You believe it, so it'll make it all right for someone like you to be with me. With someone as messed up as I am. If . . . if you just want to fuck me, Benn, that's okay, I like the way you fuck me . . . better than anyone else."

She laughed silently, I didn't.

"Dayita, you've gotta stop talking and thinking like that. Like you're nothing." Her expression implied that what I'd just said was the dumbest thing she'd ever heard.

"Well, I am. The law says so and Hoppy has the legal documents to prove it. Pedigree papers for his prized pet bitch. I'm 'a pretty face and a prettier cunt,' that's all anyone wants me for, has *ever* wanted me for. Mommy always said so, that's why she had me 'fixed' and it's what Hoppy says too, constantly.

"What else could you've wanted *me* for, after that first night you looked through my window and saw him and . . . saw us . . . together. Why should *you* see me, want me differently?

"I didn't even graduate high school, Benn. I've never worked, though I could probably get a carny or circus job—throwing knives. But, I can't tolerate crowds, so, that's out. Maybe a butcher's shop.

"I'm not like you, you've been places; have an extensive, real education; and somewhere many people know you, respect you, love you, and you're very important to them. You have a *full, complete* life. You're an entirely free man, like him and can do and go wherever the fuck you want. So, for once, he's right.

"You'll want to get back into your life and you'll want a cunt you can show off on your arm in a crowded, exclusive gathering, someone who knows current topics and doesn't have a personal history that's better not mentioned in public."

She half smirked.

"Then, maybe you'll be smart and take me up on keeping me

on the side. I'm the most perfect mistress. I'm always ready to please you, nicely or nastily, and I can't run away. And, realistically, Benn, what makes the two of us together special, anyway, except the sex?"

She shrugged her bored, taking-it-for-granted sigh and continued with her frosty analysis.

"We both know it, Benn, we *three* know that when you're utterly tired of me. Of carrying me around. Of my . . . moods. Of dealing with Hopkins and his smokes and his dictating. Of having me . . . secondhand, after I shower and douche him from me.

"After you're tired of fucking me, while living, merely existing, in this fucking, little horrid, claustrophobic house—you'll abandon me here, with him, and you won't come back."

"First, Day, I'm nothing like Hopkins and he's not right, not about anything; and second, that's—."

"Not true, Benn? It's not true that what you saw of me through my window that first night, when you watched him fuck me, and I wasn't happy about it, you're going to swear to me, that you weren't . . . intrigued?

"What exactly or vaguely did you see; an unfulfilled hunger in me or just an unprotected vulnerability? Whatever it was about me that fully caught your attention, you came back to taste it yourself, to get what you could get from me. Or . . . ?

"Benn, I can keep you fascinated for a while, maybe even quite awhile longer, but you're not the kind, who'll stand . . . sharing, like you've been sharing me, forever. And, I can't afford for him to die. I'm so screwed, if he dies."

She laughed and rolled her eyes.

"Maybe I should stop trying to kill him. Well, *hell* no, *that's* just *completely* unacceptable."

She giggled maniacally then abruptly sobered.

"When he first took me out of *there*, he had to change his unlisted phone number, and that didn't work, so we moved farther out—but *they still found me,* they'd call and . . . and say *things*, blatantly ask to see me, to use me. 'Party,' they called it when I was inside.

"One-on-one. As a group. What is it about me, do I *look* like a 'party,' that I would *be* . . . the *entire* 'party'?"

She was getting angry, kneading and pulling, fretting with the flesh on her forearm then triceps, till it must've been painful. I was hurting and in hell, knowing what I knew about her and she didn't, as I heard her words, which cut into me deeper than the lengthy blade ever would have.

Oh God, Day makes me so very crazy, which, considering our circumstances, is probably not good or sexy or at all romantic.

"I'm making you crazy, Bennet, aren't I? You don't want to be reminded that you won't stay and you never like hearing about my 'misadventures' in—."

"No. I-I don't, but I *will* listen, if you need to say it."

She shrugged it off, as if entirely nauseous and bored of it. When I said nothing further and waited, she glanced toward where he was sleeping, shifted around on her tush, as if uncomfortable in her skin, then continued.

"He overheard me confiding to Elise *some* of what they'd done. I told her, so she'd understand, that I'm not just completely a . . . . He's never once looked upset, as you always do, when I tell you.

"He . . . he said I 'deserved it,' that he 'wished' he'd 'been there to participate.' Because he'd 'had' me before, then 'subsequently' I'd 'dug in my heels' and kept refusing him.

"He said I had 'no right to refuse' him, that I 'owed' him for some greasy wheel or something he'd paid so damned much for, to get me out. That I . . . 'deserved whatever they did' to me, because I never should've turned him away, once he'd had me.

"That . . . that I was his and always had been. He said she always knew that and that Mommy shouldn't've put him out of the house. She didn't want him, so why shouldn't he have me, instead? He could . . . he could 'take care' of me, and 'certainly no one else would bother with a confused little girl, a whore with a horrid temper.'"

Her voice had become incredibly small.

"That's why I never ever told him I intensely wanted out of *there*; because I knew he'd fuck me and fuck with me, somehow. He always does."

I'd been walking around the room, to get some distance, because it was too nasty to go out. The ocean was pounding the hell out of the shore and it just wouldn't be right to leave. Nor would it make any difference to put distance between us.

Whenever she talked about her past, or I found out anything significant about it, it always sucked me in closer to her.

She knows that, I'm sure.

"Benn, I was in a regular school, with regular friends, and I was regularly normal, most times, like every other kid. I'd never been with anyone; then, I almost was, in my room, with a Latino boy I liked so *very* much. A 'tenderhearted' boy, my friend, Lucy's mother called him.

"But, I went to answer the phone, in case it was Mommy. She'd always get real pissed, if I wasn't in, which I was. But, the call was some stupid hang up.

"I went back to Ray, my boyfriend, and he'd dressed, 'changed his mind' entirely, just like that, and 'didn't want' me, as if he were suddenly repulsed by me. It didn't make sense.

"He wouldn't talk to me. My own boyfriend wouldn't talk to me and didn't want to see me again. 'Ever.' He . . . he said *that* very clearly. Like his life depended on it."

The weather out was all lightning and rumbling thunder, overhead and all around us, and she was deeply upset but not exactly crying; she'd probably cried herself dry a thousand times before on this exact subject.

Day, after all these years, didn't know why the boyfriend had done what he'd done, but I did.

Stephie had found out. Don't ask. My sister can get into just about anybody's anything, with enough personal incentive driving her.

The boyfriend, Ray, had hung onto his fear; feeling guilty, ashamed, used or whatever.

He eventually told Day's best girlfriend, Lucy, whose mother told authorities. The info found its way into a half lost social record where it languished, and was later rejected for the jury by the judge; after finagling by Hopkins' solicitor at the time.

Ray's words on her behalf never fully appeared in Day's official and later sealed juvenile record.

Anyway, by then it'd been made useless and been forgotten.

Day'd been violated, "fixed" and she and 'Mommy' had had their *last* argument. And, Day was right, young Ray's life *had* "depended" on leaving her.

Hopkins, at his creepiest, was already in her house when she'd gotten home from school, and he'd hidden himself in her spacious closet from where he liked to watch her. Wanting her. Coveting her.

When Hopkins understood that Day had the boy over and was going to let the boy and his condom hit a home run, or whatever the English call it in cricket, Hopkins, under the sound cover of her stereo, speed dialed from the closet on his cell phone.

By the time she'd answered the call down the hall in her mother's room and had come back, he'd scared the hell out of Ray and literally told him to "NEVER come back," not if he wanted to "be able to continue to pee like a man."

Hopkins left the terrified boy there, probably trying to desperately get his quickly receding manhood back in his pants, while the older man slipped out of her room and into the bathroom, probably, to let Day pass him.

Then, he'd gone outside long enough to let himself back in and pretend he'd just gotten there.

Funny, the old man had never told her any of that. I decided not to, yet, as well, as I let her say what she needed to say.

"Hoppy . . . Hoppy was there, had just let himself in, as Ray ran away from me. Hoppy cornered me against the fridge. I couldn't get away from him. He said . . . . Hoppy said *things*, did—.

"*He touched me.* He shouldn't've touched me. I . . . I shouldn't've . . . let him . . . touch me, but his hands were all over me, and he was kissing on me, and I couldn't get away from him.

"He kept saying how I was so 'obviously ready.' That he'd waited so long, that 'she'd made' him wait, and that I was finally 'ripe to be taken.' *That didn't sound right to me.* Does that sound at all right to you?"

I silently shook my head "no."

"I knew he knew Mommy would be late, so I couldn't say she'd be home soon. I couldn't make him go and I wasn't 'dressed properly.' She'd hate that part a lot, say it was my fault; and he kept . . . . He kept at—.

"He said it'd 'be all right,' he'd 'never hurt' me, that it'd 'be better' with him 'than the boy,' because he was a man and I 'most obviously' needed 'a man,' 'a man like' him, and he knew me so well, wanted me 'more than the boy ever could.'

"Benn, he said so much, touched . . . so much. I lost track of things he was saying. I was crying and asking him, begging him to stop, but he kept . . . .

"He kept pushing and confusing me. With Ray it *made sense* and *felt right,* until . . . until he left me alone with Hoppy's obscenely hot body pressed against mine, confusing me. I don't like being confused. I *always* do the wrong thing, when I'm confused."

The look in her eyes was hollow, empty, and lost. A lot of emotions were coursing through her, but she took responsibility for her actions, right or wrong, confused or not.

"I . . . I let him."

She laughed bitterly, abruptly.

"I didn't 'let' . . . . He exhausted me, so I . . . stopped fighting, I thought it would only be once and, like he kept saying, Ray and I had been planning to do the same thing . . . . Besides, how bad—? Sex is supposed to be natural, isn't it? And, he promised he wouldn't hurt me.

"*That* didn't feel *natural*. Not to me. And, it hurt. Didn't like it at all, not with him, not one bit, although he seemed pretty damned happy about all his stiff poking, hurting, and puffing like a horrid beast and saying shitty 'compliments' about my being 'so mature' and . . . ."

I'd unwittingly moved to the corridor, between her and his room and . . . him, as if waiting for him, except I felt any moment I'd go and yank him from his bed, awake or not and—.

"Rapist. Hopkins, you fuckin' rapist."

If he'd appeared before me at that moment, I'd've bashed his face in to the back of his skull. I finally realized she'd stopped. She knew I was on the edge.

"Go on, Day. I want to, need to know."

She shook her head "no" and I literally tried to shake off the feeling and moved away from the short hall to the porch doors.

"It's all right. Go on."

"Mommy found out because he kept after me, kept coming back for me, at home and . . . . No matter what I did or where I went, he always found a way. The baby made me really sick all the time and she found out *everything*, when she kept asking was it Ray's.

"I told her. She was furious . . . and something . . . something else, that scared me even more, but she wouldn't explain.

"That's when he offered to 'take care of' me, like that 'Gigi' girl in the musical, but he's no Gaston. *How cool is that, a <u>fam-ily</u> film, a musical about a family of whores, oh, excuse me, 'kept women'?*

"No, wait 'courtesans.' Yeah, that makes it all better. Like that 'Pretty Woman' whore drivel from Disney, of all . . . ."

The rain wouldn't let up and Hopkins was snoring through it, like sour musical accompaniment. His sound bothered her. It's the same one he makes in her bed, after being with . . . after using her. She turned from it to face me; I stared at the floor.

"Benn, I couldn't seem to help that I . . . I responded . . . a little, sometimes; he made so much of it. But, I still never wanted him."

She was silent a long while.

"*His 'proposal.'* He planned to keep me, but not marry me. Mommy didn't like that; he said *she* should've married him herself, when she had had the chance. Too bad her chance was 'plainly long past.'

"She said she still wanted marriage for me, and 'all the *material* perks,' especially, she said, since I was 'damaged.' *She should see me now, between <u>her</u> handiwork and <u>his</u>, and my own.*"

She rubbed an itchy spot on her ankle, as my mind distantly noted it was still healing nicely, with my herbs and massages.

"They . . . they went back and forth at it, but the only thing they agreed on was 'the perfect doctor to take care of' me. Hoppy paid cash, out of pocket, and she had . . . had my . . . my baby 'removed,' and had me . . . neutered, like a randy pet, that can't control itself. As if it were all my fault.

"She told him to stay away from me, not to 'encourage' me. That I was just like him. He became impatiently incensed and screamed that I should be like him, since she always knew I was his all along and that he'd marry me, if that's what it took to 'appease' our 'provincial mores.'

"'Our' nothing, I didn't want to marry him or be kept by him or . . . .

"*I couldn't believe it.* I was still recuperating, itchy stitches and all, and they were making me insane. I cursed them both and swore I wasn't his anything and I wasn't ever going to be with him again, especially not since he'd raped me. She asked me if I were 'sure' about him forcing me.

"I just nodded. I didn't want her to know I . . . I'd *felt* . . . that he'd . . . confused me. 'Confused girls go to the asylum.' She'd always said that to me, as far back as I can remember. That's when she locked him out.

"That was real hard for her, Benn. Doing the right thing. He'd taken care of a lot of our bills and . . . and fucked her, when they thought I was asleep. She didn't like to work hard or much, and was too lazy to go sex pro or whatever her problem was, I guess.

"She said it was okay I didn't want to marry him, but it was good I was fixed. 'Just in case.' She didn't say exactly what the 'case' would be or what specifically she was afraid I'd get myself into. Maybe his saying she wasn't good in bed anymore was true. Or she was afraid I'd liked it with him so much that I could get his money without her.

"Hell, I was tired of pretending to sleep and shriek like I'd had a nightmare, to wake her, because he'd leave her bed in the middle of the night to pee, then stand over me feeling himself, whispering horrible things. Things he wanted . . . to do to me.

"Mommy never liked me, not really. I always knew that down deep, from the very beginning. His not begging to get back into her bed, and having said I was 'more sensuous,' 'better on my back,' than she . . . she became . . . less satisfied with me, and picked and prodded and pushed and . . . and then all that *other* stuff happened, and I-I was sent *away*."

Dear, sweet man. Any information, any lie Hopkins told to cover his ass, for some reason the authorities believed. They certainly didn't believe Day, in her "confusions," with her "hearsay" about her money-grasping Mommy.

"Benn, instead of coming to torture me, one day, as usual with his words and his anger at what *I'd done to her,* he took me home with him. One of the nurses said it was 'a good thing' and 'really nice' of him to 'take responsibility' like that. 'Responsibility'?! He'd barely gotten me in the door, before he . . . .

"It still wasn't as good as he said, not even for him. He said it was . . . ," she frowned, forgetting the right words, "He wanted me 'alert and responsive,' then . . . the sex between us would be . . . .

"The meds they had me on kept me foggy and irritable, suicidal, so he took me off them. It took forever for the meds to get out of my system.

"Even then, *I still said 'no' to him, that it 'didn't feel right'* and he said I was his to 'do with' as he wished because the state said so.

"The state papers—he showed me, I couldn't understand them. He said that they said in 'all practicality' that he owned me, besides what he wanted of me wasn't anything I hadn't done before with him or wouldn't've done anyway with Ray. But, he said 'the boy,' instead of 'Ray.'

"He wouldn't leave me alone, but I thought, at least it wasn't *all* of them, like at . . . . He said even my 'lackluster lovemaking' was better than being with her, with my . . . with Mommy, because of how I looked and felt in his arms, that he'd find 'a key' and 'get to the fire' in me . . . 'cause it'd 'be well worth it.' 'To die for,' Lucy'd say. I miss her some- . . . .

"Y'know, Benn, he says *things* to me, burning whispers in my ear. *Nasty things.* They don't sound bad nasty when *you* say them, but . . . . He has *things* he wants me to say to him, to call him. Things that if they were true would be, *have* to be *illegal, and immoral.*"

"What words, Day?" She shyly refused to verbalize them.

"I was told, Benn, that Jesus was 'innocent.' People say I 'look innocent,' that I *am* innocent. But, it kinda implies stupid or ignorant, doesn't it?

"I asked a minister, a special day resident, what *exactly* 'innocent' was. He said 'knowing what the possibilities are,' 'knowing what the choices are,' and 'knowing full well what will be, and yet doing it anyway'; that's 'innocent,' like Jesus—knowingly going to his death. Innocent—not stupid or ignorant, like most people think.

"It seems laughable, I know, considering all I've done, what I am, but being *with* Hoppy, *is* far worse than being with all of the others all together. I know that. *That* place was killing me, and yet *this feeling* about the wrongness of *him* never leaves me. It's like being encased in a solid, prickly, brick wall.

"I couldn't, I can't go back; I couldn't, I can't stay. I'm exhausted, burned out. And, no matter how many times I've told him 'no more,' he says—."

Hopkins seemed to have a hell of a lot to say, when he could cut the heart out of someone. The rain was thinning.

"He still says what he said then, Benn. That he was tired of my 'hemming and hawing and holding out like some untouched virgin,' and if I didn't behave 'like the whore' he knew I was and should be with him, he'd invite them, *all* of them from *there*, to 'party' with me. He said *that,* to me . . . " she had to think, " . . . the same day I had my acci- . . . . When I cut—."

I hugged her tightly to me, content to merely hold her, until realizing she was feverishly kissing me, touching me, intimately, through my clothes, as if I were fresh water she was thirsting for and needed for her very existence.

She began undressing and fiddling with me; her softly probing, wanting hands on my needy, wanting skin.

Hypocrite that I must be, I hated Hopkins and I hated *them* for using her for their own lusts.

A complete and practical satyr, male or female, would enjoy working with people with little to no legal recourse and little to no social credibility; mentally imperfect or disturbed people. They're often extremely libidinous, not that I myself wasn't, too, especially, whenever she crossed my mind or line of sight, or touched me like this, with such desire for me that it was as palpable as the rain and lighting and thunder.

I let her do whatever she wished with me, as she indulged herself with tasting me, touching me, watching how she affected me, until bluntly indicating she wanted me to eat her out.

No complaints here, especially since I wasn't yet in intensive care, bleeding out from some body part sliced clean through.

I pulled up a chair, pushed up her skirt, and the sight of her, the smell of her passed through me, like the sensuous, intimate touch of soft silk on a bare, aroused nipple.

But, I delayed our satisfaction, as I massaged her feet and legs while she laid back, luxuriously stretching out across the dinner table, confident that I'd get to all the best parts, in good time.

I knew she was overdue, and so was I, when her fingers tantalizingly produced a stream of juice that flowed from the deepest valley of her sex. I dove in, tongue first, until her gyrations against my face were so rough and inviting and in desperate need of me, that I had to push her farther onto the table and mount.

I'd barely sunk deep into her sopping heat—.

Day pushed me.

"What?" She was playing some game, toying with me, knowing I was in full heat for her.

"Ravish me. Rape me."

I was afraid her wide-ranging mind was where it'd been the last time she'd requested that of me, until her legs opened wider to me and her ankles locked firmly against my thighs for leverage, as she fucked up against me. The brightness of her eyes said this wouldn't be as that time, as her cunt maddened me and she gave me more incentive, with a devilish look and cunt squeeze around my engorged cock filling her.

She pushed against me again.

"Fuck me hard, Benn, use me rough." My crotch was driving me insane, as—.

"Hold me down, control me."

Her ankles were definitely in much better shape. I grabbed both of her wrists and *almost* had a complete second thought about what I was doin—.

"Hurt me, if you want. I won't mind bruises from you."

I held her down on the oak tabletop and fucked hard into her the whole time she coaxed and swore vilely at me, squirming and struggling enthusiastically, fucking me back *more and more* furiously.

"Don't be *nice*, Bennet, be selfish, use me for your own—."

She moaned, opulently, and I let go of one of her hands to grab her elsewhere and she slapped me across my face; obviously, a seductive challenge.

I let go of her fully and grabbed hold of the table edge with the other hand.

The salad oil bottle down the table rocked and teetered, as I cruelly seized her asscheek. My grip was tight on her; she'd have fingertip contusions . . . bruises. She ruthlessly clenched a handful of my hair, as I lost all control and bore into her, forcing my tongue deep into her mouth against hers.

We were all fury and passion; uncivilized.

I'd never been . . . .

I came with no concern for her needs, which is what she'd commanded of me, which, I'm sure, made me completely just like *him* and *them*. The only exception being that she'd demanded and commanded me, the entire time.

My uncontrollable cumming triggered hers, and she was wild beneath me, as her lust was successfully fulfilled.

No one else is like her.

She knows that and let me know, while her sexual power was still radiating like electricity through me, she let me know.

"Miss your old Arabella, or anyone else?"

Hell no. But I said nothing, knowing she was putting in her next bid for keeping me with her. Addicted to her. Obsessed with her. Because she already knew the answer and she just wanted me to realize it.

She'd stayed her hand and hadn't shoved nine inches of stainless steel into my flesh and was now, once again, taking the reins of my soul, which I hadn't used for anything but vanity for too many years, anyway.

I glanced at Hopkins' pix with the blade point in its eye and heard him mumbling back up the hall in his dreams, about Day, I think.

She heard it, too, and scowled a moment.

I quickly forgot him, since my body and mind were still in their own energized Day zone, as I removed myself from her and sat back in the chair between her feet, which I kissed.

The scents and heat of lovemaking kept us connected and

the feel of her was still with me, not to mention her cunt was open before me, calling me by sight, by nostrils, and cock.

She leisurely rubbed her toes, soles, and heels against my penis and balls, getting me up again, before she resituated her pelvis and opened her thighs wider, looked at me and opened her cream soaked pubes and labia with her fingers.

"Want more of me?" *As if I'd still had the power of speech.*

She evidently tightened her interior vaginal muscles and I watched her juices and my semen stream from her and down between her asscheeks.

I slid my fingers into her hole, as she pulled up her knees high and flexed open the puckered, wet lips of her anus, then looked again at me, her meaning obvious, as she handed me the salad oil from the table rack.

I was very glad he was out cold for the night.

As I did what I was bid.

As I *wanted* to do with her this time.

As I rimmed and tongue fucked her tart bunghole, oiled her, then cockfucked the wanton slut's beautiful ass, without fear that I'd hurt her.

I pulled fully out, to Day's disappointment, as I grabbed her up and carried her over to his favorite armchair and sat, ignoring Hopkins' scent and the nostril burning smoke smell that always reeks from it.

She was spooned against me, reimpaled by me, except that I kept her thighs together with both her knees over one of my forearms, as I controlled her body, making circular thrusts, as I slowly fucked her, on 'Hoppy's' throne.

Her hand slipped behind my head, to entangle deep in my hair, as she moaned and whined then seized a handful of mane, to draw both our heads closer.

A delight. She was a total delight, as she whimpered once more and breathed her question to me.

"He still thinks he owns me, but you own me, now, don't

you, Benn?" That statement nearly paralyzed my tongue.

"No. Dayita. *You.* You own you."

I was holding her at an angle and she could see my face, but twisted around farther before fully comprehending that I wasn't teasing or lying.

She didn't say anything for a long time, as I kept at her. She leaned her head back against mine, to coax and huskily beg me, in heated whispers, to fuck her shithole harder and harder, until, holding her tightly—my nads contracted and my spunk exploded from me, and deep into her.

I slipped my long fingers into her hot, grasping cunt and her back arched sharply, as her "pretty pussy" gushed its sweetly salty cum, which dripped past her asshole and drenched onto my blissfully, languidly expiring shaft.

We held in that position a long time, sharing the same breaths, kissing long and deep, in his precious seat of power.

I eventually glanced up again, some long time later, in after coital bliss, as I cleaned up the place—Mrs. G discovers enough crap around here on her daily rounds.

Day's deadly accurate knifeblade was, of course, still wedged in Hoppy's picture blue eye, slicing it out of existence. I really liked it there, a whole hell of a lot.

The curiously odd thing was that, even after I'd yanked it out and locked it away, neither Mrs. G nor Hopkins mentioned the obvious damage to the photo.

* * * *

Hopkins woke the next day to find me yet alive and still in devoted attendance to Day's amazing needs.

"*Very* disappointed," as Chuck used to quote some always dismayed and thwarted TV antihero.

I wasn't at all nice or delicate about taking the nasty old guy's blood that day, either; by self-serving, personal choice. Since then, however, everyone in the house, uncharacteristically, has been unusually well tempered for quite some time.

Day and I were alone.

Mrs. G had taken him to his doctor's for a checkup, and I was lying down, glad not to be presently responsible for the care of a man, who wouldn't care less if I dropped dead of natural or other causes.

I was *chillin'*, as another friend of mine still always calls it, when you're just lying about, doing absolutely nothing plainly useful. I was nursing a small but stalwartly persistent headache, which was finally receding, in its glacially slow threat to abandon me.

I'd long ago checked and logged out of email to let Day randomly search my encyclopedia files on my durable and abused PowerBook, which she was abusing more because it wasn't doing what she thought it should fast enough. She stopped in midbanging frustration to glance guiltily back at me, when it "bombed."

I winked at her and reached over fixing it. That's why I got it, its an exceedingly well-designed, forgiving of neglect, sturdy machine. I can be a *bit* careless with it, especially with all the travel time I've logged with it, and all the "air" time it's logged flying over a certain, self-involved, nameless, auburnhaired Satan's spawn.

No one I've mentioned, or ever will again.

The next time she had a problem with it, Day managed to fix it herself, without overdisciplining it. Fast learner. I really should run the self-healing, diagnostic maintenance program.

She was lying on her stomach and I was stroking and kneading her firm, peach round backside, which lay, naked as usual, beneath the soft fabric of her dress, as she lay across my lap. There wasn't anything particularly sexual about us at that moment, just the familiarity of two people intimate with each other.

I believe that even if we hadn't been lovers, but had become merely friends, we would still find ourselves in this position—*minus, perhaps, stroking the meaty round globes of her wonderful ass.*

When my mind wasn't specifically focused on her, I was going over and over and over a few intersecting things in my mind, such as that I once flipped through a singular book.

I don't remember what it's called or who wrote it, a grad student I knew when I did a semester or two in the District had loaned it to me. She worked in the library over at American University on Massachusetts Avenue NW, DC, and was a far more sensible film and video student than my old roommate.

In her shelf straightening, while keeping an eye out for the library supervisor, so she could warn her study weary coworker, Serbo, who'd nap in the stacks, she'd come across this book.

In it was a dissertation on what I've chosen to internalize as Shirley Monroe.

The book was on sex as presented, visually and subtextually, by Old Hollywood in their movies. In the reigning days and afterwards of child tap queen Shirley Temple, before she became Black and a successful adult woman, it postulated that the perception by most, that all the child screen goddess' fans were mothers and small children, was bogus; a misconception, a misperception.

Most of her paying fans, by statistics, were adult men.

I won't get into how her character parts were queerly designed and had her playing the littlest "Lolita," blatantly manipulating men—"Daddy," "Cap," or whomever, by being a darling, tear jag pulling, cuddle kitten, to the point of spiritual incest.

The point is that the men fans later found a less demanding yet more yielding Shirleylike child replacement in the woman's body of the voluptuous iconic persona of Ms. Marilyn Monroe.

Both Shirley and Marilyn were, *are* still vastly fantasized about by tons of males, and both—*child and woman*—were literally, but in different ways, deified and shamelessly used, then discarded and vilified.

And finally, redeified.

The only difference between them was, is, and yet still remains is that a horny man can safely, publicly vocalize his intense sexual desires for Monroe, but not Temple.

Nasty.

My longwinded point being, that Day has something of that same quality. Maybe a lot of women do, since we men never can seem to remember to card the young ones before we date them, or worse.

Some of us don't even care—if she appeals to our eyes, our cocks must have her, no matter the restrictions and taboos.

I've done things, plenty of things, but nothing, as yet, as heinously, legally, or morally completely wrong as . . . .

Do remember to save that last thought for later.

Some of us, to segué to another nebulous point, can gaze on our lovers, as they abuse our computers and wish, as she wished, to see the sweetness, the petulance, and the many other qualities good and bad, that she has, in a child of hers. I can understand how Hopkins may have become fond of her as a girl.

Day had to've been a beautiful, delightful girl, but to overstep the emotional and physical barbed wire, sexual boundary around any child . . . .

To not, in a good way, spoil a child with benign love and affection, as my sister and I were raised, but to seek to defile her with premature, adult sex and horrid, personal loathing is inconceivable to me; and I can conceive a hell of a lot.

Some things should just not, should NEVER be done, no matter how many times they cross our minds and settle there.

It should be the same as when most of us find it an interesting concept, yet remember *not to actually* stick our hand into a roaring, hot flame or to beat someone to death, even when we *really* want to.

Plus, hatred from a father is bearable, for the most part, but it isn't from your mother, especially if she is all you have.

I know people who've sought their whole lives for their "real" mother; they haven't looked all that damned hard for their "real" father.

Our Dad, for instance, isn't a super wonderful person, but he never allowed us to think he hated us or that he detested the very blood in our veins.

Day's "Daddy"?

I don't know anything concrete of him, except that he was of mixed blood. In America, who isn't?

I did clearly know of her pained avoidance, when forced to consider him; when asked she won't discuss him.

That's not completely true. I do know a thing or two about him. More than two, actually. I had someone I trust check a bit. The emailed report about him was incredibly short and unpromising, which in and of itself says much.

How could anyone leave *her* lost, alone, and unprotected with those who hate her so plainly?

And, leave her with people, who'd abuse her, castrate her, and leave her to be cast up on this beach, without a secure mind, a secure life, or a chance to redeem herself in her own children, like so many of the rest of us do?

Her Dad must have assumed that a man can just go about *doing man things* and not bother with any *fatherly things*, once the girl reached a certain age. He seemed to assume that a mother is easily and automatically *motherly* and kind and gent—?

I must've audibly sighed. Day looked around at me, and it was plain she was reading my anxiety.

"What? *Benn?*"

I simply said, "It's nothing."

* * * *

Sid came over, interrupting dinner, as he smartly avoided me as much as possible, justifiably afraid of me.

He needed Hopkins to sign off on legal changes requested. Day was very interested in that, that's when I remembered what she'd wanted from Sid when I'd retrieved her from his office. Dinner got pushed aside.

Hopkins, healthwise, all in all, wasn't as bad off as many often are after a stroke, but he was still slurring his speech and having some basic motorskill problems, although his mind had cleared immensely.

He flipped through the updated pages of his revised Last Will and Testament, and pulled out one page, scribbled a wobbly "no" on it, then handed it to Day, who didn't want it, but he demanded she take it, "since [she'd] ordered it, and paid so casually for it."

She took the page, holding her head high, until she glanced at it before dropping it and coming to me for comfort. Mrs. G retrieved it, read it, then handed it to me, while Hopkins, still holding sway as local resident despot, slurred his demand that I attend "a little meeting" in his bedroom, "away from the ladies" and even Sid.

Day made a slight, piteously pathetic sigh, before hotly whispering "no" in my ear, as she clung to me to detain me from him.

I made her let me go and handed Day off to Mrs. G before following Hopkins, in his protracted retreat to his room.

We were locked alone together in that smoke-filled confinement for quite awhile, as the sun set, dragging the warmth of daylight away with it.

Eventually, he called in Sid and Mrs. G, who'd turned on lights throughout the house and the central heat to low, to remove the unseasonable chill. Hopkins signed his shakily handwritten instructions. I signed. Mrs. G signed off as witness with no idea of what specifically she'd signed.

Sid did what legal stuff he had to do.

The other adult in the house was left aside like a child and not asked to participate.

Sid gathered up everything and left.

Mrs. G finally went home, after I assured her, then reassured her, that I'd "take care of Day," that I'd "take care of" myself, that I was "taking care of everything." Period. Even after she made me reaffirm it once more, even after she said I "looked pale" and was, perhaps, "too tired" or "ill," I promised "to eat," to "get Day to eat," and to go "to sleep early."

I pledged a great, great deal that long, strenuous evening.

Day was on the sofa, waiting for me, her knees held up too

tightly in her arms, to her chin. I made her unfold, because her toes were turning purple.

"What happened, Benn? Why were you in there so damned long? What did he want?"

I would've sat beside her—just my body beside hers would have comforted her, and me, but I was too tired, just too, too tired.

"I can't tell you." Still on the sofa, she got up on her knees to scrutinize me closer, to focus her considerable, seductive persistence in my direction.

"Of course you can."

"*No.* I can't. If I tell you or Mrs. G, he'll be able to tell, by your actions, or by your words." She wanted to comment but couldn't figure out what to say or ask. "He . . . he knows I'll be with you when he . . . whether he's completely incapacitated, or dead—."

"He threw away the thing I *needed*, Benn, that I . . . that I worked so hard for. That I . . . that I made you so angry about. With Sid. When you left me. You *have to* tell me, Bennet. What you did, what you said back there, in whispers behind locked doors. *It's my life!*"

I swallowed hard because she was not going to like this.

"He expressly has it so the judge will ask if I've divulged what he's told me, to you or Mrs. G. If I have, and slippery Sid's job will be to make certain I haven't, but if I have, I'll have no say at all in what happens to you."

"But . . . . No. *No.*"

"'But,' he understands that I have a way with you that he never will, and if I do as Hopkins wishes, I get a say in what happens to you, a very *generous* say. I'm not going to piss that away for your curiosity, no matter how well-founded."

"What do you mean, 'a way' with me?"

I was too tired to answer because it would've required another answer and another. I shrugged off her question, as gently as possible.

She pouted deeply, staring at me, as if nauseated, as if I'd betrayed her. She had a pouting, mute point; I was quite apparently on "Hoppy's" side, whatever that exactly entailed, following his maxim of "his house, his rules," full against her in this critical thing.

She sat back into the lamp's bright light, yet her expression retreated into sheer darkness, as she emotionally sharply withdrew from me, which I didn't like but didn't mind, because there was absolutely no way she could stay angry with me for very long.

Which proved to be a slight miscalculation on my part.

The next three withdrawal-like nights and days—without her connecting with me in any substantive way, as she refused my presence, my very existence—*those hours, minutes, seconds would feel interminably long.*

I once again let her have her way, knowing that whenever she wanted me again or felt I was about to be lost to her, she'd seduce me, entrap me in her fully addicting, mind and body-enslaving way.

Having Day in charge of me is not the worse thing I've ever had happen to me in my life.

Neither is having her suddenly appear, in her thinnest robe, with a sheer stocking dangling from her hand.

Didn't realize she had any.

I was on my third sleepless night in a row, sitting on the sofa with my pained head in my hands, when she dropped the nylon in my lap.

She knelt on the sofa beside me and slipped her naked fingers through my hair, along my touch-deprived scalp and temples, before gently massaging them down my piercingly aching spine, as my head nestled against her soft, fragrant bosom. Even if she hadn't touched me, just her mere presence, her barest, slimmest attention to me would've eased my entire universe.

Day sat down beside me and without preamble put her knowledgeable, stocking covered palm to my lonely crotch, and took me.

It wouldn't take long—make up or torture, it wouldn't take long.

Her instructing me to tell her when I was cumming was nearly ludicrous, she . . . she knows me, knows my body far too well not to . . . .

I could barely form the words anyway, before she slipped her warm mouth around me to catch the hot, plentiful spill, then straddled me and soul kissed me, sharing the taste of my own spunk.

I'd eat my own shit off her tongue.

She also gave me that leading look, which I could and never will be able to describe, but always felt . . . *can* still feel, like a warm, delicious breeze over naked skin.

Following her to the kitchen, she both ignored me, yet enticed me, while simply pouring out apple juice and drinking it. Then, she leaned, elbows on the center counter, just leaned, presenting.

I pulled up the tail of her thin robe and took her slowly and thoroughly, with tongue and finger and cock, savoring every bit of her, every new moment with her, caching to long-term memory every sensation she drew from me.

I heard Mrs. G drive up to start her workday, as Day came hard and took me over that heady, dizzying cliff diving edge with her.

Then, she huskily whispered, "I'm not done with you yet," before leaving me to pick up her dressing gown and shake off my pants that were suddenly choking my ankles too much for a quick escape.

I swiped up our spills with the robe and ducked into my room with her, before Mrs. G had the misfortune of catching my naked ass.

I closed and locked my door, and tried to slow down; the lack of sleep, the distress of the last few days, the sudden onslaught to my sexual senses of this beautiful woman. I almost never call her "beautiful"; she doesn't like that.

Day suspects deceit in those who flatter her too much; even with the truth.

Moreover, it's obvious from my eyes that I love the look of her.

I decided a while back that she was the most dangerous kind of beauty, in that she radiates it from within besides having the perfect surface; the two types of beauty together *is* the deadly part.

More deadly for her than me, perhaps, because of having gotten her into things and involved with people she has not wished to be involved with.

I was still standing aside, watching Day a long while, as she lay on my . . . her . . . our mattress, the thick futon on the floor, a pillow under her pelvis as she lay on her stomach, feet scissoring over her round, brown tush. Despite her being pissed with me these last few days, I'd noticed her ankles had been stronger of late, her limping less pronounced.

My interrelationship skills—nay.

My medical skills—yay.

Her knuckles were propping up her chin, as she gazed at me, gazing up and down me.

Her gaze is like an intimate physical touch of the hand or more like someone blowing their soft breath across the most vulnerable parts of you—*I have mentioned that before, haven't I?*

She was indulging *me* now, as I postponed going to her, because she knew she had my *full* attention or at least enough of it that I wouldn't be wondering off anywhere.

Day excels at getting a lover's full attention, even when she doesn't want to, but most especially when she does.

I abruptly considered myself some guy in an old fairytale or Arthurian Knight's tale, who'd turned his back on one materially successful life and gone off wandering, hoping against hope to find meaning and justification.

I'd found a Princess, a Rapunzel, or Sleeping Beauty held captive by spell, by devilment . . . by a hideous ogre.

The Hero Knight-Prince's bewildering path always leads directly to *(if she's the reward)* or through *(if she's the trap)* The Beauty with the soft, entangling hair, who's vulnerable and unable to say "no" to him.

Or some Revisionist's Satanic Siren, the never forgotten Babylonian Whore type, who sought to keep the good Christian King Arthur's pride and joy of a he-man warrior locked up in her vaginal "garden" or "enclosure" from his more manly path—the pursuit of public success and killing things.

All this, by merely offering herself to him.

Hmm, pride or pussy, one or the other, never both. That's truly not fair.

But, I like fairytales and folktales, when the religious types aren't rewriting the cool out of them. There's a lot of truth in them and a hell of a lot of latent sex, if you pay attention.

The moral of the story is . . . .

I wasn't certain yet what the moral of *this* story was, or if I might still, possibly, want out. I felt there wasn't, but logically speaking, there were things I didn't know yet that I most certainly should know BEFORE my last and final decision to "forever after" with *this* particular Beauty.

You know, except for Stephen Sondheim, they never tell you exactly what the "forever after" stuff is.

That can't be good.

I had a somewhat nasty, self-centered thought—as beautiful as she is, she is most beautiful when her face is suffused with enjoyment; preferably, the enjoyment of her climaxing all around me, with me doing likewise deep, tight, and cozy inside her.

That thoroughly incorrect thought *(as real and personal thoughts often are)* is fed by things, various little bits of things, she's said to me or that I've heard in earshot; things so like wishes or prayers.

And, I'm a total sucker for being her Genie, fixing things for her, and Day's sweet, little offhand, whispered for my ears only wishes and prayers often blatantly imply, that my ejaculations bathing her womb's door is a cure, so, I've never told her everything.

I *am* potent, in the sperm department: twice—once by condom failure and once by overheated carelessness.

Aborted chances and God-sent miscarriages.

Let's just say that both sexes, female and male, "trick" each other into and with the baby situation, which subliminally explains my initial carelessness with Day. What a nice little surprise for me, a disappointingly horrid little surprise to at last find someone I . . . to find her sterile.

I don't know if other men dream of . . . .

I dream of children, by her; I see and feel them near, especially, in those long, delicious moments when I'm blissfully inside her, and she's "inside" me. Beautiful, wide-eyed, delightful children with the best, and/or worst of us both.

I know—as boldly as I know I can comfort and heal—that much of the joy, the ecstasy, the lust she has for me is not just for my limb and back strength.

But, in that innate knowing of hers of my most secret heart and mind. And whether it's logical or not, she feels—*and feeling is almost never a logic function*—she feels that if anyone can break and supplant her sterility and enforced fallowness, it would be me.

I swear it's not just my overinflated ego speaking, this time, but truly a great part of her motivation toward me.

So, she keeps me heated and aroused, *spunkily* blasting and battering her highwalled aloneness, cut into her flesh when her mother, with Hopkins' money and sanctioning, and for their own most individually selfish reasons, severed her from her full womanhood.

Day sat up on the edge of the mattress, a little impatient at my dawdling, and I went to her, loving her kisses on my knees and thighs, on my belly, on my cock, of her knowledgeable hands on my nads, on my buttocks. We . . . explored each other and renewed our intimacy in many ways and physical angles.

Yes, she may have *me,* by my equipment, but I have *her* by hers as well.

And, more than that.

It's the "attention" subject again.

Arabella never gave me this kind of intense, personal attention and thorough awareness; and no, I wouldn't expect it so often or so intensely from a working woman; but, how about *some?*

And worse, Ara would never let me fully focus mine, as intent as a laser, on her. She was always deflecting it, putting it off, saying it was "too much."

Aborting it.

What is "too much love"? Or "too much lovemaking"? I don't know. I don't think Day knows either.

And so, the big Hero question: Is my path *to* Day or *through* the trap that is Day?

We were done, happily satisfied for the present, lying sixty-nine, her one chilled foot beside my head and the other on my chest, under my chin, as she lay draped and asleep across me. I felt watched and looked behind me, toward the open bathroom door.

I had to tilt my head awkwardly to see properly . . . .

Mrs. G smiled, unabashedly pleased at the sight of us so comfortably together.

I fell back into sleep right away, then woke, feeling watched again, no, I heard a thump.

I twisted 'round, as best I could, suddenly realizing Day had managed to get a fair grip on my cock in her slumber, partially immobilizing me, turning me into her security blanket.

It was Hopkins. Smiling.

I was thinking that wasn't right, that it must've been visual distortion from my weird angle or more likely, that I was probably still asleep.

When I looked again he was gone.

Later, I realized the sun had moved between glances, because I'd fallen asleep, so I'd missed his leaving, if he'd truly been there at all. Hopkins *NEVER* smiles at me, not without malice, and certainly not while I'm in "possession," so to speak, of the woman he desires.

I extricated myself from her grip and turned around to get us both under the covers; she sat up frenetically reaching and mumbling my name.

When I pulled her back and kissed her cheek she relaxed beside me.

Day's done that before and I've asked her what she sees because her eyes open, with the most plaintive expression, and she reaches—unmistakably disturbed in the most heightened and unsettling manner—yet she's fast asleep. She never remembers it, or at least wants to believe she doesn't, whenever I ask.

But . . . .

* * * *

But all of our making up hadn't happened yet, as I heard Sid's voice from Hopkins' room, while they discussed his Will and codicils and whatever else goes into a Last Will and Testament. I was still standing tiredly before her, as she sat back on his sofa.

I could feel the angered, cutting coldness of Day's disappointment in me, in not telling her what the old man and I had discussed alone, of her suspicion that I was yet another selfish, heartless fuck, taking private, secret lessons from THE MASTER on how to screw her over.

She glared at me, as though she hated me, completely and most totally detested me; so, it was a cinch she wouldn't eat dinner.

Sorry, Mrs. G.

The justly nauseous look of anger and disenchantment on her incredible face remained before my mind's eye, even after she limped away and left me there alone. I was exhausted, with a gnawing pain deep and centermost in the soft tissue of my vulnerable brain.

I nauseated myself, having formally contracted, having shook on it—*hand-to-hand, man-to-man*—to close the deal I now secretly and formally shared with Hopkins.

* * * *

Y'know, you never really know who watches you, from the advantage of near distance.

Penelope, Hopkins' neighbor watches. Watches us. Watches me. She said I was "exceptional" with Day, "who seemed a nice . . . ." She couldn't quite apparently make up her mind on whether Day was spoiled, corrupted, or simply troubled.

She never finished her sentence and she never did quite say it plain out.

Almost no one does.

Penelope did realize that my lover can be a difficult person, sometimes a delightful person.

But, our neighbor wasn't sure "the why" of Day's "extreme mood swings" and just assumed it was "the physical convalescence," as Penelope nervously babbled on, nearly stumbling into the mental tar pit of revealing that she wasn't really quite certain what the sexual context was among the three of us.

Our interrelationship was plain enough to confuse her and intrigue her, and she, along with her husband Steve, had obviously given it considerable thought of some kind, which especially embarrassed her in my presence. I'm fairly certain Steve left out his witnessing and participation in the exciting floor show we'd given on our porch.

Penelope wanted something of me, and I had no clue.

She had all kinds of kudos for my being able to handle Day, when, on occasion, even Mrs. G couldn't.

Why Penelope's very busy life wasn't busy enough for her to not notice any of this, I wasn't sure and didn't ask.

However, she asked if I could watch her kid, a two and a half your old, "just for a few hours."

She had "an emergency" —everyone seemed to have emergencies in this area. Her sitter was nowhere to be found, and she was pressed for time.

I got the *very* distinct impression, by something she let drop and tried to backtrack and cover, that she was making bail, of all things, for her hubby and didn't want the kid involved—*probably afraid* baby'd tell his sitter or buddies in pre-preschool about the wonderful cops and station house he'd visited.

It's amazing what little people remember when you don't want them to.

But, I really didn't think she wanted to tell me and I really didn't give a shit about Steve, so I didn't ask.

Penelope's a tightly wound woman, so the fact that she considered me was nice, and desperate. Too many have found out too late that one doesn't usually leave your baby with a man, not even its own father—for fear of the child's safety.

I said yes; she needed the hand, Mrs. G'd be back soon, in case I needed backup with the dangerous critter, and Day, standing out of Penelope's view, had a heartbreaking, pleading look on her face.

That look of Day's was the true cincher for me.

The "rambunctious boy," Toddy, loved visiting, loved exploring, and I loved that he proved extremely useful when he managed to chase the blustering Hopkins back along his smoke trail into his room. Our beloved Hoppy's stroke was slowing him down about dictating; should've been taking his prescribed meds, along with my professional therapeutic attentions.

Day was, as Mrs. Gorbachev said, "Darling with the child," and became tangibly bereft after he left, waving, looking back over his mother's shoulder with his happy eyes fixed on his new play buddy, Day.

Day abruptly tumbled into an emotional, abysmal void in the child's absence, so Hopkins left her to me to deal with.

He abhorred my presence, except at such apt times, as these, *and* when the sex turned in his favor, then he was *very* glad to have me around.

About five minutes after the boy was out of sight, Day quietly went directly to lie on the futon. Seeing another side of her, her aunt . . . mother side, instead of just imagining it, had made me want her, a lot. Shamefully a lot.

I always wanted her; and I greatly appreciated that in the child's presence, she hadn't forgotten me in her playing and teaching him, which was extremely adult of her.

To tell the truth I'd been a little, a *lot* jealous of the little guy receiving her attentions, which was stupid, but we guys do that even with our own children, let alone someone else's.

In my case, I'll blame a bit of it on genetics. Right, Dad?

I can't say how very much I loved the longing, mellow looks she gave me, as if she wanted to mount me, as soon as viable, to make a few little Toddies of our own.

Then, she'd sigh, from holding her breath, until it broke forth of its own accord, before she'd look off then finally refocus on the boy.

I went to her, she was lying down, faced away from me, sobbing quietly, and barely allowed me to hold her. Actually, she didn't. She was indifferent to me, to everything; she was obtusely numb, and I held her to comfort her, but it became more for my own solace than hers.

We men like to fix things for our women, which is something we can't always do, and unfortunately I'd come late to this game and Day's problems didn't need anymore "fixes."

When I abruptly awoke, cold and startled by her absence, I distantly heard Hopkins shouting. They weren't in the house but outside. She was using his physical weakness against him to violently force him off her and he fell heavily in the sand. I went to him and he slurred that he was "fine," to "get her, stop her."

Day was in the water, heading out deep. It wasn't winter but the Atlantic was fucking cold to me—which it was, but the intensity of the situation didn't warm the water's temperature. She was an hysterical, angry demon, who fought me hard, until the ocean's chill bit into and sharply cramped her legs, taking the underpinning out of her rage.

She couldn't get away from me or outfight me and finally permitted me to carry her in.

Hopkins managed to crawl back to the steps and get himself up and mobile.

I deposited her in the tub, plugged it, and began filling it with cool water, very slowly warming it to heat her trembling, ocean cold stiffened limbs. She was in pain, but she wouldn't cry out despite being curled up in its grip, then abruptly, fully submerged in her anger, her loss.

She actually tried to inhale, right in front of me, and I dragged her back up to air, coughing and pissed to all high hell.

"Leave me be!"

"I'm not letting you drown right in front of me!"

"Then, look the hell away, Benn, 'cause I'm drowning every-day anyway. Let me go!"

I let her go, prepared to grab her again.

Hopkins lumbered in and sat down heavily on the toilet's lid. She turned her back on us both, coughing and sputtering out water. She was very determined at this; if I hadn't woken from my deep sleep, simply because my body'd missed hers, she'd be dead.

That's when I got a searing insight I didn't want.

"That's what you were doing on the beach, when we met."

She didn't look around or make a sound, only shrugged.

Hopkins made some kind of strangled noise. I wasn't certain his sound was comment, fright, or a mere bodily malfunction.

She was coming down from the rush and resignation came out on her like a cold sweat, as she trembled. I needed something to do, to reground me, since my brain was suddenly absent. I touched her leg.

"Don't touch me."

It was a serpentine hiss of a statement, and I ignored it, with prejudice, as I slipped my hand along her inner thigh through her wet dress.

"Benn, don't touch me, please."

She softly pleaded this time, trying not to look at me, as she shoved my hand away. She never shoves me away, especially when she's feeling badly.

I'm pretty certain she wouldn't have argued, if I'd touched her again and I was about to when Hopkins cleared his smoker's throat, the sound of which stiffened her spine straight as an unstrung hunting bow and caused her to focus like a laser on him.

"Have I expressed to you lately how very much I *detest* you and hope you *die* very *painfully*, very *slowly*, very *soon.*"

"When I die, you'll go back."

"I don't fucking care."

"Day?"

"Stop being nice to me, Bennet! I'm not your fucking project for your next seminar discussion."

I wasn't happy with drawing her ire, then she went back to him.

"You've asked me why I don't 'love' you, after 'all the things' you've done for me. Well, Hoppy, I do love you, as much as you love me. *Wait!* You don't love me, but you most certainly love possessing me, using me, requiring me to be *nice* to you for my very little 'freedom.' Well, it is not worth it anymore."

"Day?"

"Shut up, Benn! I'll get to you, when I'm done speaking to my *guardian.*"

I was unthinkingly going to interrupt and she could see it

on me. She has a razor mind and a laser tongue when she needs to cut someone.

"I know what you are, Bennet, I'm not stupid like he is. I have no old friends or dinner companions or portfolio monies to count or *anything,* to distract me from comparing what people do against what they say, or don't say.

"I know the truth and the lie when I hear them, even when they fit so nicely together on a tongue as articulate and sexually facile and useful as yours."

It wasn't very specific, her accusation, but I felt a deep coldness run through me, much like the shock of when I'd stepped into the Atlantic to retrieve her—it wasn't the water's cold I'd felt, then or now, but *her coldness.*

"Leave the lad alone, Day." She laughed, broadly, theatrically.

"'The lad'? When did the man you hate more than any other man I've ever known you to hate become 'the lad'? If he were the type to run away with me, you'd pull 'favours,' spend all your estate to find us. You'd prosecute him to 'the fullest extent of the law.' Money and the law, and me, all made just to serve *you're needs.*

"And, you'd separate us and hand me a blade and lick my ear with your suggestions, like a serpent, like you always do; murmuring, hissing hints of whatever you'd think would get the best effect, for you—that Benn's abandoned me, that I was going back, to *them.*

"Then, you'd step back and watch my blood flow, because you're too weak now to have me. Without help. To control me. You won't need control, if I'm dead; and dead, nobody else would be able to have what you can no longer have."

She appeared tired of it all and closed her eyes.

He, for his part, had looked guilty at every word, as if he'd considered exactly what she'd said, in gruesome detail and really had wished I'd run with her. To punish us both, especially since his wanting her now required my assistance to keep her reined.

He'd probably thought of it a lot lately, it wasn't as if he were in any decent *[now there's a word]* condition to do much with her any longer.

Consider, if she'd never given him the full attention he'd wanted before, even with me in the balance, *he knew she'd never give it to him.* After my exit.

So, he'd fuck us both, somehow, and not prettily.

It hadn't been that long ago when he and Steph had messed with her and she'd fallen to desperate pieces, or when he'd cocked her trigger and she'd gone hunting for a knife to bury in my flesh.

Her anger and her eyes had held him there, and with her lids now closed, he used the time to laboriously escape, without giving me one glance of, "Come on, lad, before she crucifies you, too!"

It didn't matter, I'd never needed his encouragement before when it came to her; I'd come into this and stayed, with every eye opening revelation.

Why run now?

The main problem now was that she was worse than Stephie at getting under my skin, deep into my head, as I endeavored to prepare myself for a mental and emotional skin- and fleshpeeling.

"I don't have anything, Benn. Nothing of my own, and even what's supposed to be mine, isn't."

Her eyes were still closed, and I knew she'd heard him go and had let him go—*theirs was an old war with a foreseeable end,* particularly with his physical health deteriorating. He was an easy target, she needed her strength to work on me, and her eyes were abruptly on me.

Those eyes, in that face. Happy or sad they get to me.

Day suddenly looked down and away, then physically turned to not look at me at all—happy or sad, I get to her, too.

"Leave, Benn. Just leave. You're going to go one day anyway, so go right now."

"If I'd thought Toddy's presence would hurt you like this, I'd've—."

"Kept me safe? From everything? All the harm that can be done to me is done or in place to be done, and it doesn't really seem like you'll be able to do too damn much about it, now or later.

"*I'm tired.* I'm so tied up in legalities. In strange, bewildering confusions. In never-ending punishments. I don't want you here, anymore. I can't afford it, anymore. It was a very nice little pretend at . . . at being grownup, at being sane, but you can . . . ."

She was staring at the shower curtain and then the tub wall. Anything but me.

"I know what you are, Benn, he doesn't, because of the way you've acted and because you're skin's the color it is. Besides, you're not money and you're not me. His two most favorite things. Which explains the lack of investigative interest about you on his part.

"At least Hoppy's stroke and the medicines are slowing his lust. So, I don't really need you around, anymore. I can trip another handsome cock on the beach when I wantta get fucked."

She still wasn't looking at me, hadn't once glanced at me, she always looked at me, especially once she understood *how clearly I really saw her*, and not just her looks or the lies she'd long ago stopped telling me.

She wasn't presently lying to me or to Hopkins or herself, as far as I could tell. She really didn't want me with her anymore, although she clearly did have a need for me, but she wasn't going to indulge in that need again was the tone and meaning I heard and felt from her.

Day was holding herself closely, trembling in the cooling tub of water, still slightly turned from me, in her soaked dress. I reached to turn the hot water up, but she kicked me. Not hard, it could've been harder if she'd wanted, without hurting herself.

The kick was a warning to stay out of her space.

There'd never been space between us, not since that first

night together, when she'd offered all of herself to me and I'd hungrily taken what she'd had to give.

I was starting to itch all over. I'm slightly allergic to the salts and crud of these more northern waters. I peeled off my clothes and she tried hard not to look, as she scooted into a tighter ball to get away from me, as I stepped in and showered off—to rinse me and to warm her.

I hooded my eyes to watch her and she finally gazed up at all of me, especially at my cock, which was close enough for her to grab, then she caught me looking at her, at her budding desire for me, and turned again from me.

"Just pack and go, Benn. Right now. I won't drown myself or even get a glass of water, just—."

"Didn't I ask if you trusted me, Day?"

I stooped to be closer to her.

"Trust me. I'm not going anywhere."

The glare she gave me, cut, but I bled, without a whimper, unseen, into myself.

"I'm not going."

"Yes, you will, so it might as well be today. Elise will be here soon, I won't try to get the knives or break glass for a cutting shard. I'll behave myself, day and night. I don't need you baby-sitting me, carrying me, or holding any part of me to make it all better!

"IT'LL NEVER BE ALL BETTER!"

She was shaking, from the adrenal rush now, because the water she sat in had been warmed by my showering. I turned my head to turn off the shower, which was splattering us both, and she threw the soap at me with a vengeance.

New bar, quite large, my cheek would continue feeling it awhile. I got out, but not wanting to leave, I sat, naked, on the rug.

"Stop taking care of me, Benn. Stop playing the fucking savior."

She let the water run down the drain, which was where she was trying to send me, then abruptly moved closer to me, without getting out, the cold tub wall between us.

Whatever she had to say was just between us.

"Maybe you've noticed. I don't get out much; but, I've been around enough of *your* kind to know one when I see one, hear one, feel one of you touch me. I've known, almost since you tripped over me, though you, you nearly threw me. I so wanted . . . .

"I understand what you did and didn't tell me at the house, *your* house, not Chuck's.

"You ran down this strip of sand, Benn, between civilization and wild, open sea, because you were completely empty and lost. Well, thank you for happening to land on me. I appreciate it. It felt like I had something for a while; not bad for a girl with a fucked up past, a fucked up life, and no fucking future.

"But, you're going to want a woman, who's a woman *all the time*; a woman you won't have to give tons of explanations about; a woman you can trust to not get confused by what others say to her, and bedded by them, while you're gone for two seconds. Someone you can trust as much as you want me to trust you.

"I trust you, Benn, I do, but I can't be your perpetual damsel in distress, or your toy, or your whatever it is you think we can be together, with Hopkins in tow. Not forever. Your *other* life, the one you had before me, the one that called you away when he and Steph—.

"Bennet, I saw you, y'know, on that entertainment show with that nicely dressed guy with the mustache. I saw you with some famous and rich Hip-Hop artist, who's husband was hurt, and you ducked the cameras, but I *know* you."

"He doesn't allow you to watch television."

"Stephie did. Internet, streaming video on her laptop. News clips. Music. Anything to get at the parts of me I was giving to you."

My face flushed with heat.

"She didn't see you, but I did. She and Hoppy were huddled

together, figuring out something to fuck with my head.

"The mustache said who you were, he said *your* name, how smart and important you were, how others'd been seeking you, but your spokesperson, a Chinese lawyer said you were "unavailable" and would be again, that you'd come in from 'an extended sabbatical,' just to help your friend.

"*All that was just icing.* I already knew, before I saw the back of your head ducking into that limo. *I knew.* I just didn't know *how big.* How hugely important you are to others, *to the world.*

"I can't take that kind of stress, not that I'd ever see it. I'm not a girl you can take anywhere. Not to places *you* get to go, with the kinds of people *you* get to help, with, I'm sure, incredible, billable hours."

"I'm done with that." My words were quiet and sincere, and my tone softened the way she was speaking to me.

"No you're not. You have a 'gift,' that medicine woman, the curandera, said so. *I* say so. You have to use it or you'll never be happy."

"*I wasn't happy!* I choose to be with you, Day. No, I take that back. I *have* to be with you, because I don't want to be with anyone else."

"That's only because I'm so fuckin' eas—."

"I don't want to hear that shit!"

She stood up with great dignity and petulance, peeled off the sopping dress, letting it plop back into the tub, before sitting on the rim to swivel on her tush to step out, which is a method less stressful on her hampered legs.

I should get her a swivel tub sea and, did I tell you, I love her body? Oh, yes, I did.

"You want me, Benn, a lot of people *want* me. Maybe when I'm too wrinkly or too something, all of you will leave me the fuck alone. I'll sleep peacefully in my bed, without someone sneaking into it or dragging me from it. I'll bathe without someone 'accidentally' coming across me there.

"You *are* the *first* person to give me what *I* want, but *your life* won't let you keep me, it won't let you stay. A life like yours has a momentum of its own, an energy you can't always control with just your will of wanting me.

"You'll never outrun its reach. And, even if Hopkins did let me keep you, and if that great life of yours did . . . ?"

I rose up on my knees, but she put her fingers near my lips to stop me from speaking. She never touched me though.

"No matter what I give him, it'll always, *always* end in punishment for me. Your staying longer is just more pain, because you'll have to go in the end anyway, and I'll have to . . . .

"I know, I understand that I . . . I completely understand what I did, then. That even if I 'don't remember everything.' That though 'I was upset.' It doesn't matter. I *have* to be punished for it. But, all this other bull, and now you . . . .

"Benn, no one cares what I want, and before you burst in screaming that you do, that doesn't matter either. It just doesn't fucking matter."

She glanced off, seeing things, remembering things I'd only heard of.

"I once wanted a single, intimate moment with my boyfriend. I'd thought out the consequences of that, like Mommy finding out, Ray not liking me, the condom breaking, which would've been worth it, because I wanted babies of my own, or adopted.

"I wanted a mother, who *liked* me. I wanted a happy life; a loving husband; friends, who understood me, despite me. And, a clear mind.

"I wanted to be able to go and come as I pleased, or to stay where I wanted to because it was pretty and felt good or because I just *wanted* to—*I get none of that.*

"I'll never get any of that and you're being here and still not . . . .

"I'd prefer to no longer pretend I have a future; that I have people to meet, children to love, or any of that." She frowned, then rose and was leaving. "I just no longer need or want you."

"Do you know what 'doesn't matter,' Day? That I truly don't give a shit, at the moment, whether you need or want me."

Her back remained to me, but she stopped her exit and crossed her arms, which aren't long, so I knew that instead of lying under her full breasts, like an underscore, they'd be across them, as if lying on top of a puffed pillow.

I said nothing for a long while, which made her turn to see what was on my mind. Her nipples were obscured by her arms, which left only her exquisite patch visible.

She saw my cock was hardening and thickening and she tried to glance away, and couldn't, especially not after I stroked myself, knowing the gesture would please me *and* catch and hold her eye.

Also, knowing her, I knew that beautiful, soft bush of hers veiled a salty little sweet river that was freely pouring out its hot welcome for me to come and take a leisurely dip.

"You're a liar, Day, you want me badly."

That made her angry, that she'd gotten so quickly side-tracked from her pursuit to shove me aside, before I'd abandon her.

She sharply half turned away, which plainly caused her leg pain.

"Damn you, Day! All right. You're right. Straight into my head right. I had . . . . I lost myself and more, *much, much more.* It wasn't the business, hell, I can't make them *stop* coming to me for help. It was . . . .

"I thought losing Mama was the worst, yet somehow I was ready for that, even though it happened so quickly, but not losing Chuck, too. And, after all these years of apprenticeships and intense training, I most certainly don't appreciate having a *'gift'* that can't or won't help the ones I . . . ."

I stopped for a moment, not fully certain what I was blurting out or thinking or feeling.

Numbness, a lukewarm, screaming numbness, when I'm not in her arms, is my natural state of being.

Being in total control of myself and all around me had been my forte and reason to be, and now, like the life that'd turned and rolled over me, like the proverbial steamroller, now, I couldn't control my desire for this one woman.

I could control her, but not my desire.

And, perhaps the point, after all these months, was that I wasn't supposed to.

"Mrs. G'd told me that 'being lost together' wasn't such a bad idea. I'd blown her off when she'd said it, but . . . . No one tells me to leave you, Day, not even you."

I was still on the floor, on my knees to be precise, like a supplicant before the Mount of Venus. Day stared at me sidewise, with icy curiosity and unveiled suspicion, before finally limping a few, hesitant and stiff, pained steps toward me.

The possibility of her coming to me just to bitch slap, again, me was a definite thought.

Stiffness had clearly settled in her limbs, despite the tub water and the central heat coming on.

Hopkins must've turned it on before hitting the sack.

It was probably because she hadn't used them since I pulled her from the cold tide, and because of the freezing tension between us.

I reached down and gently rubbed her legs and ankles, and she winced.

I kissed the inside of her elbow, then her soft belly, as I felt her cool hand slide through my hair and along my nape line, then down my spine.

If I hadn't been stone hard before, I was after her touch. Unable to resist, I grabbed her by the back of one of her full, strong thighs, just under that lovely round lip of her ass, and pulled her to me to brush my lips across her pubes, which made a little regret-laced sigh issue from her.

I got her off her feet, as I settled her down on the thick, soft rug I'd found for her, to keep her feet warm and cushioned from the cold, hard bathroom floor.

Day cradled my face in her palms, staring at length at its composition, before lying back and, with great handfuls of my hair, compelling me to go with her, pulling me to her, between her legs, until my cock felt the chilled surface of her belly.

"What's been done to me, Benn, by people I've had to trust, isn't fair, but if I . . . I can't tell if you're lying to me, or just holding something out of range of my sight."

She sadly laughed a bit.

"I guess, despite what my medical files say, that alone makes me *exactly normal*, like everyone else."

Her face changed in a flash, as it so often did, in expression, in temperament; adult to child, child to adult. Her quick changes, sometimes, were endearing, other times, as now, heartrending.

"Benn, I can stand it from everyone else, but if you're . . . insincere. If . . . ?"

I didn't move. I said nothing, because I hadn't a clue what to say. One huge, silent tear rolled out the corner of her eye. Hell, water was about to drip off the tip of my own nose.

"Please, *please*, don't hurt me. Go now. Don't . . . don't stay, just to hurt me. Everyone, nearly everyone hurts me. I'm used to that; but, if you do, too, no part of me could endure that."

'Endure.' The words this girl uses sometimes.

She half sat up to tentatively kiss me.

Both of us kept our eyes open, as we did, then she lay back. And, eventually, her face changed again—*from lost child to sultry adult*—as she leisurely fingered my nipples to distraction, before sliding her soft palms down across the sensitive terrain of my abs, as she purposefully opened her legs wider to me, and I entered.

* * * *

Day, at that moment, was more than physically naked and open to me—in ways no one else had ever been; and, I know plenty of hard guys, who'd pay tons of cash to taste that kind of vulnerability.

Not to keep it, but to possess it and control it, and her for . . . .

At that moment, there was virtually no deception on her part. Not intentionally.

No high sophistication, as a jaded and calculated façade, nor a detailed, hidden agenda. Just her willingness to be who she truly was—*a fucked up and naked "innocent."*

And, not to be underestimated or undervalued was her willingness to be what I needed and wanted, in her hope that what she'd found as a refuge and security in me, I wouldn't take away.

Day was helplessly, willfully dependent on a childlike, great hope that—*I must add here*—had always obviously failed her.

* * * *

I was standing over her, weeks later, mercilessly teasing Day, while she sat on her bed, which I'd just gotten out of recently, when Hopkins entered in a slurring, loudly demanding fit.

This was "his time," which accounted for the partial erection pushing out against his closed robe.

His stentorian, apparently vehement rage at me confused her, she feared for me, and probably thought he'd send me away. She put herself physically between us to protect me.

I don't know why he overplayed his entrance, his whole manner. It wasn't necessary for *my* benefit, except, I suspect, as another vicious mind game against her.

It didn't help her thought processes, when I confused her more by agreeing with him, that it was "his house," and she was "his."

Day didn't like my words and wanted me to remain with her; but I had an important, previous . . . *obligation* to fulfill, by meeting the minimum, prescribed terms of; and I've never reneged or not fulfilled a major contract ever.

She didn't make him happy. She told him he was "half dead" and still "trying to dictate and own" her, that what he wanted of her "was grossly wrong" and always had been.

But, she also said "no"—*and she had the presence of mind to say the right thing, to explain it*—because she'd hurt him, like "last time," when she'd evidently "nearly killed" him with the stroke.

She didn't "want to hurt" him "worse."

She'd "heard of men dying like that"—*"in midfuck"*; but "never women, except when ganged up on, or in childbirth—."

She abruptly stopped there, having wandered a bit off topic.

I said *it* again. I quietly put in my *official order.* I told her to *be with him,* anyway he liked. Her face snapped around to look into mine, as she stared at me a long while, as if not comprehending, before finally answering me.

"No."

Hopkins, tired of standing, sat with a grunt, dipping the bed, which made her move from him and closer to me.

"Make lov—. Lie with him, Day."

She didn't want to argue with me, she loves pleasing me; I *love* being pleased by her and pleasing her in return, because there's truly nothing else in the whole of existence, like pleasing her, but . . . *this* . . . this was cold, necessary business.

"*No*, Bennet. Please."

I held her head in my hands and whispered for her ears only, and watched her expressive, open face change with the realization of what I was *absolutely requiring* of her.

"Day, you said you'd 'do anything' for someone you truly wanted. You want me, don't you?" She finally nodded, suspicious and in shock. "Do as I ask then, Day. Fu—. *Be* with him, as if he were me. Just, as if he were me. Or . . . or we can't remain together."

"That's completely unfair! You can't . . . ! You don't know what you're asking of me."

"*Yes*. I do. I know *exactly* what I'm asking."

She looked disappointed and disheartened—*I think my golden armor in her eyes had just tarnished. That hurt, but it didn't matter, it just didn't fucking matter.*

"No, Bennet, you *can't*. I *can't*. You *know* I *swore* I'd *never—*."

Ironically, after living with her like a wild Bohemian Gypsy, doing whatever I pleased.

Which'd been pretty much just about pleasing her, about letting her have her head, her way in nearly every matter, except only when she could harm herself, by limb or life; ironically, she could hurt me all she wanted, and I'd take it and come back for more.

That'd been the way I was as a kid.

I never minded getting hurt by *some* people, if I felt they were worth it, but I'd grown up, toughened up, and I'd ended up ruling anyone and everyone, being the one who hurt others, whether it was necessary or not, because I could.

And, they'd often perversely thank me for it.

Even Stephie never really could govern me, not if I didn't let her, which I often just choose to let her do.

In my life, that distant, *other* life, before this one with Day, I'd become exhausted being the king and absolute ruler of everyone and everything, yet unable to help the ones closest to me, who'd needed my help the most.

Unable and ceaselessly unwilling to let go and accept what was out of my control, but out of my control it remained.

And still remains.

My healing mentor says some people are incurably ill, as a spiritual lesson of help.

A lesson for the patient to receive and become "grace in discomfort," by allowing others to do for them and to be gracious to those who need to give them help.

A spiritual lesson for us to give help, even when we know or at least believe our assistance is wholly superfluous, but to learn that our help may yet give "a small bit of comfort."

She says that some people die to show us how to live life; to live well, and in the *now*, in the *present* moment. My mentor says a great deal—*and she's pretty damned smart*—she says that for me, I need to learn "when and when not to control" with my iron will.

I'd rarely been ironwilled or hardassed with Day and had loved spoiling her, letting her have her way with me. I loved spoiling myself doing it. She was presently so upset with me, though; I could feel her pain in my own chest.

"I know what you 'swore,' Day, to *never* fully give in to him. I also know you will not say 'no' to me again, in this matter, in any way, shape, or form, or I will leave and be absolutely done with it. With him. With you."

She stared down, suddenly, unable to meet my eyes, then, eventually, nodded, vaguely, without looking up again.

I left them; actually, I only went as far as her bathroom doorway, so I could see everything.

His back remained to me, as he scuttled backwards on his elbows deeper onto the bed, then lay back, opening his robe, revealing his fully nude anticipation. I knew his eyes were locked on her; they always were, when she was in sight.

Day, however, closed her eyes tightly and admirably went at him with her hands, doing what I'd comman- . . . .

Yeah, the word is *"commanded."* I waited, and waited—*his body not yet being able to remain up for the activity he'd demanded, and I'd signed off on, leaving her to do the dirty and immoral work.*

I left for a brief moment to get a pack of cigarettes and a bottle. By my return, as I'd suspected—*very little had changed.*

It was like one of those proverbial train wrecks. I didn't want to look, but I'd seen everything else, since my first night under his roof; I might as well watch this, too.

It was painfully obvious she didn't want to look at him or in my direction.

I watched the hatred for the task and me, for that matter, and the inevitable anguish in her expressions and movements and sighs, as his sick body lethargically refused her hands. She unhappily put her mouth to him; then, his sick body, finally, hardened enough for her to use.

She mounted and was *active* with him, as "if he were me," as I'd requested, had demanded of her. He was "lucky" I'd been . . . . I'd fucked her not an hour before, so I knew she was still slick.

It was his luck because the tension I felt from her now would've made her too dry to be of use to him, if I hadn't gotten *there* first.

He coaxed a little, "kibitzed," as a perpetual acquaintance of mine calls it, and per his instructions, she tried to be vocal, as he preferred, pausing in her actions once, when her eyes unexpectedly opened fully on mine.

It hurt to see the expression of so many distressed emotions fighting within her, as she followed my orders that were slaughtering yet another part of her, probably the last vestiges of any true, childlike innocence she had left.

Butchered soul by Bennet Gillespie, blackmailing, coercive lover.

She tightly squeezed her eyes shut against the sight of me.

My stomach didn't become queasy once during the whole affair. Go figure.

Hopkins and his messed up body, with its badly miswired bloodflows, took an eternity with its erratic, unstable erection and forced her to masturbate, while riding him, which wasn't working for her, I could tell.

She was also forced to stare him deep in his eyes, as he wanted. It was too obvious to me that she was never going to cum, but she was faking the bodily contractions and giving him the convincing sound effects, the extra-satisfied sounds, like the ones she has with me, which he'd always wanted and expected from her.

She'd told me she'd never cum with him or because of him, not when she was a kid, nor since he'd brought her to stay with him.

That was a partial lie, justifiable and forgivable, but a lie.

But, this time it wasn't.

I watched her play act her desire and "reward" him with the tangible external representations of her seeming lust for him, as she "made love," in a fine, award winning performance.

But, her subterfuge wasn't working, since his prick wouldn't hold its firmness, despite her fine try; and fake all she wanted, he wasn't letting her get away with not getting him off.

Day was losing it.

Her tears silently cascaded down her soft cheeks and off her chin, as frustration and fear came out all over her like sweat, as she began glancing my way, not certain to meet my eye, beg for help, or just quietly implode to death—*I've had patients, interns, residents, and, even full surgeons, look at me in much the same condition.*

Hopkins slapped Day.

"That's not what I want, you ungrateful . . . ! You'll fake your way back—!"

"Hey!"

They both looked at me. She was off him and holding her knees to her chest, he was up on one elbow and not in full control of anything.

Of course he wasn't, that was *my job.*

I've always been in control.

Until I get fed up with it all. It's what I do, so well. Did well. Am about to do.

"This isn't acceptable, Mr. Gillespie. Not acceptable, not at all. I thought you controlled—?"

"Shut up." She was about to protest a question to me. "Both of you, shut up."

I checked his pulse and his eyes, and was surprised he didn't argue when I did. I opened the recycled water bottle I'd prepared days before of tea and other herbs, a recipe older than any formal country in this part of the world.

"Drink this." He didn't want it; he wanted her. *Like I wouldn't know that?* "If you want *her*, you have to drink *this*. Trust me. Though you deserve it, I haven't poisoned you so far."

He sat up and drank while she studied me through her long, dark lashes and tears. Day was trembling and I knew it wasn't because she was physically cold, she was reacting to *my* coldness and the fact that she couldn't, at present, get inside my mind or away from what I'd asked her to do.

I slipped my shirt off and she ceased clutching her knees to her naked breasts to slip it on and hug desperately to me.

I hugged and squeezed her in return, kissed her neck and cheek, felt down her backside through the cotton fabric. I raised the shirt up to fondle her buttocks and to show him I, literally, had it all in hand, as he put aside the empty bottle, his color better, his mind and then hand also on her ass.

She reacted, but I held her, distracted her with *my* mouth and *my* hands, and she ignored his attentions, as I gave her mine, which didn't exactly make him happy, though watching her react to me always did.

Yes. I do mean that I know he hadn't always been entirely asleep or completely gone or distracted these past few months.

That he'd watched us fuck and make love more than I mentioned.

I most definitely didn't mention it, because it's a distracting and disturbing thought you didn't really need to know or to have mucking about in the back of your mind.

I'm sure his mind always pretended she was reacting to *his* touch, *his* kiss, and *his* stone hard cock the same "all-encompassing" way she nearly always did with me. I'd known he'd watched us and I'd chalked it up to another *worthy* price to pay for having her, under his nose, in his house.

"Mr. Gillespie . . . ?"

"Shush. It may still be *your* house but you're now under *my* rule." He didn't like being shushed or out of the loop of control, so I asked him a question. "Have you ever had her, shared her simultaneously with another?"

I felt her stiffen, defensively, in my arms, as his eyes lit up with the novelty of it, with the knowledge that sharing Day sexually with me should guarantee a lively time.

That thought and the bottled tea both kicked in, as his manhood stiffened considerably.

"Benn?"

She wanted to say "no" to this whole thing, but was afraid to say it to me. She was quiet and trying to trust me, and was confused, *dreadfully* confused.

She knew full well how much I never liked sharing her, even though I always had. She also knew how much I detested his touching her in any manner, but now here I was permitting it.

A necessary evil.

"I'm taking care of everything, baby. Give yourself to me as always and I'll take care of everything. All I need is for you to be an adult. I need the woman not the little girl, Day, can you do that?"

If he hadn't been touching her sensitive ass, I probably would've gotten an affirmative sooner. The silent, weepy nod came.

I kissed her deeply and long and he was feeling her, kissing and biting at her asscheeks, and despite him she melted against me into my arms, as her flesh became hungry and yearning for me.

He was touching her between her legs and feeling, smelling the wet changes I wrought in her, the changes he desired.

I reached around her and checked his pulse again from under his chin, and again he uncharacteristically didn't protest.

I removed my shirt from her, leaving her naked before his starving eyes, before I ripped off a sleeve and playfully tied it over her eyes. I laid her down beside him and aroused her head to toe, before spooning against her backside and putting her head again to his gray crotch, as I entered her and she felt his cock against her lips.

"It's all right. Take it, baby, I have two cocks and I need to be inside you front and back."

She balked, but I leaned to her ear and said things that slithered through her mind, that she likes to hear from my lips and told her again, with my blindfold over her eyes, that I had two cocks, both for her, both needing her desperately.

Hopkins slipped his uncut meat into her mouth, and I let him, welcomed him to her services, as I pimped—*to my late mother's eternal shame and my twin's eternal amusement.*

I was neither ashamed nor amused. "Business is business" and, well, "strange bedfellows" and all that.

Dad would probably not be overly prideful of the situation, but he would appreciate the fact that I was working on getting what I wanted, even if I had to "do some serious damage" to get it.

Dad always said I had "a tendency" to be "too nice, too accommodating," and "not ruthless enough"—*he hadn't seen me in the past few years.* I'd changed a lot since those many years ago when he'd first bemoaned those little "weaknesses" in me.

Old man Hopkins was east of Nirvana, now, and since I was running this fuck I made him pay a little ahead.

"Hopkins?"

He was pretty far away and was annoyed at a direct interrogative, from a male voice. He glanced my way.

"Swear on your *honor* and your first serious hard-on in an eternity, now in her mouth, swear that it's all legal and valid. Swear or I'll leave you with a cold, limp biscuit, dried up on your thigh and no way to find her, let alone have her.

"You know me, I don't mind running every day."

"It's valid. *If* I get . . . ."

The rest of his answer was lost in a moment of sheer pleasure.

She'd done something that melted his mind, and since his penis hadn't collapsed in a while, it was time. I pulled out of her, leaving her hungry to have me, as I ordered her to keep the blindfold on, to keep loving my other prick, and to keep her mind focused on me—*my voice, my touch, etcetera.*

I'd take care of everything.

I kept one hand busy with her, as I pulled a container from my discarded pants, lubed up, then slid balls deep into her receptive anus.

I drew a nice little moan from her, before pulling her off him to have her restraddle him; we both did, since I remained inside her.

I resettled her sopping wet cunt over him.

Even fucked up and half dead, he managed to eagerly stuff himself up into her, like one of those old Saturn Five rockets. I more than half expected him to fall away to pieces like one of those S5s, but he held on, as he zealously fucked her, like he hadn't been able to in a long time.

He shouldn't've been so eager, he didn't need to work so hard for it, I had her going hot enough to take care of his needs, but Mr. Hopkins is a greedy fuck.

He ordered . . . .

Then backed off to beg her to remove the blindfold and open her eyes to him, because with her hotter than hot, with us both inside her, correction, both of *my* cocks inside her, he wanted to see her eyes, her whole face, when she came, while riding him.

He'd never had her react to him with this kind of enthusiasm.

Never.

I slipped my torn sleeve off her eyes and told her to open them; that I'd stay with her the entire time, that she was fucking killing us both.

It was clear he loved her eyes on him, but I was in her head, conducting, and he didn't seem to realize she was somewhere near that mental place; her fugue place. That dream place she went when she'd sit up and reach in dreams—*eyes open, but not seeing at all what I plainly saw before her.*

Hopkins was losing his staying power, his thrusting strength, but he was still hard enough, so she used him and rode him like a stationary dildo, as I continued fucking her in the ass, until Hopkins finally shot his wad with a throat-constricted, choking whine.

She tried to wiggle off him, but I continued fucking her and pushed her all the way down onto his diminishing shaft, knowing his pelvic bone was forced against and pressuring her clit, and that she'd be coming soon.

"Let go, Dayita, let it go. I want it all, every last drop."

It's not lost on me that double penetrating a woman with another man is not unlike masturbating him, at least I think it must be, because the wall of flesh separating your dick from his is negligible.

She reached back over her shoulders to hold me by my hair, as she shuddered and came and triggered me.

Good ole "Hoppy" was still hard enough and still deep enough inside her to feel her fantastic contractions and my multiple recoils.

Odd that so many things that are vile, can also be pleasurable.

He immediately went soft and was expelled, along with his feeble cream, by her constricting muscles, but I continued pumping at her and felt her tremulously cum a few more times before my slick cock fully emptied into her, gave up the ghost, and slipped like a robber from her.

* * * *

Lucky is the man, who gets what he wants, or is it what he deserves, while screwing over and using whomever to fulfill his wishes?

It looked highly probable that I'd get what I wanted, because Hopkins had at last gotten exactly what he'd wanted, through me.

* * * *

Day lay quietly against me, with eyes closed tight in postcoital rest, not paying him any heed, preferring to shut his complete existence out.

The call of nature got me up for the piss pot and I started to take her with me, but I was just relieving myself and rinsing my face.

I heard her, and came back out in time to see her staring intensely at him, before abruptly falling from the bed, entangled in bed covers. She came crawling and half-stumbling to me, straight to my feet, as quickly as her jangled nerves and stressed ankles would let her.

She reached for me, trembling, but stopped inches away.

Instead of touching me or permitting me to touch her, she headed for the tub, as always after her encounters with him. She did smell of him, hell, I probably smelled of him.

I recall thinking, with a great deal of pride for her, that it was an interesting point of personal integrity on her part, that even after such a traumatic, intimate display—*that she still refused to allow me to touch her,* after him, *with his small amount of residue yet marking and staining her.*

I left her long enough to check his vitals—*none.*

At least he hadn't died alone or unhappy, his corpse had a self-satisfied little grin on its "sleeping" face.

I shut her bathroom door between us and him, then watched her douche—*washing away evidence crossed my mind;* but, it was "normal" behavior, for her.

I got into the shower with her, and took over her roughly frenetic and becoming more so hair and body washing.

She became tranquil, as I gently cared for her, rinsing soap-suds and him from her, from me, for the final time.

She stared at me a long time, looking me up and down, as I squeezed the last of the cleansing suds from her hair. Although I didn't mention it to her, I was very glad she appeared pleased with the sight of me still, despite the past hour or so.

"Benn, I'm yours, now, and no one else's."

I nodded. Those words and their meaning, and the feelings generating them meant a hell of a lot more to me than I could ever say to her.

"Did I do what you wanted, Benn? Did I do it correctly?" I nodded again, but it was too apparent that she wanted, no, *needed* to hear my voice.

"Yes, Day, you did exactly what I wanted, in exactly the right way."

She was fingering my mother's beat up, gold locket, lying in the middle of my hard chest. So I slipped it off me and onto her.

Day smiled, brilliantly, in blinding innocence, then nuzzled me and became intensely desirous of me very fast, which was very good, since I'd never totally had her all to myself. Not without the smoky specter of Hopkins lurking.

I still wasn't entirely certain his lingering, choking smog was cleared away, though.

He'd signed off on me having a "generous say" about her and sworn on his extremely dubious "honor," but he was Hopkins and had never been honorable when it'd come to Day before.

No matter how long or little time I legally truly had with her, she was at present utterly mine, and I utterly, thoroughly, claimed what was mine.

Mrs. G "discovered" the body, hours later, and called for me.

I didn't like using her like that; but, everyone had a part in this play, and it was certainly a lot less than I'd asked of my lover, or myself, for that matter.

Day didn't want me to go "back in there," but I explained that I had to, and did.

There are no words to describe the expression Mrs. G had on her face when she completely realized that not only Day's things were on the bed and floor beside her cold and deceased boss, but my things, as well.

I'd thought to get my pants and whatever of mine lay in the room with the body before bedding Day once more, but decided

Forensics would figure it out anyway.

Day stayed in my bed, never again going into her room, and we had to remove some of her things to my room for her.

The paramedics came, then the cops, "routinely" making certain there was "no foul play."

There wasn't. No. Really. Think about it.

The master of the house asked for a service, and received it, in full. What's sinister about that?

The two detectives and uniform kept us all separated: Mrs. Gorbachev in the kitchen; Day in my room, cowering from their intrusive authority on the open windowsill.

Later, she'd try retreating from them out to her side porch patio chair, guarded by those lovely and picturesque jumper bars.

I was on the beachside porch, chain-smoking, leaning against the porch rail, looking out to the eastern horizon, when they finally got to me.

They had my official stats by then.

"Mr.? Uh, *Dr.* Gillespie? Orthopedic surgeon?"

"Technically."

" 'Technically'? "

"I don't think much of titles and honorifics, just because you did the homework. I actually prefer my licensed curandero status, so 'Mr.' is fine by me."

I don't think they'd ever heard a doctor say such a thing and didn't really believe it.

"Yeah, well, *Dr.* Gillespie. The ladies of this household have some *interesting* stories."

Short version.

They found all the intimate details that came out about our private lives "interesting" and plainly "suspicious."

Well, it's not like a DNA sampling of the bedsheets wouldn't have told a good deal of the story anyway. Besides, it's their job and their nature to be "suspicious."

Plus, it was obvious they didn't know of any other "gifted," nationally known surgeons apparently egoless enough to do physical therapy and healing duties for minimum wage, but then again, there was the lovely Ms. Day—*an obvious work benefit, even without any insurance plans.*

They seemed quite fixated on a "few facts," like that this was an "interesting sexual triangle" between an ill and now dead, wealthy elderly man and a quite healthy younger man.

Also known as a dead white man survived by a live red one.

They weren't certain how well-to-do *I* was financially, yet; however, I was—*as I always was in school*—first, on their to check further lists.

I was their man of the hour.

A younger man with "advanced medical knowledge." A man with "sexual and emotional motive," if Day were evidence of such. A man with, "perhaps, financial motive" against a "poor old guy with one foot in the grave."

You know the usual, all wrapped in a deadly, gossip friendly, one for the memoirs, "kinky threesome."

"Jeez, Doc, sounds like death by—."

Sex? Premeditated death by sex?

Will that really fly with the courts? The media, yes, but the legal courts? Besides, I don't think you have that one on your books, which was the gist of my reasonable answer.

I didn't mention sodomy, which may still be on this particular State's law books, and prosecutable.

Unless, of course, that law had been for same sex partners only. Then again, well, I'm not a lawyer licensed by this state, am I?

They'd doggedly followed my lead down the front stairs and out onto the gritty sand.

"One of your neighbors swore the deceased called the young lady inside his 'daughter'?"

What do you take me for? Take any of us for? Which got

a scurrilous look out of them, but they kept their responses to themselves.

"*Who* inherits?"

I do, as far as I know. *Confirmed later by Sid.*

And again, as everything always circled around and returned, there was delicate "Ms. Day," and *her* legal, criminal background; and the whole matter of who was or wasn't "responsible for her." Etcetera.

Chuck's sister, Cinda, arrived in her corporate limo, fresh off the corporate jet, with her phalanx of competent assistants. I'd phoned and emailed every pertinent thing I could to her around when Mrs. G'd called emergency.

Any calls going out too early to her would've been red flagged by the cops, as "very suspicious," whether they ever gained access to the privileged info discussed or exchanged.

Cinda, ESQ, removed and tossed her expensive, raw silk high heels to one of her lackeys before hitting the beach like D-Day, waving a perfectly manicured, chastising forefinger at me, and then the officers.

She was not happy with the "unwise and unsupervised" communications I'd been having with the cops, "without proper counsel," and forbade me saying anything else to them, no matter how seemingly benign.

She knows I'm no idiot, but the law *is* a tricky, slippery thing, even for the *completely innocent,* which I've never ever been accused of.

She put out her palm and I put the pocket micro recorder in it that she knew I'd have on me, taping since the first question.

I'd given Mrs. G one and placed one in Day's pocket, too, for Cinda's edification, so she'd know *exactly* what had been said, during the private conversations, because we weren't under arrest or under any kind of oath.

The Police were extremely unhappy about all that and very dearly held to their suspicions, as they worked their "evidence."

But, nothing was legally wrong and would be fully confirmed by the autopsy and by the fully authorized letter, promptly dropped off by Sid, which Hopkins had presciently had drafted for the occasion.

Like an occasional greeting card. How nice of him. And grateful.

The letter stated that I'd "taken care of him," as he'd wished, he was "contented" to leave me everything, including and especially the charge of the "special" young woman, Day.

Motivewise, I had "access," but I also had my own considerable amounts of personal "money"; I had "the woman," exclusively anyway, since his illness.

And, he was on doctor's orders to exercise. He stubbornly and perversely chose sex as his usual and only sport. *His* choice.

The private terms of his blackmail to control her custody and whether she would stay with me or go back to the lockdown were couched in legal language so carefully opaque and oblique, that the cops believed they understood, but couldn't actually confirm it as motive.

Even the District Attorney's Office really couldn't be fully adamant on its meaning.

And, medically, he was DNR *[Do Not Resuscitate]*, which protected my nonusage on his behalf of my "advanced medical abilities."

The detectives had eventually left by the last of the sun's waning light, leaving a small contingent of uniforms to keep a perimeter—*the media had picked up my scent around the dead, wealthy elder, and were starting to descend from wherever they descend from.*

Cinda instructed me she'd take care of "any announcements" and teased that for trying to hide I wasn't doing a very good job of it, but that, "after getting a gander" at Day . . . .

Cinda's got a sharp mouth, a sharper mind, and a sharp body for that matter, but she is a lot less vicious and more graciously sympathetic than Stephanie will ever be.

I was truly surprised when Stephie didn't call, email, or just show up to rub my nose in my own fragrant shit.

How so unlike her.

Cin went to successfully joust with and win the media and the law for me. She always jokes that *no one* turns *her* down, *except* me. The woman is hotly desirable, there's no doubt there; however, I love her too much to accept.

Plus Chuck'd come back from the grave and haunt me to death, if I didn't do right by her—*I'm serious, I swear, he told me so.*

Besides, she doesn't need rescuing, she's my legal rescuer, and Cin's not particularly open about her love matches or her lovemaking—*major minuses for me.*

Mrs. G came out on the beach, where I was still chain-smoking and watching the cops and Cin dispersing the carcass eaters from Hopk- . . . *my* doorstep.

"Mr. Bennet?"

"Hm?"

"She's not at all happy here and won't come back inside. Not without you. And, even then, I fear . . . ." I'd figured as much.

"Call the hotel, see if they have a suite or two connecting rooms, and I'd greatly appreciate it if you'd stay there with us, with her, she's justifiably upset. And, I'll surely be a little busy the next few—.

"Oh, and you don't have to pack much for her, I still have the suitcase full of her new things from our trip, hidden in my trunk."

Mrs. G was quiet; but, the wheels were noticeably reeling round her handsome, wise noggin.

"Mrs. G, what is it?"

"I saw, I've overheard . . . today . . . ."

She didn't want to say precisely what she saw, or "overheard," in god only knows what kind of language.

Evidently, she hadn't asked Day, or her Ms. Day had refused to tell her exactly what the older woman already knew. Mrs. G is not stupid, just a bit obscenely optimistic.

"What . . . what you *did* . . . was *that* for . . . was *that* . . . was *it* . . . necessary? Did she have to . . . ?"

"It wasn't for . . . pleasure. Not for mine or hers." I left out that we both had felt pleasure, but she didn't need to or want to hear that.

"And, you know how he was about her, her participation was required. I tried to make it as . . . painless, as possible for her."

She frowned hard enough to shatter her face.

"Mrs. G, I know you've thought about it more than you want to and if I could've taken that bullet for her . . . I—."

I had to shake my head on that one, to get my own thoughts clear of the obstacle better known as Hopkins.

"If there could've been another path to hell, I'd've gladly taken it alone in her stead.

"You have to have known how intensely he wanted her, and how . . . . He had us entirely boxed in. It . . . . *What* he wanted needed to be done, *that* way. To get her free of him."

I left out the fact that I'd sent . . . *commanded* Day to go in alone to him. Into the lion's den. Into the circle of fire. Alone.

Cowardly, practical, expedient, covering my ass—*sometimes different words and phrases mean the same thing.*

Or at least feel like they do.

"Hopkins flatly, vehemently refused to give me custody of her, otherwise. It's *actually* in the codicils to his Will. In black and white. What a fucking, controlling, motherfuck—. Excuse me. I apologize."

She shrugged off my language and the next thing she said was so softly spoken I could just barely hear it over the Atlantic behind me.

"Ms. Day has always fervently denied it, but . . . but, he'd say things. About being . . . *related.* Was . . . was . . . ?"

Mrs. G couldn't even say it and sometimes, even the strongest, most pragmatic people don't really want to hear . . . .

Then again, sometimes, they need to hear it anyway.

I did the "guy thing," the "take charge" thing, the "surgeon is god and knows best" way out and decided for her.

"You know him, how manipulative he was."

Mrs. G's doubts and fears and moral revulsions visibly dropped from her like heavy, overripe coconuts into the sand beneath us, she smiled to herself then me and went in to make our arrangements.

We were finally getting out of his claustrophobic, death box of a house, that'd never been a comfortable home to anyone, except its previous and now dead owner.

For me at least, there'd be weighty, legal decisions that had to be based on more than my substantial libido and my ego's considerable desire to be stroked by the young mistress of the house.

Real considerations had to be taken of whether she could be "handled," "controlled."

Without Hopkins in the picture, she should have fewer "killer mood swings," but even with my penchant since childhood for, pardon the phrasing, handling dangerous vipers, and my new skill of talking the knife out of her hand . . . .

Day had said she'd "share" me, with "a wife," to appease me, to appease my career, my rather large life.

But, she doesn't want to share me and she's clearly too dangerous, blade in hand or not, for me not to give the new parameters of a sans Hopkins life, all alone with her serious, *serious* thought.

The sun was flaring one final time on the horizon behind the house, as I walked back, in a slight proprietary haze.

The house and everything in it, like her, were now all mine, as I put out the end of my last, not fully smoked cigarette, slit it open, then sifted the remaining tobacco onto the wind.

* * * *

The judge gave us a short recess from the hearing, and I dashed out, as if my hair were on fire.

Cinda let me go, she was only "observing." I'd asked her not to come, but she'd come anyway, "as a friend," after getting all my "legal ducks in order" and was "just keeping an eye on things" on my behalf.

Stephie obviously disappointed slimy Sid by following me, instead of staying to talk with him.

She caught up to me in one of the consultation rooms, where I sat, thinking—*well, trying not to think, trying not to let the feelings I had, the thoughts I had overwhelm me.*

She had a bright green file folder in her hand and opened it on the table, displaying every grisly, graphic photo before me.

"Knowing and seeing," Day had always said.

I already knew, because, before we'd signed his Last Will and Testament, Hopkins had given me a long and specifics-filled explanation of *this*, of Day's physical responsibility in her mother's death.

I hadn't wanted to believe most of it, as I now turned each hideous photo face down.

It was curious that he had left out his own fumbling, greedy seduction, statutory rape, and subsequent out-and-out rape of a confused, emotionally assaulted child; that he'd left out his *help* in having her castrated, his soiled part in all the rage, that had led up to these same pictures.

It also occurred to me that with his cash and connections he . . . .

It was odd to think he'd had copies of these and had felt kind enough not to've shown them to me.

That, of course, really didn't sound like Hopkins, in any configuration. He was probably more afraid the photos would kill my libido and any possibility he'd have to control her, if I left.

He wanted me gone, but he wanted Day's full, sexual attention much more.

"I worked damned hard to find and get those released," Stephanie was saying in her disappointment, as I walked away from her, and them, until I abruptly stopped at the window, which faced a wall—brick. *Ha!*

"Stephie, when she's back in lockdown, in *that place,* confined for life, medicated out of her will, and at any and everyone's mercy—or lack thereof . . . . So, Steph, besides Mrs. G, are you making plans to be her cherished, outside lifeline?"

"Interesting, Snake Boy. You didn't say *you'd* be her 'lifeline' and visit."

Yes. It *was* interesting.

"She belongs there, Benn. She did *this.* I'm a registered, card-carrying bitch, licensed to wield a scalpel, and even *I'm* not capable of *this.* If she hadn't been judged insane, she'd be on death row."

She had thumped on the picture backs, while stating her point.

I bet she'd gotten them from Hopkins, perhaps as a thing to do upon his happily satiated death. One last, final, vicious turn of the cold, hard, straight razor in my heart.

"Benn, these don't just show five or ten inappropriately, yet somewhat justifiable, angry slashes, but nearly a hundred. The mother was like hamburger, parts of her nearly severed by sheer volume and impact of the lacerations.

"Your little darling, *our* little darling was found more covered in her mother's blood than on the day she was born."

"*Yes.* I get the picture." I really didn't want to talk, but I knew she'd never leave it alone.

"I *know* you, Stephanie, your clit's aching for her right now, while you're busy trying to cut her out of *my* life. You're harder than I am on your lovers. You won't mind seeing her in *that place* and you'll go to be with her, *there.*

"And, no matter what she's done, she doesn't deserve *those* jackals.

"But, that won't bother you all that much, will it? You'll simply *arrange* conjugals, somehow, and take what you want from her, then leave. Without a thought of her in *there*, not until you get another deeply randy itch for her."

I saw the reflection of the negative shake of her head.

"I won't. I've reconsidered."

"You'll reconsider your reconsideration." I heard her sigh.

She didn't want to be sidetracked by her own lust, while still trying her best to get me to end this "little affair," as Steph was still calling it.

"She killed him, Benn. On purpose. You know, *murder?* Little Ms. No Panties sucked you into . . . What'd the media call it? Shit, it was so stupid. What? Uh! I can't remember.

"The old man wanted her too much and compromised his health and then his life, letting her fuck him, while you were losing all control of your spine to her, letting her get you off, and off the track of controlling her, as well.

"She wiggled off your leash, that fat, hungry dick of yours, just long enough to hop on his and coolly finish him.

"Then, what, Benn? She came back for an encore with you? Is this particular woman's cocksucking and cockcatching so fantastic that it's worth your life?"

Steph held her scalpel of a tongue, for all too brief a time.

"Twin Benn, I know you think you can control anyone and everything, but you can't. Her own mother and Hopkins both thought they could, and, gee, they're both very dead.

"You've never seen it happen, but one day, you'll leave out a knife or something else hard and sharp and she'll repeat her killer performance. This girl does not like authority figures over her. She kills them."

I was really coldly tired of my amateur psychologist sibling.

"Stephi, authority figures have always let her down, viciously.

And, as for you. You tried controlling her, Big Sis, and *you* certainly weren't fucked to death."

She chose to ignore my sarcastic observation.

"Get wise, Benn. The both of you, Hopkins and you together, with all your emotional and physical snares tripping her up, could barely control her sometimes. Face it, the only way for anyone alone to rule her, is to keep her *in* lockdown with more than three overindulgent people watching her."

She paused too briefly, before proceeding.

"Despite all that, yes, *I do want her.* She's very easy on the eyes, is sexy as hell in that deceptively ingenuous, innocently passionate, volatile way of hers. She's an incredible lay. Just think how grateful she'll be to see a familiar, friendly face that isn't staff?

"Besides, Little Brother, no matter what I actually think or feel about her, I don't want what she did to them done to you.

"So, don't forget, I know you, too. You come across all sensitive and Prince Charming and crap and you do have your moments, but let's face it, a woman needs to be damned tough of the mind and heart to be with you. Not to mention taking your being intensely in perpetual heat for her.

"Lord knows dear Arabella wasn't tough enough, she's just barely getting her—pardon the pun—*shit* together, since you abruptly and harshly cut the umbilical between you two.

"You and I both know you're a lot harder and a damn sight more selfish about taking what you want, and playing all the games, like the sex game, than you let on. The only problem is, is that you get exactly what you set out for, all the time, then throw it back, because you decide you no longer want it; careerwise or romancewise."

"Why the hell do you care, Steph? You never liked Arabella, so *that* point's wasted. And, contrary to what you've thought, and done, Day is none of your business, either."

My hackles were all the way up.

And, I was ready to unleash.

Forensics had put a great deal of Hopkins' final moments together, but beautiful and deadly Cinda corked it before it could get out to the street.

Presently, I was getting a headache and my stomach was starting to act up. Stephanie has no qualms about putting a ton of pressure on anyone, including me to get her way.

I can stand pressure from nearly anyone and anything, except the women closest to me. I very much wanted her off me, and especially off Day. I had enough I had to do yet about Day without—.

So. I succinctly informed Dr. Stephanie Gillespie about *who'd been in charge,* when Day had fucked her guardian to death—*that shut my sister up.*

And sat her down.

It's something so incredibly huge that I know she'll never hold it over my head, and to tell you the truth, it scared the hell out of her, that I'd go that far, for this one woman.

Or, more precisely, to paraphrase my twin, who knows me damned well—it scared the hell out of her, how far I'd pushed this one woman, to please me.

Silence fell heavily between us.

Eventually, I let her hug me before she left, then I looked at the photos again, while my stomach ached painfully. Maybe I should go back to work; my gut never bothered me at work.

The judge was done speaking in private with Day, who was trying not to wear her fears on her face. She looked great in the suit Mrs. G'd picked out for her and I'd bought.

For the most part, though, she looked like a nervous child in a woman's suit, but she was probably just tired. She'd barely slept in her agitation; then again, she may have been just tuning into my own restiveness, which was partially based, as Steph had said, in the debate of *having* versus *wanting.*

I asked the judge if I could speak with Day, and she gave me ten minutes in the consult room. Mrs. G was going to leave us, but I asked her to stay.

Day instantly stared at me, attuned in that hypersensitive way of hers to every shade of my moods and every subtle tone of my voice. It's probably one of the things, which makes her such an incredible bedmate.

I put down the photos, one by one.

Mrs. G valiantly went through each, the scowl on her face deepening with each one and her ability to swallow plainly starting to fail; Day, I think, gazed somewhere past them, her eyes never seeming to entirely focus on them.

Mrs. G quietly restacked them and handed the green folder to me. I shoved my fists into my pockets, not wanting it. She folded it, then stuffed it in her handbag.

Day didn't look at me, she merely slipped my mother's locket off from around her neck and laid it on the table, stood, and walked to the door, then just remained there.

I suddenly, finally, realized why she sometimes did that, even at the beachhouse, before a drive or when we'd gone to the bed and breakfast.

I'd mentally filed it, at the time, reasoning that it was an ego trip, a control issue, a way to get others to do a kindness for her.

Stephie and I had seen that behavior in the lockdown; but, it hadn't registered with me, not until that moment.

Even if a door were unlocked, the inmates weren't allowed to open the door themselves, at least not without specific permission.

She glanced forlornly at Mrs. G, then back at the door, like a pet dog waiting for walkies—"walkies," how British was that? Hopkins was gone and still hanging over us, at every moment, like acrid smoke pollutant in your clothes and on your skin and hair.

Damn, I wanted a cigarette.

The judge stated that the Will would stand, especially considering Day's "continuing condition."

Like Cinda had advised, the ankle trick, even though it was

considered "an accident," didn't "have the right feel" to the judge, even without actual proof of Day's or anyone else's "violent intent."

Day's pittance of an inheritance from her mother would stay with Hopkins' estate. It'd grown quite well under his administration. Everything else was all in order, per Hopkins' last changes witnessed by Sid, Mrs. G, and myself.

Once Mrs. G's modestly generous amount he'd left her was paid out, and since he was childless and spouseless and a coercive, blackmailing bastard, I was uncontested "full executor" of Day's funds and "sole heir" of Hopkins' considerable estate and holdings.

Mrs. G couldn't somehow get her mind around any of it.

"*What?* Could you please repeat that?" The judge graciously did. "He left no trust maintenance for her, outside of custody as Mr. Bennet's ward or as a state ward?"

No, Mr. Hopkins did not. The only provisions are in the hands of the executor and sole heir per the private and legally documented agreement he had with the deceased.

Stephie said, "All right, Benn."

Mrs. G's temper snapped and she stated something foul in reference to me "stabbing Ms. Day in the back," having known and "manipulated what exactly was in the Will," and "taking everything from Ms. Day, leaving her with nothing, after all she suffered and endured. Leaving her nothing, except *that place.* That place Ms. Day detests and fears."

From the angle I sat, it caught my attention that Day was sitting beneath a wall design of an eagle, at full wingspan. She was staring at the floor with her feet turned in such a way, as to seem disjointed, unconnected, broken.

Mrs. G was still not happy and Day grabbed her hand, while never looking up and gave the older woman's hand a sharp yank. Mrs. G sat and shut up.

I stared at them boldly, as only a man, who fucking owns the world, her world can, before urging the judge to "please continue and get this done, as soon as possible."

The forms lay side by side.

My signing one set of forms, would give me official control of Day's and Hopkins' monies, and the legal right to keep her with me, as full guardian.

If I signed the other, she would go back to the lockdown, with no foreseeable chance out again and I'd still keep everything that was cashable, which really was a cherry of a sum, not that I was hurting for any.

But, you can never have too much cash and I really do like not having to work everyday.

Mrs. G protested that she could care for Day, but the judge denied her verbal petition on grounds it wasn't in the Will, and not in Day's "best interests." This hearing was for Day's "own good."

Laughable, especially since "for Day's own good" wasn't why he'd put me in charge and given me ownership of everything that should've been hers.

Besides, Mrs. G was still a resident alien and although the Cold War was over, there still could be some questions about her husband's Soviet Russian background.

To translate the judge's speech my way, Mrs. G would never have enough power or money to get Day out.

I glanced at Stephanie, who was smiling ear to ear; she loves seeing herself and Dad in me. She understands and approves of me most when I'm selfish, insensitive, and cold to any woman, but her.

Being a twin with a woman can be a particularly peculiar and intimate relationship; warped, yet, a *forgivably* warped relationship.

I sighed. I signed. The paperwork was done, once Cin gave it her once over to her satisfaction. Everything was in order and the bank was waiting.

I left.

Actually, before I left, I had something to say.

I needed to say it to her face, to Day's beautiful and sometimes coldly serpentine face of innocence and pain, that beautiful façade of the child woman, who could take her own mother's life so graphically, who could attempt to sever her own feet, while she was still wearing them.

And, who even in the middle of her mental and emotional anguish, managed to simultaneously string along two grown men, no, make that three; forgot about slick lawyer Sid.

And, maybe Steve and Pizza Yutz should be lumped in together with Sid.

Or, am I missing someone?

I have my moments, too. I know I'm not *the* sweetest man on the planet. I've been called a bastard, and worse, oftentimes deservedly, to my back and my face, and I will be again.

But, being a bastard, a pimp, a stud is never as insulting and denigrating in tone as being a bitch, a whore, a slut.

My new American Heritage Dictionary has a comment entry, a "usage note," under "mistress" stating that one of their researchers compiled a quick list of licentious names for women, which stopped at 220 words, both old and new.

She located only 20 comparable male terms, then 500 for "prostitute," femaleness, of course being implicit, while for a male of the same, a mere 65.

Plus, being a pimp, a stud, or a Casanova is considered an approving pat on the back in comparison.

All that may not have a lot to do with anything here, but it is *interesting,* and *enlightening.*

"Words have power."

Words that label.

Words of the Law and Justice.

Words of sex and proper deportment.

Words your mother repeatedly whispered softly to you, as

she lovingly tucked you in for the night or pushed you in front of a hungry man, who was starving to defile you.

The list goes on and on.

And, all things being equal, which in some ways, they probably won't be, for quite awhile, women need to cover their asses, their vaginas, uteri, and any other part, physical or mental, we can invade.

We men can't be trusted to take care of *your continuing problems*.

We say we will, but *everyday* childrearing, the female *monthly*, and all those complicated, "soft" and messy things are your worries.

WE MEN are busy.

We're setting and attaining records and goals, which sometimes coincide with your goals, until the next one you set for us gets too hard and we're embarrassed we'll fail or "punk out" or simply "don't know what to do."

Or, until we think we're being ignored.

Or, taken for granted.

Sounds like a woman, doesn't it?

Or, we feel overpressured, by the world, our job, the weight of our own personal problems, or by you, our lovers.

And, then, it's adios and goodbye, Baby.

Day once told me about using what little she had to get what she really wanted.

The bitch sitting before me at the hearing appeared as innocent and vulnerable as a child, and was just as amoral and dangerously captivating in her methods as any dangerous, angry little girl.

She's incomparable in using all her charms: body, face, emotions, problems; whatever would best cut a man off at the knees, put a bull's ring through his nostrils and lead him around by his aching nads.

Believe me, that is an incredible, mind-hobbling ache she can generate, whether it's to her advantage, or not.

And, nasty, controlling old Hopkins, with his blatant lust for her, detested her.

He never loved her. Not enough to get her anything she truly wanted. Except the ice cream.

Nor did he get her anything she truly needed. Except Mrs. G.

Hopkins only wanted to *own* Day, as a possession.

Never to *claim* her, in love, as his.

He was very much like the first investment guy I ever saw face-to-face, as an undergrad. The man, who wore a tacky tie with stethoscopes on it, owned Norman Rockwell prints, not because he loved or respected them, but because they were worth cash. Because others desired them, therefore the price was worth his attention.

I don't know, perhaps that is the way to invest for value, but I always wondered if he'd still feel so comfortably smug about his smart purchases when the market for Rockwells bottoms out and he's holding tons of prints he can't sell and doesn't love in the least, outside their crapped out investment value.

Anyway, the bastard Hopkins left everything to me, his rival, regardless and careless of whether I kept her or not, whether I actually loved her or not, as long as I made certain she gave him "no more of her lackluster participation" in bed with him.

That was "THE DEAL" between us.

Still love me?

I made her actualize her words, that she'd "do *anything,*" for me. When she "swore" she'd never fully capitulate to his will, I emotionally blackmailed her, until she did.

"For her own good," or at least my own.

I've always pretty much gotten my way, no matter how difficult the odds or the person opposing me. I'm used to leading people, who are too afraid, too squeamish, or too prideful to do what they know they need to do, without a hearty shove.

But, by the time I'd tripped over her, I was exhausted of making life and death choices for people, who refused to face their own music and make those decisions.

I was tired of having to carry extra malpractice insurance because *I was* making those kinds of decisions, in their lazy stead.

I'd "sworn," as I left on sabbatical, that the next time I made a life and death anything for someone else, I was gonna get paid a hell of lot more than my usual fee or the usual effusive, grateful thank you's.

And especially more than the I-love-you-so-much-Dr.-Gillespie, BUT "oh, by the way," second-guess lawsuits.

Promise kept from me to me.

The old man had correctly surmised, especially after our porch exhibition in front of both him and Steve, that I could get him what he wanted, that she'd "do anything," probably anywhere, maybe anyone, to please me.

Then, he and I had, literally, in his smoke-filled, back bedroom, shaken hands on it, over his Last Will and Testament.

I was to give her to him, when he came for her.

And, as you well know, I did.

I even went further and jumped in and shored up her jangled nerves and his anticipated equipment failure, and he'd died happily, feeling he'd gotten what he'd wanted from her.

He *was* grateful in his warped way—that I'd allow myself to be maneuvered to serve his favor, because without me, he'd never have gotten her to so utterly "yield" to him.

Although, she was truly only fully yielding to me.

And, it was very much in *my* best interest to manipulate her, until she did, because he meant nothing to me personally, except when it involved Day, to whom he unfortunately meant too much.

Part of him had, I'm certain, counted on her never giving in to him, making it so much less problematic in continuing her life sentence, after his demise.

He'd have never rewarded her or Mrs. G the slimmest dim chance of receiving the illusive key to her freedom, without me— *satisfied or not by her*—even if she had freely given him her "full [sexual] attention."

To be that generous, you would have to love that person, truly be grateful, and care a minimum about their personal welfare.

If he had apparently died of anything other than what he blissfully died of, if I hadn't delivered her to him, on the proverbial St. John The Baptist gold platter, his formal instructions made certain that his estate and final wishes wouldn't have benefited either of us.

All of this for the complete rule of one, fucked in the head beauty, whose mother had failed, pointedly, in trying to do the same—to *control* her.

But, of Mommy, Hoppy and myself, of the three of us taking turns holding her psychologically and physically hostage, only I had actually controlled her, when she was emotionally uncontrollable.

* * * *

Okay, you're silently screaming, "YOU FUCKING, EGOTISTICAL ASSHOLE, SHE CONTROLLED <u>YOU</u>, SUCKER!"

Yes.

I'd let her control me, to and beyond a point or two, when it served my needs; and she'd let me control her will, because she'd wanted me, emotionally and sexually, and, despite all, still desperately wants me.

More than her pride. Which, as she's pointed out, she hasn't any of.

Yes.

She had me, has me by my nads and my ego.

However, remember, in this particular world we all live in— wherein things have changed, but not all that damned much— that I'm also everything she isn't.

I'm a free man, a sane man, a legally powerful man with quite a bit of cash in my pocket.

I can do whatever I damn well please. Hell, I'm a man.

Jeez, how unPC of me.

* * * *

Day is absolutely none of these things and is legally and emotionally only in a position to beg or barter for her freedom, her sanity, and her power.

I sincerely hope that's not a surprise to you.

It's not to her or me.

And, certainly wasn't to Hopkins.

* * * *

Yes, I adore the quixotic her and her incredibly "slamming" body and her fluid mind slipping in and out and around and through . . . ruling my mind.

I truly enjoy being ruled by her. But, I still control her, and "nearly" always did.

Because I let her.

Because it feeds my ego and hers.

Because I so completely get hard and get off on her feeling powerful and manipulating me, of her wooing me, of her getting so completely *inside of me.*

No lover before her ever so intensely wanted me, wanted me enough to whore herself for me; to put aside her personal "sworn" ideals, not even for one breathless moment—*to please me; appease me; to keep me.*

It's entirely selfish of me, as sweet, not so benign Stephie so insightfully pointed out; but, we all pay.

That was Day's high price to have me.

Hell, it's always been my price, with anyone, and she inherently understood that, sometimes better than I did.

God, I can hear you frowning and frothing with indignation and outrage.

Don't get all . . . .

There's no conflict.

Day understands lies and intimate deceit and personal treachery better than I ever will, and with this last "courtly" episode, sponsored by Hopkins, unfolding around her, she knew what I'd done, without being told.

All the veils we'd both persisted in putting up between us were gone, we were both startlingly, unpretentiously naked to the other and she was trembling, but forced herself to stillness, when she saw my feet before her.

Stephie in her usual, emotional semi-obtuseness patted me on the back, on her way out.

Which meant, as usual, when the emotional stakes were high, Cinda at least stood nearby to make certain I was all right, while my beloved twin ducked out on me.

Meanwhile, Sid still hadn't figured out the beautiful and hard to get Stephie and trailed her out.

Idiot. Fired idiot.

Mrs. G stood to defend her charge from me.

Day tensely gestured her away, stood, and met my gaze full on.

I'd told her before, on *that* last day with him, that I'd known *"exactly"* what I was asking of her and I'd known she'd made herself believe that I hadn't.

I also knew, she understood exactly what had happened with us, and why. That I couldn't've been any more open with her.

That I had to usurp control of her, "for her own good," because *she'd withheld from me,* as she'd accused me of, when I'd never mentioned being a surgeon.

And, that even in spite of denying it to herself, I had *truly* stomached and bore for her, her darkest, most shameful secret and its morally heinous repugnance, which far outweighed my being a closet surgeon.

It's odd how, with all that has insidiously pervaded everything around her, Day is still more innocent, in any manner you wish to define "innocence," than I am.

But, legally, that doesn't matter, does it?

I could tell by her eyes, by her anxiety that she wasn't sure what exactly I'd say, in my final decision.

Unlucky her, the one time she can't get into my head.

She'd been right previously though and completely insightful that she could never handle the kind of public life, full of people and worldly concerns, I'd had and which would never fully let me go.

Another hard price. The price of being excellent at what I do.

And, she too is excellent at the many things she does to survive—*one of which is sizing up men.*

When Day'd met me, she'd wanted me because she'd instinctively *known* I was hard, shrewd, and wouldn't fold or let Hopkins completely overrun me.

So there's no surprise to her, deny as she might, that the final choice is mine and mine alone, not hers. She gave it to me. She chose me as her advocate, and, it would seem, unfortunately for her, so did he.

And, to the *highest bidder* I went.

Day was abruptly bone straight; having become the young lady her warped mother had raised, yet hated.

She was the one, who had survived her insane and unloving parents; her unknowledgeable mother, who didn't seem to know that most of those soft, strong ladies of old were exactly like Day.

They survived, as best they could with their bodies and minds, as their only assets or weapons.

Survived against envious and stupid mothers, who threw them to the frenzied sharks; better known as men.

Survived against men, who wielded hard, blunt weapons, such as man's law and his church against them.

Survived against men, who lied to them, used them, discarded them, leaving them with nothing, by callous design or unhappy flaw.

As endearing or frustrating as Day could be as a "child," as a woman she has no peer.

And, she was at that moment, without coaxing, most definitely and defiantly a woman standing before me, facing the results of the role of the dice she'd thrown, and so I quietly said my short, bluntly direct piece.

Mrs. G cried out, while Day, literally, crumpled silently at my feet, her teary face against my legs.

* * * *

Just so you know, I never told Day the exact contents of the conversation between Hopkins and myself, that evening, when Sid came over for his signature for changes to the Will.

That night Hopkins'd sequestered himself and me into his bedroom, and we came to an agreement.

I'd gotten him comfortable and, per his request, I'd popped a noisy video into her machine and left her door open to cover our discussion from the others, in that intimately claustrophobic house, before locking the door and taking a seat across from him.

"She's going back, and soon, Mr. Gillespie."

"There's no need for that. *I'm* here."

"Yes, you are, but you may not be, before long."

"I am so fucking tired of . . . . What game are you playing at now, 'Hoppy'?"

"The *big* game, lad. She's no longer heeding me, because of this damnable, half-crippling . . . . *But mostly, because of you.* She has no right to deny me—."

"Let's not start that again. She has the right, the obligation to herself to say 'no' to you, if and when it pleases her."

"*No, she does not.* Not before pleasing me. And, neither do you."

Angry red silence fell between us, as he studied me and I tried to figure his angle.

Hopkins' angles were always far out of any ken that I'd ever known, or had cared to know. He asked me to bring a file to him that was lying on the bed. I got it for him, but he wouldn't take it.

"Read it, Mr. Gillespie. I wouldn't want the two of us not being on the same page in the same book because crucial information was withheld from you. You stayed with us with your eyes wide open, now look a little deeper. Scorch your eyes right out of their sockets."

He nodded to the blue file and was silent, while I read. I glanced, then read a little deeper for confirmation before casting it down on the table between us.

"I already knew this." My statement amazed him.

"*Really*? She would *never* tell you *that*."

"No, she didn't. She doesn't know, she doesn't *want* to know. It kept bothering *me* though, constantly. *THE* lie. The one *most* unsettling thing here, among so many unsettling things. It wouldn't leave me be, so when an opportunity finally presented itself . . . ."

I gestured slightly to the dark blue file with the official pages inside.

"I received the exact same results."

He nodded thoughtfully, understanding fully when and how, and now why.

"No wonder you were so cruel and bruising with that needle. I'm a little surprised that you stayed once you had the results; then again, perhaps I'm not. The information, I'm sure, added to the *heat* of the situation, and she is a great—."

"*Don't* say it, whatever it is you want to rub my nose in and denigrate her behind her back with, don't bother. You know. I know. You don't care and I don't care. Neither of us has a moral backbone.

"Let's move on. What the fuck do you want with me, here,

now, in this room?"

"The same thing I always want."

"Well, I can't give it to you. I'm not her."

"On the contrary, I've seen you do things with her, that . . . . She'd do *anything, for you,* if that's what *you* want. And, I'm quite certain, *you* can make her do *anything.* I no longer can and never could to the remarkable extent that you do.

"Presently, she barely heeds me, as it is, and will barely allow me to . . . . She's *concerned* for me, to preserve my 'fragile' health, of course, which doesn't matter to me. Not with all the ground I'm losing to it, and to you and your desire to own her—."

"'Own her'? Slavery, even white slavery is illegal, you know." He smiled, grimaced really.

"Well, lad, we all tell lies to ourselves, don't we? Her most of all. Why not you, as well. You don't want to 'own her,' but nevertheless, I will *leave* her to you, *if* you will order her to—."

"I'll not 'ord—."

"*Don't interrupt me, boy!* I'm not one of your fawning surgical staff."

He let up on his flash of anger and laughed.

"The anger, the frustration, the . . . desire. You understand desire, obsessive, addictive desire?" He chuckled under his breath.

"Of course you do, don't you? Well, it's too much of a strain, especially with you pulling her away from me. You'll wait, I'll die and you'll quietly take her when no one is noticing. *That will not happen.*

"I have full legal control of her and any money due her. My full, personal estate—*everything*—will be yours, because I have no one, who is worth leaving it to and because there's no way she could handle it anyway. I know, Mr. Gillespie, you don't need it, but money is always such a nice bonus incentive, isn't it?

"And, 'you can never have too much of it, not really.'

"That *is* what your father taught you, isn't it? Besides, you can always humour her, by saying you didn't *want* it, you don't *need* it, but what the hell, keep it. But, then again, how will you keep it from becoming a wall between you and her?

"Personally, boy, I don't care; I only care how *you* handle *my* wishes.

"All of this is, *Dr.* Gillespie, on stipulation, of course, of if I die of 'natural causes' and no obvious 'foul play' *and* with you fulfilling my following request. Only then will any judge, who draws the final ruling for my estate, find you in the position, by my written permission, to keep her, as her legal guardian.

"I get pushed down the beach stair or my neck gets snapped from an alleged fall from my bed, at her coaxing or by your inordinately strong hands, or I die of some "mysterious cause," and the bitch goes straight back to the daily, institutional hell she deserves."

"Why?"

"Because I can. Because she has always, in one way or another, been mine, and yet defied me. *Because I will have what I want.*

"Because, if Twyla hadn't interfered, trying to get something for nothing, I would have had all of her long ago and today there would be no question of Day completing her required duties to me, and . . . there'd be no you."

I didn't want to ask and my voice was softer than I'd meant it to be, I knew what he'd say, but I asked to be certain.

"What 'request'? What *exactly* do you *want,* from me?"

"I've seen her bend to your will, seen her go far out of her way to curry your indifferent favour and win you back, while she thumbs her nose at me, defying and denying me. For all this, I ask only one simple thing of you.

"Deliver her to me in the manner you know I want, whenever I choose to have her or, should I say, receive from her what I want, per your directive."

He didn't say anything for a long while.

"If I die or am worsened by it, by her active, full submission to me, of her full and lustrous participation . . . .

"In my incapacitation or death, if there is a smile on my stricken face, no one need be concerned.

"Everything, including the woman herself will be yours. It's that easy, boy. I've already had Sid put it in black and white, all nice and legal for you. Just sign and deliver."

"You're vile and insane. Completely, indecently insane."

"It's congenital, I'm sure.

"I have also taken note that you have not flat out, self-righteously said 'no.' What do you say, lad. Is there someone else, more intriguing waiting in your old life for you? How untaintable and sanctimonious are your morals and ethics? What exactly do you call honour?

"And, the BIG question—is there anyone you want more than my beautiful, sensuous Day? There isn't anyone else for me and so I believe we two are on the same page."

We weren't quite on the same page—same book, same chapter, but . . . .

My brain seized and shut down in large sections, while other parts of my "grey matter" became fluid and raced swiftly and vigorously.

How could one woman, without a dime to her name, without any ambitions or desires, except having me, wanting me . . . ?

This kind of intense inflation to my ego by her, this perpetual contamination by the both of them, this onslaught to what Mama called my "moral fiber" cannot be a great and wonderful thing.

But, then dancing with the Devil is always a learning experience; a samba, a tango of seduction.

And, besides, I wasn't exactly pure when I arrived on his beach.

I'd also noted that he'd said "anyone [I] want more than." That was eerie.

It was exactly what she'd so perceptively asked me the morning after our first night, when I was already finding it difficult to be apart from her.

Great minds think alike. Right?

I also guess the one outstanding thing about wanting her to be shamelessly open and demonstrative with me was that everyone seemed to think they knew everything they needed to know about me; to blackmail me, to coerce me, just because they knew who I wanted.

Because they perceived inequalities, between Day and myself.

Inequalities I myself never really saw as entirely unassailable handicaps or weaknesses.

What couple is absolutely equal in everything anyway?

And, aren't "inequalities" the spice that surprises, that blows your eyes wide open, that momentarily snatches your breath away, or is it just, maybe, the most delightfully sublime experience?

Collectively, all the repulsive things I knew, at that specific moment, didn't matter.

It just didn't deter at all, for one goddamned millisecond, the fact, that sitting before his sick half smile, I still wanted, needed her terribly. Beyond logical reason. Despite the official and ugly report, lying on the table between Hopkins and myself; with its nauseating confirmation of the "official test results" I'd had run previously by my own regular lab.

I made the pact, the Devil's Pact *with him, to have what I wanted,* because simply, I couldn't possibly just trust and wait for him to be kind or die. Not with full and confident hope I'd be able to break the back of his legal wishes.

Bastards, like him never die, when you need them to and their advisors, though they may be spineless wretches, can draw up flawless, titanium-clad legal papers, that even Cinda, ESQ and Associates can find difficult to break.

So, very technically, I . . . *betrayed* Day into his hands, into his lap, and he paid me well, in full, but although successfully accomplishing my mission, some things just never leave my sensitive stomach alone.

Or my too self-absorbed mind which, possibly, found a few of its well-learned, ego-stroking judgments were in error.

Self-realization, self-clarification makes the feet cold, and entirely changes where you thought you were going.

It makes one shrug slightly, then sit quietly, frozen still, like a not yet detected rabbit in a den of slavering wolves, until everything is all clear and balanced—*if it ever is clear and balanced.*

* * * *

The day before the hearing, we were still staying at the hotel, when I took Day aside, in her nervous apprehension.

I reminded her of what I'd told her, in that last hour or so alone with him, that I'd known *exactly* what I'd asked of her, *exactly* what both of us were up to our necks in.

She shook her head in frenetic denial and I put it to "Ms. Day" plainly, about her *secret*, which she'd always feared to think, let alone, admit to or tell me.

The most intimately private thing at the core of, and tainting everything; what her mother knew and that her father, the man married to her mother, was finally informed of, when he was told the emasculating truth, by his best friend, which was why the husband, Day's "Daddy" had left.

The so called best friend, her *"real"* father, just didn't want to be a father, but once she reached a certain age, he did intensely want to be Day's lover, which her "Mommy" said "no" to, then, reluctantly, threw him out.

The woman had a motherly backbone for a day or a week.

Her action was already too late and only a morally righteous reflex and was soon undermined by an amoral, emotional engine, fueled by hatred for her own life in general and for her daughter in particular, and a weakness for money and not working for it.

The woman, without conscience and in full self-involved

determination weakened.

Mommy's calculated, thoughtless solution was to retrench, recultivate and sustain a strange, unhealthy home environment, which included having her only daughter's fallopian tubes severed- —*a tubal ligation; having her "fixed" as if broken,* as if something'd been horridly wrong with Day.

It certainly wasn't done for the girl's health.

All of this was done with the "father's" blessing.

Mommy then offered Day up as sacrifice to his lust and her own lazy avarice.

When Day told her "no" with a long knife, many, many, *many* times, the woman, who'd reneged on throwing Hopkins out, was busy wheedling, arguing, and inculcating the "benefits" of her case to young Day for a permanent, sexual match between the unfortunate girl and her own genetic father.

Day's most private, secret of secrets.

Day slapped me, open-palmed. It was a tapping sting, compared to when she'd bitchslapped me with the back of her hard, little knuckles.

She looked terrified, and her copious, silent tears were back.

"Benn. I'm sor—! You shouldn't—."

Her voice fell in volume, it was almost inaudible. There was no one in the suite but us, and still she didn't want the world to hear.

"No. No. That's not true. That's not true. That's not true. No. No. No. No. *No.*"

She was so intensely upset and in such monumental denial, in this blatant, repeated, emotional lie, for which I had blood and DNA matched, official test results of the physical truth.

She was so intensely upset, that her sharply heightened anxiety, as if it were my own, overchurned my stomach, before I could think some mind trick to quell it.

I just made the "porcelain receptacle," as I emptied everything but my stomach's lining into the toilet. It was not unlike that first night, when after she'd seen me watching her with him, I'd puked our combined, bewildered anxieties out through the jumper rails.

That first night, the first time I'd seen them together, and she'd turned her face from his, toward mine, as he . . . .

Day'd followed me into the bathroom; it was an automaton motion on her part. I closed the lid and flushed, then she sat quietly on the toilet lid.

I proceeded to brush and rinse the stomach acid from my mouth, knowing it was highly possible my guts would roil inside out again, because there was a sharp, hard cramp inside me still, from her.

She held her knees pulled up tightly in her arms, with her head tucked down.

A human, fetal football.

She said absolutely nothing and absolutely did not move from the spot. Silence and immobility and something about her kept me from picking her up and carrying her out to at least a softer seat.

Silence and immobility, for hours, till I was out of the immediate area for about thirty seconds, signing for room service— *more ginger ale for the nausea,* when she ghosted herself from her potty perch to lock herself in our bedroom.

Fairytales require odious fiends and dire, personal straits and a certain ironclad aptitude to sustain and live in a dream, even if it's not a tangible actuality.

Or, in easier words . . . .

I should've kept "my knowledge" to myself, kept that sheer veil of *pure* renunciation between us, at least one more day, since we had court the next, which was enough strain.

But, it had seemed a *logical* bit of business to get out of the way between us; removing the last bit of . . . .

Only actually doing it, quite plainly, didn't make as much sense, as I'd thought. Stupid me, thinking she'd be relieved to know that I knew her truth, that she wouldn't have to lie anymore—*at least to me,* if not to herself.

I was first in every graduating class I ever belonged to. Some days the brains don't show at all, do they?

Mrs. G was totally pissed at me when she got back and found our little mistress silent and barricaded in, without much for explanation from me.

I wasn't going to tell her.

Plus, my stomach was killing me; Day was mutely ripping me apart.

Mrs. G went to bed angry.

I slept on the sofa, and only woke when Day touched my face. My gut, which had finally quieted, was flip-flopping again in her presence. I didn't turn on the light, even though I couldn't really see her full expression in the near pitch dark of the room.

She was still without speech and staring at me, eyes like saucers, and no, I wasn't afraid she'd stab me with something, although, I'd left my titanium pen in my coat in the bedroom—.

UNLESS IT WAS IN HER FIST!

Which it wasn't.

Sorry, just fuckin' with yah.

I did think of that later, but not right then. Right then she was a cold, lost little girl, who'd been unloved by her mother and loved in the wrong way by . . . .

I pulled back my cover and she slid in against me, naked as nearly always. My cock ignored my gut and went granite immediately at the feel of her abundant curves and soft skin on mine.

You know how cocks are, you try to keep them civilized and restrained and they spring up, without warning or discretion, with a lot less provocation than a naked, voluptuous Day.

When I did nothing about it, she didn't like it, as I interminably waited for my dick to soften and relax. It'd been a bad day among many other bad days, and tomorrow would be even more stressful, standing before the judge.

Day faced me, pillowy breasts and silken pubes brushing and pressing hard against me, which didn't make my "granite" situation easier, most certainly not softer.

And, her voice.

It's amazing how much biting pain and pleading anguish can be expressed in a barely audible whisper.

"Don't you want me, anymore?"

* * * *

She'd been wrong that afternoon when Steve watched us, Day *does* have "shame"; strong, personal shame, and there are some things even Prince Charming, The Gallant Knight, and The Swaggering Hero all combined would never be able to "take care of."

Or "make better."

And, it's not really unusual, in *everyday life*, for a disenchanted Hero, some idiot, who believed he was "head over heels" and entirely shielded from all doubts, becomes abruptly disillusioned by a frigid, breathstealing submersion into reality, to find himself entirely not able to stomach that reality.

He's reminded he can't control and fix or love away everything that happens to her, whoever *his* her is, which means he is not a HERO, merely a man.

Small "m." Small "a." Small "n."

Scary, isn't it?

And, in this cold sweat realization, he . . . runs. Bolting through the cluttered jungle underbrush, like a frightened, juicy tapir before a starving jaguar.

And, he never returns.

I've seen that happen, a lot, a hell of a lot of times.

In fact, it's in *my* bloodlines, genetically encoded, practically, which is why Stephanie and I have so few pictures of Dad.

Speaking of frigid splashes of reality, remember, my own little handshake tête-à-tête and "legally signed"—*if such an im-*

moral contract truly is legal—pact with Hopkins, was long before I ever saw *the* pictures, the graphic, informative photos of what was left of her mother.

All the little chiseled bits and splattered blood, in full color.

It messes with your head and is a true walk-up call when you equate those pix, as the result of a real and furious, blade-wielding hand; the same talented hand, which so adeptly strokes your piece to iron hardness, and caresses and holds your tender, vulnerable nuts in her gentle palm.

Funny.

Hopkins did have a set, of pictures.

I found them in his bedroom, when I went back to the house, while getting his things in order, before going to the hearing. They were *innocently* lying on his bed in a large envelope. He must've pulled them out just before going to her bed that last time.

I won't speculate what kind of juice he and Sid must still have had, post mortem, in order to get the cops to ignore or put those hideous things back, and not mention them.

Or maybe weak Sid had dropped them off, later, either way . . . .

I burned them. Didn't want Mrs. G or Day seeing those. Not then. It is odd though, that Hopkins'd never shown me.

He probably was truly afraid they'd make my nads shrink in terror to the size of hard little aggie marbles, my cock a mere "dinky pinky," making me completely demoralized, keeping me from my appointed rounds, as official harem master and cunt wrangler.

Thank god, for big sisters, who love photos, too, right? Nothing like a second look at those lovelies.

By, the way, I literally had "Hoppy" buried face down. *No joke. No shit.* That's what you do to make certain anyone digging themselves out of Hell and the eternal grave can't get back to you.

That's not a family, cultural superstition. I saw it in a horror movie once, seemed totally appropriate.

You'd've loved the "official" explanation I gave the funeral coordinator for *that* little request.

* * * *

I sold the Virginia Beach house; he was the only one, who liked it and I put the money from it into a considerable extension and upgrade of the Yucatan beachhouse, shared in the winter with my cousins.

Stephie, in her usual peculiar intensity, didn't like my final decision to not share as much of what I'd received, as she'd wished.

She hates the Yucatan in any season. Tough.

She'll get over it, she always needs me before I need her anyway, but since I'm such a lady charmer, maybe I'll grovel and give her an ego boost. Our birthday's coming up.

I do what I want, when I want, which means pretty much nothing's changed, and I consult and keep my hands in the game, when it's a good idea.

I finally married and rent out Hopkins' forest house and my house when we're not around.

We usually spend summers in Scotland, since our honeymoon there.

Day *loves* it, the grey granite, the heather, the thistles, and the hardy, humorous, and directly honest people. They've welcomed us, the "exotic" Americans. Quaint and sweet of them, they could say a lot worse, since I am the only man for kilometers with a nanny for my wife, not my kids.

My Day can now stand most crowds pretty well and can make a crucial decision without help from either of us. For instance, choosing a fruit preserve for her peanut butter no longer puts her off her game.

I quietly had Cinda and her law pack contest his Will, in her favor, as his sole surviving blood kin, with "extenuating circumstances," meaning I did it "quietly," because I did it behind

Day's back and Mrs. Gorbachev's.

Day's still not admitting the blood tie and Mrs. G . . . .

I'd never tell her, unless specifically asked to by Day.

It's been pretty much all to naught anyway, but Cinda's working another angle, because even in death, he screws his one and only daughter over. She remains destitute and in *my custody* or it's back to *that* place.

And, if I muck with the Will in too much detail, trying to deconstruct it, it ALL goes away.

I believe she should get what she deserves; but . . . .

The money, the properties, and the stocks, etcetera don't really matter at all, only Day does, and he had it so tightly set up that, when it all goes away, the first "thing," the very first "item" on the list to go, of course, will be her.

She's tied to his estate, like prized livestock. She's *still* his "property" or, perhaps, I should say mine.

But, I won't.

He desperately wanted her hamstrung and dependent, even now that he's gone; it kept him hard when alive, knowing that, and probably still does.

It is a "loving father," a "good man," who thinks of everything and fully provides for his child.

Surely hope he likes burrowing to China. Via Hell.

Day has a generous allowance though, but still doesn't want much, except me.

Yeah!

She smiles a lot now.

You should see her.

She likes being able to do things for others and getting out, which are two things that make her "feel powerful" and "free."

Also, she can run fairly well for short distances, to her pure enjoyment; however, she oftentimes has darkly sad moments, after playing with or patiently giving simple dance instruction to some of the local kids.

I . . . I abhor those moments.

So, next week, we take the leased jet back to the States, to confer with a couple of friends, who specialize in reproductive microsurgery, and their med group on our fertility options.

They're a great couple and already have both Day's operative and pathology reports from her forced sterilization, and think our tubal reversal prospects look fairly good.

Crossed fingers and knocking on wood.

By medicine, God, or adoption, I'll make this work for her, and me.

By the way, Mrs. G can't wait till we swing back to Mexico for our next visit; she has a mutual crush on one of my cousins, even though she's still a little pissed with me. Although her absolving me would be a bonus, it isn't necessary to my personal peace of mind.

She can't quite yet completely forgive me for the things she now knows I did, to get custody of her "Ms. Day."

Day told her *quite* a bit.

I wouldn't've, but Day didn't want another lie between them. I do know she hasn't told Mrs. G about her paternity. I think she will, eventually.

Nevertheless, Mrs. G is softening in my favor, because she always did like me, as a choice prize for her deadly young lady and, besides, *I'm just so thoroughly charming, as well you know.*

And, *My* Day, *Ms. Day Gillespie,* forgave me right away, of course, standing beneath the eagle on the wall, at the custody hearing.

When I proposed a life of freedom for her, imprisoned in my arms. She even forgave me for holding out on her, after I shook hands with Hopkins.

Behind her back.

She forgave me, because she understands I'd "do *anything*" for her, even ruthlessly, shamelessly swallow my personal pride and shed any moral prejudice I'd had remaining, to use her against herself.

To *her benefit* and my own, and hopefully, our future child.

Because I really and truly "only want" Day.

—oo—

www.Neale-Sourna.com

or

http://hobble.neale-sourna.com

Aegis
A Novel Fable of Sexual Control, Compulsion, and Release

by

Neale Sourna

[more previously]

Let's just say I was feeling *very* mean.

I'd called Jilli and the little one; but, Grandma Jilli was out or still just shunning me. I left a message, then did what I do, when I'm mean and went to Gina Torres' place.

Dancing is a fair replacement for sex, why else do you think the Puritans had it banned?

But, that kind of potent, lively energy isn't always easily stoppered or redirected, productively or harmlessly. That explains why so many Puritan women ended up dead, by judicially sanctioned drowning and hanging.

I bet a Hell of a lot of them "disappeared," "kidnapped by *Indians*" and such, or more likely a neighbor with an unquenchable, evil thirst and itch.

And, a durable shovel.

I danced hard and passionately, trying to burn out my own "unquenchable, evil thirst and itch."

And, it would appear that some easily misguided men really have a thing about a strappy bra top and pants of pink leather poured over a woman's body, like butter.

Apologies to Gina, but I kind of was the center of a *little* fight between two jerk offs, who looked like they could probably fight better than they could fuck anyway.

My favorite bouncer and all around good guy Che sent me

to the roof to cool off, while he and his boy tossed them.

* * * *

She'd stood out pale, still, and out of place on the energetic dance floor, in that diversely colorful crowd. The same could be said when Cassie followed me to my roof.

My temperature was already running too hot on a chilly night, my jacket'd cast aside, as I lay on my precarious, stories high, cold, stone ledge, nearly exactly where Guy'd come to me that first night.

I was feeling the driving beats from the dance floor below coursing through me, when I asked her what she wanted. Not what the *Hell* she wanted, merely what she wanted.

"Ren." Wow, she's so come to the wrong person.

"Well, Cass, since he and Guy both simultaneously cut my name from their dance cards, I suppose even *you* could arrange that."

She seemed really odd, more so than usual. Normally, she was sort of annoying and cloyingly perky, tonight she was solemn and *driven.* As if she'd come hunting. A predator Miss Cassie is not.

Yet, she'd stepped deep out of her comfortable, private country club zone, deep into "ethnic," "urban" territory looking for *me,* in *this* place, where it was painfully obvious she was unfamiliar with the terrain and terrified of the locals, yet had known *exactly* where to find me.

Someone was tickling her keys, getting her to play a tune she didn't know or could ever play correctly.

I almost felt for her.

"He'd said he'd sent you packing—."

"'*He* said . . . .' Ren *told* you that?"

"Oh, yes, that and lots more. Whore. *(Ouch.)* The *things* you've *made* him do. Pulling him *down* to *your level.* No wonder that . . . that last time with me, he was so—. Why won't you leave him alone?"

I didn't answer that.

Angry people, especially ones feeling righteous, never shut up, so you might as well preserve your energy, until the opportunity when they wind down or worse.

"He . . . he actually *cried*, he came to me for solace and forgiveness and . . . ."

'Solace and forgiveness' . . . and *tears* from the hard-ass king himself? Pun intended.

Someone must've gotten laid very "tender" and the like.

I didn't have to ask, I knew.

Ren'd gone to her, wound her spring ever so well and gently, as she likes and craves, then sicced her on me. *Goddamn that Guy.* This was some of his shit, coaching Ren to use Cassie to fuck with me; and Ren, no doubt, having a fine time of playacting sweetness and gentility.

I am so not having this.

Fuck that innocent dupe crap, fuck them, and fuck her for being so fuckin' stupid not to know that silver spoon up her tight ass sphincter had evidently been stolen from some truly innocent dupe, by her hardworking, underhanded moms.

God! She's still talking, I wished she'd shut the fuck up!

I jumped down.

That scared her.

I was gonna hit her, but freaking her out seemed instinctively a more fun thing to do, which is what happened when I grabbed her by the back of the neck and kissed her, hard. Tongue and all.

It wasn't great. Not because she's a woman, but because she's Cassie.

She shrieked from the back of her throat, as well as she could, since my tongue was deep in her maw, as I also fondled her. It took her a while to think of it, and even longer to get up the nerve to do it, but she finally shoved and I let her push me off her.

Interestingly, she didn't wipe her lips, or spit. Isn't that what most people do when something *wrong* gets in their mouths?

"Ren was so right about you; he said you weren't my friend."

"*I* always said I 'weren't' your friend."

"You want him for yourself. You're in love with him." *I am not being nice to her anymore.*

"I suck his fat cock, the way he likes it sucked, unlike you, who doesn't know what to do with one. Then, he fucks me, down my throat, in my cunt, and up my ass, until his cum shoots out my nostrils."

A visual, physical exaggeration, but she got the picture.

"That's our 'love' making. We 'love' what we do with each other and to each other, and Guy watches us, then Ren watches me do Guy with whatever nasty little things Guy and I 'love' to do.

"Same bed, at the same time and sometimes, *many times, most times*, they are both on me or in me, at the same time.

"There is *no* 'love.' And, you, silly bitch, are the furthest thing from Ren's mind when I'm riding his brother's impressive cock, and his own long, thick dick is shoved, like he loves to shove it, to the hilt up my ass."

She punched me.

Well, *at* me, missed my face, and hit my shoulder. It wasn't a Ren punch, or as powerful as any number of other punches I've received from loving admirers on dates or on the tenuous front line between Crime and the Law; but, I wasn't feeling very Law-like, was sick of her not getting the point, and just really—.

I hit her.

She went down in a gush of blood, and I went down on her.

Well, more precisely, I jumped her ass to beat the shit out of her.

Someone, someone(s) were screaming my name, as if I were doing something outrageously wrong.

Come on. An annoying, rich, former private school bitch like her needs to get a good beat down at least once in her—.

Che yanked me off her and flung me aside, as Rummel checked to see if Cassie were too damaged.

I never noticed how badly off she might've been, since, when I landed, I saw, several yards away—Guy standing and Ren stooped down a few yards behind him. Both dark, part Asian predators watching the show.

If Che had charged a roof admission, he'd've cleaned up.

Guy tossed his fine, Irish linen handkerchief to me. *Oh, red on my wet, hard knuckles.*

Rummel called on her cell phone for an ambulance and asked Che to carry the bloodied princess away, then she asked me to come with her. I heard her and turned to answer, but heard and felt Guy move closer to me, a few paces behind.

"No, Jilli."

"Artemis . . . Arie, come with me." She'd grabbed me.

"No!" I shoved her away. *Hard.* Which scared both of us.

We'd never—.

"This isn't like you, Artemis." Take note, she glanced at Guy with great hatred. "You're falling too far, and when this woman presses charges—."

Guy cleared his throat; he was laughing, but *half* attempting to hide it from Rummel, as he spoke.

"She *won't* press charges."

"And, how may I ask, Lieutenant, *sir*, do you know that?" Jillian Thelma Rummel can be real imperiously snotty sometimes. *I like that in her.*

"Cassie's pride won't let her, and her mom won't either." He and Ren both snickered. I smiled a teensy bit.

Jilli was not pleased with any of it.

"No, really, Detective Rummel, there will be no charges pressed, I can assure you of that. God or the Devil only knows what got inside her and possessed her to come way down here in the first place.

"But, it's really good to know you're on the ball. However, we have private matters to discuss with Detective Belladonna. You're dismissed."

"Arie?"

I backed away and stopped when I felt Guy behind me, his fingertips brushed slightly down the bare skin of my back, then across my ass. An *extremely* sensitive part of me. That was all. I couldn't leave.

Jilli saw my face change and her voice changed in urgency to match.

"*A-Arie?!*" I *wanted* to go to her, to please her—.

"Detective Belladonna, come to me, please?"

I felt a flush of heat, as I managed a glance at her, before turning to go to Ren, who was still kneeling a few yards back. I think she said she "never" wanted to see me again, then left, but I'm not absolutely certain.

Not with Guy and Ren both in my head.

"Cassie's not too bright, is she?" as if Ren needed to clarify that obvious point. "And, I think, *finally,* she'll not want to ever see either of us anywhere near her again. Gosh darn."

Ren looked up at me and softly stroked my crotch, which ached terribly to have him, as I felt it cramp and wet its starving palate.

"I told you before how you should come to me."

I got down on my knees. No hesitation, no thought in the matter. Ren stood to his full height over me. His crotch at my face.

"Now, tell us. Who owns you?"

Since childhood, through job interviews, whenever I've been asked to describe myself, to say what is most important to me, as if I were dissolved like a chemistry project down to one element, the *strong* answer has ALWAYS been one word—independent.

My answer now was *weak.*

"No one—."

"Stop being a child, Arte!"

The vehemence in Ren's frustrated, impatient voice should've, would've frightened anyone else; it made me remember his delicious impatience and force whenever he wants me, when he's inside me.

God, no wonder Jilli looked at me that way.

But, I didn't blush with hot shame this time when I thought of her. There can be a lot of power in—*no shame and no pride.*

Oh, yeah. Here's where I piss away my independence, as well.

"I'm yours." He was reaching for my face, when Guy spoke— *his tone a warning.*

"Ren?" Ren ran that same hand over his hair, instead.

"She said it, Guy."

"She didn't say the proper words."

"'Proper'?"

"It matter—."

"You and your—. I *really* want to fuck her, Guy! *Now.*"

"Like Tsianina?"

After the mention of Ren's homicide deceased wife, the rest was a chastisement in that odd Pidgin of theirs, of Chinese mixed with French and Portuguese. They only do all three languages when something's extremely critical.

I gotta get into Berlitz®, Living Language®, or something.

Ren stepped aside, taking my power over him away from me and giving it to Guy, who waited, still as death, while his brother paced, barely contained, for me to say the magic words.

"You . . . own . . . me." I knew it before I said it that that wouldn't please the number one guy in my life.

"Who owns you?" Guy asked. Okay, the *right* magic words.

Guy knew I knew he had me. That he was breaking me first. If for no other reason than he's far more patient than I am.

"René and Guy Fellowes *own me.*"

He nodded slightly. Ren snatched me to my feet to stare at me as though to kiss me, but instead, tore away my bra's leather lacings . . . .

END OF EXCERPT ONE

www.Neale-Sourna.com

or

http://aegis.neale-sourna.com

LIBIDINOUS 1:
Erotic Exercises

featuring

Steve's Monkey's Paw
(aka: Steve's Poe Paw)

Whoever came up with "guys don't make passes at girls, who wear glasses" was seriously stupid.

Alex's Managing Executive, Kara, wore horn-rimmed eyeglasses, conservatively classy office dress casual, and her dark hair smoothed back in a no frills chignon; all to no avail. She was "definitely, definitely"—*I felt as half-witted and out of my depth, as that idiot "Rainman" around her.*

A brown goddess, who was wholesome, yet unassumingly sultry.

And, in my exceedingly well-educated opinion, she was entirely failing to hide her mischievously bouncy, firm breasts and ass under the crisply bland professional façade.

The façade, which I couldn't believe was deterring Alex, the biggest, most successful and unrelenting sexhound I'd ever known.

It'd been a long while since he'd seen me, so, I'd decided to come out of hiding.

I was visiting him at his office and catching up on the last few years and all that kind of thing. He was installing a new piece of phone equipment and software himself.

Not good.

Alex likes to do things himself, that's why he'd opened his own successful business. The man's a true god working with people, female or male, especially female; but, he's all left thumbs with anything with cables.

"Um, excuse me, Kara. Alex needs you." She immediately

got that look smart women get of "I knew Mr. Know-It-All would need me."

Alex had changed.

When her incredibly fine ass accidentally brushed against his well-educated crotch, as she entered his personal desk space, he didn't even smirk, let alone attempt to spoon her, as I've often seen him do to those with less obviously well-endowed charms.

He wasn't the same.

Kara is *a big girl* in <u>*all*</u> *the good ways*, yet he actually backed away, as she took the cables of the new hardware and deftly switched the end connections, which we two smart frat men hadn't figured out.

Why study instructions, which are so often badly and confusingly done these days, anyway.

Besides, *Ms.* Know-It-All didn't look either.

However, she did look at Alex. A lot.

Which he, of course, would never notice, since he *always* gets looked at a lot. The thick, Black Scot-Hispanic hair, the perfect skin and musculature, the clear blue eyes, with "all that abundant charm glossing over all that reckless danger," or so states my kid sister, repeatedly.

Lucky Alex.

For myself, women of Kara's quality, *never* look at *me* that way.

I'm "not hideous," as my small-brained sister once pointed out, but "well, Alex is well Alex."

Me, I'm just a generic looking Polack, who doesn't turn heads or get the hot cream liquefying and rushing down the insides of welcoming thighs, just because I'm in their proximity.

We'd both watched Kara return to her office, which was across from and in full sight of his.

"She so wants you, man." I got a blank, unfathomable stare from those all too perfect eyes of his.

"What?"

"Kara wants you."

Reading faces.

When you go on cat crawls and bar hops, also know as "pussy prowls" and "bunny hops or skips," with Alex, you become a genius at reading faces.

You, also, hate it. At first.

Later, you get addicted, watching too eager faces, too afraid to approach *the godling,* but who ask *me* tips about how best to approach *him.*

Oh, yeah. Put out, then I'll inform you that *I may take Alex' leftovers, but he* never *takes mine.*

On reading faces.

Alex had gotten some subtle, new expressions, since last we'd faced off. New subtle expressions to hide showing his true feelings for people constantly falling all over him.

He's harder to read now, but for a man known for his genial casualness, he was proving with Kara to be unmistakably *too* concise about nearly every movement and tone of voice of his that could be construed sexually.

I mean he has the utter command of whatever the rest of us will never have, including never having to worry about being taken to task for sexual harassment—*except perhaps as a plaintiff not a defendant,* with the constant offers and innuendo that can gravitate to the man.

And, here he is tipping on rice paper and eggshells with a bombshell in his sights.

Just look at her.

Just listen to her, with a voice as smooth as warm cum sliding down cool crystal glass. She *had* to be at the extreme top of his "to do" list, but he wasn't acting like it at all.

Something huge *had* made him change.

Reading faces.

Kara's expressive face is a true joy to read; especially, her very dark, old soul eyes, which, I absolutely swear, *sparkled* when interacting with Alex. How the hell could he not—?!

"I repeat, again, Mr. Hearing-Impaired. The lovely Ms. Kara wants you."

"She's my exec, Steve, employee technically, though I'm asking her to go partners. She's brought in so much lucrative business with her innovations."

He shook his head, in *my* complete disbelief.

"Kara's a friend. Smart, exceptionally capable, absolutely indispensable, a brilliant researcher and innovator. Did I say smart? And—."

"Stunningly beautiful. Seductively gorgeous."

He was silent, then shrugged, as if *that* didn't matter.

Was this Alexander "The Horn," who'd always received comprehensive BJs, handjobs, or fucks in any aperture of his choosing, from practically anyone he chose for the blessed opportunity?

He really *couldn't* see Kara's obvious but reserved interest? Her seductive . . . everything?

"You're *not* dating her?"

"N-no." Nice, but how to get her to notice *me*, beyond basic, common civility because I was in the room, let alone go out with her, was another matter.

Bright light bulb over head.

Our minds can forget a billion gazillion things, then, at the most crucial, Lucifer-illuminated moment, it's there. The number of that cute, dumb girl, who'll do *anything* for very little coaxing.

Or Grandma's monkey's paw.

Damn hideous thing!

Gave me nightmares, as a child. Inherited it with a box of other "memorabilia," better known as old lady crap.

Gran'd sworn someone in the family'd gotten it directly from

Poe, who'd written *THE* story. You know, *The* Edgar Allen Poe and "*The* Monkey's Paw".

Oh, yeah, I believed that.

Although, it is amazing how much we don't believe, until an intense, longing desire makes it all believable.

Alex and I watched the new toy giving number, name, time of call, and tons of other profound data; "even from voicemail."

He was proud. It was so exciting. Oh, joy. Neato. Yawn.

He was fascinated by his new plaything, while I watched Kara moving around interacting with the others outside his office, envisioning her strong and well toned, shapely legs vised around me.

And at their center, her dark and humid triangular arrow of lust pointing me, directing me . . . .

I'll hit that target, if he won't.

"Hm? What, Alex? 'What am I thinking?' Nothing. Just nothing. Let's go eat."

Long lunch. Catch up.

Here and there pick info about Kara. More catch up.

It's been great seeing you, Alex. See yah again, soon. No, I won't wait so long, next time.

The usual, insincere bullshit.

Fast car.

Home.

"Where's that damned box of yours, Gran?" Monkey's paw, monkey's paw . . . *paw.*

Ugh! Still goddamned hideous!

I grabbed the brightly furred, bony, black-skinned thing, then put it back, dropped it really, as if it were a flaming, taboo object.

Thought hard and long.

I needed to be unambiguously, absolutely correct, and not

mess up, like the silly and pathetic, old geezer couple in the story.

Heart pounding, I held that cursed thing and silently wished the precise words of power I felt would work perfectly. Remember, "in the beginning was the Word."

Of course, typically, it picked then to storm and rage overhead, complete with lighting flashes and tons of rain.

I waited.

And, waited. Nothing. *Nothing.* For the better part of an hour.

Fuck it.

I went outside to watch bitchy Mother Nature's little I'm God show, and my own vaporizing breath in the chilly, wet suburban night.

One minute later, a sports car pulled up in the wrong direction and jerked to an abrupt, screeching, haphazard stop at my curb, as if it'd been turned off while still geared in drive.

Eventually, Kara stumbled out, and hesitatingly walked across the expanse of my yard.

No umbrella. *No shoes.*

What I'd mistaken for a trench coat was a thick bathrobe getting soaked heavily with rain.

Disbelieving my eyes, I breathlessly jumped off the porch to meet her. She came straight to me, and I removed her rain-streaked horn-rims.

Her magnificent eyes were scared, confused, and . . . obstinate.

You get ten novena, Gran. Thanks.

"Come inside, Kara."

* * * *

I locked the door, then walked around her.

Beautiful, simply stunning—even drenched, pissed, and trembling violently.

I reached for her robe; she tried to stop me.

"No, Kara."

She . . . let me, against the hard and futile resolve in her burning, dark eyes . . . .

[more, available at www.neale-sourna.com/steve1.html]

Silver Pole
(from Libidinous 1)

by

Neale Sourna

[more previously]

G'd left for a last minute upscale, bachelor party, when Max, I-Am-An-Ass-And-Completely-Spineless, said Dark had finally "requested" I dance for him.

Yes, Max made finger quotes.

I'd asked Ginger once if she liked dancing for Dark. She giggled.

Remember, with G, giggling means me, or money.

Translation, she doesn't like men, but she'd even fuck him, since he pays well.

He'd better because I can charge more than the others. I get the patrons to come inside, and bring their friends, and I keep them all there longer and cumming right here in my hot, little hand.

I really considered not dancing for that imperiously bossy snot though.

But, maybe I'm stupid, because Dark's sudden interest in a private dance, after ignoring me, except for my general dances and to taunt me, had me a smidge intrigued.

Well, actually, more than a smidge.

* * * *

He didn't want me on his lap, so I and my delicate, gold Egyptian bracelets gyrated and twisted, and displayed and fingered and shook my more obvious assets from a distance.

He seemed pleased, while Shadow *[his huge bodyguard]* looked on.

Minutes later, Shadow put down lots of Mr. Franklins. I guess his boss didn't want to get his hands dirty.

I was reaching for the loot.

"Again."

"They're your Bennies," I said.

This close to him, this long, it was starting to get to me that he never looks at me like anyone else does.

Not like his Shadow, who was trying hard *not* to look at me. I know when a man's looking at me, and Shadow'd lost the battle.

The hard proof being the growing precum stain, from his stiff billy club in his pants that he tried to modestly shift to a more comfortable position.

Unless, of course, he had a big thing, for his boss.

"Come here."

The sahib indicated I may now approach, and buff his lap, which I did thoroughly. The song ended. Shadow piled on the Poor Richards.

"Again." Greedy bastard.

Dark peeled off his long, stylish jacket. A little warm, I guess.

Y'know, others want lots of dances, too, but they don't have the cash or credit, or they're afraid they'll cum their slacks.

Dark seemed to be holding his cream, but his trousers were becoming less slack the more I rode his very expensive imported, custom tailored fabric.

Then, he touched me.

"No touching!"

I'd dismounted so fast, I don't think he'd expected it. The look on his face said touching me was no overinfatuated mistake.

As *they* always say.

Tiny Natalie'd had some queer *lick* her ass just yesterday.

Totally creepzoid.

We do a lot. But, it's a *service*, a *special service,* and it has its limits.

Let's face it; we're vulnerable—*naked, outweighed, unarmed, with help far enough away that we could get seriously damaged or dead before the bouncers get to us.*

So, touching me . . . us is very much breaking the law.

And, *my* law.

Most people still like to think we're wearing pasties or nude plastic or Sally Rand feathers, "if these kinds of places must exist," they say.

But, no, the law says nude's—*fine, opening my legs*—fine, touching myself or another performer's anything is—*fine*; but customers touching us . . . me is forbidden.

As I rub my body against theirs.

I'm on . . . I *am* that *thin, fragile* line between voyeurism and participation, stripping *(Since I'm naked, I strip your mind, not my clothes.—Good, huhn?)* and prostitution.

"Dez, it was just your waist I touched."

"It doesn't matter, Dark. *You* touch nothing."

"All right. I'll behave. Finish. Please?"

I didn't like the look in his eyes, I couldn't read it, and, the pit of my stomach churned. Never a good sign.

"If you want more, Dez. A penalty fee?"

Where was Shadow pulling those bills from?

He never put his hand in a pocket, no bill fold or wad seemed to be in his huge hand, and then *Blam!* He put down ten of them this time, for his master; fanned so I could count.

"You're not stupid, Dez, you know I like you. I just momentarily forgot proper decorum."

"Bullshit." He smiled at my anger, which pissed me good.

"Okay, Dez. One last dance. You get paid, and I'll go. I'll never come back here to Max', unless you give me permission."

I had to think about that one. The money was better than great, and there'd be more, he always pays, even if he only watches for thirty seconds. And, then his dark, royal pain in my ass would leave; he could dry hump himself.

I wished he'd stop looking like he knew exactly what I was thinking, which, of course, I knew he did.

So, I Salome'd again, and he asked me to straddle him, which is not unusual, especially from a high-paying client.

I mounted him and his eyes held mine for a long time, his prodigious bulge between my legs, throbbing deliciously, making my bare pussy dampen its tongueless mouth. I tried to move off the expensive fabric, before I—.

"Wet it, Dez, I don't care."

How'd he know I was getting so wet? I thought to disobey, but I liked the constant throb his cock was singing to my cunt. I wanted more. He could tell.

"Put your hands on my shoulders, and lean into me."

I hesitated, but finally did it, and it felt *wonderful,* but I was loosing control, and the position put his hot lips too close to my breasts. If I'd been flatterchested we would have stayed within the law, but my tit brushed his hot mouth and he grabbed me and sucked.

Pulling away made him suck harder, biting just a bit, and his pants got wetter, at least from my side.

He smiled, mouth full of me, knowing he had me, knowing he was getting my body, that's controlled by me, that serves me, to betray me.

I pulled away to dismount, and his teeth let go, but he held me on his hard bulge, pushing it up into me.

I wanted it, but I wasn't having it, as I shoved to get away. He grabbed a handful of hair on the back of my head.

Piss me! Tryin' to <u>control</u> me.

I backhanded him, and, suddenly, he had a switchblade at my ribs.

"She's thinking whether or not I want her enough not to slice her beautiful body, or if I'm afraid someone might hear her call out, and come for her."

He pulled my head to his.

"Delectable Dez, who's going to run through *that* door and into *him*? And, if they got past him, who'd run up on *me*? Even for you."

"What d'you want?"

"Control of you." Thought so. I elbowed him in the neck.

He let go.

I screamed and made a break to pass the huge guy, who moved faster than a guy his size usually does. I think he's made out of granite, too.

And, by the way, I didn't hear any help coming.

Goddamn that mouth-breathing Max.

I knew it was stupid from the start, but I kept going anyway, and turned around. Dark was able to inhale and swallow again. Scarily, he'd let me go, but the knife'd never left his fingers, which it did now, as he threw the blade point into the floor.

At least he really didn't want to cut me.

I ran past him to the other door, a sometime dressing room/ stage exit.

I never made the exit, as he pinned me with his hard body, titside, to the cold wall.

"Let's talk, Dez, or rather you listen. Your buddy Ginger's working a *very* private party.

"*I'm* throwing *that* party, so I can have this one, with you, without her overprotective and intrusive interference.

"Which all means, that I know you, that you'd probably let me hurt you, just to not *obey* me, therefore, *you will obey me* or it'll be one call, one word from me, and she'll discover the unspeakable joys of a gang bang."

Damn. I couldn't even hit him with an elbow or knee.

"You're insane."

He ran his hand down my bare curves and behind, then slipped his long fingers deep inside me. My gasp wasn't because it hurt.

"No. I just get what I want. And, you know exactly what I want from you."

He removed his probe to smell and taste me off his fingers, let me go, and sat down. He pulled the blade out of the floor and put it away.

"You're taking too long, Dez. Unzip me and mount up. *Now.*"

He smiled in that all too annoying, owns-the-whole-fucking-world . . . and-you-too way of his, knowing I take direct orders badly, but, because of Ginger, that I was taking *this* one.

I went to him . . . . [more]

END OF EXCERPT TWO

www.Neale-Sourna.com

or

http://libidinous.neale-sourna.com

All Along The Watchtower
From Book Two

by

Neale Sourna

anahk Tor The Destroyer, The Mother and Child Killer, and The Betrayer of All Whom He Loves tiredly swallowed down the bitter last of whatever he was drinking.

He had presently forgotten the name of the strong, dark liquid, which meant it was doing what he wished of it—*making him forget, anesthetizing his hurt mind.*

Keeping the hideous past at bay.

It did nothing for the present, however, as some portentously loud idiot, who thought himself more important than anyone present, and perhaps *more important* than anyone else in *all* the dusty city of Tash'k't, including the high royals themselves, was berating and beating a half crippled youth.

The boy was covered from head to toe, face heavily swaddled in the veiled Tuareg manner, as the Fool beat him, because the boy would not fetch for him.

The youth was not one of the family, who ran this . . . establishment, this foul piss-hole, nor did the boy work here.

If the colossal Fool had truly been of any import, he would not have been in *this* place.

The boy took the unjustified mistreatment and retrieved what the man wanted from the barmaster, then returned quickly, and spilled most of it.

The drenched Fool did not find it as uproariously amusing as Tor and pretty much everyone else in the place.

And the useless buffoon did not notice, as he further beat the youth, that he would not be able to pay his way. The youth had fast, subtle hands that had liberated the bully's money bag from him.

No one noticed, except Tor, who had been intently watching the Thief, as soon as he had entered.

His eyes stalked the youth, now especially, as if he were prey, because there was something disturbingly familiar in the way he moved, in the way he held himself, despite the fact that Tor had never seen this boy with the lameness of leg and arm before.

Tor allowed his interest to wane once he lost sight of the Thief in the noisy, jostling crowd, and was now half listening to someone with an unfamiliar accent woefully going on and on beside him, about all the city gates being locked indefinitely, before asking him what he thought.

Tor leaned his aching head back against the wall a long while, because he did not care to think, which he truly could not at the moment.

He did agree to whomever had spoken, that there had to be some way out, but for himself, it was not worth the trouble or blood to draw his axes; despite the fact he was not finding much comfort from his vexations in the drink, the herbs, or the company.

"Surely, anahk Tor of The Csokas, you have seen and caused *worse* 'vexations' than you now feel. So, do not bother lying to yourself or to me, or bother trying to drown and numb your senses, Betrayer."

Tor swallowed hard the last of the spit that was quickly evaporating from his mouth and throat.

Except *her*, no one these past years had ever called him "Betrayer"; not directly to him, not if truly knowing who he was. They said it of him, in general reference, never knowing who he was.

Those unfortunate few who had recognized him would approach in anger, then fall back in their alarmed and wiser cowardice of the infamous Magyar-Egyptian. They would abruptly find their lives far more cherishable than whatever grudge they held against him and his broadaxes.

And, their grudges were great, and intensely personal.

A large minority, who were too stupid, too hurt and forlorn, or too something would fling themselves at him—in suicidal madness, because *they could not kill him.*

The Mare or Whoever would not permit it. He was protected. At least from the stupid ones—*seeking justice.* The others, who recognized him and feared him, avoided him.

This curt person with the strange accent did not fear him or avoid him, and yet knew him.

Tor turned to see.

The Thief's dark, burning eyes seared deep into his from above the obscuring, swaddling face veils for a brief eternity, before Tor realized the boy was slipping away, leaving. He was already far across the room, before the former, too loyal General, the former, treacherous Prince Consort truly realized it.

The Thief left, and was gone.

Tor bolted to his feet and, stumbling into things and people, as he followed.

To him, this was further proof Dara was purposely driving him insane, from wherever she was, as she physically hid herself from him, these past years, as she callously and incessantly tread through and stalked his mind.

There was no doubt in that, *he knew it was so.*

Whenever he sought hard to find her, whenever he knew he was close, that someone had *recently seen her* and he was nearly in reach of her—something, ALWAYS something, or *someone* worked against him.

Most times it was simply misinformation from people too ignorant of terrain and human character or of hunting others to give him the correct intelligence to track her.

Sometimes it was nature or The Great Mare, or whatever Great Power guided and shielded her and kept a man, kept *him* from finding the one woman, who had most reason to abhor every last bit of him—*the woman he loved, the mother of his lost child.*

Whatever it was, whatever Power Dara commanded, it usually detained him when he was close enough to follow Dara's trail with his eyes, so close he could nearly smell her, taste her.

That was ALWAYS when the skies or the earth or the rivers would decide to send an early, violent tempest or tumult before the usual early, violent tempest or tumult season.

And, her trail would, literally, be erased from before his eyes.

Now, he was shakily tracking a slim creature through the late day's crowded, dirty streets of Tash'k't, tracking a slim creature he believed, so wanted to believe, was so afraid to believe was her.

It . . . he . . . she could not be.

She had kept him far, far from her all this time, in her utter contempt of him.

Why would her Ka just now appear, as a shade . . . an eager ghost, as her Beguiling and Dangerous Double seen by others, to hurriedly lead him now, down twisting, nauseatingly winding streets and foul, congested alleys he had never cared existed?

He momentarily lost sight of the troubling spirit around a double corner serpent turn, which sent his anxious heart and mind into greater despair, in his blind, exhausted pursuit.

Then it was there. The shade, the youth, this Thief . . . Dara . . . Dara's Double, whatever it was, was waiting for him.

Tor slid along the wall to it, coughing harshly because of the dust and because he was fatigued from miniscule sleep.

Sleep that, when it did come to him, was restless at best, and whose troubled content stampeded and trampled his dreaming mind with extensive spirit herds of wild horse, sent after his disconsolated soul and lonely life by her, by His Dara, The Little Mare.

Tor was also weak from imbibing a great deal more mind and pain numbing liquor and bhanj, laced with opiates, than he consumed food.

It . . . he . . . she beckoned and he went to it, and did what it beckoned him. It wanted a boost, a leg up.

Tor was too mentally, physically, and spiritually fatigued to question. The creature had weight and smelled of leather, dirt, and animal musk, as it lightly stepped onto his thigh and into his palms, then vaulted over the wall to disappear.

Tor switched to the far side to see where it had gone.

He could not see a thing and so plopped down to sit in the dirt to wait. It was gone the better part of ten minutes before sailing over the wall in a tumble, to land directly in front of him. The phantom that was haunting and taunting him had obtained a rather heavy looking package, which was strapped to its back.

"Run."

That was all it quietly, emphatically said, then lightly, swiftly ran off, up the alley. He heard sounds of weapons clanking and angry men's alarmed voices from behind the wall, as he left them behind in his frantic pursuit of this slippery, elusive thing, this Mind Thief.

Not because he feared the men or their weapons, but because the Thief, the torturous spirit, the whatever, whoever it truly was, was leaving him.

He saw it enter an old house of old money, and followed, stepping from the late day sun into the dark shadowed interior, without doubt or personal mortal fear.

He was in error not to be.

The rich, old house had many doorways, too many rooms for someone so tired to search.

And, she . . . he . . . it was not in any of the ones he peered into, not before an intelligent Boy of twelve or so quietly appeared, wearing a natural coloured tribal gown and skullcap of one of the local tribes, yet he himself was plainly of far eastern blood.

The Boy was alert, apparently expectant, yet not frightened at his dark, looming presence, as he asked Tor to please follow. Tor hesitated only a second, before doing what was asked of him.

He was shown to a comfortable place to sit and was brought food. He did not ask where the *thing* he had been pursuing had gone because his mind was now in blank exhaustion, in the receding aftermath of the tension of pursuit, and could only do what it was told, as long as he remained physically unthreatened.

If he had felt true danger, he would have become alert; however, even then, probably only to acknowledge that he did not care if he were or were not in imminent danger of forfeiting his life.

He ate and drank what was initially put before him, but mutely refused additional servings. His body was hungry still but again he did not care and felt what he had ingested would sustain him and nominally show he appreciated the hospitality.

The Boy led him deeper into the large house, into a mosaic walled room with a hot, pool bath. It, like the entire house, had been sumptuous in its day, but was now chipped and faded, yet serviceable enough.

Tor welcomed the bath without complaint and thought he dimly remembered having fully cold bathed perhaps a month before.

He did not know what sort of soap the Boy provided, it had an astringent in it and burned slightly but not too badly. Its plant scent reminded him of soap Dara made for those who might or did have infections, cuts, or bugs of the skin and hair.

The bath was made in such a way that one could rest or sleep upright quite comfortably, without slipping to one's blessed death under the water's calm, hot surface. And, sometime during one of the times he was fully submerged, rinsing hair and scalp—soaking his head, the Boy left with his filthy and only clothes.

And, his hand weapons. He sighed and let it go; if this were a trap, he would die clean and relaxed.

He laid back his distressed head, his loosened black hair of dreads and waves floating, long and away from him, along with his troubled consciousness, as the edges of his mind slipped between the peaceful feel of the hot water on his warm, dark skin and that windy, desolate steppe of heightened mental and spiritual torment where wild horses and other wild beasts, commanded by Queen Dara, Shaman Prime of The Children of The Great Mare viciously hunted Tor's spirit and sanity.

He heard someone slip into the water or, more accurately, unalarmed for his life and just as uncaring, he did not perceive the other enter the water at all, but did hear whoever it was smack the water's surface to gain his attention.

Tor sat bolt straight, in awed terror, upon seeing, or believing he saw—*Dara*—naked and moving towards him through the water and steam.

She was thinner, which made her appear more muscular than when he had last seen her, because the pregnancy weight she had had then was now gone, and so was some of her regular weight.

In another time and place, it would have bothered him to see her so thin, although, she was not unpleasantly . . . .

It had always secretly delighted him that she seemed thinner with clothes on, because when, in their intimate privacy, when he would remove the layers of fabrics she wore, the true delicious fullness of her naked body greatly pleased his eyes, greatly pleased all of his hungering senses.

This Dara, however, was starkly slimmer, or more precisely, sharper edged, to his eye and her hips were somewhat wider to his discerning eye, plainly from bringing a child to full term in her womb.

Somewhere outside of him yet intimately close, as if spoken in his ear, he heard Krel's bodiless voice call him "Midwife" and laugh softly at him.

Tor closed his eyes a moment hoping the semi-floating, nude phantom with the mirrorlike dark eyes and His Brother's warmly amused voice from beyond the Veil of Death would for once both leave him be or outright kill him, but not minisculely torture him anymore.

His eyes involuntarily opened when he felt her hot and real against him. There was a patch of silver streaked through the beautiful creature's hair. Dara did not . . . had not had that, before The Betrayal.

Tor cried.

And, she . . . he . . . it pulled back, aghast.

"So, anahk Tor, *The* Destroyer cries? What have you to cry about, *Murdering Betrayer?*"

He said nothing, only silently cried, and shivered with dread, as he reluctantly gazed away from her.

Her full lips touched his cold ear, her hot breath heating the inside of his tortured mind.

"Do you love me, Tor?"

His tears came hotly, mutely, flooding unchecked, from the belly of his soul. He finally answered; avoiding gazing upon his lovely nemesis, his throat constricted, his voice a bare whisper.

"Yes. But, you are not *here*. You are never *really here*, with me. I never found you. You forbade that I should."

He stopped a long while, and she . . . it patiently, petulantly waited, and still he could not look in its . . . her eyes.

"Before I . . . wronged you, I never truly believed there were . . . events . . . demons that follow us day and night, that torture those of us who do . . . unjustified . . . evil."

He braved to look full into the unearthly, burnished mirror eyes, of His Demon.

"I was wrong."

She . . . It . . . stared at him from the deepest, hardest depths of its dark, fathomless eyes and he loved the feel of her, of *it* against him, yet wanted her . . . *it* to leave him be.

He had often, too often "felt" her against him, had "felt" himself deep within her and . . . ALWAYS IT WAS A LIE; a lie of insanity or wine or—.

He felt her mouth on his, her . . . its . . . her questing tongue against his own, for too brief a time.

He yearned to have her, as he had so many previous, phantom times, and sighed, loudly and disconsolately.

When he had indulged that greatest of desires, to have her and had met her—*like this, in a waking dream, awaking inside another dream,* in that part of him where he could *feel* he actually *touched* her, was actually *touched* by her, like *this*.

This torment!

Like this, when he knew he was truly *least* sane; *least* sober; *least* fully himself.

Returning to the "normal" afterwards, to *everyday* consciousness *always* "betrayed" him, because "she" would be gone; he would be, alone, soaked and spent from his own intense desires, but not from the sweat and lust of hers.

It was what she did to him. It was how she punished him, tortured him.

Sometimes it *was* just an insubstantial dream.

Sometimes, on rarest of occasions, it was . . . Her . . . Her Spirit's Double; substantial and actually touching him. Unfairly arousing him.

Most times he could not tell which—*Double or mere dream*—when fully engrossed by Dara's phantoms. Nor did he truly care, because no matter who or what came for him, in her stead, they were too much a part of her not to fool him, not to win him, and confuse him.

Plus, Tor wanted to be fooled, *anything* to have a bit of her with him.

Today, though, *this . . . creature was too . . . tangible.*

She . . . It . . . *She felt, tasted,* and *smelled* so . . . so very *real.*

Who better to torment you, than someone, who once loved you greatly; and, who now abhors you?

Someone with the Power to caress you to desire with love or strike you with fulfilled promise of a slow and shriekingly painful death . . . from a great, great distance, with no other "real" weapon save Her Will's Hand?

A near goddess Betrayed by Her Mate—Tor.

END OF EXCERPT THREE

www.Neale-Sourna.com

or

http://watchtower.neale-sourna.com

FRAMES
by

Neale Sourna

[from the completed screenplay]

FADE IN

EXT. LURID, RED DREAMSCAPE

ADULT MALE, BARE FEET RUN SLOWLY, THICKLY through a prickly nightmare, which ABRUPTLY SPEEDS UP.

CAMPBELL RADETZKY frenetically carries and runs with two apparently biracial CHILDREN (LIZ, 12 and RAY, 6). Campbell's terrified, soaked wet with sweat, tired but proceeding over and through nightmarish obstacles.

He clutches the children to him and they look too tired to care to be scared. They're nearly rag dolls from exhaustion.

>   WIN (O.S.)
>   Campbell?

His footsteps slow until an OILY DARK SHADOW oozes swiftly after them. It has substance, a core, as if it were a person—a woman; its SOUND is eerie, as eerie as a banshee's scream over tearing metal.

>   WIN (O.S.)
>   It takes two to make a seduction . . . and two to
>   make true love magic work. You're problem . . . .

Campbell redoubles his PANTING steps, his HEARTBEAT pounding out of control, as he runs through a FOREST OF RED TREES, which seem to protect them, until they close in and he realizes with horror that both children are gone from his arms.

>   WIN (O.S.)
>   Campbell?

He runs more frantically as the Oily Shadow Woman SCRATCHES at him, PULLS at him, TRIPS him. He gets some distance and enters a CLEARING with TURBULENT SKY AND CLOUDS above, RED RAIN

FALLS, STAINING HIM like blood. APPROACHING SOUND of the Oily Shadow Woman forces him across the wide expanse.

                  WIN (O.S.)
    Bell?!

A lone tree is before him and he HEARS HIS CHILDREN and runs to the tree, which ABRUPTLY HE SPEEDS TO AS IF YANKED TO IT and finds his kids wound within WRITHING BRANCHES, which are SNAKES NOT WOOD—and he reacts.

The kids are held out of his reach by what is no longer a tree but a RED MEDUSA WOMAN, who is terrifying, yet beautiful.

Campbell tiredly acquiesces and collapses to his knees at the PLANTED FEET of the Red Medusa, but before he can touch it, the Oily Shadow Woman overruns him and DEVOURS HIM, HIS BLOOD SPLATTERS THEN RUNS FROM OUT OF THE BLACK OIL.

INT. CAMPBELL RADETZKY SLEEPS - NIGHT

He writhes and turns in bed in emotional, mental pain but does not wake. Then he settles, a RED HANDPRINT ON HIS ARM and a RED DOG LOOKING BITE AT HIS THROAT are apparent. He swallows with difficulty, MOANS in pain, yet still does not wake.

The MARKS RECEDE but REMAIN. HIS EYELIDS indicate intense REM dreams . . .

INT. STUDIO, CAMPBELL'S LOFT - DREAM, DAY

He's dreaming in low contrast, muted tones of HIS HANDS STA-PLING WOOD FRAME BOARDS together, stretching and stapling new CANVAS taut over the large rectangular frame. Of spreading plaster white GESSO onto the fabric for a base.

Of painting in 2D: muted gold, muted brown, and a muted red.

                  WIN (O.S.)
    Campbell?

He pauses his activity . . . touching the WOMAN'S BROWN, PAINT-ED HAND, which TOUCHES him back, and EVERYTHING SHIFTS FROM 2D INTO 3D then 4D. The COLORS NOW SCINTILLATINGLY BRILLIANT, and . . .

                  WIN (O.S.)
    Bell?!

. . . REAL fabric that he slides off her caressably real skin; and red—Yes, China red lips, that he fervently kisses. And, truly startlingly bright ey—.

                         CAMPBELL (O.S.)
          Ow!

                         [script break]

INT. STUDIO, CAMPBELL'S LOFT - EVENING, SAME DAY

Campbell quaffs a GLASS OF MILK. He's in a good mood, humming and preparing a CANVAS. He pauses to stereo channel surf with the REMOTE in one hand, AIRBRUSH and SABLE BRUSH in the other.

He finds SCOTTISH MUSIC, decides he likes it, bops to it.

INTERCUT WITH - INT. FRAN'S BEDROOM FLOOR - SAME

O.S. SOUNDS—a MAN'S HEAVY, EXITING FOOTSTEPS, a DOOR OPENS and SHUTS.

Fran pours a MILKY URINE COLORED LIQUID from a DARK DRINKING GLASS into a SMALL BOWL. It SMOKES a bit and TURNS BROWN.

She's sweaty, her hair tousled, ROBE barely covering her naked body as she sits middle of her bed—which is in SHAMBLES.

Campbell PAINTS.

Fran places the smoking bowl beside Campbell's photo. Scooting across the bed she removes a DARK CURLING LOCK OF HAIR hidden behind her HEADBOARD.

Campbell paints—a woman.

Fran gets off the bed, pulls back the sheets. Her MATTRESS IS STAINED WITH BROWN STREAKS.

She dips her fingers in the bowl and flings small cascades of the YELLOW BROWN "solution" across the mattress. The liquid SMOKES A BIT THEN SOAKS IN, WITH A LITTLE SIZZLE.

She dips the hair in the solution, before squeezing it straight between her fingers of excess.

Campbell paints—a woman, a dark-haired woman.

Fran winds the wet curl tightly round her index finger, then strokes it down her neck, between her breasts . . . all the way down her torso.

She drapes Campbell's hair across his photo, then PHONES.

Campbell paints—a woman, a dark-haired woman. Maloy. PHONE RING.

ANGLE - MINUTES LATER

Campbell's on the phone; listening, painting, scowling.

> CAMPBELL
> Why'd you call me with this? I already told you,
> I've got a job tomorrow. Y'know cash to pay bills
> and eat?

Campbell impatiently wipes paint from the canvas.

> CAMPBELL (continues)
> You want me to play . . . bodyguard while you
> meet some ex, because . . . ? Why would I possibly
> care?

> FRAN
> Please, just come with me?

> CAMPBELL
> It's a setup.

She reacts as if caught, almost. She purposefully grabs the lock of hair from the photo.

He pauses indecisively then, robotically adds fresh YELLOW PAINT to the canvas.

> FRAN
> I need your help. That's all.

> CAMPBELL
> Fran, you're giving me a pain in the head for God's
> sake. Just tell me exactly what it's about.

She yanks a hair from her head and tightly winds one pale end around reinforcing the already blonde-bound brown lock.

                    CAMPBELL (continues)
          Damn it. What'd I just say?

He falls silent a long while, abruptly stopping, looking at his work,
falling back a step, then another.

She draws his hair around and around in a little, doodling circle on
the brown-stained mattress.

                    FRAN
          Say you change your mind, and come downtown
          with me tomorrow. Please?

He continues staring at his work, while stretching and rolling his
neck around in a tight circle.

She stops the circling.

He stops rolling his neck and shrugs himself out of it; however, his
voice is barely audible, resigned.

                    CAMPBELL
          All right. All right.

He quietly disconnects.

Fran kisses the lock, then resecures it to the headboard using her
own golden strand. She dotingly slips it behind, into its hiding place
where it swings side to side, out of sight.

And, Campbell, sickly displeased, plops down before his FRESH
PAINTING of Maloy—her face partially smeared away —part of it obscured and overpainted with Fran's features and hair.

INSERT - EXT. RTA TRAIN, DOWNTOWN BOUND - DAY

The "Egyptian Business Man with Briefcase and Tie" GRAFFITI
passes by the window as the RTA LIGHT RAIL TRAIN RATTLES under Eagle Street Bridge, then deep into the dark rail tunnel under
Tower City's skyscraper.

INT. MALOY'S PERSPECTIVE, CAMPBELL'S NIGHTMARE - DREAM,
NIGHT

A SMEARED, MOVING LIGHT STREAK with RED EAGLE FEATH-
ER WINGS, stops, it's Maloy arriving in Fran's SKEWED DREAM
HOUSE, taking another spill, when she stops and looks about . . . .

                    MALOY
             Where the hell—?

A STREAM of SYNTHETIC MUD with SOMETHING MOVING IN IT,
flowing past. She follows it upstream through the house to . . . .

INT. FRAN'S SKEWED DREAM BEDROOM - DREAM

 . . . Fran and a MORPHING 3D SILHOUETTE OF A MAN/WERE-
WOLF/DOG fucking in a soft MULTI-COLORED COCOON SAC,
which spits out the unnatural mud substance, that flows into a
maggoty mud Hell pit, of which Medieval artist H. BOSCH would be
proud.

In it Campbell struggles slowly, trying not to ingest, or drown; failing to reach an edge. Parts of him stiffen, like the mud INTO CON-
CRETE, his skin becoming the same dead color.

Maloy compassionately reaches to him and her touch rejuvenates
him immediately. Their hands clasp, but a HUGE RED HAND
snatches her very unwillingly away from him.

                    MALOY (continues)
          NO!!

INT. CAMPBELL'S LOFT - SAME NIGHT

                    CAMPBELL
          NO!!

Campbell's standing, asleep, eyes open, before the duo painting;
a sleepwalker with body on automatic in one place and his active
mind in another.

Garbage's "Push It" PLAYS on his radio, while he dismantles the
painting's STAPLED PINE UNDERFRAME. The PIECES DROP, with
HIS FINGERPRINTS HOTLY SCORCHED into them.

                    CAMPBELL (continues)
             Maloy, where—? Oh, there you—.

His eyes close, a moment later, he jerks "awake" again—somnambu-
list "awake," then almost immediately he's in full REM, asleep on his
feet, while WINDOW LIGHT BLINKS ACROSS HIS FACE.

INSERT – STUDIO/CORRIDOR/ABYSS, DREAM VOID

"Push It" THROBS, as part of his dream environment, luring, prodding, following Campbell, who STEPS THROUGH Maloy's gold painting, into a CORRIDOR edging an ABYSS . . . where he totters.

Behind him—is a GOLDEN-SKINNED FRAN, naked and seductive; but oddly artificial, HER VOICE A DOG'S, DISTORTED TO SOUND HUMANLIKE.

Eyes wide open, Campbell turns from her to intentionally FALL INTO THE PITCH BLACK DEEP, as an EAGLE CRIES.

INT. CAMPBELL'S PERSPECTIVE, NEAR SATURN - DREAM, NIGHT

In the PLANET'S BILLOWING DARK SHADOW, ITS SURFACE MOMENTARILY HAS MALOY'S FEATURES, as Campbell LANDS, painlessly, naked, and comfortably alone, but expectant.

A SOFT BREEZE and his own HEARTBEAT are the only SOUNDS, until Jordan the dog, HER HEART BEATING, SNIFFS up to him, sniffs him approvingly, then DISAPPEARS.

ANOTHER HEARTBEAT, ANOTHER BREATHING. He smiles knowingly, then pleasantly feels Maloy's naked body on his back, as her legs and arms wrap around him.

INSERT - INT. RTA STATION, TOWER CITY – EARLY MIDDAY

COMMUTERS, SHOPPERS, and TEAM SPORTS LOVERS boisterously disgorge from the RTA train.

RESUME SCENE

Campbell's still enwrapped in Maloy's arms, losing his concentration to her touch. Their SEPARATE HEARTBEATS BECOME ONE. HE'S SUDDENLY FACING HER, inside her, moving together in love.

INSERT - INT. MALOY'S BEDROOM - SAME TIME, NIGHT

Maloy lies on her stomach clutching her pillow, turned sideways under her head and chest. She rises up enough to shuck off her tee, then pushes back the covers to cool her skin, while never really waking.

Immediately, she's back in REM sleep . . . .

RESUME SCENE

. . . stroking her nose across Campbell's chest, inhaling the scent of him, kissing down his tensing stomach muscles—.

INSERT - FRAN - SAME

FRAN AWAKES—uncertain suspicion wearing hard on her face.

RESUME SCENE - CAMPBELL, LOFT - SAME

SOUND—SMOKE DETECTOR

Campbell startles fully awake—and finds the new canvas in his hand . . . ON FIRE.

CAMPBELL
Ah. OW!!

END OF ALL EXCERPTS

www.Neale-Sourna.com

Dear Reader:

If you are interested in **prenotification, info, or availability** of the completed novels or impending promotional incentives *(posters, photos, etc.)*, please contact:

www.Neale-Sourna.com

book title = hobble, aegis, libidinous, watchtower

Neale Sourna

PIE: Perception Is Everything

Box 192

12600 Rockside RD

Cleveland OH 44125

www.PIE-PerceptionIsEverything.com

www.PIE-Percept.com

Thank you,

Neale

PIE: Perception Is Everything™